the summer of firsts and lasts

Also by Terra Elan McVoy

Pure

After the Kiss

the summer of firsts and lasts

Terra Elan McVoy

Simon Pulse

NEW YORK   LONDON   TORONTO   SYDNEY

SIMON PULSE

An imprint of Simon & Schuster Children's Publishing Division
1230 Avenue of the Americas, New York, NY 10020
First Simon Pulse hardcover edition May 2011
Copyright © 2011 by Terra Elan McVoy
For information about special discounts for bulk purchases, please contact
Simon & Schuster Special Sales at 1-866-506-1949 or business@simonandschuster.com.
The Simon & Schuster Speakers Bureau can bring authors to your live event. For more
information or to book an event, contact the Simon & Schuster Speakers Bureau
at 1-866-248-3049 or visit our website at www.simonspeakers.com.
Designed by Mike Rosamilia
The text of this book was set in Adobe Garamond.
Manufactured in the United States of America
2 4 6 8 10 9 7 5 3 1
Library of Congress Cataloging-in-Publication Data
McVoy, Terra Elan.
The summer of firsts and lasts / Terra Elan McVoy. — 1st Simon Pulse hardcover ed. p. cm.
Summary: When teenaged sisters Daisy, Violet, and Calla spend their last summer together
at Camp Callanwolde, the decisions they make—both good and bad—bring challenges to
their relationship as well as opportunities to demonstrate their devotion to one another.
[1. Sisters—Fiction. 2. Camps—Fiction. 3. Interpersonal relations—Fiction. 4. Dating
(Social customs)—Fiction.] I. Title. PZ7.M478843Su 2011 [Fic]—dc22 2010039638
ISBN 978-1-4424-0213-3
ISBN 978-1-4424-0215-7 (ebook)

For Erika and Brae, of course.

While all of the other polygons can be bent into many different forms that are NOT regular polygons (with many different angles in each polygon), the triangle always keeps the same shape. It is the strongest polygon.

—Roger's Connection

DAISY

The way Calla's marching back and forth up there with her white shorts and her important-person headset, you'd think they really did name this camp after her, instead of the other way around. She was bouncy and excited when Violet and I arrived for check-in yesterday, running over to grab us in a hug before we were hardly out of the car, but this morning I can tell she's nervous. Tenser than normal, anyway. It could just be from her job working in the camp director's office, and the stress of the first gathering. Or it could mean something's already happened with Duncan.

I bend as subtly as I can to see where he's sitting with the kids in Muir cabin. He isn't watching Calla, but that doesn't say much. Duncan's seen her get uppity. He's even seen her in those starchy white shorts.

I can't look around too much though, because I know Violet's probably watching me, wanting to check if I'm okay. But I'm fine. I know Flannery from my cabin last year, and there's this girl Manon who I already really like too. The best way I can reassure my older sisters about how no-sweat I am, really, is to not even look around. Last summer, sure, I needed Calla and Violet both to help me figure out where everything was, to teach me the warm-up dances ahead of time so I wouldn't look like an idiot, to tell me to avoid the sausage links and other vital information like that. But this summer I'm going to be fine. Calla's got her job, anyway, and now this is Violet's last summer as a camper. It's better with me out of their hair.

I need to be discreet this morning for another reason, though. I still don't see that guy Joel from last night, and I'd feel better if I knew where he was sitting. But I don't want anyone (especially not him) to catch me searching, either. I'd noticed him staring at me during more games after dinner, so it wasn't so weird when he came up to congratulate me and my partner for beating them in the three-legged race. But going on to find out what cabin and concentration I was in, and where did I live and what music I was into? Let's just say last year I was on the sidelines, listening to Violet scoff at the boys who wanted to know that stuff about her.

"Finally. God," someone murmurs behind me, as the Whitman cabin comes in wearing the same color T-shirts and their hair all in pigtails. They're singing the "Whitman Yawp" (a tradition that is half football fight song, half jazz hands) and doing their *Wizard of Oz* skip into the auditorium, coordinated and cheerful as always.

"You've got to be kidding me," Manon mutters, while on my other side Jordan, a girl whose name I remember only because she has it embroidered on her pillowcase, goes, "We should've thought to do that together, coming in."

Manon rolls her eyes. Our placements are supposed to be done randomly right before we arrive, in order to encourage us to get to know girls from different hometowns, grades, and backgrounds. Though most of us end up in varying cabins every summer, somehow Whitman always houses girls who've either been in it before, or else are willing to conform to Whitman legacy. There are lots of traditions here at Camp Callanwolde—most of them emphasizing care for the environment, ourselves, and our community—but even in all this transcendentalist equality, Whitman's the sorority. You'd think Deena would have done away with it when she took over as director a couple of years ago, because it's pretty exclusionary to everyone else, but watching them come in, up there onstage, she has a small, almost proud little smile on her face.

"I'd love to get into Whitman and really sabotage those girls," Manon leans forward and hisses.

"Yeah, or just cream them in the Olympics," Jordan whispers back.

I nod my agreement, even though they aren't really talking to me.

Deena finally steps up to get our attention, and the entire formerly-squawking-with-girl-and-boy-chatter hall drops to a total silence. Deena presses an appreciative smile between her lips and says, "Good morning, campers, and welcome!" We all erupt into cheering, officially starting up our camp session.

First are warm-ups, which are basically these stupid dances to a bunch of different songs. Then there are announcements. Among other things, Deena explains the selection process of choosing a former camper to work for a summer in the main office, and Calla comes up on the stage. As Calla waves to everyone and thanks Deena, Duncan lets out this huge hoot of approval. I clap for her too, but both Violet and I know better than to make too much of a scene. Still, I'm glad Duncan made a big deal out of it.

Next the counselors are introduced. When Duncan stands up, his whole cabin jumps up and "Whoomp, whoomp, whoomps" around him while he smiles under his long honey curls. My eyes shoot to Calla, but since she's sitting now, I can't really see more than the side of her face and the same "You're amazing" smile she's been giving him since they met four summers ago.

Deena moves from the counselors to the concentration instructors, and I zone out a little, checking people out around me without moving my head too much. My favorite instructor from last year, Coach Haddock, got a new job at some college and had to be there this summer, so I'm pretty disappointed. I'd liked running before, but I hadn't really known I could do it until I met her. I wanted to work with her again. I wanted to try to get really good. As soon as Calla got here for training before first session, she'd e-mailed and said the new coach was really nice, but I want someone who is going to give me a challenge.

Just as Deena says, "Now I'm happy to introduce to you our new track instructor . . . ," I see Joel, only four rows in front of me, unmistakable with that white-blond hair.

". . . Sterling McKensie, who coaches track at Oakwood High, just a few towns over from us."

My eyes are yanked back to the stage.

I feel the blood rush up to my face, and then rush again because I'm embarrassed that I'm blushing. I don't know if it's because of Joel's proximity (how did I miss him before?) or the new coach or both, but around me the whole room is tittering with girls, so it's more likely the latter. Coach Haddock was strong, lean, and yes, a little leathery; her hair was always in a braid and she never did makeup or anything. But the new coach up there with Deena? Calla somehow failed to mention that he is so good-looking it makes your eyes hurt.

"McKensie? She means McDreamy," says my cabinmate Olivia. She's going to be in my track concentration too. The same pink that's in my cheeks is revved up in hers.

"You can pretend you're chasing him on the track, then," I whisper back, trying to sound like I think she's immature for even noticing, the way Violet would.

"I know. Thank god I picked it, right?" Her face is actually hopeful about this. I don't say anything back. The new coach takes the mic and talks about how excited he is to be here. It is, I have to be honest, pretty incredible how gorgeous he is.

He sits back down and we meet the other instructors, then Deena goes over changes and upgrades around camp, reminders about safety, blah, blah. Next it's time for keynote—a twenty-minute devotional on the topic we're supposed to focus on each day. Today it's "Beginnings," and the presenter is the new Languages instructor, Helene. She takes a minute settling both the mic and her glasses in the right position, but then she talks about what it was like when her family moved to America from France when she was thirteen, how no one understood what she was saying, and everyone thought her clothes (very stylish in France) were funny. She hated the grocery store, she tells us, and missed the outdoor markets. Movies made no sense for years.

"I still consider myself French," she says, voice lilting on different syllables. But now the United States is home to her too, and she doesn't even mind the grocery store.

It takes us a minute to realize she has finished, but finally we're clapping. I think there was supposed to be some kind of point there, with the grocery store mention, but she hasn't really said more than, *If you stay somewhere long enough, you'll just get used to it eventually.* And maybe that's comforting to some of the new campers, who aren't positive about being marooned here, cell phone– and internet-less for three whole weeks—kids whose parents never heard of Callanwolde before, let alone spent every summer here like our mom did. Maybe last year even I would've benefited from it, if I hadn't had my sisters, but now it pretty much seems like covered territory.

To finish things up, we go over all the camp rules and say the pledge. *(I vow to be mindful and respectful of myself and others at all times. I promise to uphold the standards and traditions of Camp Callanwolde.)* We all stand up, and each cabin gets to scream a Spirit Splurge cheer to the whole room. Then all that's left is the whole neck-craning, head-turning, body-shifting shuffle to find our instructors, who are standing in different places around the auditorium. I don't mean to check, but I watch the Water Sports instructor until Joel shows up beside him. It was weirdly a relief last night to hear he wasn't in Drama, or Vis Arts.

Around me a couple of my cabinmates who are already "best friends" hug each other good-bye, squealing, "See ya at lunch!" It's annoying how girls who were strangers a day ago pair up before we've even been here twenty-four hours, but then again, I am pretty glad I have Flannery around. I tell her I hope her concentration is good. She wiggles her eyes over at Coach McKensie and says, "Yours will be." We don't hug or anything, but she waves happily, and then I take a deep breath and head over to meet my companions for the next three weeks.

VIOLET

rinity's still complaining about how we're not allowed to have cell phones here—*duh, it's totally in the camp rules and that's probably why your parents sent you here, you text addict, so chill*—whining how many cool things she's probably already missing out on at this stupid place, but I'm only kind of half listening to her. Maybe not even that much. The rest of me is looking for Brynn's blue-black and turquoise-streaked head. She said when we met last night during the shoe game at the bonfire that she was in Alcott, but they're sitting a few rows in front of us—beyond the empty ones reserved for Whitman, whenever they get their preppy show-off asses down here—and she's definitely not with them now. She wasn't at breakfast, either, which is weird. I don't want to turn around or make it too obvious that I'm looking for anyone, mainly because Daisy will think I'm trying to check on her—and it's not like Brynn and I are BFFs—but as Whitman files in with their stupid pigtails and their bouncy smiles and their dumb song, she's still not there with the rest of her cabin. So I can't help but be seriously curious.

One person I do see though is James. Again. Every time I saw him yesterday I sort of couldn't believe it was him. Not that I didn't recognize him—even though his hair is shorter and he's kind of thinner in a more angular way. It's just that I couldn't believe he was here. Here and a counselor. Here and so gorgeous and funny and cool, instead of like he was two summers ago: just this guy in my concentration, a buddy you weren't upset about being stuck in a canoe race with. I saw him as soon as we all split up: Calla returning to her check-in duties, Mom and Dad going over to meet the concentration instructors, and Daisy off to see who her cabinmates were. James was standing with the other counselor for his cabin under the Audubon banner, shaking hands with dads and high-fiving this really overeager freshman-looking kid. And it was like, I don't know, balloons should fall from the ceiling or something, seeing him. Which was weird, because it barely registered to me that he wasn't here last summer. We'd become friends in Vis Arts, sure, and I thought he did good sketches, but it's not like we were sobbing in each other's arms when camp was over. Seeing his face light up when our eyes met yesterday though, feeling the thrill of being thrilled together, balloons from the ceiling was kind of the right response.

I felt it again at dinner last night. Everyone was sweaty and laughing from the first cabin get-to-know-you games, and there was a huge grill full of tofu dogs and hamburgers and big bowls of chips. The lightning bugs were going, making it seem like we were in a movie of camp instead of actual camp. Daisy was standing with me and two girls from her cabin, plus some girls from mine, and we were all just talking and laughing and waiting for the people in front to move forward. When he walked directly in my line of vision, all the way on the other side of the picnic tables, moving slow to catch my eye and totally staring, I couldn't help but feel thrilled. He smiled and gave me a single wave, lifting up his paper plate as though in a toast. Daisy pressed her sneaker against my bare calf. I bent my knee a little to press into hers.

Now, watching for Brynn, James is hard not to see. He's not looking around for me, which is nice, actually. After dinner, at the bonfire, I kind of wanted him to come over and talk to me, but after he didn't right away, then I didn't want him to. We knew we were there. We were glad to see each other, even though it was kind of odd to be so glad. The silence, the not talking, became this fun little game that was just ours. As soon as we talk, everyone will know we knew each other from before, and because everyone is the way they are, they will start asking what's up. And then we'll be acknowledging that something is maybe actually up. When all we've done is smile at each other. Incredibly happily.

So, as long as we don't talk, everything can stay electric. I can be curious about what he's been up to, wonder what he's into now. I can keep it magical. Like last night. I had fun with my cabinmates and my sisters, singing and marshmallowing around the fire, yeah, but the whole time there was this other layer to it: knowing he was there, knowing he was seeing me, no one else knowing about it. Not even me understanding all of it.

I wonder how long we can keep it up.

Deena starts the announcements and the introductions and the la-dee-dah welcoming, most of which is boring and the same from the last three summers. Calla's watching from where she's standing up front, not immediately next to Deena—more kind of in the wings, over by the stairs up to the stage—but still definitely up there. I wonder if that's where Deena told her to stand, or if Calla's just there trying to be helpful—ready to do whatever, since it sounds like Deena's a pretty control-freaky boss. When Deena introduces Calla as the new office assistant it makes more sense, her hovering, but I still wish she didn't look quite so eager.

I know Calla's stoked to be working at camp, and that she admires Deena and practically wants to *be* her, but my sister has a tendency to get really cranked about things on this crazy-maniacal level, internalizing any kind of even minor criticism and then working twice as hard to overcompensate for what might be perceived as a mistake. This is what worries me about this summer. Calla actually got an ulcer when she was in seventh grade—which, hello? What twelve-year-old gets an ulcer, except my sister? Graduating and finalizing everything to attend Smith in the fall has chilled her out a little, but she's never going to get rid of that need-to-please thing she's got going on. (Notice how she's gotten a job, instead of just staying at home, lying out and reading magazines for three months.) I don't want this stupid summer internship or whatever to take some kind of serious toll on her. What she goes through with Duncan is definitely enough.

Sure, Mom came here as a camper, and she and Dad met here (he was the Water Sports instructor and she was a counselor). Sure, Calla's even named after the place, and, knowing Mom and Dad, was likely intentionally conceived here during one of those gross Callanwolde alumni reunion parties, but still.

It's only summer camp. It's amazing and incredible while we're here, yes, but it's not the rest of our lives.

And yet, admittedly it is hard not to act like it. For most of us. So I also understand her intensity about it.

Everyone's stood up now and we're doing the whole cabins-screaming-chants thing, when finally I see Brynn. She comes slowly down the side aisle to join her cabinmates, practically wincing with each step. She's got these huge sunglasses on and keeps lifting her hand to her temple in this fragile, pained way. Unbelievably, instead of standing for her cabin's cheer, she sits. I lose her after that, in the blur of sorting ourselves out into our concentrations, finding our instructors, heading out to HQ, but something suddenly tells me that my curiosity (and the curiosity of everyone else) is exactly what she's looking for behind those dark glasses. That headache of hers is probably a whopping fake. But instead of being annoyed by this, it makes me even more curious. With Dover off in Greece this summer with her family, I need a new camp best friend. Maybe this year I'll surprise everyone with my choice—including myself.

CALLA

As a camper, this day was always my complete, absolute, total favorite. Maybe it's because this was when Duncan and I first noticed each other four years ago, when we had that I Need to Know You moment during warm-ups that I'll never forget: bopping around with our cabins, our eyes meeting, and that total recognition between us of *You look like a fun person*. But really, I think it's more than that. There's always something about this first morning session, the first gathering of camp, that's hugely exciting. You're seeing all your old friends and checking out the new ones. You'd had some time to make alliances in your cabin and sniff people out the night before, but now, sitting together as a cabin, it really meant something. Meant you were going to be together for the next three weeks and you were going to learn things and discover yourself and tough it out during hard times and it was all so—promising and exciting and great.

Now, being behind the scenes, it's still exciting, but in a different way. It's more like an anxious excitement: Is the sound working properly so that it cuts out Deena's headset mic when the new instructors are talking into the handheld one? Is everything running in the kitchen the way it's supposed to so that lunch will really be ready on time? Did Nathan go get the new bow he needs for archery this afternoon, or did that never get fully explained to him—that it was his responsibility, and that he'd just get reimbursed by the office? All this background stuff, it's so cool to know, and to help make happen.

Now that this is second session, and I've had four weeks and a first group of campers to learn a lot of the ins and outs around, it's even better. I am so glad I didn't go the standard route and just become a counselor like most everyone does after graduation, but went for it and applied for junior assistant to the director. The last four summers, Camp Callanwolde has been this totally magical place for me, this place where I've been free and excited and sort of . . . I don't know . . . open in a way I can't be at home. I loved the first gathering, because I knew it meant my time—*my* time—had finally started. And now I get to be a part of the mechanics that make that happen for a whole new crop of kids. (I put that in my application essay, and I *meant* it.) Even though there's more work than magic this morning (so much I don't even get to try to find Violet or Daisy in the crowd, and only know where Duncan is after he screams out like that when I go up onstage), it makes me respect camp in this whole new way. Like how you don't really know how much you like this one girl in your class, until you have to do a really hard research project with her, and it turns out she has some wicked ideas.

Everything goes smoothly with the gathering though, and when I do get to catch Daisy's eye before she leaves, she gives me that little pressed-between-her-lips smile and a tiny wave. I tiny-wave back so as not to embarrass her, even though a part of me wants to be like Mom and stand high on my tiptoes and wave and wave my arm as hard as I can until she's totally gone and there's no way she could possibly still see me. I also want to be like, *Hey, that cute boy who talked to you last night is right over there*, but there's no question about how dead I'd be if I did.

After everyone's cleared out, I go outside to stand in the warm sunshine a minute, watching them disappear in the direction of their concentration headquarters. I see Violet, but her back is to me, so I just send her thoughts for a good morning. I'm about to head up to the office when Duncan runs up, making a beeline for the auditorium door, though not in so much of a hurry that he can't come over and wrap me in a hug, lifting me off the ground.

"Fun morning, eh?" he asks.

"Always is."

"I know, right? Though it's weird a little, that we'll have four of these 'firsts' before the summer is over."

"What, you don't want more chances to do the Star Trek dance with me again?"

"Are you kidding? It's the hundred and twenty obnoxious high schoolers in there with us I could do without." He bounces around, doing the Klingon part. I pretend to shoot him with laser beams, hoping my face doesn't give away the thought of us being here, together, alone.

"Well, I better, you know . . ." He extends a hand toward the auditorium door.

"Go, go, go. I've got work to do too." I shoo him with my hands.

"Wave to you at lunch?"

"Not if I wave to you first."

We smile again, and he darts inside the auditorium. I'm remembering my very first summer, when I didn't know anyone and had never been away from Mom and Dad or Violet and Daisy for more than a long weekend, back when I was homesick and sad and scared and worried I'd mess up all the time, that no one in my cabin would like me, being even more terrified too that my fear would show and then everyone would make fun of me. How, though, after that first gathering when Duncan and I spotted each other, when we were buddies in an instant and best friends after one conversation at free swim, well, just like Helene said this morning, I got used to it and flung myself into about the most fun I ever had for the next three weeks. We've had the same kind of fun every summer since, and now, even though we've both got our responsibilities this time, I'm so glad that we're here together, like always, him and me.

VIOLET

Ten minutes into Writing, and I've forgotten all about Brynn or James or anyone else. I feel like the next three weeks are going to be *terrific*. For one thing, our instructor, Kelly, is immediately fantastic in the way you can just tell about people—something in her smile or body language, something hard to articulate and impossible to deny. The way everyone's got their pencils working over their notebooks already, frowning with concentration, staring up into nowhere to glimpse the right word or idea, is also just the most energizing thing. I hardly know these people (except for Reena and Iris, who've been here the same session as us the last two summers), but just glancing at everyone's ease and focus tells me we're going to be a good group.

After our quick warm-up, Kelly tells us how she's always hated her name. "Kelly." Her voice is overly flat and dull. "Not exactly the name of a famous literary novelist, right?" She giggles when we giggle. "And Franklin? As in, Benjamin Franklin? That dowager-looking guy with the mullet and the tiny glasses? No thanks." She sighs. "Not all of us are lucky enough to have parents who manage to name us just the right thing. A lot of us have, like me, wished we were named something else. So, what I want you to do is spend the next twenty minutes freewriting about that. Write about your name, how it makes you feel, and then write about what you wish you could be named. My only rule is that you keep the pencil moving constantly."

She explains further that when we stop to think, we actually stop the unconscious flow of our thoughts and ultimately our words. So it doesn't matter if we get stuck and write the same word over and over, or if we write "This is stupid, why am I writing this?" What matters is to keep the pencil—and the words— moving. Eventually, she says, we'll punch through the obstacle and get our thoughts moving again. So keeping the pencil going is really important. And I love this idea. But it's exciting to see everyone else at the table getting into it too.

I try not to think, and just write. Start writing about how

abnormal it is to be in a threesome of sisters all named after flowers. How everyone refers to us as a bouquet, and how we have to just stand there smiling while Dad's fellow professors loom over us at the department holiday party, congratulating themselves on coming up with the line, *Goodness, Mike, how your girls have blossomed.* I move into how stifling it is to always be defined, even by our names, as a unit, instead of as three individuals. And how being named after a flower is nowhere near as unique as even being named after another person. I mean, everyone already has these set ideas about flowers, and what they symbolize to them, and usually it's pretty banal. All I can think about when I picture violets is this gold-rimmed miniature tea set I was given by some relative when I was little, with violets painted on the side: lovely and delicate and only semi-useful. Certainly not bold, challenging, difficult, intelligent, fierce.

What I end up writing most about though—and end up sharing, after Kelly instructs us to read over our work, underline our favorite and strongest thought, and work it into a serious, developed piece to serve as our introduction to the group— is the nicknames my sisters and I have for each other. Daisy, as one might imagine, is Daze around the house all the time. But somehow, once Calla got into middle school, she wanted to differentiate herself from the rest of us and started calling her Dizzy. So I started doing it too, of course, but then, for some reason we can't really explain, that shifted into calling her ZeeZee or Zee, as well.

My nickname from Calla—since I was around six, and told everyone at the dinner table that I did not enjoy being referred to as Vi or Lettie (Mom still likes to tell this story)—has been Vivi. But sometimes, usually when she's being sweet or silly, Calla calls me Shazbot, Bot, or Shaz. This we got from an old TV show Mom and Dad loved about an alien; they spent one Thanksgiving break forcing us to watch the whole first season on some DVDs Mom got for her birthday. It actually turned out to be a sweet and funny show, even if it was mostly corny and so dated. Anyway, we thought "Shazbot" was hilarious, but even funnier as a nickname, so there you go.

Calla used to be just Sissie, since that was what our parents called her when talking to me or Daisy when we were little. (As in, "Pass Sissie the butter please, Vi," or, "Daze and Vi, let Sissie stand in the middle because she's taller. Now one, two, cheeeeeeese.") But Sissie has become pretty interchangeable for all three of us at this point—an easy thing for Mom or Dad to say if they can't remember which daughter they're talking to.

The main thing we call her instead is Cow, which most people don't get, and that's a lot of why we do it. Cow sounds like a clipped version of Calla in some strange way (like if you are trying to say "Calla" with your mouth full of ice cubes), but really it comes from a night a couple of years ago when Calla (we'd called her La-La before this, after the Teletubbies) came home completely hysterical and crying from a double date with her best friend, Madeline. Madeline liked this guy Timon, but was too shy to go out with him by herself and wanted some backup. So Calla agreed, because she is that kind of good, supportive best friend. But the guy Timon picked to hang with Calla that night was Gregor Sykes—a soccer stud who moved here from Norway and thinks he is entirely above all American high schoolers. He barely speaks to anyone. Which we thought Calla already knew, but somehow she was actually thinking she and he might hit it off. That this would be her chance to show everybody she really did *not* care that Mitch Oberston had asked Skyler Susskind to Homecoming instead of her.

They went to the arcade and played video games and Skee-Ball and air hockey and ate nachos, and the whole time Gregor said barely a word to Calla. Apparently it was so awful that even Madeline and Timon felt weird and wanted to leave early, which meant Calla felt guilty about ruining her best friend's date. When she got home, bursting with the frustrated, embarrassed tears she'd held in all night, we sat there—me on one side, Daisy on the other—at the top of the stairs, clutching her knees and hugging her while she did this horribly mocking (and actually, horribly accurate), high-pitched imitation of herself trying to get conversation out of him.

"I'm sure he's posting right now about what an idiot I am," she wailed, her face wet and red. We handed her tissues that immediately became soggy and gross in her hands. "A prattling, babbling idiot. I'm such a cow," she moaned.

At which point I should not have looked at Daisy. Because Daisy was suddenly trying very hard not to laugh. And when Daisy tries hard not to laugh, she presses her mouth into this almost invisible line, but her nostrils flare out really huge, and they quiver with the power of her restrained giggling. So I looked over, saw Daisy trying not to laugh, and then suddenly *I* was trying not to laugh. And then there we were, trying to comfort our humiliated sister, but trying even harder not to laugh. Which then made the need to laugh even more impossible to hold back.

Calla must have felt our shaking shoulders, because she opened her eyes, pressed a crumbling-wet tissue against them, and said in this adorably pathetic voice, "What?"

Which meant Daisy and I could do nothing but erupt with our giggles. I didn't even know for sure what we were laughing about, just that it was hilarious. Fortunately, seeing us rocking backward, practically choking over *what,* she wasn't sure, Calla started laughing too.

Eventually Daisy got enough breath to say, "May-may-maybe that was the problem. Maybe he—" Moment of silence while Daisy laughed silently into the open air of our staircase.

"H-h-he was just waiting for you to tell him you were . . . you were in the *moood.*"

This idea was so dumb and crazy and random that Calla and I started laughing even harder. And then the three of us sat there, laughing so hard we couldn't breathe, each of us trying to re-create Calla's failed attempts at sexy conversation in Moo-ese.

And then Mom and Dad came home from their dinner out. They, as usual, wondered if someone had drugged us in their absence. And from then on, Calla was Cow.

"What's important about these nicknames," I finish, standing in front of my fellow campers, reading my completed piece, "is that they were something we created. Us. Together. For and with each other. And while the names our parents gave us are still important, are still who we are, these names we call each other ring in our ears with a different—with a chosen—kind of power."

It's much longer than a paragraph. And it doesn't really address Kelly's original question about what we wish we were named, but from the faces of my peers—and my instructor, and from the way I felt reading it, the way that last sentence just sounded around me when I said it out loud—I know it's good.

DAISY

To all our surprise, Coach McKensie doesn't take us to the track right away after keynote. Instead he leads us over to the arts building and into the smaller of the two dance rooms, before he disappears again into the hall. There are nine of us standing there—five girls and four guys. The boys naturally hover together. Me and Olivia and Montgomery glom together too, being in the same cabin. I also know April, this junior from last year, who ran in the relay against me. When I catch her eye, she gives me a little smile. Nobody says anything—all of us just kind of stand there waiting for Coach McKensie to come back in from wherever he went, all of us shifting in our running shoes and our shorts. I picture Violet in her writing class, probably playing some name game.

"Okay." Coach's loud, happy voice echoes in the wood-paneled room. He's carrying a water bottle that's dripping wet, and this incredibly old portable CD player. "Everybody know each other?"

Our eyes flick from face to face, embarrassed. We shift our clumps into a loose circle and go around, mumbling our names. When I say who I am, this tall, freckly redhead says, "You're Calla's little sister, right?" and when I nod, she gives me a big smile. "We were in Alcott together my second summer."

"So, good." Coach claps his hands and smiles at us. "So, who can tell me some of the most important things in running?"

No hands go up. I'm thinking: *breathing, pacing, stretching, focus . . .*

"Nobody has any idea? Nobody run before?" His face is entertained by us.

The freckly girl who knows Calla says, "Well, speed."

"Good, good." He nods, shifting back and forth on his feet. "And you are—?"

"Lena."

"Good, Lena. Speed is important. What else?"

"Pushing through even when you think your lungs are going to explode," one of the boys says. The one who will maybe make good backup if Joel, who is apparently already (already?) into me, doesn't work out.

"Good." Coach nods, making his eyebrows ask the guy's name.

"Finch."

"Excellent, Finch. Yes, pushing through is important, especially for distance. But there's another thing I'm looking for."

"Um, your shoes?" Olivia guesses.

"Your shoes can count, your shoes can count." He is nodding but has gotten tired of our lameness now. "One of the most important parts of running"—his hands rub together in this twitchy, nervous way that makes him less hard to look at—"is stretching. Stretching and strength building, actually. Now, I don't mean strength in terms of a lot of weight lifting and bulking up and that kind of thing. But it is very important, in order to avoid injury, that your muscles are strong. Strong and flexible."

I'm secretly pleased I thought of stretching, but glad I didn't say it.

"So, before we even look at the track today, we're going to work on both things. In that closet back there there're some mats. Not sure what condition they're in, but go get yourself one, and take off your shoes. Then come back out here and find a spot where you have plenty of room. Four-foot clearance at least, got it?"

We shuffle to the back closet, none of us sure about what is going on. Olivia looks at Montgomery and they both giggle. The tallest guy is making himself Mr. Helpful by pulling the mats out one by one and handing them to us. They are gray and smooth and smell like must and something synthetic. We take off our shoes, lining them up in a row, like they're an audience, watching. Montgomery and Olivia go up front, dropping their mats down with perkiness. I move behind them, far to the left. April puts her mat a few feet away from mine. We swap small, unsure smiles again. All I'm thinking is, *No way.*

"Good, good," Coach says. "You might want to, ah, move in a little there—" He's wagging his pointer finger, aiming at one of the guys far over on the right. "More to the back than the side. You'll need to see, see?"

Once we're all positioned, he pushes play on the CD player, and this Celtic flute-type music comes out. Olivia giggles again. Definitely no way.

"So, one thing you may not know about me is that aside from coaching track, which I do, I'm also a"—he drags out the "a" and stops, faces us—"yoga instructor."

I can feel the guys giving each other glances, but I keep my own eyes straight on Coach, my face expressionless. I am trying to clench myself against my own doubt about all of this.

"So you're thinking, What the heck does *yoga* have to do

with running? I mean, I signed up for *track*, man. The hippies are all in the art studio painting pots." To this he gets some genuine laughs. "Well, I'll tell ya, there is nothing, my friends, like yoga to help you with your running. It increases blood flow, strengthens and lengthens important muscle groups, helps you regulate your breathing, and above all, stretches you out much more completely than pulling your foot up behind your butt cheek a few times."

More laughs. He's winning us over. The "Good Lord, he's so hot" intensity has definitely dropped for me, thankfully, but he's still pretty charming.

"So we're going to get started. I'm going to teach you some basics first, but then I'm also going to move around and help you with your positioning. So—" He claps his hands together, looking at all of us. "Are we ready?"

"Yes, Coach!" Olivia pipes, like we're the soldiers and he's the sergeant. Montgomery shoves her, but they both giggle. Coach gives Olivia a funny little look, and then I see him look at me, his eyes going, *These girls are a little hyper, aren't they?* My eyes don't know what to say back, so I just look down, at my socks, shaking my feet loose, pretending I'm preparing myself.

Coach pushes another button on the CD player, making the flutes start over, and we begin, doing our best to follow him. Nobody can keep from laughing at first. For one thing, the music is awful, and then there's Downward Dog, of course, with all our butts up in the air, including Coach's. On top of that, in spite of the flutes, this isn't soothing, wind-chime, green-tea yoga—he's moving us pretty quickly from pose to pose, and it's hard sometimes to keep up, hard to hold all the positions. It doesn't take long for my breathing to speed up and for me to sweat a little.

After a few Sun Salutations and Chair Poses, Coach starts moving around the room behind and between us, which is a little distracting, because I don't want to be doing things wrong and looking stupid. The boys seem to need the most help—their knees are all bent, legs crooked—so he hovers over there, putting his hands on their shoulders and turning them just slightly to form a straighter line, showing them how to raise their chins and lengthen their necks. Of course this gets Montgomery and Olivia giggling again, which makes me happy I'm behind instead of beside them—harder to see.

We go into another Downward Dog and have to hold it for a while. My hands are slipping on the mat from being sweaty, and I'm concentrating on pushing down hard, trying to keep them still, when I feel Coach come up behind me and put his hands square around my hips, firm and unapologetic. And then of course all I can think about is how gorgeous he is again, yoga dork or not. He raises me up and pushes me forward a little, one hand moving down between my shoulder blades, pressing a bit. It is startling how strong and direct his hands are, how he is not gentle or shy but not rough, either—just very sure-feeling. And how much better it feels in this position now. Olivia is watching me from under her own arm. Coach murmurs, "Better, yeah?" before he moves away. Next time I look, Olivia's staring at her mat.

After about half an hour or so, we do some cooldown floor stretches. My body is warm and tired. Lying here—legs spread wide and forearms down on the floor—feels great. What Coach calls the Happy Cow is also terrific for my tight hips. The final five minutes is just this guided meditation thing, where we lie on our backs and listen to Coach talk in this slow, quiet voice about visualizing all the cells in our bodies vibrating with happiness. I'm expecting more giggling, but surprisingly, everyone is calm and still, breathing. It's so quiet I can hear the music from the dance class in the big studio next door, the footfalls of dancers thrumming through the floor.

"Okay, when you're ready, you can stand up," Coach says, having returned to the front of the room. He tells us we did well, asks us how we feel. There are nods and "good's" and a general feeling of "yes" in the room. Coach says that's great, because this is how we're going to start pretty much every day—yoga before we do anything else.

"But let's get out there now and see what you can do." His hands clap once. We put our mats away and our shoes back on, take a break for bathroom and water, then go up to the field, around which there is a worn dirt path about two runners wide.

"Now, this isn't a competition. Not today, anyway," Coach tells us, squinting in the bright sunlight. "We're just going to take a few laps around here and I'm going to watch your form, see how you do. So we're not showing off speed, just finding a good, comfortable stride and sticking with it. My understanding is that once around this field is not quite half a mile. We'll do some off-sites later on, get on some different surfaces. But for now, just show me what your normal stride looks like."

The boys head off right away. The freckly girl, Lena, trots off after them, starting a little short in her step. April waits a minute, gives me a little wave, and hits it too. Montgomery and Olivia and I start off together, at the back of the group, them a little in front and me very last.

By the second curve we're all stretched out in a line. Mr. Helpful is way in the front, having pulled ahead of the other three guys, who are evenly spaced behind him. To my surprise though, Lena isn't far behind the guys, and during the next straightaway she actually pulls ahead of two of them. April is steady and even, ahead of me but not in a hurry. I've had to go past Olivia and Montgomery, finding my rhythm, evening my breath between the one-two of my feet.

After that I don't think about the running, or who's ahead of or behind me, though I do say hey to April when I eventually pass her. I am listening to my breathing, in-out-in-out, one-two, one-two, but mainly I just let my mind go and let whatever comes up come up. I picture Calla in the director's office, working hard at whatever it is she's doing, picture the other girls in my cabin, doing pottery and riding horses and other camp-y things. I picture Mom and Dad at home, reading books or magazines together, able to listen to as much jazz as they can stand without the three of us in the house.

And, yeah, I picture Joel. It's nice that he doesn't have braces. And his short white hair is just cool enough to look cool, without it seeming like he's trying too hard. At least not with his hair. Coming right over to me like that was pretty bold, though. I'm still mostly astonished he did it. And it's very possible that after five minutes of chatting with me, he's decided I'm not worth it. I guess I'll find out at lunch. Or tonight. It occurs to me it would be nice to just have a guy at camp already, though, rather than spending the first week deciding who I liked, and the next two trying to get him to like me back, which is the drama I watched pretty much everyone in my cabin do last year, and is why I didn't bother at all.

Coach startles me, suddenly being there, running beside me, working to match his pace with mine, his breaths going in and out with our one-two. I realize I've gotten closer to the closest guy, and that the guy ahead of him is slowing down. I don't know how many times I've gone around the track.

"You feel all right?" Coach says.

"Yeah."

"Hips a little tight, after a long run?" he wants to know.

I glance at him. *How did you know that?* "Yeah."

"We'll work on that," he says, nodding. "There are some exercises you can do."

"Okay," I say. We are closing in on that last guy.

"You go ahead." He juts his chin. "I'm gonna check on this one. Tell me your name?" He squints at me, only a little bit of sweat on his forehead, and under his nose.

"Daisy," I tell him.

"Daisy. Good, then. Keep it up."

We jostle together in the path a little, him going wide to let me by. The sun is warm but the air is cool, the ground not too hard or dry, not too muddy or soft. I don't have to think about my breathing anymore—it's just coming. I pull up even with the guy in the lead. He glances over and smiles, the blood up in his cheeks and his hands loose at his wrists. I like his pace, so I stay there with him at the front. We go around, and then around again, passing other runners—Olivia and Montgomery just walking now, talking, like it's PE or something. Coach has gone out into the middle of the green, hands on hips, watching all of us. Circling the field is getting a little boring and I wish I had some music, but mainly this feels great. Too soon Coach blows his whistle and waves us in.

It's pleasantly surprising, knowing I could've easily gone longer. Even after my Olympic triumph last summer, I was too embarrassed to try out for track at school. In the spring, classes got crazy and there was the chorus musical, which Calla would've been upset if I wasn't in with her, even as just a dancer. I did go on some runs during the year, but until the summer started creeping up, I wasn't really thinking about it in a serious way. Not until it hit me that this was going to be my concentration and I really didn't want to look like a total amateur. So I got Mom to take me to get some decent shoes, and every day for the last five weeks I've just been going on runs around the neighborhood. I don't even know how far. As soon as the sun goes past the line of trees and beyond the hottest part of the day, I head out and just run until I don't feel like it anymore, sometimes more than two hours. The first couple of times I had to stop and walk a little to get the stabbing in my side to go away, and some mornings I wake up with these old-lady pains in my hips, but I was surprised to be able to go a lot farther than I expected.

"So," Coach says to all of us. "You guys look good out there. Very good. Got some sprinters, it looks like." He nods at Finch, the cute one. "Also got some short distancers, some of you with long-distance potential, lot of leg in you." This to me and I-Have-Got-to-Learn-His-Name, the guy I was running with at the end. "All of you need a little work on your technique in different ways. I've got some exercises in mind for specific areas, but in general a good, good-looking bunch." He smiles at us without showing his teeth, nodding, making him look like a boy in an old photograph. He is definitely cute, but now he's a lot more accessible and human. "So, why don't you walk a couple laps, shake it out. We'll do some final stretches together, and then—" He checks his watch. "Whoa. Whoops. Later than I thought. If you want time to shower before lunch, we'll have to—ah, yes?"

He looks at Olivia, who has her hand up. She giggles.

"Coach, I just wanted to know if we should, like, be eating a bunch of carbs or something."

Montgomery elbows her and chuckles. "Gawd." To Coach she says, "We were just wondering, you know, about our diets. What we should focus on to, you know, maximize our potential."

"Well, that's a good question, Olivia. And—Montgomery? Good question. If you all were doing hard-core training, like say for a marathon or a serious race, I would mainly encourage you in the direction of lean proteins, actually. But this is summer camp, right?" He holds out his hands to grip the sunshine around us. "So marshmallows and hot dogs are pretty much required. Which means, Olivia, you can eat whatever you want. Running makes you hungry, but in a good way. Just listen to your body, all right?" Clap.

He sends us out to walk it off. Olivia and Montgomery are together up ahead, so I find myself with April and Lena. They're both older than me, and I don't want to seem annoying, so mostly I just walk and listen to them ask each other a bunch of questions, answering when things are directed at me but trying not to horn in too much.

We do our final stretches right there in the grass, which is warm on top but deep and cool near the roots. It's been a great morning, and I've got free swim this afternoon with two guys' cabins and I think Violet's, too, which is extra fabulous. It'll feel so good getting in that lake and then just lying in the sun for a couple of hours, especially on top of how satisfying track's been. I do allow myself the small thought, though, as we walk back to shower, how much better today will be if free swim also happens to be with Joel's cabin.

CALLA

It's kind of unbelievable how cheerful our receptionist Sally is, every day, no matter what's going on, no matter how cranky Deena's being or how much work there is to get done. Even on a crazy day like this—first official day for a new batch of campers—always, every time, whenever she talks, Sally totally sounds like someone's Southern aunt: this soft, light, airy voice all twanged out in just the right places. Her sweetness and delight to see you are particularly noticeable when you yourself are not certain you are excited about being awake, even at your favorite place in the world. But Sally is 100 percent all smiles always, her front teeth almost all exactly the same size, shape, and color, like a ventriloquist dummy's teeth, and just a hint of a silver rim near her gums. She totally looks warm and cheerful too: tiny wrists and ankles, and actually fantastic legs, with her middle all bunched up and doughy starting from about her shoulders to her belly button, in this way you can just see is really comfortable to hug. When I come back into the office after the gathering, there she is with her V8 and her big, toothy smile, saying to me, "Why good mornin', darlin'! How'd it go?"

It is a quick little burst of enthusiasm that at first kind of got on my nerves, but now I really like it. When Deena's stressed-out, or I look at the schedule and see that Duncan's busy with some awesome thing I'm missing out on doing with him, Sally's sugariness is totally buoying.

Not that Deena's been mean. Or ugly. It's just that she has a lot she has to juggle and a lot that's on her mind, and there are, like, a million crazy things for her to handle and respond to at once. Sometimes, for those of us who work closely with her, she just gets, you know, tense. I don't take it personally, though. In fact, I enjoy knowing what's going on behind her moods. Like for example, in the last four weeks I've learned that sometimes, even when Deena's voice is all cocktail-party hostess, and maybe she's squeezing your shoulder in this friendly, helpful way like you're about to be her new future sister-in-law, what you can tell, under her smile and all her effort at helping you understand her position, is that she is *pissed*.

Which, again, I totally can't blame her for, especially now that I see how many things there are for her to keep track of, how much she needs our help to run everything. The parents' expectations alone take up a big part of her time, not to mention the needs of the campers, or the camp itself. It's a huge stress, and if anybody understands how hard it is to have to be nice all the time when you're stressed, it's definitely me. So I want to do everything I can to help. I want to be someone who learns from her, but who also makes things flow. Someone who comes up with good ideas, instead of this dumb high-school-kid hindrance or annoying obstacle in her way.

Duncan thinks Deena's just mad all the time because she'd rather be working at some high-gloss marketing firm, which is what her degree is in, but his parents were good friends with Bob and Tina, our directors from before, so he has this automatic thing about her no matter what. He won't call her a bitch in front of me—not after I punched him in the arm a couple of weeks ago for it, and his first-session campers made fun of the bruise until it faded away—but I know he's only glad for me about my job because I am. I reminded him that one of the qualities he likes so much about me is how I set my mind to something and then just do it, but I'm not sure he bought it. (I didn't actually buy it either, since setting my mind to making him realize we should be together hasn't worked out so well yet.)

But I did set my mind to this job, and I'm so glad I got it. Since I'm interested in doing resort management, I thought this might kind of help in that department, but the main reason I wanted it was to really see how camp worked: to be part of the guts and lungs and heart of it. I wanted to know all the gritty details inside, not just the beautiful exterior. Like, one thing I figured out fast in my first week was that being surrounded by people who wear bathing suits most of the time is no excuse for coming to work in a wrinkled sundress or capris and a sloppy tee. You never know when a local alum might drop by, and it's important to make a good impression, even to campers, which is why I made sure to iron these shorts this weekend, even if Daisy and Duncan say they make me look like I'm pretending to be on a yacht.

But if I took my wardrobe cues from Duncan, I'd wear Chacos, hoodies, and cutoffs, and that's pretty much it. Deena's a much classier bet. She has on ivory today: shorts to her knee with a thin pinstripe, an ivory sleeveless cowl-neck T-shirt, and even spotless ivory Keds. Her gold earrings and bracelets (big enough to notice but not big enough to be gross) shine with a honey gloss, and her hair falls in perfect straight sheets on either side of her small, pointed face. Everything about Deena is small and pointed, except her eyes. Those are huge and brown, though right now they're kind of squinty, already back in the office and staring at the computer.

It's nice being back in the cool quiet of the office though, and getting serious. I'm glad the rush and craziness of arrivals yesterday, of this morning's gathering, are all over, and the three of us can settle into our regular tasks. I get myself into a good rhythm for the rest of the morning: Come in, say hey to Sally, see what new things have been added to the to do list, pick up the stack of things left for me that Deena brought in from last night, settle in at my desk.

One important task is to continue my work on the introductory e-mails to send to new schools Deena's visiting in September. Somehow I still cannot get them right. There's also a new note about canceling her hair appointment tomorrow and trying to reschedule it, plus the ongoing brochures project, which I love, where I read through all these brochures from other camps so I can see if there's anything interesting that I think Deena should consider doing here. Plus entering and fixing stuff in the database—that's an ongoing thing too.

But those introductory e-mails need to go out right away, so I start with them. I thought they were done, but on Friday Deena'd dropped the printed-out versions in the basket on my table/desk, with marks that Sally had to help me figure out said "tighten" in Deena's crazy caterpillar-crawl handwriting. I'd used the e-mails Sally sent out last year as templates, but for some reason I'm just not saying things the way Deena wants me to. I mess around with them for almost a half hour, cutting words and adding a few more—even going on dictionary.com to the thesaurus section to see if I can find some better ways of articulating things, but mostly it feels like pushing your food around your plate to make it look like you've been eating.

After I feel like I have them pretty good, I print them out and drop them in Deena's basket on Sally's desk, so that they'll go in the folder that Deena takes home with her every night. In my basket are updates for the database, so I hunker down to get those changes and updates in before lunch.

Duncan thought it was so nerdy when I told him about the database's amazingness, but still, it is that cool. I have no grasp at all on all the different reports it can run, but inside it is basically information on every camper who's been here since 1978. Sally had some software grad student come and build it when Bob and Tina hired her almost two decades ago. Everything was only on paper at that point, so she went through all the records herself, entering everything in by hand—camper by camper, parent by parent, counselor by counselor, employee by employee. Now we can totally search who's sent how many kids, who's come to what alumni gatherings and referred which campers and who's hosted

Deena—plus Bob and Tina—and we can compile information about every person who's ever worked here, even the exterminator. But it constantly has to be updated, because people are always moving and changing e-mails or getting different jobs and asking to be taken off the mailing list and stuff like that. So that's where I come in.

Sally's husband's truck guns up to the front drive, right as I finish clicking the two Brown families to "inactive" and find the kid who just graduated from Eckerd and needs his forwarding address updated. Sally smiles and says, "I guess my date's here." Though I'm surprised to see it's lunchtime already, I'm not so absorbed in my concentration daze that I don't wink back at her as she heads out. The two of them are totally cute. Sally always trots out in her little skirts and wedge sandals, and they go to lunch—sometimes just brown-bagged sandwiches she made that morning to eat by the lake. He comes to pick her up after work, too, and I imagine them going home to sit on their lakefront deck sipping drinks out of Mason jars and talking about the day, sometimes having dates to go dancing or play bingo. When she told me how they grew up together in the same town, going to all the same schools and running with the same bunch of friends all their lives, but that it wasn't until she came back from two years at the vocational school that he perked up and noticed her, it gave me a ton of hope that one day Duncan and I will wind up like them.

Watching her go, and hearing the camp bell ring for lunch, I realize I'm totally hungry, on top of stunned about how fast the morning's gone by. Violet and Daisy have both had their first mornings at concentration, and Duncan's been enjoying his free time going fishing with the guys while his campers are occupied. So much has happened around me, while I've stayed put in this office chair all morning.

I pop up, stretch, start looking forward to seeing Violet, Daisy, and Duncan. Deena locks the office, and we're heading down to the dining hall when she suddenly whips around with this anxious look and goes, "What time's my appointment this week?" I remember about rescheduling her at the hair salon. So then I have to go back up and spend the next twenty minutes being on hold or talking to the really prissy receptionist, who is probably, like, my age by the sound of her. We go back and forth a few times before I finally nail something that will work. At that point there's only time for me to run down to throw a sandwich together and grab an apple or a banana before Sally comes back, but at least I'll get to catch a glimpse of my sisters. And maybe there'll be time to get one of those hugs from Duncan again too.

DAISY

Everyone complains about afternoon swim, because it's not as cool as the ropes course or riding horses, doing zip lines or blindfold hike. I don't get what's so bad about it, though. While everyone else fusses and scrambles into their swimsuits—trading tops, advising on different bottoms—I just sit on my bunk swinging my legs. I'm still warm and happy from my run this morning, from the yoga stretches. Lounging in the sun, Joel or not, is going to be the cherry on top.

When we get to the lake, I can see Violet stretched out in her one-piece. A second quick scan makes it clear Joel's cabin is not part of the group. But it's okay. It would've been nice, but I realize it's almost better that I can just hang out with my sister and my girlfriends, without worrying about some boy seeing me in my bathing suit, or having to prove my cleverness. I don't go over to Violet right away, though. Flannery wants me to play this dunking game girls in our cabin are all excited about, and that seems like the perfect kind of brainless fun. The game turns out to be Twenty Questions, basically, but if you're the one guessing, you get held by two other people, and for every question with a "no" answer, you get dunked upside down. It's a dumb game, but it attracts attention, with a bunch of boys hopping around us shouting out random annoying questions like, "Is it bigger than a bread box?" and "Could I hide it in my pants?"

But after Olivia gets three wrong questions in a row and practically chokes to death inhaling half of the lake her third time under, and when she starts shrieking that Manon and this other girl from Violet's cabin held her under too long, the game breaks up. I stride out of the water with Olivia up to the beach and try to see if she's okay, but she shrugs me off and grabs her towel from the sand, charges over to one of our counselors.

When I get to Violet, she's up on her elbows, shielding her eyes, watching me.

"Bit of a hysteric one, eh?" she says.

I shrug. "She got scared, I think. And embarrassed."

Violet makes a *pssshhhh* sound. "Cabin dramatics."

"Most of the girls are cool. I like Manon a lot. Her parents are from the Ivory Coast or somewhere, I think. I like her accent."

"Anyone in your concentration?"

I can't help a wry smile. "Olivia." I point with my chin. "And her friend Montgomery."

Violet laughs. "Eeeesh."

"They're not so bad. Just giggly."

"You like it, though?"

"What, running? Yeah, I think so."

"More than just the coach?" Her eyebrow is arched high.

"When you see him up close, it's not that big a deal. He always claps to emphasize different words. And this morning he made us do yoga."

"Wait a second," a girl on the other side of Violet says, reaching over to put her hand on Vivi's knee. I forgot there were other people around. This girl peers at me over her sunglasses. "You mean to tell me that Coach is doing *yoga* in track?" She whistles. "I would like to see some of that."

I can tell my cheeks are pink. "It's really good for your body."

"I bet it is," the girl says.

Violet shoves her off like she's a puppy with a licking problem. "Shut up, Trinity. Not everyone chose their concentration to scope out boys."

Trinity makes her face completely blank. "Really?" She's convincingly dumbfounded. But two seconds later she breaks into a deadly grin. "Are you insinuating that I am in Water Sports for some other reason than the fact that most of the kayak and canoe trips are shirt-optional for my male companions? It totally helps them paddle. Or steer. Or something. Right?"

"You're sick," Violet says, but she is smiling. She rolls over onto her stomach, hooks her chin on her shoulder to look at me with some meaning. I flip over onto my stomach too, so Vivi and I can talk without so much eavesdropping. There are things, after all, we need to talk about.

Speak of the devil, just then Duncan and a herd of boys from his cabin go charging past us, kicking up sand and honking and flapping their elbows like wings. They run as hard and fast as they can into the water, see who can run the deepest before they fall down. A couple of other counselors shout half-seriously at them to cut it out. The herd starts a splashing war in the middle of the lake instead.

"I hope something happens finally," is all I say, watching Duncan.

"God. Are you kidding me? I don't think I can take it again. I really don't."

I can't help but groan a little.

"He doesn't love her back," she says, serious and flat. I think it too, though we haven't said it that plain before. "If he did, they'd be a couple now in their fifth summer of love. I'm telling you. But I wish I could tell her."

I look at her. "You mean, like you and . . . whatever that was last night?" She knows what I'm talking about. I don't want to say too much because Trinity might still be listening, but I don't have to. It may have only been a tiny thing, James waving to her like that at dinner, but I know my sister and I know boys around my sister, and I know when something suddenly becomes a lot more than you think it could.

She chews on the side of her lip. "I'm not sure. I mean, weird, right?"

I can see how just even the sideways mention of him makes her sparkle.

"You talked to him yet?"

"You talked to that boy from the bonfire?"

Both of us smile, caught, knowing both answers are no. But still I'm excited, each of us having someone new to be thrilled about, someone interesting in this wholly surprising way. Violet's never serious about all the boys who flock around her at school. She'll go out with them, yeah, but she always comes home rolling her eyes and cracking jokes. When she saw James at sign-in, I swear I saw her . . . glimmer. Even though I was like, *Huh?* I still thought it was great.

"The counselor thing is tricky," I say, trying not to even move my lips.

Tricky because of the rules, but also because of Calla. Even before she was staff, Calla didn't need any camp rules to make her against camper/counselor relationships. Sitting here with our sister, I practically hear what Calla would think about Violet being into him, and I know so can Vivi. But seeing Violet so enthused, even without saying much, I want Cow to be here, to be excited too.

"Maybe I'll talk to him tonight," I say finally, bringing the focus back to Joel.

"You gotta make him come to you, right?" She is sly-grinning again.

"I don't know." I shake my head. Suddenly, being here next to her—being close to the aura that is Violet and her intense passion for everything, thinking about my new romance compared to what hers will probably end up being—I feel kind of removed from the excitement that came over me last night when Joel was clearly interested. Like my emotions still aren't on par with hers. Or Calla's.

"You still burned about what happened with Dylan?" she wants to know out of not-totally nowhere.

"I won't break Joel's heart with my 'acute coldness,' that's for sure." I snort.

Violet scoffs. "That was *lame*."

"Yeah, it was lame." Although I don't know what was lamer—being dumped for not wanting to tongue someone at my locker every morning when we'd only gone on one single "date" at the mall, or that Dylan had his sister drive him to our house so he could dump me face-to-face. She waited out in the car the whole time. With the engine running.

"I mean, who says that? I still don't even know what that means," Violet goes on. "Does he think he's John Mayer or something?" She's laughing a little now. "'Acute coldness.' That's like saying 'Abstract frivolity. I can't go out with you anymore because of your abstract frivolity.'"

"Your obtuse fragility."

"Your isosceles thoughtlessness." She tries to say it with a straight face, but can't.

"Yeah. I can't go out with you because of your isosceles thoughtlessness."

"Your taxonomic hypocrisy."

"Oh god. Your photosynthetic mysteriousness."

She sits up. "I'm afraid, dahling, your osmotic shyness has put me quite off."

I clap my hands as though summoning the girl waiting in the car parked in the driveway. "Sister, away!"

Violet's face is scrunched up now with laughing. I can feel

my cheeks up to my eyes too. I'm not even sure this is all that funny, but that's how we get.

A multiheaded shadow falls across our towels. We freeze, mid-smile. Violet squints up.

"Hey, Satch," she says to this huge totem pole of a guy standing over us. He's brought two other guys and a thin, pale girl wearing a purple tie-dyed bikini that only makes her look more wan.

"'Sup, Vi."

"This is my sister Daisy."

"'Sup."

"Satch was in Vis Arts with me last summer," she explains. "You doing it again this session?"

He nods but has other business for us. "Up for some chicken fights?"

None of the other kids with him are looking at us, all of them scoping the beach for potential other people they could be talking to. It's only Satch who wants to be here. And he only wants to be with Violet.

"I don't think we're up for it today, Satch." Just like that, she tells him, straight-out. No excuses or flirty lies. Which I know, even if she doesn't, means she is truly intrigued by James.

He nods. "Sometime later then."

"Later." She gives him a little wave. We both turn to watch him go down the beach, one of his friends gesturing to a group of girls sitting closer to the water, girls who look the opposite of wan in their bikinis. Suddenly I'm irritated. She should've gone with them instead of staying here with me just because I'm not keen on chicken fights. She should know by now all I really care about is her being happy. That, and that she doesn't feel like she has to look out for me all the time.

I sit up fast, surprising her. "I think I want to swim."

"You're not even dry yet."

"I want to dry off on the floating dock."

"Out there?"

"Why not? Manon's out there. It's cool if you don't want to go."

"It's not that I don't want to go." She sinks her head back down on her arms, shifts her hips so that she can settle flatter on her stomach. "It's just that it's so *nice* right here."

She says this when we are curled up in blankets on the couch too, and she wants me to be the one to get up and get us more cookies or Coke or whatever. I look down at her. Her shoulders are getting pink.

"You need some sunscreen."

"Give it to me, baby." She points in the general direction of the pile that is her T-shirt, shorts, and sandals. I squeeze some out onto my hand and smear it onto her shoulders, down her back. She lifts her curls off her neck so I can get her there, too, though her hair is an impenetrable curtain through which no light could fall.

"Okay, well, enjoy your swim," she says, something weird in her voice I can't pin down and also kind of want to ignore. I toss the sunscreen onto her shorts after swiping a bit on my own cheeks. I haven't actually managed to swim out to the dock before, mainly because last year it was dominated by a bunch of seniors and juniors preoccupied with perfecting their backflips off the edge, but I guess I'm game now.

I walk past the bikini girls and into the water, veering far right to give Satch and his friends—they found enough girls, plus two more guys—plenty of room. I start to paddle. Flan's dolphin face pops up next to me, wet and smiling.

"God, you scared me." My foot stretches down, tiptoes touching the sandy bottom, barely able to keep my face above the water.

"You going to the dock?"

I look out at it, gauging the distance. I can make that, sure.

"You wanna come?"

"I been out once, but sure!" Her head goes immediately under, and I see the pale twins of her legs kick out before she's down deep, pushing herself into the dark water like a happy mermaid.

I stick to the surface and take it slow, my swimming more

like dog-paddling than anything else. It's not that I don't know how to swim. I just don't like how water completely surrounds you, keeps you from seeing very well in any direction. It's better to stay up top, where at least you know what's coming.

When I get to the dock, Flannery's already there, sitting with her legs stretched out with Manon, Jenny, and Jordan, plus some girls I don't know from Violet's cabin. They're playing Would You Rather, trying to gross out and shock each other. I find a space next to Flan. Little beads of water cling to her thick eyelashes. A cloud goes over the sun, and I get goose bumps.

"Would you rather," Jenny is saying, taunting each one of us in the circle with her snappy blue eyes before asking the question, "have to wear only giant, thick maxi pads or use those tampons with no applicators?" Everyone's faces scrunch up and there's a lot of embarrassed giggling, groans of "gross," and "ew," though a couple of girls roll their eyes. Going around the circle, most everyone picks the pads, but when it gets to my turn I say I'd choose the tampons, since I already know from Violet they aren't that bad.

"Ew. You'd put your finger? In there?" Jenny says.

I just shrug at her.

"Why let a boy do something you're too afraid to do?" Manon says, mocking. "Tampons, definitely. They're better for the environment, too." She winks at me.

It goes on like that. We all lie down on our backs, heads

in the middle of the circle so we can hear each other, though it still sounds like the girls who aren't right next to me are talking underwater: Would you rather have a boyfriend with a pimply butt or a really hairy one? Date a guy with a dick for a face or a face on his dick? None of these girls have probably even *seen* a dick—most of us are fourteen, fifteen—so it's funny how they talk like they know. It strikes me that everybody always thinks boys are the trash-talkers. They obviously haven't hung out at many floating docks in summer camps.

The sun moves in and out of the clouds. We dry off, dozing, talking about stupid stuff. At some point Flannery takes off to swim some more. New girls and a few guys come up and join us—I don't really follow much of the conversations, just enjoy lying there and half listening, being part of a group without having to be. Eventually the counselors start hollering for us to swim back, get ready to clean up and come in. I didn't mean to not hang out with Violet this much. I thought she'd come out to the floating dock. As I swim myself back to the shore, I can see her, bending and shaking out her towel, looking exactly like Mom, though she'd hate me if I said so. A girl in a green tankini says something to her and she laughs. Violet's curls are dried and fluffy around her face. She doesn't turn and look for me as she heads up toward her cabin. I guess she figures I'm okay on my own. I realize, for the most part this afternoon, she's right.

CALLA

During the rest of the day, I'm honestly way too busy to really think much about Violet or Daisy or camp and how much fun they're having and what's going on or Duncan's afternoon with his cabin or any of that stuff, though as I'm going down the stairs to dinner with Deena, I do wonder if Duncan's going up to the fire pit after lights-out, if I shouldn't drag myself up there just to make sure he's still on his weird (but wonderful) streak of not being into any other girl for what's becoming the fifth week.

Even with that thought though, sitting in the same room with (if not at the same table as) the three people I love the most, talking to the instructors about the day and all of that, half my head is reminding myself of the things leftover from what came up this afternoon that I need to finish off in the morning, the list I should make when I get back to my room. I should be excited about seeing my sisters at the bonfire after dinner, excited about getting to talk to Duncan about how his new campers are settling in, but the truth is I'm kinda tired and don't much want to drag myself up the hill for all that cheerful singing. Daisy and Bot will be distracted with their new friends anyway, and Duncan will have his hands full. Look at me—half already not going, and I've barely lifted my fork.

I am able to register what's going on around me enough, though, to notice Violet up at the salad bar, and this weirdly muscled-but-thin girl with black hair and annoying turquoise streaks sliding up next to her. Violet's face immediately goes into that supercool, nonchalant thing she does, which is funny because it's obvious the other girl is the one who wants to do the impressing: picking up a hot pepper and popping it, whole, into her mouth. I know Vivi's bummed that Dover's not here this summer, but *ugh*, I really hope she's not going to hang out with some poseur punk girl who's obviously trying to make sure we all know how different she is.

Focusing on them actually keeps me from seeing Duncan, who comes up behind me from I guess the drink station to

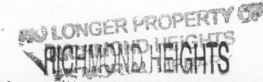

61

squeeze my tense shoulders in his hands a few times, the way he used to in Drama, the way I tried to—still try to—pretend I didn't think meant something. It's not a big deal—everyone knows we're best friends—but surrounded by all the instructors, it does mean something, right? Him coming over like this. I hope some of the other girl counselors are noticing.

"How's the paper pushing, chief?"

"Probably easier than corralling a bunch of fourteen-year-old boys. Although . . ." I put my finger to my chin. "Maybe I'm not sure."

"At least the girls in your office don't stink."

I look up at him, astonished and sympathetic. "They haven't been here a full day!"

His eyebrows go high, leaving those blue-and-green-flecked eyes big and round and twinkling. He waves a hand in front of his nose. Last session he and his co-counselor actually had to throw a kid in the lake because he wouldn't shower.

"Tell me I didn't smell that bad when I was one of them," he pleads.

I take a big whiff of him. He smells like outside. And oatmeal soap. And, okay, a little bit of boyish sweat. But in a way that means he's been having fun, being the totally-throw-yourself-into-things boy I love.

"You smell like a prince."

He steps back and bows. I try to shut out the image of myself as Cinderella.

"Either that or . . . a ham sandwich. I'm not sure."

"Nice, Cal. Nice. Once again, I am so glad I can count on you to pull me up."

I look sharp at him. "You know you can."

His hand goes back to my shoulder, and his face stops laughing. "Absolutely I know." He pats me again before slipping off to refill his glass. He might be thinking of last summer, when his dog died while we were at camp and I sat with him while he cried by the lake, scared anyone in his cabin would see. Or maybe our first year, when Molly Eberstein dumped him three days into camp, and I listened to him recount all her bad qualities, my heart beating in my throat the whole time. Or that I always helped him finish memorizing his lines when we were in Drama. It doesn't matter which time he's thinking about, just that he is. And that he said it so seriously, so definite. And I think probably I will absolutely go hang out at least a little tonight.

Although, admittedly, my own evenings have turned out to be kind of pleasant. Once the first-session campers got here, after our first week of training—when evenings didn't matter because everyone was exhausted from those ten-hour days Deena put us through—I didn't really know what to do with myself after dinner. Sometimes I'd hang out with Kesiah and Lucy, my suitemates in the instructors' lodge. It wasn't that awkward, except when they wanted to go down the road to the Hook 'n' Mouth for beers. I tagged along then and still do sometimes, mainly because it's fun to shoot pool, though all I can have is ginger ale or cranberry juice and it's so obvious I'm underage. Before first session, though (was it only a couple days ago it ended?), I got really, really psyched and was all, *I'm going to do everything in the evening and show everybody how awesome camp is and that even staff like me can still get into it.* I thought maybe there'd be some junior who'd need a mentor, and that we'd be friends and she'd come visit my campus in the fall when she was looking for colleges, stuff like that. I thought, stupidly, that Duncan and I would get to sit and sing together at the bonfires like we always did before, that we'd be on the same teams for the games, that I could squeeze his hand at the graveyard ghost stories like I have to. But I guess as a camper I never paid much attention to what staffers were doing, because after two bonfires and camp sing-alongs, where Duncan spent most of the time watching to make sure his campers didn't set each other on fire, after one night of camp karaoke and then playing Flashlight Capture the Flag (which was actually a lot of fun, because me and Duncan were on the same team and we totally made up these G.I. Joe codes and scared the crap out of a bunch of sophomores who thought they were too cool to really play), I realized I was basically the only staff person besides

Deena who was around, and even she was camper-focused. It felt almost silly for me to be there.

Which was and is okay, mostly, because I'm so much more a part of things in the office. Yes, the counselors are in the thick of it, but they're pretty myopic. They don't know small things like that Deena was on the phone negotiating a major donation from an alum right as they barged in saying there's no more jewelweed soap for the poison ivy kids. They still have their free mornings to just do nothing, while I'm getting to help make the whole system run so smoothly they don't even notice. I'm the one who orders the jewelweed soap, after all. I mean, yes, Duncan and Hailey and Adele—who I know from camp before—all of us love camp, love being here to help out the summer before we go off to college. The difference is they're all still mostly just playing around, while I know how much they get paid, and when there are problems and how they get dealt with, and all of that. So, the few times first session when I did go to hang with Duncan and whoever else was up at the fire pit after lights-out, even though Duncan was happy and we leaned on each other and laughed, I still felt kind of—outside. Plus after about the second or third time, it really seemed like being the one staffer who was going up there meant I was kind of condoning what they were doing, even though we all know it's totally against camp rules.

I thought when Bot and Dizzy got here second session, it

might be different. That I could go hang out with them and we could do stuff together. But of course, looking over at both of them at their cabin tables, it's not like I can really just go sit with them without it being like, *Hey, who is that staff person sitting with you?* I don't have time to go to keynote every morning like Deena does, so I won't be able to connect with them there, either. And during evening activities, they're supposed to be hanging out with their cabinmates, and I honestly want to do the evening routine I've established for myself, to make sure I'm in bed early, so I can be sharp and focused and fresh like Sally in the morning.

It might be dorked out of me, but staying in my room and reading, or writing notes to my sisters or Madeline back home about random things during the day I want to tell them, or working on the Sudoku book that Duncan and I swap back and forth (writing smack-talk in the margins, which is hilarious but also this fantastic, energetic conversation between just us)—it's turned out to be pretty luxurious, actually. At first I thought it was totally lame and boring of me, something I would make fun of girls like Miranda and Cath back at school for probably, but now it feels really . . . grown-up. After work I'll go on a walk or jog, do my sit-ups and push-ups, then shower before dinnertime. Maybe if I feel like it I'll go to whatever the evening activity is so I can see people a little—can give Duncan the nasty charred outsides of my marshmallows if we're roasting them, since I'm the only one who knows how to scorch them just right for him— but usually I won't stay the whole time. I'll come back to my sweet little room and slide into my pajamas and turn on the lamp by my bed, get a big glass of water, and then just curl up in my bed to read.

I've actually gotten pretty obsessed with trying to get through all those classics we didn't do this year in AP Lit—books I some-how managed to graduate from high school without reading. I mean, yes, *The Glass Castle* and *The Absolutely True Diary of a Part-Time Indian* are totally good books, but hello? How can I go to college not ever having read *A Tale of Two Cities*? Or *Pride and Prejudice*?

I finished *Jane Eyre*, *1984*, and *Catch-22* from our leave-a-book, take-a-book shelves in the common room during first session. Now I'm on *Anna Karenina*, Vivi's dog-eared copy that I brought from home. I'm annotating my thoughts in my note-book for her, so she and I can talk about it together later this summer. After today, and my brain-scramble feeling, Anna and Kitty and Levin and everyone sound pretty wonderful, although that shoulder rub from Duncan felt pretty great too, and I know I could get him to give me a full-on one if I went back up there tonight after lights-out. But I'd have to make myself stay awake past midnight before I even headed up, and after rising even earlier this morning because of the gathering, I'm not sure I have the physical ability to do that.

While I'm debating all this, as well as whether I'll have banana pudding or a slice of watermelon for dessert, I see that turquoise-streak girl showing her whole table how she can balance a spoon on her nose. Duncan, helping his campers construct some sculpture out of toothpicks and watermelon rinds, catches me looking at him and gives me a wink. When I look away from him, I see that white-blond kid who was talking to Daisy last night, and he is definitely looking over at her. So, tired or not, strange or not, I'm thinking that even if I don't know what dessert I'm having, with everything that's going on, I should really go to the bonfire after this.

VIOLET

After dinner at the bonfire is pretty fun. We sing stupid songs, and I chat with Cow for the fifteen minutes she stays up there before yawning and saying she has to hit the hay. She apparently doesn't even remember James from two summers ago, because we don't discuss him at all. And even when she asks me what I think about that Joel kid and Daisy, she still keeps one eye on Duncan, which is a little annoying, but even more so when it's clear the reason she's leaving is because Duncan is pretty preoccupied with helping Adele teach both their campers some crazy clapping game.

A while later, everyone tries to out-pysch each other with

ghost stories—a normal night around the fire, except of course me and James looking at each other and then looking away real fast. When some girl from Whitman screams and has to run back down to her cabin because someone's flung a half-roasted marshmallow that lands in her hair, even that's normal. But during this Brynn leans into me and says, "Meet me at the boathouse at midnight," and it shocks me so much I just nod. I don't think how I will do it. Instead, just like that, I nod, and I'm in.

I have never snuck out before. It's not because I don't want to sneak out, or because—like Calla—I have some kind of superior morality complex about what is and isn't right. Just a kind of unnameable discomfort with it. Like something could go wrong.

So now I'm lying here in my bunk, listening to my cabinmates settling down from their giggling and gossiping, drifting to sleep (lights-out is ten, since we all have to be up and to breakfast at seven), and my body is rigid with conflict. On one hand I'm trying to sound and appear as though I, too, am fast asleep. I'm doing the regulatory breathing thing and leaving my mouth partly open and all that, but the other half of me is SAT-prep alert, clenched with anxiety, worried that, in faking sleep, I actually *will* fall asleep, and thereby win Brynn's disdain and mockery forever. I don't know her at all, but I know I don't want her thinking I'm lame. So I've got one eye closed in repose, the other staring fixedly at the little digital clock down by Trinity and Aislin's bunk.

Which is why I nearly leap out of my own bunk when, at eleven thirty, our counselor Natalie slowly creaks up from her single bed by the door, fumbles a minute for her flip-flops, and quietly lets herself out into the night.

This leaves me lying in a state of semi-more-relaxedness for the next while, waiting for her to maybe come back. (At least Natalie thought I was asleep, or else doesn't care either way, and our other counselor, Emma Jane, didn't even budge, so that means either she is dead to the world or doesn't care either.) I occupy myself with wondering where Natalie went. Is she hooking up with another counselor? And if so, who? It takes me rejecting all the boys before it even dawns on me that it could be one of the girls. Natalie and Nyasiah could make a good couple, maybe.

I shock myself out of this, though, seeing the clock at 11:56. I almost jump right off the bunk, but Emma Jane is still at the front of the cabin, so I slow myself super way down, moving like a scene in some dumb action movie where they practically stop all motion so you can see the bullets as they make impact, the blood splooshing out, the tough guys' faces in exaggerated agony. I almost make myself giggle out loud, grimacing like one of those guys as I lift my foot s-l-o-w-l-y and silently over the edge of my bed and onto the first rung. I have to stop there for a full thirty seconds before I'm sure I will neither laugh nor slip down the rungs on top of Emily, who is sleeping in the bunk underneath me.

When my feet finally hit the floor, my heart feels like it's going a hundred beats per minute somewhere six inches outside of my chest, and I'm breathing these little short breaths out of my nose that, in my head, sound like the snortings of an angry bull. It takes twenty or so of these breaths before my toes find the edges of my flip-flops (at least I hope they're my flip-flops) stuck under the bed. I pick them up and press them to my chest and then begin the very, very, very slow and I hope silent path toward the front door. But I can't be too slow. It's already 12:01.

On my scary creep to freedom, Emily snorts in her sleep twice, Bo—I think—murmurs and does a complete 360-degree turn from stomach to back to stomach again, Emma Jane scratches some part of her lower leg with her foot, and somebody up high starts that gargling breathing that isn't quite snoring but isn't normal breathing either. Each time, my heart pounds, my joints absolutely freeze, and my ears nearly strain themselves off the sides of my head, listening for the change in sound that means someone is really awake and I'm caught. I hallucinate the lights flicking on so clearly I have to press my eyes closed for a minute, just to make sure they're not. And yet also, the whole time I'm wondering what has made me such a chickenshit. I have got to get outside. My new friend is there, by the boat-house, waiting, and if I don't hustle some muscle it's going to be a long, boring summer.

Once I'm finally out of the cabin (cracking the door only barely big enough to get through, and then moving it millimeter by millimeter back to its safe and shut position), of course everything's fine. It's almost weird how not-menacing everything looks—each cabin with its warm, safe light glowing by the front door, everyone silent and innocuous in their bunks. No alarms sound, no dogs come barking after me. I walk (well, quick-walk) myself down the path to the boathouse with no inci-dent whatsoever. I don't know what the heck I was so afraid of.

"Jeez gah," Brynn hisses when she sees me coming. "Take forever. What'd you do? Full makeup or something?"

She's mad, but she's also looking to check I didn't really put on anything—maybe, it looks for a second, a little scared I might've shown up prettier than her.

But she's not ultimately the nervous one. "C'mon." She grabs my wrist like I need leading, like I'm her kid and neither of us wants to do the grocery shopping.

I don't ask where we're going. She lets go of my wrist and we walk, sort of side by side but her a little ahead. Being in the woods in the middle of the night isn't that scary. At least not with the security lights shining bright enough so that you're not in strict dark for very long. Brynn takes me down to the water so we can walk along the darkest edge of the lake, as far from the lodge lights as we can manage without swimming, then up around the arts building, and diagonally across the pitch-black field and up the hill to the fire pit.

Even before we get there, I can hear people talking. Brynn's not hesitating about there obviously being counselors hanging out, so I try to be cool about it too. When we reach the top of the hill, about five of them are sitting on the ground, talking and poking sticks occasionally into the black smoldering mess that was our campfire tonight. My eyes have adjusted enough to the thin light of the moon, to see—*oh shit*—my own counselor Natalie is one of them.

"Dude, nah-ohn," Heath says, standing up. "I thought no campers this year, man."

"Chill," that weird surfer-stoner counselor at our feet says.

"Shut up, Carp," Heath aims at him. "I'm serious. This is lame. I'm goin' back." He turns as though he really is going to leave, but does it slow enough to make it clear what he really wants is for them to make us go. I flick my eyes at Brynn. Maybe it's better if we do just leave. But she's standing there boredly looking at Heath, just waiting for him to shut up so everyone else can get on with the night. I guess I'm staying put.

"Dude, calm down," Natalie says, while at the same time, Duncan's unmistakable Prince Charming voice goes, "It's not like we didn't do it last year, man. Just chill. And there's no way to keep them from coming up here if we are."

When it seems Heath's not saying anything else, Duncan adds, "Hey, Violet."

"Hey, Dunk," I say back, still unsure. Brynn's bony elbow bumps slightly into my arm. I don't know if it's because she didn't know I was tight with one of the guys already, or if it's because she's just seen James like I've just seen James, as he's moving over to hand Natalie another beer. There's no way Brynn knows anything about him, but you'd have to be dead from the waist down not to notice his hotness. Or maybe it's not about James. Maybe she's doing it because she didn't realize my own counselor was going to be here, and thinks it's weird. Maybe it's because she wants to go, though I doubt it.

"So, I'm guessing this isn't about any disaster over in Berry," Natalie says next. I can't tell if she's annoyed or kidding.

"Here, guys." Duncan brings over beers—something in a can, and not very cold.

"Is it—okay?" I can't help asking, sort of holding the beer there. Most of me still feels like we should just go back, even though the rest of me is dying to stay up here with James. This is counselor chill time, and I feel weird that we're encroaching.

"Sure it is, man," the surfer guy, Carp, says, laughing. "Wouldn't be camp if we didn't have some little turds sneaking up, trying to party with us. Take a seat."

So Brynn gives me another poke with her elbow, and that decides it. We move around the edge of the pit, and I angle myself to sit down by Natalie and Duncan. When Brynn starts chatting with Carp—who is obviously the one who invited her—I lean over to Nat and ask her if she's sure this isn't too weird. Really, what I mean is, *I'm not in trouble, am I?* She must be able to tell, because she just squeezes my knee and tells me not to worry about it in this resigned-and-amused kind of way. She clinks her beer against my still-unopened one, dumb there in my hand.

Where I'm sitting, since the fire's not lit anymore and the small moon seems to be tucking itself behind the treetops, I can't see James but I can hear him. Or, I can sort of hear him. Between Brynn and Carp's snorting and giggling, and Duncan and Natalie talking about something in basketball that I have no idea about, I can make out the little agreeing or disagreeing sounds he's making as Heath delivers some monologue about his idea for—I don't know what because I'm pretending to be listening to Nat and Dunk, or else pretending to laugh at whatever Carp gurgles in my direction from time to time. But he's . . . there. And in the dark, across that fire pit that is no longer burning—I can't really explain it. But there is this tingling feeling in my neck. I can tell he knows where I am too, can tell he's over there listening for me. And even if he doesn't say anything to me for the rest of the night—until I decide that Brynn and I should be polite and leave before we're asked to—we're up here, together. And I know it matters to him, just as much as it matters to me.

Tuesday

VIOLET

The morning comes way too fast, and even though I didn't end up drinking more than about three sips of that warm canned beer, I feel like lead. Half my cabin is chirpy up-and-at-'em, though, so I have to fall in quick, or else I'll get stuck with the shower on the end, the one with the weird pressure that half the time just trickles a thin little stream. A couple of times I try to catch Natalie's eye and again express my gratitude to her for being cool last night, but she and Emma Jane are too busy making us all straighten our bunks, helping us find stray flip-flops, brushes, and shampoo bottles.

Breakfast is pans of eggs and packets of oatmeal and big,

lopsided bagels accompanied by messy bowls of stabbed-at cream cheese and something that might, in some hemisphere, be butter. There's another big metal pan of shriveled-looking sausages that I know from my first year ooze half their weight in grease the second you bite into them. I grab half a bagel and head over to the line by the toasters, already imagining the dry bites gluing my mouth together.

Which is maybe why I have nothing to say when Brynn saunters right by me—plate piled with eggs and sausage and Binky's potatoes, too—and raises her eyebrows, saying, "Look sharp, Cap'n" just as James crosses the other way past us both. He is wrangling two of his campers to the back of the toaster line, saying something jaunty about politeness and ladies preferring gentlemen, but as he says it, his teeth and his eyes and his smile all go in my direction. It's not much of a moment between us. With Brynn there in the same space at the same time, though, having already somehow picked up on the something I barely understand, it feels like one. I know I'm red, and I don't want to be. I don't want her to be here, seeing it.

But instead of moving on to her table, she sidles up to me, like she's going to slide those sausages right in the toaster.

"So, what?" she says, with that elbow.

"What, what?" It is almost my turn. I finger my bagel, as though trying to decide which way to put it in.

"You've got a thing for James? I saw you last night."

"We didn't even talk last night." It is defensive and dumb, how I sound. I slip my bagel onto the mechanical roller through the toaster.

"I know you didn't talk last night." She guffaws. The girl ahead of me at the cream cheese station glances back.

"It's no big deal. He was here—" I try to make my face look like I'm trying to remember. "Not last summer but the summer before that. Just a guy in my concentration. He's a counselor now, anyway. Whatev." I shrug just as my overly browned bagel drops with a thunk in the bottom of the toaster. *A guy who did the most amazing charcoal sketches; a guy who always had encouraging things to say about everyone's work; a guy who I stupidly thought was super great but not cute enough to pay attention to before. Just a guy. Right?*

"Wanted to make sure he was free pickings, is all." She winks, snatching up a sausage and biting into it, grease spreading across her lips before she saunters away. She's just kidding—at least I think—but the idea of James with anyone else, even if I haven't even talked to him yet, makes my stomach burn.

I drop my tray with my half-black bagel and a glass of orange juice at the seat next to Emily.

"You were smart with the bagel," she says, playing her spoon around the glob of goop that is her oatmeal. "I didn't want it to get too runny, you know, so I didn't put in enough water."

Complaining about breakfast, talking about what boys everybody's scoped out, whining about concentrations, and wondering what our afternoon activities are going to be—this talk surrounds me, but I'm not really focusing. There's no way James would go for Brynn, would he? Although he is so cool now. Maybe he would. I can't help it—I pretend I'm looking around for Daisy, whose table is near his, trying to be sly. But the minute he sees my head turn, his eyes are on mine. Yeah, there's no way he'd go for her. I try to hide my smile by taking a bite of bagel.

Speaking of cool, I'm kind of amazed at Natalie this morning. Down there, joking with Trinity and Bo at the other end of the table like nothing happened last night. She doesn't even look tired. It's not like we didn't know counselors snuck out at night—Calla always had all these great fantasies about a counselor's life after lights-out—but having been there, having seen it, having had her let me stay, I feel like the one person in the audience who knows how the magic trick really works.

I watch Brynn, three tables over, talking with her mouth full to some girl in her cabin. She's still so hard to get, like why she pegged me for her sneak-out partner or anything. It seems like she couldn't care less about anyone here, but now, without knowing I'm watching, she's yukking it up and goofing off with this total prep girl like, well, like they could be friends. Like they both belong.

Which makes my head crane up to see if I can spot Calla over at the instructors' table.

She looks cute this morning. But I feel bad for her, not being able to wear T-shirts and shorts like the counselors, having to make an impression and set herself apart by dressing professionally.

Besides being dressier than most of us, she's also doing a lot of listening over there, it looks like, which is somewhat out of character. It strikes me that she seems really calm, though, and sure—like she doesn't have to work to make everyone like her. Probably because they already do like her. A ton. Most of the instructors I don't really know, because unless you're in their concentration you don't see them much, save for the fifteen minutes they give at keynote, or helping with evening activities. Watching her with them, for a weird second I have this flash of jealousy; Calla gets to hang with the twenty- and twenty-five-year-olds, listen to them talk about jobs and studies and trips that are way, way, way beyond Callanwolde's fences. She's part of the grown-up tribe. She can do pretty much what she wants now. When I notice the way she moves her head, though, how her spoon hovers over her oatmeal, not taking a bite—suddenly I know she's not really having a good time.

My jealousy disappears. It's not fair for Cow to be here, her favorite place in the world, and not be having a blast. I want to take my plate and go sit next to her, start quoting lines from *South Park*. I want to make her crack up, get her to do her Wall-E impersonation, let her be silly, try to enjoy herself.

But I can't do that for her forever, it occurs to me. Soon she's going to be at another table, in another dining hall, far away. I won't be able to help her out then. In mid-August, she's going away and she's not coming back. Not except for Thanksgiving or winter break or perhaps for half a summer. I've been trying not to think about it, because we knew we'd be together here at camp, but even after Zee and I go back home, Calla will still be here, without us. And even after only a day, watching from across the room, it seems like she's kind of already without us. And we're without her, too.

DAISY

During yoga this morning, there's a little less laughing and goofing around. Except for the part where we're supposed to grab one of our feet and then raise our leg up behind us in some sort of "bow" position. That almost no one can do, and even Lena groans and giggles through it, falling over and nearly taking Finch with her. Coach moves around to the front and does the pose for us again, reminds us to go slow. Except for hard new ones like this, I'm glad I don't have to watch him constantly to see what our position's supposed to be—enough Downward Dog and Chair Pose and Warrior, I can just go straight into them.

During our stretches near the end, when we're sitting on the floor with the soles of our feet together, leaning as far over them as we can, Coach comes over and puts his hands on my back up near my shoulder blades, presses gently down. I feel my hips stretch further, but not in a painful way. The weight he adds on my back feels good too. But then, after a minute, I'm just aware that Coach is standing there, hands on my back, leaning on me, and it's kind of weird. Not weird in a creepy way but more a *Hey, maybe someone else needs a turn at this* kind of way. But he stays there, gently pressing, until he tells us to come up and we move to a different stretch.

"Better?" he wants to know.

I nod for him. He means my hips.

"Good." He goes over to help Finch.

Outside on the field, he divides us into three groups: Me, Rutger, Lena, and Daniel are together.

"Okay, so—" His hands clap together. "You guys"—he points at the four of us—"are going to be distance. You've got long strides, high endurance, and it's obvious you love to run. So I want you to take off from here and give me two full laps around the camp. Up here"—he points off toward the road where it runs along the hill up to the fire pit—"and over around the whole thing. Okay? Two times, but I want you to try to stay together. That's your challenge. Try to find a good pace for everyone. I don't want one of you running back up, with the rest of the pack five minutes behind you. All right? May be too hard or too frustrating in the end, but I want you to just trust me and try it, okay?"

For Finch and April he says to do the same route, only once around.

"The rest of you, you're going to stay here with me, and we're going to work on short distances and sprints." His hands clap again. "All right? You got me?" He takes a stopwatch out of his pocket. "I'm going to time you all, so first group, get ready." He holds up the watch, squinting at it. "And . . . go."

The four of us start a slow jog across the field and up to the road, which we cross so we can run on the grass along the farm. The Agri kids are out there already, weeding, a few of them taking what look like soil samples, measuring for acidity or whatever they do. Cross the road again, down around the woods-facing side of the instructors' lodge. I'll have to ask Calla which one is her room. When things spread out to the wide expanse that is the basket/volleyball court, the Ball Sports kids are playing an already vicious-looking game of dodgeball, and beyond in the low field, it looks like Margaret has the dancers mimicking grass in the wind or something like that.

By the time we cross the wooden bridge over the lake's neck, we've separated out a little: me and Rutger spaced evenly in the back, Lena and Daniel about ten feet ahead of us in the front. I can feel my breathing, but it doesn't hurt. Everything inside me is warm, and sweat coats my forehead. At the top of the lake, about halfway through our first lap, I don't have to think about the running anymore, just watch Lena and Daniel ahead of me, let my feet match the sound of Rutger's. Past the boys' cabins and then behind them and back up, to the field. Lena slows down a little, and Rutger and I try to work our way by. Daniel, as we pass, has an uncomfortably red face.

"Should we slow down?" I ask Rutger as we pull a few more paces ahead. He nods, and like a car shifting gears, suddenly we're both one-two-one slower. The sweat is dripping down into my ears now. I don't know how far we've gone. When we pass the field, Coach looks up and waves, looks back down at his stopwatch. I wonder how we're doing time-wise. It's getting awfully hot.

We pass the farm and the main buildings again, down beyond the girls' cabins. When we get to the woody end of the lake, something's wrong. I've fallen behind Rutger and even Lena, and I just want to stop. I want to be like Olivia and Montgomery and walk the rest of the way. My knees and hips hurt, and my legs feel heavy and uncooperative. My breath's not coming easily either—like I have to grab for every inhale. But Rutger's still a steam engine, chugging ahead. So somehow I just make myself keep doing it. *Keep going. Keep going. Keep going*, I tell myself, trying to concentrate on my breathing the way Coach says to in yoga. I try to imagine every cell of my being vibrating with joy, but really it's just from my skeleton hitting the ground over and over: one-two, one-two. I slow down even further. We're at the top of the lake—not much more to go—which makes it feel even more stupid to keep running. We're almost done. We might as well stop. But Coach told us to stay together, and I don't want to frustrate Rutger.

When we curve around the last cabin on the boys' side, start to head back up to Coach and the other runners, the bizarrest thing happens. My mind suddenly clears. It's like the edges of my vision open up, and the trees and the grass and the sunshine all gain a sharper edge. I'm breathing hard but not uncomfortably. I focus on Rutger's back, feel myself pushing closer to it.

By the time we get back to Coach and the rest of them, I almost think I could run another lap. But slowing down to a walk also feels great. My blood is thrumming through me and my entire body is coated with sweat, but it's a good feeling. A healthy feeling. Coach claps us in and then tells us to circle the field, walk it down. Lena and I trade small, satisfied smiles, tinged with only a little embarrassment about our crimson faces and heavy breathing. Rutger juts his chin out in affirmation and offers a hand up to Daniel, who collapsed down in the grass the second we got close enough to hear Coach's clapping.

As we walk, we watch the rest of them alternating in dashes of some kind. Coach has marked off the distance with powdered chalk he has in a big white bucket, a scoop jammed down in the thick powder. Coach's hand drops down—he must also say, "Go," and Finch takes off, leaving Olivia easily ten feet behind. She's running like one of those little trains they have at the mall during Christmas, the ones kids can ride in waving to Santa, perched on his throne in the middle of everything. She slows down way before she gets to the finish line, trotting in. Coach stops his stopwatch. He isn't smiling.

At Coach's command, the four of us take another cooldown lap, bodies calming, the occasional breeze lifting and cooling our sweat just slightly.

"You on track?" I bring myself to ask Rutger.

He looks down at me, nods. "This guy is cake compared to my coach back home. I'm just doing this to stay in some kind of shape over the summer."

"Dude, you are a killer," Daniel says. The top half of him is still hanging somewhat limp over the rest of his body.

"You ever do a half marathon?" Rutger asks. We all just look at him, impressed. He shakes his head a little. "Walk in the park, this. I'm telling you."

"I about died, man," Daniel groans. "Wall hit me, like, right when we got to the bridge. I was a zombie, I'm telling you. You were a brain sandwich, was all I could think. Just watching you go, go, go, thinking, 'I got to get that guy or I ain't going to eat.'"

Rutger laughs. I am not sure what they are talking about.

"Doesn't look like you punched through much, my friend," Rutger says, only half being funny.

"Dude," Daniel says, shaking his head. "Coach should give us some water, something, man. This heat."

Lena and I walk together behind them, trading grins. We are a part of them and yet not. It's a good and pleasant feeling to be both.

We get back to Coach and see that along with the chalk, he also has a bucket, water bottles floating in melted ice inside. All four of us crack open bottles, begin chugging. A lot of it spills around the sides of my mouth, down my chin and onto my shirt, but I don't care. I consider pouring half of it over my head, like Rutger does, but I don't really want to turn this into a wet T-shirt contest.

Coach lines up two more runners, and I move over to Montgomery and Olivia to watch with them.

"How's it been?" I want to know.

Olivia looks at me, eyebrows in a half frown, but she doesn't say anything. Montgomery doesn't even look over, just keeps staring at the runners.

"You need any water?" I try again.

Olivia barely shakes her head in a silent, curl-shifting no. They must be hot. Or irritated with running the same thing over and over. Or something. Though that's not much of a reason for Montgomery to act like I'm not even standing there. I decide to just stay put and watch, not moving away but not trying to engage them anymore either.

Coach calls the smaller, freshman-looking guy, Will, and me up for the dash. He beats me by several strides. Walking back to the start, I see Montgomery mouthing something to Olivia, their eyes coming over to me. A creepy feeling goes along my back. I'm probably just imagining that they're talking about me or saying anything bad. But it doesn't stop me from feeling like they are.

"Okay." Coach claps. "You guys have worked hard and well today. Hard and well. So it's almost, uh"—he looks at his watch, face moving up in surprise—"almost eleven thirty, so I guess we'll just do a couple more things before we have final stretch. Daisy?" He points at me. I nod. "You ran the relay last year, am I right?" I nod again, cheeks flaming for no reason. Of course there's probably some record of everyone who's ever won or competed in camp Olympics—I just didn't think about Coach McKensie looking at it.

"So you come up here with me," he instructs, "along with, let's see, April"—he points—"and Montgomery, and Rutger."

I hear, distinctly, Montgomery make a sound that is half disgust, half hocking a loogie. The creepy feeling crawls along my spine again, and I think even my ribs are blushing. But what am I supposed to do? A crappier job just so I can hang with them?

Coach has already marked out several distances three-quarters of the way around the field. He sends me out to fourth position, Montgomery third, with Rutger at the first handoff and April starting us off. I'm stretching the backs of my legs, hands on knees, watching April dash with long, even paces to Rutger. Their handoff is uneven, and it slows Rutger down—he probably isn't used to running with anyone else—but he makes up for it in the last few paces, getting to Montgomery faster than I expect. She's at least making an effort, but her elbows are way out from her body and she obviously doesn't know what she's doing.

At our handoff, I don't know what happens. She doesn't slow down or I don't start up, because she kind of just collides into me. I see her coming and I'm trying to line myself up with her, and then she moves one way and I move the other and she moves back again and then we're on the grass.

"Are you okay?" I reach my hand out to help her up.

"My ankle" is all she says, feeling it with both hands and scowling.

She stands up without any assistance, bounces around on one leg. I reach for her again, but she waves me off.

"Well, we'll definitely be practicing more of that," Coach says, coming up. "You okay there?" He's looking at Montgomery like he doesn't believe she's hurt. She nods, unhappy, but she's still not putting her foot on the ground.

"Well, we'll check that out in a minute. Good job today, all of you. Good job. Let's walk a final lap and then we'll stretch and go." He gives his signature clap and sends us off, turning his attention to Montgomery.

Olivia stays behind to check on her friend, so I walk our final lap with Lena and April. Because of the relay, we aren't really going to have time to shower before lunch. I don't want Joel to see me like this, but I'm also way too hungry to care much. Plus, since he hasn't said anything to me since Sunday, he's probably not even looking, anyway. Maybe I should start talking to Finch.

On the way to lunch, Montgomery seems to have recovered pretty well, though she's still scowling. Behind me I hear Olivia say, "Well, at least we don't have to go into lunch all sweaty and *gross*," as though screwing up a relay is better than looking like you worked hard to do well in one.

When we get to the dining hall, I look for Flannery, which means I also spot Calla at the instructors' table. She's in the middle of telling some story to her tablemates, most of them hesitantly smiling, not sure where she's going with it. (Calla loves long, rambling, twisty stories with lots of side parts you're not sure are going to matter until she ties them all together, brilliantly, right at the end. Shaggy dogs, she told me they're called, because a shaggy dog looks all big and pouffy, until you get it wet and see there's just a skinny little creature under there.) She moves her eyes to each staffer as she tells the story, drawing everyone in, and I remember her talking once about her old friend Paige, explaining that the best way to keep your enemy from stabbing you in the back is to face her bravely and keep her hands full with a friendly handshake.

I know I can't charm anybody as well as my biggest sister can, but seeing her makes me steer around the emptier end of the table and head back over with Flan to sit directly across from Olivia and Montgomery. I don't believe what happened during the relay was on purpose, but I want to make sure she knows I hope she's okay. Both she and Olivia are already deep into complaining to Abby and Esha, who are groaning about their own concentrations as well. I wait for a small slice of pause, and plunge in.

"It was so boring, running around camp. You'd think they'd let us have our headphones or something." I think of the tiny bit of acting I've had to do in the chorus shows with Calla and pretend I have a role in the musical *Act Like You Like People Even When You Don't*.

"Can you think of any good songs I should have going in my head?" I ask Montgomery, making myself keep my eyes on hers.

"That Black Eyed Peas 'Tonight' song," Flannery says, her mouth still chewing on a bite of her sandwich.

Montgomery's face barely moves, but her disapproval fans out like an odor. She watches Flannery for half a second more, then moves her eyes to me. She shrugs. "Lady Gaga's always good." She rattles off five or six more groups I've never even heard of. But I nod as though I know who she's talking about, make my face grateful. My own iPod's full of weird indie music from Violet, plus a lot of singer/songwriter kinds of things, and some nineties stuff that Mom started loading for me, after she caught me singing along to Sinead O'Connor in the car.

It's not much, but at least Montgomery has acknowledged me again. I'm trying to think of something else casual to ask her, when the Whitman girls stand up together all at once and launch into one of their Spirit Splurges, which means we're about to have a cabin showdown. It's a fun and kind of dumb tradition at the same time. Duncan's cabin, Muir, stands up to do their chant before Whitman's even finished. They're shouting about redwoods towering over everyone else. This gets the Thoreau kids on their feet. They do call-and-response, screaming that the rest of us, too obedient, are "Just! Like! Slaves!"

Flannery's smiling next to me, watching this, while Esha and Jenny are hissing at each other and everyone else around the table, squabbling about which Emerson chant we should do, the

one about the only way to have friends is to be one, or the fool-
ish consistency/little minds one.

Nobody gets a chance to holler back, though, because somehow, right in the exact pause of space it takes for Thoreau to
finish shouting and before another cabin stands up to respond,
that girl Violet was talking to at the bonfire last night—the
super-sinewy one with the black and turquoise hair—stands up
and shouts, "Hey, guys! Here's where I put all my camp spirit!"
And then she turns around, pulls down her shorts, and moons
everybody.

The dining hall explodes with noise. Everyone's laughing,
and two-thirds of the boys are on their feet, clapping. Deena and
the counselors and instructors all go into Major Crowd Control mode, commanding everybody to sit down and shut up.
One of Moon Girl's counselors grabs her by the arm and practically yanks her out into the hallway, straight upstairs to Deena's
office. I see Calla jump up from her seat, toss her dishes in the
collection bin, and take off after them. Everyone around me is
babbling their surprise, shock, and amusement. Flannery's practically cutting off the circulation in my arm, she's squeezing it so
hard, her forehead pressed into my shoulder, laughing.

Montgomery's the only one around me who isn't cracking
up. Instead I hear her, voice thick with contempt, saying to
nobody and everyone, "I'm not sure I want to be in the same

camp as someone like that. Somebody should do something. A girl like that doesn't belong with the rest of us."

Flan's head jerks up, eyes wide and blinking from how mean Montgomery sounds. We look at each other. Suddenly it isn't funny. And I can't help but think what a long three weeks it's going to be.

VIOLET

When Cow comes and sits down next to me at dinner, I have to admit it's a little weird. None of the other instructors have sat with the campers yet, and though everyone in my cabin knows Calla is my sister, it still seems kind of odd, especially since she comes up right when Aislin is telling this horror story about field day at her school. It's kind of an interruption, having to make room for Cow. Though I'm glad to see my sister and glad she'll get to meet my cabinmates, after the fun we had horseback riding as a cabin this afternoon, it's sort of a strange energy shift. Especially since I know she's just got her panties in a wad about lunch and is here merely to find out what I know about Brynn.

"I don't think I've ever seen Deena so completely calm," she says, not looking at me. "It was scary."

"Is she getting sent home?" I don't want Brynn to be out of camp. Especially not after only the first day and a half. I've barely scratched the surface of her.

But Calla shakes her head. "After she left, Deena said the last thing Brynn needs is reinforcement like that. That the worst thing—and, you know, of course, really the best thing—we can do is keep her here, keep encouraging her to get involved with her cabin and the rest of camp, not make her feel like an outsider who has to act out in order to get attention."

"She said all that?"

"Everyone thinks Deena doesn't care about the campers, but it's totally not true. She has, like, this amazing understanding of exactly what kids need, you know? But she isn't all gushy-feely about it, is the thing. She's more just working behind the scenes doing stuff. Stuff you don't even know is happening, but that really helps make this whole experience better for everyone."

I want to say something about how that sounds like Kool-Aid–drinking talk a little, but I know Calla would get offended. "So, what was Brynn's punishment?"

"She had to sit her activity out this afternoon, but, you know, duh about that. And tonight at board games she'll have to apologize to everyone, but that's it. Deena says pushing her out isn't going to help her get more invested and involved."

I can just picture Brynn sitting there in the director's office, glaring at everyone, kicking the table leg over and over just to be annoying. Glaring at my sister without even knowing who she is. Although maybe now she does. I wonder if she's really going to apologize tonight. I wonder if she won't just flick everyone off instead. But I also doubt she really wants to be sent home. I see a little why Calla thinks Deena is so great.

"I'm glad she's not leaving," I admit to Cow. "I think she's kind of cool."

"It's funny that James is here," she says next, from out of nowhere, low and quiet so no one else can hear. As though by day two I hadn't been able to figure that out. I shrug, my stomach trilling anyway.

"He's way cuter than before. Is it his clothes?"

"We haven't even talked," is all I say, nonchalant. Of course she's noticed that he's hotter. But it's weird that she, like Brynn, can sense something between him and me, and is bringing him up now. At lunch earlier he was standing just a few people behind me in line, and I really could've hollered a joke at him or something, lobbed some friendly goof that would reveal him as just that plain nice guy from before. But again, when I barely turned my head, he glanced up and winked, and it was like there was this silent, electrified space between us that would stand everyone else's hair on end.

"You're glad to see him," she says—half question, half statement—looking at me out of the corner of her eyes. Her fork pauses over her plate.

"Well, yeah. I mean, he's nice. We had fun. And plus, I'm not dead." I keep my voice light, my smile mysterious.

"Lots of less illegal fish in the sea, though." She smiles back, finally pushing salad into her mouth.

"You know me: big bucket of bait," I joke, washing it down with more Coke and letting it go at that. "But what about you?" Duncan being a good distraction from James, though I have to be careful not to say his name where my cabinmates might hear.

"I don't know," she admits.

I want to warn her that he may've finally picked out his summer fling, the way he was talking to Natalie last night, but there's no way I'm telling her about sneaking out. She'd completely freak.

"It's definitely good whenever we can hang out. The way it always totally is with us at first." She rolls her eyes. At least she's able to make fun of herself a little. "But there really hasn't ended up being that much time." She sighs, her eyes sadder than she knows.

"Cow, why don't you just tell him?" I'm keeping my voice

quiet, but I mean it. Mean it for her, for real, and not just because I'm so sick of this whole Duncan thing—her reading something into every single conversation or gesture, imagining things that aren't there, and then the days and days of crying and moping when he hooks up with someone else. Really, she just deserves to know. She deserves to get her heart busted if necessary and then to get really over it and then find someone way, way better. "I mean, how bad could it be? At least then you'd know. Why not get it out in the open? It could be . . ." For one second James's face flashes in my brain. I also remember Duncan massaging Calla yesterday at dinner—easy with her in that way that really is noticeable, and wonderful. "It could be amazing."

"We're about to go off to college," she whispers fiercely. "So if I mess things up this summer, then I ruin it between us forever. At least I have his friendship, you know?"

"Yes, I know. You've said it a hundred times. I just think the whole unrequited thing is . . . overrated."

"Of course you do. Everyone's always in love with you, is why," she sulks.

"That's not true." It's annoying, this delusion of hers that everyone falls all over me but never even glances at her, because mainly she is only ever thinking about that one Valentine's Day in eighth grade when three different boys brought me candy and flowers and cards, which was more embarrassing than anything

else. She benefited from it too, because we spent the whole afternoon pigging out on their chocolate and making fun of the sappy
messages in the cards together. But she's struggling, I guess, and
she needs somebody, so I let it go.

"Sissie," I try again, "I'm just telling you because I hate seeing you always get so hopeful about him, and then end up getting crushed. And if you just tell him how you feel, at least then
you'll know. And if he's stupid enough not to be in love with
you back, then you have the rest of the summer to hook up with
some hot camper."

I arch my eyebrow at her, try to look lascivious.

"Ew, no way. Campers and counselors is totally, like, incestu-
ous and gross. Not to mention forbidden."

"You're not a counselor," I mutter back. I knew she would
say that, know she doesn't know how I feel when James looks at
me. I can't be mad at her. But I am.

"I know, but still. That would totally mess up the whole
dynamic of trust and everything. I mean, parents are paying my
salary to help run this camp, not, like, prey on their children."
She gives an exaggerated shudder.

So why do you care that James is here, then? I want to fire back
at her, but I'm being Strong and Comforting Sister this round.
"Well, Daisy's coach is pretty hot. Staff and staff can hook up,
right? I mean, what else are they going to do all summer?"

"Double-ew. He's Zee's coach."

"Only for the next couple of weeks. You're here until August."
I'm playing around, trying to get a rise out of her, get her mind
off Duncan.

"Did Daisy tell you he's making them do yoga?"

"Yep." I suck some more spaghetti off my fork. "I think
it's cool."

"Oh, I do too. I mean, totally smart and cool. It's just, you
know, funny."

I'm not even going to ask her why she thinks it's funny,
because she doesn't mean it's funny, anyway—she means what
we all mean when we buzz and whisper about Coach McKensie;
she means it's hot. But she's too proud or embarrassed or whatever to say it, so instead she just says something else she doesn't
really mean. I want to ask her sometimes: *Isn't it exhausting, being
you? Worrying all the time what other people are going to think?*
But she'd probably just blink at me, worrying about how best to
respond.

"You need to talk to Duncan." I mouth that last word, try to
convey, *If nothing else he could help you have some fun*, with my
eyes. Everyone's gathering their dishes and standing up, so we're
going to have to get going.

"I do talk to him."

"No, I mean, *talk* to him." My hand goes on her arm. She

looks down at it, then at me, her face a little sad, a little resigned. "Maybe this is the summer you play it different, Cow. Maybe this is the summer something actually happens." I want, suddenly, for her to sneak out with me tonight. But she gives this little shrug, and then we both really have to move to the aisle and head to the trash and dish bins, because there are people behind us waiting to get past too.

"I'm glad you came and sat with me," I tell her while we squeeze hands together, before we have to go in our different directions.

"Thanks for letting me," she says.

"You coming to games tonight?"

She turns. "I don't know. I'm not sure I can take more of show-off Brynn today. And maybe—" She glances, uncertain, over at the other instructors, most of them already heading out.

"Okay I'll see you, then. But remember what I said."

"I'll remember." She smiles. "But that doesn't mean I'll listen."

CALLA

I am not going to throw myself at anyone, no matter what Violet says. Yes, I want to be with Duncan. Yes, I'm maybe sometimes bored and, okay, a little lonely. Yes, it's weird and a completely different camp experience this summer. But still.

I don't know really what my problem is, but I always just feel so much like an outsider when I'm with the other instructors or counselors, even in the midst of being included by them. Even still, when Kesiah turns to me as we walk back to the lodge from dinner and says, "Hook 'n' Mouth tonight. You in?" my sister's voice isn't too far away from my ear. I consider my options: board games in the dining hall (which would mean a chance to play something with Duncan, maybe, though board game night isn't even all that fun when you're a camper), or else another night curled up reading by myself, which Violet would not approve of.

"Who all's going?"

"Us, Forrest, Chad, probably Steffie and Kelly, too. We haven't asked everybody," Lucy says. "Alexander might come."

I find myself nodding then. It may not be stepping out and confessing my love to Duncan, but it gets me out of my room in the least lame way.

"Ready in about twenty?" Lucy makes sure as we split up.

Dressing for the Hook 'n' Mouth is a little tough, though. You don't want to be so done up that you stand out and the local guys sitting hunched at the bar eye you coming in, and then play "Uptown Girl" on the jukebox, but going there is sort of going out, and some of the guy instructors are pretty cute, so cargo shorts or something feels sort of stupid too.

I decide on my yellow tank dress, which is basically a long, sleeveless T-shirt. It's comfortable and cute, and I can throw on flip-flops and put my hair up and that's pretty much it. Being dressed up and knowing I'm going out actually makes my whole spirit feel lifted a little. Maybe it's the yellow or something, but when I leave my room and cross the lounge to knock on Lucy's door, I'm feeling a little excited. Violet, I guess, was right—I should be doing more of this.

And at first, it is fun. We all gather in front of the lodge, saying hey and talking about our days, waiting for the camp super, Alexander, to come around with the big van to drive everybody, which he can totally do because it is, essentially, his car even though it has the camp logo on the side. In the van everyone is laughing and groaning and complaining about different campers they had to deal with today.

"Oh god," Ed, the Vis Arts instructor, heaves. "I swear—it's just decoupage, people. You don't have to freak out every time you lay a new image down and call me over to make sure you did it right."

"I know," Steffie, one of the Water Sports instructors, says. "I feel sorry for them, really, though. It's like their parents must hover over their every move. They're all so afraid to try anything. So afraid to make mistakes."

Mistakes make the difference between passing an AP exam and getting college credit, or having to repeat a class all over again and waste tuition money, I want to tell them. Mistakes equal low test scores, which mean all kinds of things, like scholarships and money for your school, even. But I keep my mouth shut.

"You should see them in archery, then," Nathan chimes in. "Not afraid to miss the bull's-eye—by eight feet—in there."

We get to the bar and everyone crowds into two booths, orders pitchers. They even get a mug for me, forgetting. I guess

I totally could have some—who cares, right?—but I don't want it getting back to Deena in any way that I was out boozing with the instructors. It just doesn't seem like something she'd be very pleased about. Not that anybody would tell, but you just never know what's going to slip out somewhere, and it's better to be smart, I think. Even if it means having to snag the waitress's not-very-enthusiastic attention and ask for cranberry juice.

The conversation shifts around me. My face looks like I'm listening, at least I hope, but the rest of me is suddenly dejected or something. Maybe it was talking to Violet earlier, or my yellow dress, but I was hoping tonight would be this wildly different thing than it's been the few last times. But here I am again, sitting here with my juice, talking a little bit but mostly just listening, waiting for Nathan or Forrest to get up eventually and play pool or darts. I'm horrible at both, and probably everyone will think I'm only playing because I have a crush on one or both of them, but at least it's doing something.

While I wait, my mind slips back to that empty Sunday morning before the first-session campers came, when Duncan and I decided to go out on the lake in the canoe together. Because of training I still hadn't really hung out with him yet—not just him and me. When he'd asked me to go, after our final team dinner, I was elated.

Seven a.m. is not my best or favorite time of day, but at least with Duncan I don't have to worry about my outfit as much as I do for the office. I just had to wash my face and throw on some yoga pants and a cute-ish T-shirt and my sneakers. Okay, and a squirt of perfume.

As I walked down to the boathouse that morning, I was nervous but knew I shouldn't be. We don't write a whole lot between summers—maybe we talk on the phone a few times, like at Christmas and our birthdays—but really not that much. But we don't have to. As soon as we get back to Callanwolde, we just roll right into it like we haven't been apart for even a day. We're always somehow able to understand things about each other, about how the year's been, without having to do a whole lot of catch-up.

So, even though this summer started off kind of different, with the intensity of training and all the team-building stuff we had to do with everyone else, I knew that as soon as we pushed off from the dock and got talking, finally alone together, everything would be fine. It maybe being our last summer together—our last chance—made me kind of twittery and not sure what to say to him first, though.

Of course, as soon as I saw him there, waiting for me, all that went away. There he was, with that grin I knew so well—standing in his Chucks with no socks, fists pushed down into his pockets so he could hunch and not seem so tall. I saw him and I wasn't nervous anymore. Like always with him, from the day we met, I knew exactly where I belonged.

"Hey," he said, grinning. "Let's get our gondola and away."

We unlocked the chain and hoisted up the easiest one. We carried it over our heads, without talking, to the dock. I steadied myself in the front and he handed me my oar, sun gleaming on the blond hairs along his tight forearm. He said, "Ready?" once he was situated, and when I said, "Ready" back, he pushed us off with his oar.

Before we were even a few yards out, we both simultaneously flicked our oars to splash each other. An arm of water reached up and over my right side, soaking my shoulder and part of my face. When I looked back, Duncan's knee was barely wet.

"How do you get that reach?" I squealed. "It's not fair."

"I told you, you've got to claim the back more, Cal. Steering's tough but it has its privileges."

It's too distracting if I'm in back and you're up there for me to stare at, I should've told him, but of course I didn't. Never have. It doesn't work out like that, even when I try to plan it, like three summers ago in Drama, when we got cast opposite each other as the salesman and Ado Annie in *Oklahoma!* Somehow, me wanting to spend extra time practicing (especially the couple of stage kisses we got) turned into me listening to him talking about Lyssandra and asking how to get her to see past the goofy role he was playing and take him seriously. My advice worked, of course, and there they were, a couple, for the last week of camp, locked together every slow dance on the last night. That was the summer before sophomore year. Freshman summer was Molly, then Zoe. Junior summer it was Rachel. And last summer—

"You sad Michelle's not here?" I asked him, light.

"What-ever," he mocked.

I turned to look over my shoulder at him, purposefully making my face fake-aghast. "What, you two split up?"

Michelle was a tough one, and god, was it annoying how he'd obsessed over her. *Why does she keep saying she wants to hang with me, when every time I see her she's aping around with Heath or Cage or trying to drape herself around that Muir counselor? Why does she laugh so much at everything I say and then won't sit next to me at the bonfire?* It totally tried my patience, like, totally. *Because she doesn't love you as much as I do!* I always wanted to scream at him. But at least with her, I knew by then how the last week of camp was going to go—him finally finding some girl other than me.

Not that it didn't suck when, after he finally got her attention (and some serious making out past curfew), he suddenly didn't have any more time for me, and I didn't see him again until the farewell celebration and then for a long, slightly teary hug together before our parents picked us up. I mean, it totally sucked. But that's why I'd tolerated all his suffering and moaning while he was trying to get her. Because then, at least, we were spending time together. If I couldn't be his girl, then I at least wanted to be his friend for as long as I could.

"She was weird, anyway."

"You didn't seem to think so last summer," I teased, eyes back on the lake.

"Nah, she was always weird. Way too needy, you know? I mean, you know when girls get that way? They seem so cool and aloof and happy doing their own thing, and then when you get with them you realize, 'Whoa, this girl is a black hole for attention. She sucks absolutely everything in. Planets, galaxies, supernovas—there's not enough for her. She just sucks it all in and then crushes it with her immense needy power.'"

"Yeah, I hate when girls do that."

"And then it's completely impossible to untangle yourself from the mess once you're in it. Because you've spent all this time trying to convince her you think she's great, so you look like a total asshole when, after about fifteen minutes, you find out she's not. Unlike you, Cal, who was just straight-up amazing from the get-go. No-nonsense, immediate, great. There aren't enough of you around, believe me."

"Fifteen minutes, eh? That's all it takes?" I made a joke to camouflage the incredibly deep sense of victory I felt, hearing this from him. But I remembered too the first night he and Michelle hooked up, seeing them go off together on the way back to cabins from the bonfire, remembered how Violet walked next to me just holding my hand and letting me squeeze it as hard as I wanted to.

"Well, you know," he jockeyed back, "I could go longer. Just depends on the company."

I tried, tried, tried not to let my ears burn at that, tried not to picture fifteen minutes, twenty, twenty-four hours alone with him.

"You nervous about this session?" I asked instead.

"Not really." His voice was the kind of casual that meant he was, a little.

"It's weird, not being in the cabins."

"Yeah?"

We were far enough out that behind us, camp was getting smaller. Soon we'd go out into the finger, around the bend, and wouldn't be able to see camp at all.

"I mean, I already love seeing how everything works, you know? Being behind the scenes and stuff. And I've learned so much, just in the first two days." *Like how much peanut butter 120 campers will eat in three weeks.*

"Yeah, but—," he helped me.

I didn't know how to tell him. How could I say, *But I really just want to be with you?*

"It's just different than I thought. It feels like there's not going to be as much, you know, hanging out and stuff. I mean, all you counselors were so buddy-buddy on the first day of training, and I hardly knew anyone."

"You know Adele."

"Yeah, I know Adele. And she's cool. But you guys were all bonded and everything, and it was only the first day. I didn't get to really talk to you until two days later, and even then we were exhausted. And I'm practically your best friend." I wanted him to correct me then, to say, *You* are *my best friend*, even though I know he has his real best friend at home.

"You should come up to the fire pit, then. It's awesome."

And I did not want my heart to perk up at this, to think this was a special hint to me, a hint he wanted to see me more too. But I couldn't help it—I pictured walking up there after lights-out, pictured sitting there and holding hands and laughing with our faces close together and . . .

"I don't know. It seems—"

"Unprofessional?"

I turned to squint at him, to see if he was making fun of me or not.

"Kind of." I kept looking at him.

He shrugged and paddled, thoughtful.

"It might be. But it's not like Deena's going to know, right?"

His face was frustrated. "I'm just saying you shouldn't hole yourself up in your room the whole summer if you don't want to. We're not little campers anymore. Come enjoy that. You've earned it. Why shouldn't your nights finally belong to you?"

I pictured myself again—leaving the lodge at night, walking all the way across camp, up the hill to the fire pit, waving awkwardly at the counselors there, listening to someone tell a funny story. Pictured Duncan leaning in close, his hand pulling my chin closer to his face—

"I've gone out with the instructors." I sounded pouty, defensive.

"Well, good for you."

"Wait." I stopped paddling for real. "Why are you mad now?"

"Forget it."

"No, what?"

"We should go back." He sliced his oar down in the water, and the boat began to turn.

We paddled in silence. The sun was brightening. As we rounded the bend back into the lake proper, I saw the roofs of the cabins, could picture them—a few hours from then—full of Callanwolde campers I wouldn't be getting to know, kids he would be roughhousing and singing with, kids who would—and did, and do—look at me at breakfast and not be sure what it is I'm doing here. I remember feeling the pieces of my heart shift.

"I'm not like I was, here before," I said.

"None of us are, Cal." His voice was weirdly soft.

"And after this summer, we're all going away, and—" I almost said something. I really almost did right then.

"So, let's make it a *good* summer."

"We will. But also, this is what I want to *do*, and if I don't take it seriously now—"

Another little resigned chuckle from him: "Okay."

"No, Dunk, it's just that it's not that easy—"

"I know it's not." Him, done with this conversation. Me, frustrated about how badly it had gone.

We were coming to the dock. The sun was fully shining on camp, turning the grass bright green instead of just wet and dark-looking, reflecting off the windows, warming the backs of the scrubbed-out canoes. I didn't understand why we were fighting then, and I'm still confused about it tonight, really. He wanted me to come hang out with him, and there I was, protesting, hesitating, resisting. And now—

I remember how he climbed out of the canoe, took my oar, offered me a hand.

"You'll figure it out, Cal. I know you will."

We lifted out the canoe, hefted it back up onto the rack. I felt disappointed in a way that had nothing to do with our little spat. A trickle of water ran down my arm, dripping off my elbow.

He wiped his hands on his shorts. "C'mon. Today's the only day we won't have to fight fourteen-year-olds for the waffles."

I said something back, I don't know what, but he laughed. He put his arm over my shoulder, and after a few strides I linked mine loosely around his hard, narrow waist. We walked like that, feet falling into rhythm, all the way up into the dining hall, drenched in buttery smells and buttery light.

But Duncan was wrong. I didn't figure it out first session, and I still haven't. Not really. I mean, I have my little routine. I've hung out with the instructors a few times, like the Hook 'n' Mouth tonight, did bowling and movies in town with Helene and sometimes Margaret. I'm trying—I really am. Duncan and I have even had fun at the dances and with some games. It hasn't been miserable. But now with Violet saying practically the same thing Duncan did at the beginning, I wonder if maybe I really do need to kind of change my tune a little bit. Because this summer really isn't working the way I think I want it to, even after Nathan stands up and presses his palms flat on the table, finally asks who wants to have a throw at darts.

DAISY

By our third day, the routine's established. Wake up to girls grumbling. Wait my turn at the sink, splash my face and brush my teeth. Put on running clothes. Follow everyone to breakfast (bagel with peanut butter, honey, and banana), half listen to their blabbing, go to keynote. Break up into concentrations and head to HQ, staying closer to Lena and April than Montgomery and Olivia. Yoga. Divide into groups, running. After that, cleanup and lunch. Then rest time before our afternoon activity. Back to the cabin to shower or change clothes again before dinner.

It's the evenings that provide the variety, since those involve the whole camp. Tonight we're doing karaoke.

Since everyone will be there, and most will be up onstage, we have to think about our clothes a little more carefully. This being camp, nobody tricks themselves out in minidresses or glitter or anything, but this is definitely not a shorts-and-T-shirt night. I stand over by my assigned dresser drawer, staring into it, the folded tanks and shorts and socks now a jumble, my one good skirt wrinkled from being shoved around underneath. Most everyone else is in Can I Trade You mode—showcasing unwanted camis and tops, hoping to score something unique. I would maybe try to trade with Flannery, but most of her outfits are pretty plain. The rest of the girls are deep in it, with Montgomery being the loudest and bossiest, so I just make do with the semiwrinkled skirt and my purple tank top with the silver threads in it.

I don't wear much makeup, and since I didn't bring my straightening iron for my not-straight, not-curly, muddy blond hair, I just put it up in a quick twist. Done, I go sit on Flan's lower bunk and help her with a French braid. There's a guy in Duncan's cabin I think she likes, and I want him to notice, at least, her sweet-skinned, pretty face.

"Okay, little biddies," Nyasiah hollers, hand on hip, watching over all of us. She is still in cutoff camo shorts and a tight Mickey Mouse T-shirt from canoeing and kickball this afternoon. "Time to fuss up and wriggle those butts out of here. You all look *faaaaabulous*. There's enough lip gloss in here to grease down fourteen Channel swimmers."

Everyone's heard her, but no one's listening. It takes another five minutes to wrangle us out the door, up the trail to the dining hall.

Inside, the tables are cleared away and there are only benches. As a bonus, we're allowed to sit wherever we want. Which is fun but kind of makes it harder to find people if you're looking for them. We hover near the back, still not sure where to go sit down. Beside me Flannery's craning her neck, looking for her boy.

"Don't look too hard." I elbow her, making her at least stop standing up on her tiptoes like that. Not that I'm not scanning the crowd too, determining everyone else's positions before we settle on a seat. Montgomery, Olivia, Abby, Savannah, and Esha have all squealed and gone up front with some girls from Whitman, all of them yammering together at the same time. Manon's snuck off to sit near a friend of hers in Alcott. When I see Vivi sitting near the front with Brynn, I immediately know I don't want to be Kid Sister in Tow.

Fortunately, April and Lena are together near the middle. I start toward them, Flannery close behind. When we get to their bench, April and Lena smile and make room for us. We have to scooch over again, though, when some guys they know want to come over and join in, leaving me and Flan kind of on the end of the bench, on our own.

When all the cabins have finally arrived and interspersed, when the beach ball gets confiscated after someone lofts it up over the crowd to be batted around for a while, Mike, the Drama instructor, takes the microphone and goes over the rules.

"Oh my god," Flannery says next to me, hunching down real quick. I think she's talking about Mike and his Very Theatrical voice up there, but no. "He's not cute anymore," she hisses. "How is that possible? How can he not be cute?"

I try to sneak a peek behind us and to the right a bit.

"No, no. Up there." She is pointing. I grab her finger, pull it down to her lap. "Near the drink machines."

"Okay, okay. I'm looking." I see mostly the dark backs of heads, one of them James's—unmissable in one of those thin-brimmed trilby hats everyone's wearing now. I don't really remember what this boy of Flannery's looks like, so it's even harder to find him when I'm trying not to be obvious.

She points again, though smaller, her finger barely jutting over her thumb. "Ew!" Her hands go over her face, her head shakes. "He's really not that cute."

And then I see him. Blond. Kind of rough skin. Teeth that look thick, like a farm animal's, laughing while he punches the guy next to him on the shoulder.

"He's . . . not that bad." *Just be glad she's looking*, I tell myself.

"But he's not that cute. When I saw him at free swim he was cuter."

"Maybe you were waterlogged."

She looks at me, laughs a little through her nose. "Maybe I was sun damaged."

I pat her on the knee. "You'll find someone else. It's early in the week."

She sighs but doesn't say anything, because finally the directions are over, the counselors are done passing slips of paper and tiny pencils down all the aisles, people in the front rows have jumped over each other to turn in requests, and it's time to start.

Mike gives a big game-show-host grin and calls out the first singer. She runs up and kisses him on the cheek. The Whitman girls are on their feet, most of them clustered smack in the middle and near the front. There are a few long, low hollers from various pro-Whitman boys in the room. The flute-y music twinkles out: that awful *Titanic* song. The room fills with screams and applause.

It goes on. A few boys get up and do a rap together. More girls singing cheesy power ballads, or wiggly Beyoncé songs. One of the counselors from Alcott—I think she was in Calla's cabin last year—sings "Sweet Home Alabama" and brings a ton of people to their feet. We all have to stand up to even see.

Which is when Joel's white-blond head pops up beside mine. He smiles his shiny smile at both me and Flannery before stepping over and wiggling in between us. I lean back, mouth *Sorry* to Flan from behind Joel's head. She shakes her head like she's fine and goes back to clapping with the song.

I keep my face forward while we sit back down and watch a bunch of Whitman girls go up next. Joel's here—he came over, on purpose, away from his friends, to sit next to me—but I'm not sure what I'm supposed to do. If I'm supposed to act cool or be grateful. Since he's not saying anything, I follow his lead. I'm aware of him, though—aware as his knee slowly migrates across the space between us and lands against mine. I can feel the ridge of his kneecap. The soft curls of hair on his legs. I am glad, so glad I wore this skirt, even though I'm not sure I've shaved.

And then Brynn's name is being called out. She jumps up, waves straight-armed jazz hands at everyone, and bounces up to the stage. I wish I could see Violet. Everyone is buzzing. No one is sure what she is going to do.

"'Bad Moon on the Rise'!" some boy hollers.

"'Man on the Moon,'" another lamer voice calls.

"'Moon River'!" a girl screeches out.

Brynn shakes her shiny, stripy hair and just winks at all of us. She's holding the mic in both hands. Even from back here I can see her throat working, a little like it did when she had to apologize to everyone yesterday at game night, though she seems more nervous now. Joel's fingers slowly, slowly, slowly materialize on the edge of my knee. It takes a while, but eventually his hand plants itself there, warm and moist. A guitar twangs out.

"'Busted flat in Baton Rouge,'" she starts, that crazy-low voice of hers pitched higher, more organic. Warm. It's a song I don't know, but I guess some of the counselors do, because they've immediately got their arms in the air, waving their hands slowly back and forth. I drop my hand on top of Joel's. Our fingers entwine. I wonder if Flannery can see. The song builds. Brynn is gripping the mic like she's squeezing the song out of it. Everything gets faster. She's jumping up and down, screaming into the microphone, bending practically in half, moving back and forth. Joel's hand just stays there on my knee, holding mine, unmoving. I'm afraid if I look at him he'll stop, so I watch the crowd instead, people murmuring things in each other's ears, not sure if this is awesome or just plain weird. I still wish I could see Violet.

When Brynn finishes with her wailing and writhing, half the camp is cheering and stomping, the other only halfway clapping, laughing uneasily, their faces saying *Weirdo* and *Spaz* and *What the hell?* Joel and I have had to let go to applaud. But when the next kids gets up there, his hand is back again in mine. Other than that, he doesn't say anything, doesn't move.

That's how it goes the whole two hours: Someone sings, we're holding hands, then they finish and we let go to clap, back to holding hands. The whole time, Joel says nothing—doesn't even turn his head—so I don't either. I feel bad about Flannery sitting down there on her own. But it's not like I can lean across him to talk to her.

Right before the last group finishes, Joel suddenly breaks his paralytic act and squeezes my hand a couple of times. "I gotta go," he whispers. "See you at breakfast?"

For pretty much the first time tonight I look at him—his sweepy white bangs, those pale, pale blue eyes, those confident lips. All I can do is smile and nod. He squeezes my hand again and slips over the back of the bench, disappears into the dark behind us to find the rest of his cabin. Flannery scootches back over into the space he left. Her knee bonks against mine, playful. When she smiles at me, her grin is knowing and jealous and proud. I have no idea what emotions mine is showing back to her.

VIOLET

neaking out to meet Brynn was so easy and uneventful and normal the first time, I almost forgot it was against the rules. When I see her tonight at karaoke, we don't talk about yesterday's thing at lunch at all, or her "camp apology" cloaked in disdain. All that happens is that she plunks down next to me, and then we laugh a ton together. When I hug her around the neck to tell her how awesome her Janis Joplin was, she only husks in my ear, "Tonight again."

And this time I'm way more excited than I am scared. Because of karaoke, though, it takes everyone else a lot longer to settle down to sleep, which makes me antsy. I'm a little less confident, too, since I can't tell if Natalie's really asleep or faking being asleep before she sneaks out. I am cat-burglar tiptoe quiet. But before I know it, I'm outside under the stars, figuring we're going up to the fire pit again to hang with whatever counselors are there tonight. Meaning James, I hope. Maybe we'll finally talk.

Brynn has other plans, though. She barely even says hey when I get to the boathouse, and just starts walking down to the dark edge of the lake, far away from all the cabins and their lights. Without a word, she shimmies off her pajama bottoms. She's wearing a boy-shorts swimsuit underneath.

"What are we doing?"

"Going for a swim, dummy. What does it look like?" She is half smiling.

"But I don't—I mean—"

"So swim in your pajamas." She whips her T-shirt off over her head, showing smooth white belly and too many ribs.

I go down and stick my foot in the water. It's chilly, but not totally freezing. It won't be comfortable at first, but I know I'll get used to it. But the air's too cool now to dry my pajamas before I get back to the cabin if I swim in them. And I am not very enthused about wearing wet underwear, which will then soak my pajamas, too. Taking things off and hanging them up will be a way too complicated chore when I'm trying to sneak back into my bunk. If I do this, I'm doing it au naturel.

"Or you can go back, it's cool," Brynn says, seeing me hesitate. Her voice is genuinely indifferent, not teasing or challenging. And I could go back. I kind of want to. But this is my last summer as a camper, and I don't want to be the girl who only heard about the crazy, rule-breaking things people did at camp, or saw them in the movies. I want to be the girl who did them. I want to be able to tell James about this whenever we do get to talk—to watch his face light up in surprise, imagining me out here. And naked. So off goes my top, and my sleep shorts and underpants are quick to follow. Brynn takes our clothes and shoves them in the seat of one of the kayaks chained to its rack.

"C'mon," she giggle-whispers. Something about how she sounds makes it seem like she's never done this before either.

The water is. Freezing. If it weren't midnight and I weren't breaking camp rules, I'd be squealing. Instead—somehow—I just grit my teeth and go under. It is so cold.

Hasn't stopped Brynn, though. When I come up, she's already knifing herself toward the floating dock in a freestyle that looks Olympic. I am not a swimmer. I mean, I can swim, and I like to, but we never got lessons or anything like that. My stroke is more like a turtle's.

By the time I make it out to the floating dock, I'm definitely warmer, and being in the water with no clothes on feels surprisingly good. You'd think, because a bathing suit sticks to you when you're wet and really isn't that much clothing to begin with, there wouldn't be much of a difference, but there definitely—well, there just is. I almost don't want to get out, partly because in the water at least, no one can see me. Gripping the ladder, I still get the feeling—even though it's impossible—someone might be looking out their cabin window, able to catch a glimpse.

But even Brynn can barely see me, and she's six feet away, though I'm sure my butt is white as chalk in whatever small moonlight there is. I haul myself up the ladder and sit down quick, bringing my knees up to my chest, wrapping my arms around myself and making sure my feet are blocking any view of my—you know. Since the three of us stopped taking showers together when Calla was about ten, I've really only been in my birthday suit when I'm by myself. Parts exposed, with different people, sure, but not, you know, the whole deal. I feel a little mad Brynn has her suit on. And a little proud I don't.

"You're a good swimmer," I say. My voice sounds loud, though it isn't.

I think she shrugs.

"How come you're in Equestrian and not Water Sports?"

"Their routine is messed up here," is all she answers.

"So you are on a team at home?"

"Yeah." She says it without enthusiasm, but without snarkiness, either.

"I can never get that," I say after a minute. "The arms and the head thing."

"My favorite's the butterfly. It's hard, but that's why I like it. Not many people are good at it."

And so that explains the serious shoulders she's got. Though as a swimmer I'd think she'd be more muscle-y and not so Skeletor. I decide not to ask her if she's won anything. I can't tell, from the way she's talking, if she wants me to be asking all these questions anyway or not. Though this is the first time we've really hung out alone, she's half acting like we're already best friends who are completely comfortable with each other, half acting as though she doesn't care if I'm here.

Still, I have to talk to fill the quiet. "My mom took my little sister to those baby underwater classes—you know, where you throw babies in a pool and they just naturally hold their breath and paddle around?" I tell her.

She snorts.

"But it didn't make her some great swimmer. I mean, she swims, but none of us are real swimmers."

Mom said Daisy was the best baby in that whole class, though. She'd practically leap out of Mom's arms to get into that water. Sometimes if she got fussy we'd just fill up the tub and plop her in there, even when she was really small and couldn't even crawl or anything. She loved it. Why Mom never took me and Calla to those classes, I don't know. When I asked her about it once, she just cocked her head way over and frowned into space for a minute before she said, "You know, I have no idea. But it just never occurred to me for the two of you."

Brynn still doesn't say anything. Instead I hear Saran Wrap rustling. I don't know what she's doing until there's a spark and a surprising flame, and then the fire goes up to her face and she inhales, holds it a minute, and then lets out a mossy-smoky breath.

"How can you be a swimmer and smoke?" I can't help blurting. She only chuckles. The orange dot that is the lit end of what she's smoking comes toward me.

"You want some?"

Which means it's pot. Which I should've figured anyway by the way it smelled. And it's stupid and embarrassing, but all I'm thinking is that if I smoke that with her, I won't be able to swim back. I picture myself naked, in the water, just floating there in the dark and unable to move my arms and legs, totally numb. I picture Calla having to come down to the lake to take away my pale, wet, bloated dead body.

"Where'd you get it?" I ask, big dummy. The orange dot goes back to her and she takes another inhale.

"Brought it." Her voice is tight, like she's holding in her breath.

The smoke that is somehow oilier and not as gross-smelling as regular cigarettes comes out at me again, and I feel like an idiot, sitting here with no clothes on, just some dumb girl Brynn brings along to keep an eye out while she smokes weed and drinks beers and hangs out with counselors and does whatever she wants. I don't even know why she's letting me tag around with her. She could probably care less whether I was here or not. She would do all these things with or without me. She isn't at all worried about making the swim back.

"Okay," I say.

"What?" The smoke comes out from her again. She coughs a little bit.

"Yeah, I want some, duh."

"Here," is all she says.

My fingers pinch around hers where she's holding the end of the joint out to me. It is warm, and a little bit damp. Shorter than I think it should be. The ember burns only an inch or so from my thumb. It's hard to get it close to my mouth without thinking I'm going to burn my nose off. I have to tilt my head a little. The nonburning end is mashed pretty flat, and when I suck in I'm not sure I'm going to get much, but then the ember glows brighter and a searing scratchiness goes into my throat and my mouth fills up with this grossness that is the exact same taste as the smell of flower water that's been in a vase for too long.

Like the dumbasses smoking pot for the first time in the movies, I cough and cough and cough.

"Do it again," she says in her Johnny Cash voice. "It'll help."

So I take another hit, still scratchy and gross, still making me cough, but not as bad. My eyes are stinging with water. I hand it back to her.

She smokes the rest. I don't ask for any more and she doesn't offer. I just sit there, arms wrapped around myself and my butt starting to hurt from sitting on these hard planks. I watch her shape in the dark, and the orange dot growing and dimming and moving from her mouth to somewhere down around her lap, back and forth a few times before she's putting it out and there's the sound of Saran Wrap again. She tucks the lighter and the butt somewhere and stretches out on the planks of the dock, staring up.

I'm waiting for something to happen. For my head to swirl or to start giggling uncontrollably or my tongue to swell up or the skies to explode in comets or—something. But nothing does. Only my scratchy throat and kind of a warmish feeling in the front of my face. I take a deep breath and look up at the stars anyway, because stoned or not, they do look remarkable. And here I am, naked in the great outdoors and everything.

"My stepdad—" Brynn says out of nowhere. "He's who got me into swimming. At first I hated it. My mom wanted me to is why I did it, really. She wanted him and me to have something to do together, wanted me to be active. He would get up really early to go to work before everyone else, so he could leave at three to take me to swim lessons. I was, I think, ten. I wasn't fat or any-thing, but when I started swimming I got really . . . skinny. And by sixth grade I was wearing a zero. Sure, in my school, most of the sixth-grade girls wore zeros. But by seventh, eighth, all of them started getting boobs and hips and puberty fat and all that. And me, with all my swimming, I was a total board—flat. And you know how girls are always made fun of for having no chest?"

I hear her head turn on the wood planks as she looks over at me. I grunt a kind of yes, to keep her going mostly, to see what she's going to say.

"Well, I didn't care. I wanted to swim harder, more often, more. I wanted to keep all the girl fat off me I could. And even though now I go to this school that has a pool, like, three blocks away, one I can walk to and don't need a ride anymore, my step-dad's still going into work early, still coming to my practices, all my meets."

She's quiet for a minute. "At first I hated him so much. And my mom. And he knew that, and he probably hated me for a while too, this total brat little bitch, but he just kept driving me to those swim lessons all those years and keeps on watching and clapping and taking us out for pizza sometimes afterward and buying my coach a beer—just smiling and happy and pounding me on the shoulder like I'm his real kid or something."

She's quiet, and I don't say anything. I've stopped being cold. I've stopped feeling my sore butt. I've even kind of forgotten that we're actually at camp, instead of just in some private dark place that is totally our own. Which is what makes me remember, suddenly, that we are at camp. And I'm out here on the dock, naked, and I just smoked pot for the first time, and Brynn, this girl I barely know—this tough, shocking girl—is out here with me being, in her own way, completely naked too. And I think, how can this be against the rules? How can something like this be against camp policy? Because this—this—is exactly what camp should be all about.

DAISY

After keynote I don't even bother to try walking with Olivia and Montgomery. Instead I hang back a little, waiting by the door, pretending I'm just being nice and letting everyone else push through. It's better to walk by myself than try to go with them and end up ignored. Standing there, waiting for a big enough gap, I see Joel's bright white head over by the other exit. When we spotted each other at breakfast, all we did was smile, but it felt good, seeing him light up. For a second I think of going across real fast, being romantic and bold like Violet and grabbing his hand or something, but with his friends around him, I'm not sure he'd want me to.

"You comin'?" Rutger says, suddenly towering beside me.

I watch Joel disappear out the exit and off to his concentration.

"I don't know if I can take another Downward Dog," I grumble.

"Shit, you're telling me." He smirks, letting me go ahead of him. "Yoga my ass. At my school? Coach has us doing the military obstacle course at the armory next door twice a week. Our time don't improve each time? Wind sprints. Hundreds of them, almost."

"You really don't like McKensie?" We cross out into the sunlight, making us both squint.

He shrugs. "I like the man all right. Like I said, though, I'm just doing this to stay in shape. I wouldn't want to count on him for any serious training or nothing."

I consider this. It may only be the fourth day, but already I feel like I'm learning something. And I kind of like that Coach knows what he's doing but seems so laid-back about it.

Rutger twists his mouth around what he wants to say next. "You see those two girls just walkin' the other day? That guy yesterday drag-assin' behind us, slowing us down? My coach wouldn't have none of that. You off the team, son. I promise you."

"Yeah, but it's not like Coach can kick anybody out. You should've gone to some intensive training camp or something."

We're at the arts building now, and Rutger holds the door open for me, shrugging with one shoulder and giving me a smiling wink. "Girls're too hot here, what can I say?"

I jab him with my elbow, but I'm laughing. Olivia whips her head around, but faces back when she sees I'm looking right at her. Rutger moves over to the other boys, and I decide to stick with him.

When Coach comes in finally we're surprised when he tells us we're not going to need our mats this morning. The boys all make noises of approval and give each other high fives.

"No, today . . ." Clap. "Today we're gonna take a little field trip. Going to do something a little different. What you call a little cross-training."

There is immediate chatter. I just stare at Coach and wait.

"So, let's head up to the lodge and pile into the van and we'll go from there, okay?"

"Coach, where are we going?" Montgomery wants to know, eyes big and fakely surprised.

He shrugs amicably. "You'll just have to be patient and see. But it'll be fun."

We follow him back up to the main lodge and around front, where Alexander's parked one of the camp vans. He's there leaning against the grille, waiting, staring at us as we walk up.

"Hey, man," Coach says, going up and shaking Alexander's

hand. Alexander is easily twice Coach's weight and almost a whole head taller than him. It's like suddenly Coach has just been diminished to the size of one of the boys.

"Now, no joyriding out there, Sterling. I'm trusting you." Alexander smiles his gapped smile, almost making his eyes disappear into his fleshy cheeks.

"Isn't any fun if you're not there anyway, man," Coach says, grinning. He takes the keys from Alexander's outstretched hand.

"Gas and everything in there," Alexander says. "Checked the tires this morning too. Just remember about that window back there I told you about."

Coach claps Alexander up on his arm, near his shoulder. "Don't worry, buddy. I promise I'll have it back by midnight."

Alexander waves us all into the van and smiles before pulling the door shut and then patting it twice, like a horse. Coach climbs up into the driver's seat and guns the engine. We're excited, getting to leave camp. It's not like we don't get to go for off-sites with our cabins—traveling off campus isn't that big of a deal—but not a lot of the concentrations get to do it during morning activities.

Even still, the drive into town is pretty uneventful. Montgomery and Olivia whisper together in the very back, but nobody else is really paying attention. It's annoying how they refuse to be part of the whole gang, but I'm not going to be the one trying to get them to join. When we get to town, the trip ends in this giant strip mall, at the end of which is this place with a big purple, red, and green sign that says 4 YOU FITNESS.

"Aw, we ain't doing aerobics now, Coach, are we?" Rutger says.

"You saw Jamie Lee Curtis in her day, my friend, you'd be the first to sign up." Coach winks.

We follow Coach across the parking lot and through the glass doors. While Coach signs us in, we just try to watch everybody working out without looking like we are.

"Okay, gang. They're ready for us. So, uh, come on upstairs."

At the top of the metal staircase is a large room, filled with treadmills and StairMasters, ellipticals, and a few other machines I don't even know what they do. A few older ladies are up there, working out, and they smile sweaty-faced at us as we pass them to go into another, smaller room at the back. This one is filled with stationary bikes—those high-up ones, not the ones you practically lie down in.

"So, what we're going to do," Coach says, clapping his hands together, "is some cross-training." He rocks up onto the front of his shoes as he says this, like a first grader who's been waiting to do show-and-tell all week long.

I look over at Rutger, but he's not looking at Coach—instead he's staring at the mirrors across the front of the room, looking at the reflection of the girl coming in behind us.

"This is Clara," Coach says, stretching out his hand to welcome her up front. The way he smiles at her, it's obvious they're a couple, even though Coach is trying to be all professional. I'm certain Montgomery and Olivia can't wait to take this news back to camp. "Clara is a trainer and instructor here, and she's also a triathlete. She knows a lot about training and a lot about endurance, so I want you all to give her your undivided attention."

"Well, pretty much, we're just going to get right on it," Clara says, smiling at all of us. She has the most perfect body I've ever seen: tall and lean and muscled everywhere, without being bulgy at all. Just incredibly toned. She is blond and tan, too, and coated with dark freckles.

While Clara explains what we're going to do, Rutger watches her like he's a dog and she's the one holding the Milk-Bones. Maybe he doesn't think Coach's techniques are so stupid now.

As she heads over to turn on some heavy techno music, we choose our bikes. I sit between Rutger and Lena, near the front.

"Believe me!" Clara shouts to us over the music. "You'll be grateful for this in a minute."

And oh my gosh, is she right. I can't really explain how it all goes, because five minutes in and my brain is mush. Forty-five solid minutes of biking, every three minutes or so getting yelled at by this totally fit girl, screaming, "Go! Go! Go! Level six!" over this crazy pounding music. My legs are going pump-pump-pump-pump as fast as they can to keep up, and my breath is coming out in these gusts I can't even care about. Sweat drips down my brow, between my boobs, under my knees . . . everywhere. There's nothing to pay attention to but the going.

When we finish, everyone is silent. Even Olivia and Montgomery, whom I've totally forgotten about in the intensity of the class, are breathless and red-faced and shining. I look over at Rutger and he leans across, gives me a high five. "Dude, man," he says, sweat dripping off all the angular points of his face. "Thanks for making me look like a wuss."

"Anytime," I manage to say back. We're all exhausted, with bibs of sweat across our T-shirts. Up front, Clara tells us what a good job we did, satisfied and proud. I think most of us just want to lie down on the floor.

"So," Coach says from his spot in the back of the room. He, too, is soaking wet, but smiling; clearly he likes seeing Clara do her thing. "We got it in us for ice cream before heading back to camp? Or are we, you know, too wiped for that kind of thing?"

He doesn't even need a response, really, but we groan our yesses for him anyway. Coach holds his hand open to include Clara in the ice cream outing, but she refuses with a wave. We go through some stretches together, and then thank her and file ourselves back out into the blinding heat of the parking lot to the sweltering van, all of us gasping for water, which Coach brilliantly has for us in a cooler in the back.

"Dude," Finch says, once we're on our way.

"Yeah man, right?" Rutger answers back.

"I haven't quite had my ass kicked in that way by a woman before."

Coach barks a surprised but genuine laugh.

"You're obviously not hanging out with the right girls," Lena retorts, her head lolling against the back of the seat.

"You said it," Rutger answers, while Finch just shakes his head.

I can just feel Montgomery glowering at everyone from the backseat. I can tell what she and Olivia really want to do is whine and complain, can tell they would, if there was just one more person not quite in the jovial mood. And I could be that person. I almost could. But really what I mostly feel is satisfied. That was hard, but I did it. I kept thinking I was going to quit, but I kept doing it. Doing something that isn't about my sisters, or my parents, or my friends, or anything else, but something that is really about me and my own abilities. It makes me want to do more, and better. It makes me want to prove something. Prove that I really can. And I'm not going to let Montgomery or anyone make me feel bad about that.

The shocking cold of the air-conditioned ice cream parlor

doesn't revive us much, but the idea of sugar is good. We sit together at the small tables grouped in threes and fours, licking our cones.

Coach takes a big, decisive mouthful of his mint chocolate chip. "I'm curious," he says, checking all of us out. "What do you think you've learned this week? So far."

"Running sucks," Olivia grunts. Montgomery laughs and elbows her, making Olivia blush and look as though she wasn't sure she'd said that out loud.

"Running does suck sometimes." Coach nods, considering his cone. "So why are you doing it, then?" He stares back at Olivia, who gets even redder than before.

"Discipline," April says, automatic. "And strength."

Coach nods, continues licking.

Independence, I want to say. I almost do.

"Proving something," Rutger says, quiet and serious.

"Proving what?" Coach is quick to ask.

"Proving you can do it, man," Daniel pipes up, confident under Rutger's start.

"Proving it to who?" Coach wants to know.

"Everyone," I say then. "Everyone who thinks you can't, including yourself." I see Lena and Rutger nodding.

"Well, I want you to know"—and here I can't help but feel Coach looking at me a little, at Rutger and the few of us who have taken all this seriously—"you've proven yourselves pretty well."

We finish our ice cream and don't say much else. But it's made a difference, hearing that from him. Made a difference to me, anyway. Made me feel like I've got my own place, like I belong: me, just me.

VIOLET

At lunch, after my amazing morning working on poetry forms in Writing, everybody's talking about the swing dance tomorrow night. Molly and Jamelia are both new to camp this year, and they're terrified.

"Do we have to, like, get up in front of everybody?" Molly's eyes are huge.

Aislin and Emily reassure them that it's nothing like that, that Margaret teaches a few lessons at the beginning, but it's mostly just fun.

"Nobody wears polka-dot halter dresses or platform heels."

"Not that there aren't some people who are really good," Emily throws in. She looks at Aislin. "That girl last year?"

"With the flip?"

They are nodding and grinning. They were both in Berry together last year too, but during third session. They had to pick second session this year because later this summer they're both going on a trip with their families (their dads are also best friends) out to California. There has definitely been some whining and moping about how they miss the other third-session girls they knew last year, but they're pretty cool, and we've all been getting along really well as a cabin, I have to say. There aren't any cliques or anything so far, and nobody's trying to be alpha dog, either. During cabin activities I tend to hang a little more with Trinity (because she's a senior too) and Mysha and Bo, who I know from last year, but looking around at the ten of us, chatting over our sandwiches and salads, it occurs to me that we really are a pretty good team.

"It just sucks you have to dance with boys at this thing," Bo says, frowning a little. "They never know how to do anything, and you have to lead all the time."

"Sure, if you always dance with freshmen, maybe," I tease her. Last year she had the biggest crush on this kid Jared, who admittedly had some seriously painful blue eyes, but even after she basically threw herself at him at the swing dance and a couple of bonfires, he never did anything about it.

"You didn't leave much for us to choose from," she teases back.

"I only hooked up with two of them, I swear!"

"Yeah, and you rocked their worlds so much that neither of them decided to come back."

"When you're good, you're good, what can I say?" We are teasing, and it's fun, but god, I hadn't even thought about Yoshi or Luke. Seeing James the minute I got here wiped my mind of anyone else, I guess, though if you'd told me last year this would happen, I wouldn't have believed you. Yoshi'd been an awesome kisser. And Luke was stunningly hot.

I turn back to Molly, who has no idea what we're talking about anyway. "It's completely fun. Don't worry."

We are still all chattering about it—what we'll wear, who we hope stays far, far away from us—as we go back to the cabin to clean up (ourselves and the cabin). We have a little bit of chill time before heading out to our afternoon activity, though admittedly I'm kind of eager to get going. Today it's blindfold hike for us. And it's with James's cabin.

Not like we'll really get to talk much. During blindfold hike, everyone but the counselors gets paired up with somebody from another cabin, and one of you wears a blindfold. The other person, of course, has to guide you—telling you where to step, to look out for tree branches—but they're not supposed to touch you. Halfway through the hike you swap the blindfold.

149

It's supposed to help you with your communication skills, and also teach you awareness of your different senses, and the two times I've done it, it has been a lot of fun, but this is the first time I've done it with a boy cabin, so it could just dissolve into stupidity. And plus, I might be distracted.

That I'm pretty tired from being out late with Brynn last night doesn't help. This morning after keynote I tried to be all like, *Hey, I'm dragging but that was fun* with her, but she just gave me this vague smile and told me good luck in Writing. I don't know what I expected—okay, maybe for her to hug me, or at least act like we'd bonded last night—but it seemed weird.

I'm too jacked up with my cabin friends and excitement about James to worry about it much, though. We meet all together at the East Gate, at the top of the wood line on camp property. I can't help it—as soon as I see him my face just goes into smile mode. His does too, which makes us both smile more. When I look over to see who might've caught that, Bo and Jamelia, standing together, are both grinning at me. In a way, it's kind of nice.

"Okay, kiddos," Natalie says, reaching into her canvas bag full of bandannas. "We've got twenty campers, and ten blind-folds."

She goes on to explain the rules. Molly and Jamelia move together and grab hands, thinking they're going to get to choose their partners, but as Nat keeps talking they eventually let go, disappointed.

James is busy watching over his cabin, making sure they're actually listening to what's going on. He moves over to stand between two kids who have picked sticks up off the ground and are trying to karate chop each other's. As soon as they see him even move, the sticks get dropped and they straighten up. It's funny. And really sexy, too. He sees me looking, winks. I think maybe I can't stand all this anymore.

Natalie has us count off, but instead of numbers she makes us say different animals: horse, tiger, elephant, zebra, donkey, giraffe . . . the laughing increases with every random animal that comes out of her mouth. Even Natalie is smiling at herself. Then we have to find our matching animal. I'm a gorilla. There's some muddling and confusion ("What am I again?" "Who's a giraffe, man? I need a giraffe here.") while we pair up. Half the kids have to go back to Natalie to figure out their animals, including my partner, a redheaded kid wearing a Flight of the Conchords T-shirt. I see him go over to her and am about to call out, "Hey, you—you're with me," when James walks past, leans in, and says, "When am I going to get you *alone*?" He barely even pauses—I'm not sure anyone besides my friends who are apparently obsessed with watching us would even notice—but it paralyzes me. The whole side of my face, where his breath came close, is in crazy shock. I feel the current of it running down into my shorts.

Finally we all get matched up properly. ("Clearly this whole animal thing was way too confusing for you guys," Natalie says with friendly sarcasm.) Jeremy—my partner—and I shake hands, swap brief credentials. He's a sophomore from Kentucky. His dad's a pilot. I size him up (shaggy hair, Roman nose, big Adam's apple, normal body, calm attitude, decent skin—not cute enough, and too young, even if I weren't already preoccupied), and figure I'm pretty safe from too much stupidity. At least I didn't get one of the karate-stick kids, like poor Ava and Bo.

Since Jeremy's never done this before (it rained the day he was supposed to do it last year), we decide I'll lead first.

He puts the bandanna on himself, but then needs me to help him tie it tighter. As I'm helping him, I look over and see James watching us. Every hair on my arms stands straight on end.

"Okay, gang, listen up. Leaders, you need to stay within sight of one of the four of us"—Natalie points to the four counselors—"at all times. If you can't see us, we can't see you. You must also stay. Inside. The fence. What did I just say, girls?" She whips around to Trinity and this girl she's standing next to, both of them ignoring their partners and talking together.

"Inside the fence," Trinity gives back. "We got it."

"Good. You must stay inside the fence. If we see or catch or even hear about anyone trying to climb over that fence with a blindfolded person in tow, you'll have to walk the plank. And you cannot touch your partner," she goes on.

A few "Aw, man's" come up from the boys.

"We'll blow the whistle when it's time to switch, so like I said, stay within range. And no intentionally walking people into trees or other human beings. This is about working together, not cruel and unusual mind games."

"You ready?" I ask Jeremy, who isn't quite turned in the right direction any more, trying to face Natalie while she talks. Already I want to grab his arm, turn him, but I don't. He nods.

It doesn't take long for everyone to separate out. There's a lot of laughing, a lot of "Oh god, no, wait." I'm mostly watching the ground in front of me, covered with leaves and pine needles and sticks and spots of sunlight, looking for dips or holes that might trip Jeremy up. But I have to remember to look up, too, because there are all kinds of stick-out tree branches and stuff.

"Ooh god, sorry," I say, when a small one whips across his face after I let go of it a little too soon, trying to let him past.

"Paybacks are hell," is all he says, grinning.

"Okay, watch it here. Slide your foot about four inches? Okay, feel that? It's a big root. Maybe . . . four more inches thick. Just be careful and step over."

And like that. I try to make it interesting for both of us,

winding back and forth and around between the trees instead of just marching in a straight line down around camp. At one point Jeremy says, "You're just walking me in circles, aren't you?" and I accuse him of peeking. We don't talk much though, more than me giving him directions, which I guess is good because we seem to be covering a lot more ground than other people. I can see Jamelia and her partner fumbling around, trying to get out of a tangle of blackberry bushes that somehow caught them both. Farther behind us, Molly is wheeling her arms around like a cartoon of someone playing Pin the Tail on the Donkey, barely moving her feet a centimeter at a time. Her partner is about six feet away, scowling at her, gesturing for her to just come on.

The whistle shrieks out, between the trees. Jeremy stops where he is and pulls the bandanna off without untying it. He looks around, blinks.

"Whoa. You were good. At first I thought it was kind of annoying, all the play-by-play, but it totally helped."

I try not to show my pleasure. I learned pretty fast my first year in the blindfold hike that it was a lot more fun and less frustrating for you both if the leader gave a lot of careful, clear directions, instead of just "Okay, take two steps, now move left," and generic things like that.

Jeremy hands me the bandanna, which is warm from where

it was against his face. I unknot it and turn with my back to him, bringing it up over my eyes so he can tie it tight. Right before the cloth closes down over me, the last thing I see is James, about ten yards away, back against a tree, staring at me. Then my eyes are covered, and I can't see anything else.

CALLA

After I help Alexander this morning, unloading supplies, it's postcard time. Sally's there bright and breezy, smiling her big smile and waving at me with one hand, the other already handing me a big stack of Callanwolde postcards. These are reminders for the kids who will be coming for third session a couple of weeks from now. I've already done, like, eight hundred of these, it seems like. (Not just these reminder postcards, but also a bunch of blank ones stamped and addressed to camp, so that parents can grab them at drop-off and then send messages to their camper without thinking about it during session. Mom's done it for us every year, and when I was putting those labels on in my first week, I kind of got a deep pang of homesickness.)

Anyway, I don't really know why we don't just do the reminders all at the same time—get them over with in one big swoop and then divide them into piles based on when they have to be sent—but that's not the way Deena wants it to go, so that's not the way we do it. What I do instead is sit at my little table, taking the 120 address labels I printed out all at once—before I realized they didn't have zip codes on them, so Sally had to stop what she was doing and show me how to redo the whole Mail Merge—and I stick each label on the postcard and then take them into Deena's office for her to check and sign at the bottom. Every single one.

It isn't the best work I get to do. And the afternoon isn't much better, with more database entries and then having to go to the auditorium to help Alexander get all the sound cues right for Mike's big fabulous keynote tomorrow morning.

I don't know what it is—maybe that the only three minutes of sunshine I get all day is spent walking between buildings, spotting two cabins' worth of campers lounging around like hand-fed turtles at the lake on the way; maybe it's knowing that Duncan's taking his kids white-water rafting this afternoon, which we love; maybe it's that last night was such a boring bust—but by dinner I'm so restless and itchy I feel like I'm about to crawl out of my skin. When Duncan comes up behind me in line for Seitan Surprise, bends his knees into the backs of my legs, and making me nearly fall over, it surprises me so much I let out this stupid yelp.

"Need to watch your back more, Cal."

"I thought *you* were supposed to have my back."

"I will, I guess, if you come up to the pit tonight. Rafting sucked without you."

I squint at him, fake-glaring, trying to conceal my delight. "The pit, huh? I think I know where that is."

"I'll see you there, then." He beams down at me. "And you can get your paybacks."

I'm totally glowing. I hope, hope, hope that either Violet or Daisy just saw that. All I want to do is plunk down and tell them *Rafting sucked without you*, but I guess I have to be cool. Will have to be cool for a while, actually, because there's still dinner and tonight's activity and lights-out to get through, because counselors won't be going up to hang out until way late. I'll need to kill some time. And a movie or reading is a totally bad idea because I will just fall asleep. I need some activity. I need to recruit some help.

"I feel like playing a game tonight," I say when I get back to the instructors, trying to work the whole Hey I Am the Youngest at This Table and Don't You Think I'm Adorable angle. "Does anybody have a cool game with them?"

"There's the games for game night," Steffie offers helpfully.

I nod as though I'm considering that, but I've played all the games in the camp's collection about a hundred times each.

"Ed's got Command Jenga," Lucy volunteers, straightening up. "Don'tcha, Ed?"

Ed's innocently batting his eyelashes. I'm not the only person who has perked up at this, curious.

"Ed, you holding out on us?" Daisy's coach says.

"You got something bootleg?" Nathan wants to know.

"What's Command Jenga?" Kelly asks, looking from face to face for a clue.

"Well," Ed puffs, exaggeratedly aghast. "It seems my dear friend Lucy has outed me." He presses his fingertips coyly against his lips. "And I suppose now I must invite you all over to our suite to discover just exactly how deep my secret is."

Mike and Chad, Ed's suitemates, bump fists together. I have no idea what they're stoked about, but I guess I'll find out tonight.

"Good call, babe," Kesiah says an hour later, putting her arm around my shoulders as we go up the stairs to the guys' floor. We walk down the hall to Suite Two, where already there are sounds of laughing and teasing inside. When we push the door open, Kelly—who is surrounded on the couch by Nathan and Chad and Ed—looks grateful to see some girls.

I find out pretty quickly that Command Jenga isn't any different from regular Jenga, except that when you take out one of the stacked wooden pieces, you find something written on the piece like, "Tell everyone about your first kiss," or "Sing your favorite Michael Jackson song," or "Fake a violent and bloody death," and kooky stuff like that. There are lots of pieces that simply say "Toast" on them too, so drinking is kind of automatically built in. When a beer gets handed to me I almost hand it back, but then I tell myself, *It's not like she's going to know*, and crack it open.

On my first turn, I get "Pretend you're having an annoying phone conversation," which isn't so terrible, but when Kelly has to take off her shirt and sing the national anthem, I feel really bad for her—and nervous for myself. Ed's piece says he has to act out fellatio on a beer bottle—I don't even know what that is until he starts doing it—and Chad has to pick someone in the room to slap him across the face. It's a wicked, tricky game, and I'm freaked out every time it's my turn, worried I'm going to get something totally mortifying, or else completely sick. I'm lucky every time ("Act out making a pizza," "Talk about a time when you lied to someone"), but before I know it, it's eleven thirty. When I see my watch, I almost exclaim aloud.

"What, hot date?" Lucy teases, taking a long drink from her beer.

"Oh, sit down, honey," Ed insists. "They won't be up there for another twenty minutes."

I feel my face go completely scarlet.

"You've got time for another beer, even," Chad says, his hand pushing one in front of my face.

With everyone's eyes on me, I go ahead and take it, even though I'm not sure I should. I can't remember now if this is my third or fourth. But I settle myself against the couch and get ready for another round.

By midnight those beers have definitely totally gone to my head, and when I get up to go, Chad even stands up and asks if I need someone to go with me.

"I'm fine, I'm fine," I reassure everyone. "I been here, like, five summers straight. I could find my way up there blindfolded. In fact"—I giggle, thinking of blindfold hike—"I have. Like, twice or something."

"Well, be careful," Lucy warns, her eyes on me as I get up and climb over the people on the floor.

"Thanks for letting me play." I wave to everyone, though my hand feels a little bit like it's just something I can see, not really part of my body.

I get a little bit turned around, coming out of the lodge on the woods side instead of next to the main building where I usually exit, but the lights and the giant forest help me get turned back the right way. Being outside in the fresh air definitely feels better, and when I finally make it past all the buildings and across to the big field, the thick grass is soothing over the edges of my sandals.

I'm almost totally back to normal, I think, by the time I get up the hill to the fire pit. Everyone's heard me coming and are looking over their shoulders, half with that *Ooh, goody, who's coming?* look, the other half with the *Holy shit, are we completely busted?* face.

"Hi, hi." I wave. "It's just me. Calla. From the office."

I can't really see anyone very well, because of course they don't have the fire going anymore, just a darker black place on the ground where the fire was earlier tonight, but I get the impression that people wave and smile. And then there's Duncan, popping up on the other side of the pit, saying, "Cal! I can't believe it."

"Believe it, baby," I try to say toward him. He's moved around the edge of everyone, and before I know it is coming out of the dark right next to me. His arm goes around my shoulders and I am warm, warm, so warm. I lean my head against him, hear myself make a sweet *mmmm* sound.

"Here," he says, putting a bottle in my hand. I take a sip and almost spit it out.

"This isn't beer," I squeal.

"No, it's better than that piss," a girl's voice says from somewhere to the right and down around my knees. "Kiwitastic, I think this one is."

"Melon Drop," another girl corrects. I am standing in a sea of talking. I sink down where I'm standing, right in the dirt. It's better to be low down, where the voices are coming from.

Duncan tries to tell me who all's up here, but after Heath, Emma Jane, and—well, I don't even really bother trying to remember.

"Where did you find such yummy stuff?" I feel like I am funny, like I am the Ditzy Blonde in an *SNL* sketch. "Usually it's lame semi-cold beer, if that."

"What do you think instructors are for?" a voice says from the other side. Everyone chuckles. Of course instructors would bring alcohol back from town for counselors, but it hadn't occurred to me before now. I picture everyone in pimp suits pressing hundred-dollar bills into palms, and I giggle. It's not that funny, I know, but it totally is.

"So it's like, just this big rotating party every day?" I completely should have become a counselor. Completely, 100 percent. Or at least I should've been coming up here every night. Forget this office business. Forget my lame-o book. This is how things should be from now on. I swig more of my drink. This stuff is tasty and fun.

"Not every night, man," a voice says in my direction. "Works

best on bonfire nights, because we can always say we were worried the fire wasn't put all the way out, you know?"

I am squinting across, trying to see him, and it's almost
like by squinting I can see him. Except that my eyes are kind
of sleepy, too, and keep wanting to just squint all the way shut.
I drink some more, let the cool liquid clear my throat and my
head. I feel myself say, "Oh."

"We have to trade turns, too," Duncan says, quieter, leaning against my arm to explain more while everyone else talks
about whatever it was they were talking about before I barged in.
"Somebody's got to stay with the kids, right? So we swap nights.
Some of them don't want to come up here at all, though—that's
when you're lucky."

"Does your part-partner come up here?" My eyelids are so
heavy all of a sudden. I can barely see him, even though he's right
next to me.

"Yeah, Arrow's cool. Mostly comes looking for a hookup,
but, you know."

I can feel him shrug through my arm. I can feel his mischie-
vous smile beaming on me, his wavy bangs practically brushing
against my forehead, though he'd have to lean a little bit closer
for that to happen.

"And you're not?" I'm wavering next to him. The cold swig
keeps me steady, focused.

He laughs, low. "Nah, man. We just sit up here and talk. If Amon's up here, he'll have his harmonica. Truth or Dare, if it gets crazy, stuff like that."

It's so sweet—so, so, so sweet—how he's explaining it all to me in this kind, gentle way, without being condescending, or acting like it's all too cool to even talk about. I let my body slump against him a little more.

"I love your voice," I murmur. "Tell me other things you do."

"Well, sometimes we tell ghost stories. . . ." I can totally feel his low, close, soft voice thrumming through my entire arm, vibrating around my head. I let my eyes close, let the half dark become complete dark, with only me and Duncan's voice and the place where my arm and my side lean up against his arm and his side. It's like being in a planetarium, surrounded by this huge expanse of dark that you can totally feel, with this voice-over just coming from everywhere, pointing out Jupiter, showing you the foggy sweep of the Milky Way.

" . . . okay?" I hear Duncan say, a little sharper. His body has pulled away from mine, his hand shaking my shoulder. I sit up, open my eyes, feel a sweep of cold along the edge of my skin.

"I think I need to—" But I don't know exactly what. I try to stand up. "What time is it?"

"Too late for you, I think," Duncan says. I can't get my feet unfolded right, and standing up is harder than it should be.

"Nighty-niiiiiight," a voice calls from somewhere around the pit. There are some giggles that aren't connected to anybody. Or are maybe connected to me, even though I haven't moved my mouth.

"Here we go," Duncan says, his arm going under my arm and around my back, helping to lift me up. I don't understand what's going on.

"I'm fine," I try to tell him, but then the ground drops, like, six inches underneath my foot, and I feel like I'm about to plunge all the way down the hill. I want to kick my sandals off, feel the ground better, know when it's going to do one of those crazy dips, know when a big root is coming.

"Oh no," Duncan says next to me. "You need those shoes on. Now come on—you know where we're going. Blindfold hike, right?"

I know I'm smiling. I hope he can see. We walk-shuffle like that down the hill, across the field, which is easier because of the building lights getting closer.

"There now. Emerald City, right? Just gotta push past these poppies."

This makes me giggle again. I start singing *Wizard of Oz* music. I would skip, too, if I didn't totally feel so sleepy and heavy.

"You're so fun," I tell him. "How come nobody is as fun as you?"

166

"Because nobody's as fun as me," he says, grinning down at me. He hoists my weight up a little more. It's the coziest, sweetest thing in the world.

We're in the bright light now, between the arts building and the main building. It's like staring into car headlights. It's not good.

"Oof," is all I can say.

"Yeah, I know. Almost there, okay?"

"Take me to my bed, Dunk. I just wanna lie down now." The lights are really confusing, and bright. I feel like a little kid. Everything is really washed-out white or else really black. We move around the main building into the small dark space between its lights and the lights of the instructors' lodge. It's way better there. I want to stop him. To tell him to stop.

"Where's your key, Cal?" he's saying. We're standing in front of my suite door.

"Just knock," I whine, not wanting to have to lift anything, even a key.

"They're asleep, Cal. It's late. Everybody's got camp tomorrow. Where's your key?"

I feel his hand digging in my back pockets, then into my front. It's like I'm watching him do it to someone else. The weird thrill of it makes me dizzy in a not-good way. He turns on lights. I'm sitting on my bed.

"I'm so tired," I tell him, though that's not all of it. I'm tired of pretending, tired of acting like everything's okay, tired of not being with him, tired of every single girl he ever hooked up with instead of me. I feel the weight of it inside me, inside my veins and my head and my heart and along my spine. I just want to lie down under it, I'm so tired. Only, when I do curl up against my pillow, knees folded close to my chest, suddenly everything is swirling in a very, very, very wrong way. I sit up.

"What's wrong?" he asks. "Here, let's take off your shoes."

"Something—" I'm squinting, running a mental eye over the insides of my body, feeling everything mushed up and not staying still. Feeling very, very gross in my throat. Duncan's hand lifts my sandal off my foot, and I hear the slap of it hit the floor after he tosses it across the room.

"I'm not right," I manage to tell him under the heaviness. A squeezing starts to happen in the bottom of my stomach. "I think I'm going to—"

"Here, here," he says, grabbing for the small trash can by my desk. The bag inside is thin and almost see-through. With no trash in the basket, it floats loosely, like a jellyfish, around the top. That's what I think, anyway, as I lean over it and my stomach squeezes itself clear to my spine. Everything comes up.

"Oh god," is all I can say. This is wrong, wrong, wrong, so

wrong. This wasn't the way it was supposed to happen. Hot liquid and the thickness of my dinner spills out.

"I know, I know," he tries to soothe me. "But it's good for you. Get it all out."

My body hurks again and I'm forced over the can, shoulders shaking with the effort, throat seizing up around the burning vomit, making me cough.

"Oh god. I'm so sorry." I start to cry a little.

His hand is on my back, rubbing circles. "It's okay," he says. "It's okay."

But it is completely not okay. I mean, in a way, a little bit it is, because of all the people in the world I'd want with me the first time I got drunk, besides Violet, Duncan is totally it. So it's good to have him here, because if he wasn't and I was puking and it was Kesiah or Lucy or someone, I would be totally mortified and also really scared, but it's not okay because this is not what we were supposed to be doing tonight. I was supposed to go up there and be hilarious and surprising and freewheeling and fun. I was supposed to show him that he could lean on me and kick back with me—that he didn't have to divide himself between two girls, that he could have both. In me. In me all the time, forever and always.

Another squeeze takes over my whole body. It's like I want to pour my whole self into that trash can, not just the remaining contents of my stomach.

"There you go," he says, hand patting my back. My throat convulses, and I make some of the grossest noises ever.

"This is—" I'm panting, tired. "This is what you've been trying to get me to come up to the pit more for?"

His smile is the sweetest thing. The sweetest thing, here for me. He hands me a glass of water that seems to have materialized from total nowhere.

"Well, not exactly. But you're getting the picture."

"Ugh," I say, swishing water around my mouth and spitting it into the foul wastebasket.

"Pretty much, yeah."

"I want to wash my face." I push myself off the bed, teeter a little, but not much. Throwing up has made my head pound, but it's a lot clearer.

"You be okay in there?"

"Yeah." I nod, steadying myself against every surface like an old lady on uncertain ice.

In the bathroom mirror my face is a washed-out gray-yellow, worsened by the wet raccoon rings my mascara made when I pressed my teary eyes shut to puke. My mouth hangs open, breathing. I turn away, blow my nose into some toilet paper, and don't even look to see what's there. I wash my face, using just the hand soap from the pump and not caring. I dry off on whoever's towel. Back in my reflection, my bangs are a wet, wiggly line across the top of my forehead, but at least my skin feels a little more tingly and alive. I pause a second at the sink and consider just sitting there on the toilet and curling myself up, waiting until Duncan gives up and leaves. I'm so embarrassed about all this—I don't even really understand how it happened—but more than that, I am just so tired. After a minute of standing there in the cold bathroom, I decide I care more about getting into bed than I do about my pride.

Duncan knows me well enough, though. He's ready to leave the minute I come back. The offending trash can has disappeared somewhere. He's folded back the top of my sheets.

"You want to change?" he asks.

"No," I groan, already under the cool, clean, forgiving sheets. My eyes closed now is the best thing in the world.

"You going to be okay?" He squats down beside me.

I think I nod. Mainly I am pursuing sleep as hard and fast as I can. Duncan leans over and kisses me on the forehead before standing back up. I feel the light switch off, hear my door shut behind him. It's like my whole being is centered within my closed eyes and my sinuses, throbbing. I can't think of anything else, not even Duncan: Duncan, so sweet in the dark. I can't think about him. And then—thank goodness—I really can't think of anything, asleep.

Friday

CALLA

I can't believe it's morning. I can't believe it's morning, and I can't believe that my head hurts so bad I can, like, feel it in my elbows. My alarm is positively blaring like this unholy banshee come to shriek me down with her to the depths of hell, but I can barely move to turn it off. All I want to do is stay in this bed. I am not going to breakfast. No way. Nohow. Even the thought of a whiff of the tiniest bit of that sausage link grease makes my whole body flinch in revulsion.

Resetting my alarm for forty minutes later doesn't help much, though. When it screams at me again I'm still heavy-woozy and feel like I've been run over. I think about calling Sally and telling her I'm sick. I picture myself saying pathetically, "I don't know. I think it was something I ate." But if it was something I ate, then it'd be something the campers ate, and Sally and therefore Deena would worry, maybe even go down to the kitchen, grill Binky and Carl down there, sniff ingredients. Knowing Sally, she'd come and check on me, too, and having her in my room—her perfume, her big teeth, her sweet fussiness—seems a lot more painful than dealing with her at the office.

At least since everybody's already at breakfast, I don't have to wait for Lucy or Kesiah to be done with the shower, and I can stand in there, letting the hot water beat heavily down on my aching head, for as long as I want. I move soap around my body, but not with any vigor, and I can barely lift my arms to get my armpits. Blinking under the streams of water pouring down and over my head, I piece together last night: Command Jenga, the scary walk in the dark, ghost faces around the fire pit, Duncan in my bedroom, and—ugh. The grand finale of disgustingness. So now there's no way I'm going to lunch, either. Or dinner if I can help it. There's no way I'm going to go anywhere I might see Duncan, might come across his *Are you okay?* face. I don't want him asking, don't want him checking on his idiotic, can't-hold-her-liquor, gets-smashed-the-first-time-she-lets-herself-go-drinking friend. Oh god, it's too stupid and embarrassing to even think about.

For once I don't forget my sunglasses. My eyes would melt out of my head if I didn't have them, even on the completely short walk from the instructors' lodge to the dark, cool interior of Main. I slowly creak myself up the stairs to the office. I can hear the last remnant of campers heading to the auditorium for keynote, am grateful for the quiet that fills the stairwell around me.

"Sugar, what happened to you?" Sally says the minute I walk in.

"I just don't feel very well," I half say, half whisper. "Migraine, I think."

"Well, baby, do you need to go back and lie down? The infirmary?"

Deena hears us, comes and stands in her office door, arms crossed. She looks me over—at my jeans and striped button-down, the best I could do this morning. I tuck my hair behind my ears, try to smooth it a bit. Am glad I at least put on lip gloss. God, god, please god please *GOD*, don't let her know I'm hungover. Please let them just think it's—I don't even care what they think. Please, Jesus, don't let her say anything.

"My dad gets them sometimes," I feebly explain. When he drinks, like, an entire pot of coffee in an hour, which is hardly ever, but Deena doesn't need to know that.

"The aura kind?" she says.

Since I don't know what that is, I shake my head. "I'll be okay."

"Are you sure? Because you're no good to us sick, you know."

I make myself smile a bit, nod some more. "If you needed me to lead ropes course today, I might be in trouble, but I think sitting still and working, making myself focus on something else, will help."

Deena nods. She goes back into her office, opens one of the drawers in her big glossy desk, and comes back with a bottle of pills. "Take these," she tells me. "They always work for mine."

Grateful, I pop the big white pills in my mouth, drink half the glass of water Sally just gave me. I'm not sure it's the best thing in the world to take giant painkillers on an empty stomach, and as soon as I swallow them I worry they might come back up, but there is still completely no way that I can eat anything, so I figure I'll just take my chances.

Deena goes back into her office and starts in on some phone calls. Sally takes pity on me and does half my work on top of hers—at least all the correspondence for Deena. I still have to do the database work, but for most of the morning she has me going through her files, cleaning out and shredding documents older than five years. The grating, high-pitched noise of the shredder is a little bit of murder on my head, but eventually the pain pills do start to work, and there's something sort of calming in the rhythm of feed-chew-feed-chew-feed-chew.

When Sally leaves for lunch, she asks if she can bring anything back for me. I tell her I'm thinking of going down and getting a grilled cheese sandwich, actually, because in truth the smells of lunch coming up from the dining hall two floors below are now seeming kind of good, and the idea of greasy cheese becomes appealing.

"Just want to finish getting through this pile," I tell her. "Don't worry."

Not long after Sally's left, I hear Deena shut down her computer and scoop up her keys, gather up her purse. I prepare myself to be smiling gratefully at her—*Everything's fine here! No worries! I am on the ball even though I still feel like ass!*—when she comes into the main office.

"Any better?" she wants to know.

"Those pills totally helped, thank you."

"Well, I'm meeting some graphic design people for lunch in town and then I've got a call with the accountant, but I'm going to do that at the house."

"Your hair looks good."

"What?" She swipes both sides of her hair with her hand, checking, as though maybe there's a bug in there. "Oh. Yeah. Thank you. For rearranging that for me."

She looks pained and a little awkward, standing here with me, without Sally to be some sort of buffer. Like we've been left to fend for ourselves after being introduced at a party neither of us want to be at.

"I left some things for you and Sally this afternoon, but it's nothing major. I do need to look at my itinerary again for September's Atlanta visit, though, because I think we're going to change some of the dinner reservations. The Kents can't do it at their house, because they have a fund-raiser that night, which I may even try to go to with them, but—that could make things complicated. Can you just e-mail the itinerary to me this afternoon? If there's anything immediate, I'll call in." She sighs at the end of it, almost as tired-sounding as I feel.

I stand up because it's just too weird in there with her, and I need to get some more water or something anyway. "Have a good afternoon," I tell her. "And I'll be here tomorrow to help with games."

She smiles, knowing. Cabin-versus-cabin softball, dodgeball, and flag football going on all at once, with teams rotating to different fields when they're done with one game or another, gets a little chaotic. And extremely hot. But it is exciting.

Finally she goes, but instead of following her downstairs, I just sink back into the cool of my chair, put my head on my desk, cheek straight to the cold, smooth surface. I can barely hear the din of everyone in the dining hall downstairs, goofing over their sandwiches, picking at their pasta salad. I wonder if Duncan feels as badly as I do, if this is how he feels every morning after hanging out with everyone late at night and then having to get up at the crack of dawn and herd a bunch of grumbling campers into their clothes and off to breakfast.

"I couldn't do it," I groan into the crook of my arm. "I couldn't do it."

I guess I fall a little asleep then or something, because the next thing I know I hear Sally's keys in the office door and I sit up too fast, making my head start pounding again.

"Hi, sweetie," Sally whispers, tiptoeing in, bringing with her the smell of her perfume and a little bit of McDonald's. "I know you said you didn't want anything, sugar, but I think this might help." She comes over, places a vanilla milk shake next to me. "You sip that, you'll feel a hundred percent better. My husband's cousin swears by it, and honey, believe me, he would know."

I'm embarrassed, but I guess I'm grateful, too, because the cold, smooth, sweet creaminess of the milk shake does taste terrific, and it feels like it even clears my head a little bit after only a few slow sips.

The rest of the afternoon is pretty much quiet, the both of us just working together without having to talk, but right at the end everything makes up for that, when Adele storms in, dragging along that awful Brynn, who is completely soaking wet and wearing this huge smirk on her face.

"I need to talk to Deena," Adele huffs, squeezing Brynn's skinny arm, as though she might slip out and vanish.

"Oh honey, I'm afraid she's gone. You need a towel or something?" She's looking at the drips Brynn is leaving on the carpet.

"No, just a pair of handcuffs," Adele growls. "Had some mischief this afternoon. I hoped Deena might be able to impress on our friend here how dangerous it is monkeying around in the canoes."

Sally sucks her teeth and frowns. "Now, honey. You know you ain't supposed to do that." Her voice is molasses, even though she's tsking.

Brynn only shrugs. "I'm a good swimmer."

"Yeah, but you don't know about the rest of the people in your boat." Adele turns back to Sally. "Any chance she can sit up here tomorrow during the games? Or better, I can lock her up somewhere?" She pretty much knows the answer, though. Brynn is her problem.

"Baby, nobody's gonna be up here, I'm afraid. Deena'll be here tomorrow, though, and you can talk to her then. We'll make sure she's got some time in the morning for the two of them to have a nice little chat. How's that sound?"

Brynn's still smirking, obviously not intimidated by spending time with Deena. If I didn't still feel like my insides had been slammed with a sledgehammer a few times, I might even tell her how unbelievably obnoxious, how uncool and tired it is to act like camp is beneath you or something.

Adele knows that a Deena talk is not really going to work either, though, and it's definitely not going to help her deal with Brynn tonight. Which means, basically, Brynn's getting off scot-free, because it's not like Adele can leave her in the cabin during the swing dance. For a second I think about offering to babysit her myself—telling Adele she can bring her to my room during the dance—but if I'm not going to the dance with Duncan myself, I really don't want to be stuck with this horrible girl. Violet would probably think I was the worst sister in the world, too.

"Thanks anyway," Adele says, letting go of Brynn's arm finally. "Maybe we'll just cover her in honey and tie her to an ant bed or something."

Brynn snorts. I want to kick her. I think Adele does too.

Sally looks down her nose, as though over glasses. "Now Brynn, hon, if you can't stick to the rules that we have in place to keep you and everyone safe, we will have to get your parents involved, I'm afraid. You do what you need to do to keep that from happening, though, all right?"

Sally's so sweet and so well-meaning that even Brynn knows she'll look stupid being mean back to her. "I just got carried away, I guess." She shrugs.

Adele scowls at her, but then weirdly reaches out and ruffles Brynn's hair. "You're not a bad kid."

Brynn's smile back to her is so full of fake saccharine it's creepy. Sally and I swap glances of *Those counselors certainly have their hands full.* We wish Adele good luck and tell Brynn to behave. By now it's four thirty, and Sally decides we've done enough for the day. I still feel like I've been slammed in a door, but my headache's not as bad and at least I can hold my eyes all the way open. Sally shuts down her computer, turns out all the lights, and sighs in a kind of happy way.

"Looking forward to the weekend?"

"Oh honey, I love my weekends. You know that. Couple days of quiet? Getting some things done around the house? Heaven. Just heaven. What about you, darlin'? You gonna go out?"

"Oh god, completely no. I'm totally staying in tonight, I think."

We both smile, hers with a giggle at the end of it. She pats my arm as we head out the door and says, "Baby doll, I think that might be a good idea."

VIOLET

Friday mornings we don't have to sit with our cabins for breakfast or keynote; we can eat and hang with anyone we want. Ideally I'd sit this morning with Brynn and maybe a few of my friends from Writing—or Calla if she weren't too busy, with her job I guess, to even be here—but I haven't really talked to Daisy very much since earlier in the week, so even though she wants to be doing her own thing, I figure I should check in.

"Hey," she says when I scootch next to her with my cereal. She introduces me to her friends from track, Lena and April. They wave hey but then are mostly talking to other older girls they know on the bench next to them.

"How's it going? I've barely seen you."

She shrugs. "Fine." Neither gloomy nor chipper.

"Karaoke was cool, wasn't it? I mean, did you have fun?"

"Joel came over. He sat with me."

I'm surprised, but glad for her. If I were Calla I'd squeal. "Well, that was good, right? Hooray, yeah?"

She half smiles back, flicking her eyes toward the next table at this redheaded girl and her dark-haired friend. Her voice gets quieter. "Yeah, but it's not like anything happened. We just held hands. I can't tell if he did it because he really likes me, or because he just thought I wanted him to. Or that he was just supposed to or something. I mean, he didn't say anything, and he hasn't said anything since."

"Maybe he's nervous."

She considers this. "Yeah, but then why did he come over?"

"Well, he did come over, right? So there you go. I mean, you still like him, right?"

She chews and swallows, nods. "We smile when we see each other. And I still think he's cute and everything."

Her wishy-washiness is so *arrrrgh*. "So then, what? He obviously likes you, because he came over to sit with you. Did he say anything about tonight?"

"No."

"Well, maybe like I said, he's nervous. Maybe he's a bad dancer."

"Maybe he thinks I'll be a bad dancer. I'm not the only girl in camp, if you hadn't noticed." She stares at her banana as though she's not sure she wants it anymore.

"And he's not the only boy. But come on. If he was into another girl, he wouldn't be into you."

"He could be into us both." Her face is maddeningly glum. "How do I know?"

"Well, if you don't like him, then why does it matter?"

"I do like him."

"Well, you're not really acting like it." I don't mean to be frustrated, but sometimes it's like Zee just wants to be unhappy.

"Well, maybe I just show my feelings differently than you do," she semi-snaps.

We cannot be fighting on a Friday. It's the beginning of the end of our first week, and tonight is supposed to be too fun. I decide to change tactics. I drop my voice down so that nobody around us can hear: "Want to know what I did this week, speaking of different?"

She looks at me, suspicious, but also interested. "Do I want to know this?"

I grin. "You're dying to." I look both ways over my shoulders, being dramatic, drawing things out. She kicks me under the table, insists, "Tell, then."

"Brynn and I snuck out. Twice."

She mini-glares, not sure she believes me. "What'd you do?"

"The first night we went up to hang with the counselors. It was totally cool. Wednesday we went for a swim."

"Did you skinny-dip?" She rolls her eyes.

Sometimes she can be as judgmental as Calla, I swear. So I figure she doesn't need to know everything. Definitely not about that night. Not in the middle of breakfast, at least. "Of course not."

"What's up with her, anyway?" She scoops up more cereal.

"Who, Brynn? Nothing. She's cool. Unpredictable, but cool."

"So why do you want to hang with her so much?" She's not glaring anymore.

"I don't know. I guess I just do."

And that part is wholly true. I keep thinking about all the stuff Brynn said the other night out on the lake, keep wondering at myself and why I want to hang around her, even though pretty much everyone's written her off as this unbefriendable weirdo, but it's too mixed up in my head, and I don't think Daisy would get it anyway.

We eat some more, quiet beside each other. Equilibrium has been, for now at least, reestablished.

"How's the yoga working out?"

Her eyes go to the other table again. "Interesting. Only, I wish I could do it by myself without everyone else in the room."

Which is how Daisy would prefer to live her whole *life*, basically. But instead of even commenting, I tell her about what we're writing, about how into it the group is, and how I can't wait to hear everyone's poems this morning. While I'm talking I can see her eyes drift away from me again, thinking some private thought of her own, not even really caring. I hate when she does this, because then I feel like an idiot for just babbling and babbling on, so I quit. I want her to ask me about James and I don't. Mostly, I don't want her eyes wandering off somewhere else if I tell her.

"I think tonight will be better," I finally say. "With Joel, I mean. The dance is the first thing we do where people are allowed and expected to pair off, you know?"

She looks at me, nods. And then she smiles. "Is it hard, trying to be so cool about it? When he's, like, ten feet away?"

I am blushing like crazy, and my jaw is buzzing with that electric feeling. "How come he's so awesome all of a sudden? We've barely talked all week, but I know there's something there. It's really not just me. Yesterday at blindfold hike, I thought we were both going to explode."

"I thought you were going to tell me you snuck out with him."

"I wish. But at the same time it's kind of extra-hot, the restraint."

"If you got caught, he'd get fired," she warns.

"Maybe not."

"Well, it wouldn't be good, no matter what."

"No. It wouldn't be good. But let's not talk about it. It makes me think about the end too much, and we still have two whole weeks."

"Yeah," she says, quiet. Again, those eyes of hers—the only blue pair between the three of us—drift off, over to her friends, and then somewhere else.

Which is half invitation for me to push her about whatever it is she's thinking right now—about Joel or James or the end of camp or whatever—but I know all I'd get would be more shrugs and a bunch of "nothing's" for about half an hour before she said anything serious. ZeeZee wants to feel like you care about what's going on, but she doesn't want to tell you. Or she doesn't want to tell you without you working for it. But I don't have time to get into the whole charade, because the girls across from us are gathering their wadded napkins and silverware—meaning it's time to go to keynote.

"I miss Mom, though, I think," she says, standing up. "I hope we get something from her this weekend."

I hadn't even given Mom or Dad or anyone back home a single thought really, but I guess it makes sense for Daisy to be missing them a little, since this is only her second summer. We get rid of our trays and our trash, and I hook my arm over her shoulders to give her a small squeeze. I guess it's good Calla's not seeing this, me needing to comfort our sister. When either of us is upset, Cow always tries to dispense all this advice and do these things to make us feel better, like take us shopping or give us a manicure, but what works best for me is for someone to just sort of be there. Let me know I don't have to be happy right away. Daisy isn't so different. I don't know what's bugging her right now, and half of what she might tell me is probably all stupid stuff in her head, but I can tough it with her at least a little.

Once I'm with my concentration friends after keynote, though, this huge feeling of relief washes over me—a feeling I didn't even know I needed. Here the pressure of making Daisy feel better goes away and I can really be myself. As the morning flies by, we finish our poems and share them after Kelly gives us some pointers on how to read them dramatically. She's all about the end of a line and millisecond pauses at commas and things like that, which really transforms what you wrote. You have to be a lot more conscientious about your breaks and punctuation, which is great—being so mindful that you're even thinking about a mark we take for granted every day.

By the end of concentration, we're all excited and inspired and worked up, and I can't wait for the weekend to be over so we can begin another week of writing. I want to talk to Kelly more, actually, about her own writing and what she's done to become a writing instructor, because that's something I would love to do. But I'm not staying after today—I'm hungry, and mainly looking forward to our afternoon activity, which is canoeing and kayaking with Brynn's cabin, Alcott.

Both our cabins sit at neighboring tables together at lunch, so we can start talking about who's going to be partnered up with whom. I want Bo to be in the same canoe with me and Brynn, because they're both wacky, and I think they'll really get along once they hang out. After the lunch stunt, and her crazy performance at karaoke, I've heard some snide comments from a few people about Brynn. With her sitting here next to me, talking loud and making her wisecracks, I see everyone else looking at me to figure out what to think about her. And while I understand why they aren't too sure, I'm also aware I'm the only one, thanks to sneaking out, who knows more about her. I set my face to *Make her one of us*, and watch (okay, yes, with a little bit of pleasure) as the rest of them follow.

Bo, however, is also in high demand. Jamelia and Molly want her in their canoe. Trinity wants to partner up in a kayak with her as well, and even Mysha seems like she wants in on the action. Emily and Aislin, sitting on either side of her, already have their hands in a we-are-canoeing-together death grip.

"I'ma have to start taking bids, ladies." Bo laughs. "You girls got any extra shaving razors? Maybe a big bag of peanut M&M's? I'm cheap. Just tell me what you've got."

When we finally get down to the lake, it gets straightened out. There are eight canoes and six two-seat kayaks, so we don't even have to triple up in the canoes if we don't want to. (Which is better, because there isn't really a third seat in the middle of the canoe, and if you sit there your butt gets pretty sore and wet. I know because me, Calla, and Daisy went out once on a free day last year.) So Bo ends up with Trinity. Emily and Aislin pair up in a canoe, and everyone else is sorted out. I'm glad that right away Brynn just came over and stood by me. We were automatic from the beginning.

It takes a while for everyone to get going, with the sorting out of pairs and putting on of life jackets, the handing off of oars, and then settling us into our boats two at a time and heading into the middle of the lake to wait until everyone's ready to go. For the first half hour we just paddle around so everyone can get accustomed to the rowing and steering, and then Forrest, the Water Sports instructor who is our guide today, blows his whistle and we all make our way to the far south end of the lake, where the neck opens up and we can travel down it a mile or so to the lower lake and the fingers that extend from there.

It's a perfect, gorgeous day, with plenty of sun but also a smattering of lazy, fluffy clouds that drift by and offer an occasion of shade just at the right moments. The lake is black-green and glossy, and the trees along the shoreline look like pines someone did in Painting 101: dark trunks, bristly green tops. We're not close enough to any of the other canoes to really hear what anyone's saying, but from time to time voices drift over in this lovely way, making it seem like we're in someone else's dream or memory. I wish we could lie down in the canoe and just float all afternoon. I kind of wish we had some of Brynn's pot.

"So, what's up with you and your boyfriend?" she says out of nowhere.

"He's not my boyfriend."

"Ah, but you knew who I was talking about."

I don't say anything back. I can't tell if I'm tingling out of just the mention of James, or because I'm embarrassed.

"You aren't subtle, either one of you, you know," she says after a minute. "How come you haven't done anything?"

I have to clear my throat. "How do you know we haven't done anything?"

Long silence. A single bird flies overhead.

"You're so cherry," she finally says.

The way her voice sounds, it's kind of sweet. Still, I don't know what to say back. I want to be with James, yes, absolutely, but Brynn calling attention to it makes it all weird.

"I haven't—" My head tries to think around my feelings, put

them into words, be real about it for once. "I haven't ever taken someone seriously before. But I think I want to with him. And now it's like I'm afraid to move."

"You're lucky," is all she says.

I watch the other girls in their boats ahead of us, watch the dark, squiggly reflections made in their wake. I am lucky. I am. People look all their lives for the fire I feel when I even hear his name, right? If we go further, I might spontaneously combust. But what if, when I'm finally alone with him, I find out this is all just a paper house, turned into ashes at the very first spark?

"You have to grab the ring, baby," she says suddenly over her shoulder.

"Excuse me?"

"My stepdad says it. 'You have to grab the ring.' It's an old-fashioned merry-go-round thing, I don't know. But he says it to me whenever I'm nervous about a meet, or about to start anything new, take some kind of test. It means you gotta reach over the neck of your own horse, push your comfort level, go for it, lean out. Because otherwise you'll never win the prize."

I stare at her ahead of me, at her spine poking out from her skin, the harsh wings of her shoulder blades jutting out from her tank top. Her black-blue hair stops just above the biggest knob at the base of her neck. Her arms—tough, wiry, mean arms—

push the oar into the water, cross over the front of the canoe, dip, push again. Who is this girl? I want to know.

"Here, watch this," she says, reaching behind to put her oar in the boat. We have passed the lake neck and are a little ways into the lower lake—canoes around us have spread out more, making it harder to distinguish who's who, just a blur of girls in a passel of boats.

"What are you doing?"

She is turning in her seat, creeping toward the middle of the canoe. And she's taking off her shoes. The sides of the boat rock dangerously close to the edge of the water. I grip my oar, hold it flat across my lap and try to keep us steady, watching her with utter astonishment and glee.

She waves a hand, encompassing all the houses along the edge of the lake: their big windows and screened-in porches. "All these people, they wish they could be us," she says, louder, like she's giving a speech. "Wish they could be seventeen forever. Wish they could live their lives all over again, wish they didn't have to use moisturizer and do Botox and listen to soft rock radio because it's all they recognize. We are right now what we will one day regret not being all the way. So why not be all the way, right?" She is hunched over, gripping both sides of the canoe. "Be! All! You can BE!" she shouts. Even from this distance, I can see heads in other boats turn toward us.

"What are you doing?" I insist, half-exhilarated and half-perplexed, as she goes into a crouch and looks like she's seriously about to try to stand up. Her bare toes grip the metal floor of the canoe. Brown bilgewater kisses the edges of her feet.

"I am the fuckin' body *electric*!" she shouts. "You, world, you are afraid of my power!" And then her legs start to straighten. She's standing up. Her face is wiped of everything but concentration. She doesn't even hear me laughing, probably, doesn't see the other canoes halted, two of them turning back in our direction now.

"I'm the King!" she screams. "Of the World!"

I'm not paddling anymore. Jessica—Brynn's husky counselor—is definitely headed in our direction. Brynn looks at me and winks, triumphant, victorious, and absolutely unafraid. It's shocking—and also the greatest thing ever. I watch as she lifts her left foot, puts it on the edge of the canoe.

"Brynn, don't," I'm gasping through my laughter. "Totally don't. I can't keep us straight."

The canoe dips wildly down, scooping water over the side. It occurs to me that this might not be the safest thing in the world.

"We're going to flip, Brynn. I mean it."

But I'm still smiling, until she shoots down at me, "I can swim back. Can you?"

And she knows the answer is no. But she's doing this anyway. Her tendon-y white foot is hooked over the edge. She is honestly going to try to stand on the canoe, and then we are going to flip. I'm bracing the oar flat across the edges as best I can, but I suddenly know it's not going to work. Now everyone else has fully turned, headed in our direction. Forrest blows his whistle.

Brynn ignores him and whoops, arms raised over her head, this huge smile covering her face. She stiffens all the muscles in her left leg, as if that's going to hold her up, hold us straight. I plunge the oar into the water, thinking that might counterbalance us. She raises her other foot. The boat tilts, and we both go in.

Underwater, everything is black, except for where the sun is. I am pissed and thrilled at the same time. The life jacket doesn't let me go very much under, but I'm not really worried about that. Instead I'm afraid I'm going to let go of and lose the oar. I am trying to figure out if the canoe has totally flipped over and if it's going to sink. I am kicked in the arm by, I guess, Brynn, whose face is laughing and sputtering out of the surface as soon as I break through.

"Goddamn you," I say, even though I am laughing too. *The oar. The oar. Don't let go of the oar.*

"Whooooooooooooo!" Brynn shouts out, her voice echoing across the span of the lake as she's treading water and grinning up at Jessica, who finally reaches us with a pissed-looking Natalie in the next canoe. Jessica sticks her arm out to grab the end of our boat, which, fortunately, has not completely capsized, even though it has definitely gained some water.

"You are frakking crazy," Jessica barks, that cheerleader diaphragm proving its worth. "You are so done. Do you know how dangerous that is? You are frakking finished, I'm serious. I am so over you, I swear. We are hauling you up to Deena so fast it'll wipe the smirk right off your face." She's obviously one of the cheerleaders they use on the ground, to catch the smaller, more popular ones when they do their sky-high jumps.

"If there is damage," Natalie says, much more calm, "to any of the equipment, your parents will obviously be billed." She blinks at us, annoyed beyond words. I want to hold up my arm, show her the oar still intact in my hand at least.

"This is very irresponsible," Forrest adds, arriving in another canoe.

I feel bad that Nat's pissed at me, but also, strangely, mostly I don't. We're not hurt. We didn't hurt anyone else. The equipment is fine. The only real problem is that getting yourself back into a canoe when you're in the water is much, much harder than you would imagine. Sure, you can grab the edge and try to pull yourself over, but because it's so light, there's the risk of it flipping right over your head as you try to pull yourself in. But Nat and Jessica align themselves beside our canoe and are holding it steady. Forrest starts giving advice on what to do next. Eventually they get me to toss my oar into the boat, and then I serve as a sort of stepping-person for Brynn, who's smaller and faster. She swims up behind me and then steps up onto the middle of my back while I'm treading water. When Brynn's pointy foot goes down between my shoulders, I feel like she's shoving me straight into the darkest part of the lake, but those life jackets are worth their musty stink, I guess, because I don't go under very far. Then Brynn reaches over the edge of the canoe, and with her crazy-strong swimmer strength she just about hauls me halfway into the boat in one heft. The metal edge bites into my hip bone, leaving a scrape that I'm sure will become a wicked bruise, but I make it into the boat. We get ourselves into the seats at either end, our oars repositioned. We are upright. We are safe and ready to go. Assuring everyone else—and yeah, myself—how okay we are has taken up some energy, but it hasn't eradicated the total *hell, yes* of the whole experience.

Of course, now our counselors and Forrest have decided that we all need to go back. A chaperone canoe is immediately on me and Brynn's tail to prevent any more shenanigans. I can tell some of the girls are annoyed, but whatever. It was going to be time for us to head back before much longer, anyway. Once we make it up the lake neck and back to camp, once all the canoes and life jackets are put away and Adele, Brynn's other counselor, has marched Brynn up to Main, there's really only enough time for us to get a lecture from Forrest about water safety, and then we just stand in a big circle in the grass and play Stupid Ninjas for the last ten minutes or so. It's not like we ruined the canoe trip for anyone. Not really.

Sitting there, still wet and dripping, the girls around me asking what the hell's wrong with Brynn, I feel this unexpected sense of pride and happiness. Superiority, almost, for being in the canoe with the Crazy Girl Who Stood Up in Her Boat. Weird relief, too, that it didn't even come up that I might get in trouble as well. Even though Brynn's getting bawled out in the office right now, I know she can take it. I don't feel bad about that. Mainly I can't wait to see her and hear how it went. But even more, I can't wait to find out what we're going to do next.

DAISY

Getting ready for the swing dance makes everyone in my cabin "totally retarded," to put it in Violet's words. The caliber of enthusiasm in here could be harnessed to power half the state. After dinner we all walk-run back to the cabin to get ready, which means a cacophony of girls squealing at each other, "Ooh, that's so cute!" Or, "Your hair is better up, definitely." Or, "Ohmygod, can I please borrow that tank?!"

It is humid and crowded and too loud in the cabin, but that's only a fraction of what it's going to be like at the dance. Everyone is talking at once. Abby is mad at Esha, but it's not clear why. Olivia is running interference between Montgomery and Jenny for some reason I don't know either. Today in concentration, the first time she'd really talked to me in days, Montgomery asked, half-interested, half-haughty, if I was going to hang out with Joel tonight. I'd shrugged because I wasn't sure. Swapping meaningful but brief glances at mealtimes didn't seem like much for me to go on yesterday and today. When I let my mind wander, though, I can still feel his hand holding mine, and I like it. Montgomery must have seen us at karaoke, to have said anything. For a weird second it's even affirming. But sitting above all the chaos up on Manon's bunk, watching her apply some difficult-looking eyeliner, I'm still not sure. Olivia squeals—too loud, as always— over something Esha just said. I glance at Manon and her eyes are already rolling. I smile, and she steadies her right elbow with her left hand, grimacing into the mirror, exaggeratedly bored with it all. I try to be detached too.

I wonder what Violet's up to in her cabin, though, how things are going over there. I wonder if she's watching the same kind of girlie chaos I am, wonder where the heck Calla was all day, since I didn't see her at either breakfast or lunch, and at dinner she seemed pretty out of it. Maybe she's just too into her job to bother with regular camp stuff at this point. Probably Vivi doesn't care a lick about the dance either, except for seeing James. Or maybe she's just focusing on sneaking out, since apparently that's what she's doing this week. Maybe she and Brynn have cos-

tumes planned. Or some kind of prank. Maybe she's remembering, like I am—us watching from Calla's canopy bed as our sister
darted from brush to brush and spray to squirt, readying herself
for one of the first big evenings of her life: junior prom with Max
Digby, a guy who'd come out of nowhere and asked her to join
him and all his drama-cool friends. And their drama-cool dates,
of course. A night that started with Max picking Calla up in his
convertible and allowing pictures to be taken in the front yard,
Mom and Dad trying to act indifferent. A night that ended with
Calla splayed on her bed, telling us both what a terrible kisser he
was, how much better it would've been if she'd been able to go
with Duncan, lamenting about her now-wilted corsage, which
didn't even match her dress.

Will Joel be a terrible kisser? Will I get to find out tonight?
I don't really have much time to consider either thing, because
Jill hollers at all of us to finish up, goes to the back of the cabin
to rush along the three girls all huddled together, smearing on
more lip gloss in front of the one rectangular mirror. I know
that the dance is stupid, and everyone getting all crazy about it is
even more stupid, but when they finally come out, when Montgomery and Olivia are standing near the door in their cute skirts
and their matching-not-matching polka-dot tops, when Manon
unfolds her long legs down the length of our bunk and stands
there, hands on hips, assessing, I suddenly feel like *I* look stupid.

It's going to be overwhelmingly hot and crowded, and I'm not going to be dancing that much anyway, but for a second, before Nyasiah tells us with her eyebrows that she'll have her eyes on all of us, I wish I had time to change clothes, wish I'd let myself be excited instead of all cautious and skeptical about Joel and tonight. I wish I'd put on more than regular jean shorts and this olive green V-neck lace T-shirt. Wish I'd done more than wrap my hair up in a twist, swabbed on a bit of Manon's glitter lip gloss. Wish Violet and Calla were here with me, to help me get psyched up.

But there isn't time to worry or care about how I look anymore. We're out the door. I can hear clusters of girls moving and giggling along the lighted paths, the hoots and calls of other groups closer to the lake. I wonder what Joel will be wearing, wonder if any of the guys cared as remotely much as we did.

Twenty yards away from the building, we can hear the music, which is pouring out all the windows. At the door everything is clogged. Two counselors are handing out numbered tickets as fast as they can, warning us to be sure to keep them. Montgomery leans over and says something behind her hand into Olivia's ear. Olivia looks immediately to her right and Montgomery hits her. They both giggle.

I'm craning my neck, looking to see if Violet's in there

already, also looking for Joel. But there is a crush of heads and T-shirts and arms and smiling mouths, and that's it. I picture Calla looking for a face—any face—in that prom crowd, wanting to find someone familiar smiling back. It's reassuring when Rutger's there, briefly, towering over everyone else, spotting me and giving me a thumbs-up.

Finally we get inside, and as I expected, most everyone is standing in groups around the perimeter of the room. Only a dozen or so brave couples are out on the floor, whipping and spinning and crashing into each other and obviously having a fantastic time, with Margaret stopping every song or so to give out more instructions. Violet is out there. With Brynn, the two of them cavorting and hamming, making things up, oblivious to anyone else, though James is watching them, over by the water station.

Flannery and I are standing together, arms crossed over our chests, watching everyone go through their awkward movements. It's wrong that Calla's not here, her and Duncan out there on the floor putting everyone else to shame like last year. I almost think about ducking out to find her, convince her to come out with us, when suddenly there's Joel, with one of his friends, shuffling and trying to be cool at the same time.

"You wanna try it?" he's asking me, holding out his hand. I'm completely surprised. It's so direct and so in front of everyone—I just wasn't expecting it. His friend holds his hand out to Flannery in the same way Joel is doing to me. She raises her eyebrows at me and grins, following her new partner out onto the floor.

"Can't be that hard, right?" Joel says sincerely before stepping backward into the toss and turn of the other couples. Behind his shoulder I hear Brynn's cackle. Joel takes both my hands, focuses on my face, shuffles awkwardly, trying to look completely comfortable. I feel a surge of sweetness toward him, that feeling too of *I can't believe he actually likes me.* We're both watching Margaret up front, showing everyone some steps in slow motion. We fumble through and actually manage a turn pretty well. But too soon she says, "All right! Have fun with it!" and steps away from the microphone. The music starts again. We are on our own.

I keep my hands in Joel's, jerk my elbows out, move my feet back and forth and then together, try a sway or two on one of my hips. Neither of us can look around at anyone else. We keep smiling dumbly at each other, keep looking down at our feet. The music is at least fun and good. Beside us, Duncan hoists another counselor I don't know up onto his hip, then bounces her, spinning, back off. It makes me glad that Calla actually isn't here, to see him dancing with another girl.

"I don't know where these people learn this stuff," I say to Joel, when our hands pull our chests toward each other and our feet do some kind of one-two shimmy.

"I know." He nods with extra emphasis. I picture Mom and Dad together in their twenties at an alumni dance here, picture Dad's big Adam's apple bobbing, Mom not being able to see anything else. I look back up at Joel's face; he's concentrating on his feet, his hands clutching at mine as though trying to keep himself from falling. I try to picture myself looking at his Adam's apple the way Mom would look at Dad's.

And it is really sweet, the way he's trying. Not many guys our age are even out here, let alone with a girl, and it's a huge thrill the way his face lights up, prepping me, before he wheels me around in a spin. And he is cute. And I do like him. I do.

So when he says he needs a breather, and his hand still clutches mine with our fingers all entangled and entwined, and he pulls me back toward the table with the water and the big bowls of lemonade, I'm warm-skinned and loose-jointed and happy. When his eyes go all along the rim of the room, looking for counselors looking for kids getting in trouble, I just enjoy standing there, holding his hand. We are both damp and warm and panting, but it feels nice to be in the same state together. Which is why, I guess, I don't even think about it when he nods toward the open back door and then pulls me through.

There are some other campers out here: kids just getting some air and standing around talking in the porch light, but then there are others—ones farther away, more in the shadows. Kids who look more like one unit instead of two.

"You look really good tonight," Joel says, close to my ear.

I laugh, mainly because his breath right there tickles in a way I feel halfway down my arm.

"No, really," he breathes, somewhere deeper in my neck. "You look good."

And then something funny is happening in my chest, my wrists, my knees, something warm and happy and makes-no-sense. My feet step farther away from where we were standing. I feel the shadow move over me like a cool breeze.

He says other things, asks other questions into my neck, my jaw, the side of my face. He's not going for my lips quite yet. Which weirdly makes me anxious for him to, makes my own face start bobbing and heading toward his, feeling the oily-soft smear of his skin against mine.

When he finally pulls me enough inches into the dark—far enough away from the circle of security light, just far enough from the voices and the blare of the music—I'm thrilled and a little scared, but relieved, too. *Finally, yes*, I think. But when the rude, wet, unapologetic press of his tongue fills my mouth, it's so gross I can't help but pull away for a second, fake a cough, move my hands to a safer place up on his shoulders. Either he doesn't notice or he doesn't care, because immediately there's that rubber mouth of his again, pressing against mine, pushing and squirming and, well, writhing. For a while his hands are on my waist, but it doesn't take long before they're up over my shirt.

"Hey," I say after another minute or two of trying to convince myself I'm enjoying this. I'm trying to smile even though I'm pulling back, taking a glance over my shoulder where, literally, not ten yards away, is another couple doing the same thing, though much more enthusiastically.

"What?" he murmurs. His eyes are glassy, his nose bobbling against mine, back and forth, his lips moving close again.

"I'm just—" I don't even know what.

"You okay?" His eyes stay, dreamy, on my mouth; hands are still roving over my shirt and rib cage. His hips come toward me, pressing. And I can feel him, his hardness, right there against my hip, feel him moving it, just barely, but enough. It feels impossible not to just say, "Ew," but maybe I'm supposed to like it.

"I think I want to go back in," I say instead, my voice flatter than I mean it to be.

"What?" he asks, voice still guitar-smooth, hands still gripping.

"I'm cold," I insist, stepping backward. It's the lamest thing to say ever, but at least I'm out of the cup of his hands.

In a movie I guess he'd have some kind of reply to that, about how maybe I need him to warm me up, but instead he just looks at me a second, shakes his head once, and says, "Go in, then," his left hand moving weakly by his leg, as though he's forgotten exactly where the door is but is still trying to show me.

"Are you coming?" I feel weird—like I've made some kind of mistake. I don't want to be kissing him, but I don't want to leave him either. "I mean, we're going to dance, right?"

"Sure," he says, pushing the dirt around with the toe of his sneaker.

A minute, watching him. He doesn't look up.

"So you're coming, right?" I try to make my voice, my eyes, my face flirty. I do want to dance with him. I still like being close to him, just not this way, this gross.

"Yeah. I just want to cool down some more." He's not really looking at me, not looking anywhere.

I step closer, put my hand on his arm. "Joel—"

"What?" He nervous-laughs. "We're cool."

I don't know what to say. There suddenly isn't much of a "we" to be either cool or not cool, really. I was hoping there would be more with us, just not this much more, this fast. And that it would be . . . better.

"Okay. Well, I'll be waiting then, okay?"

"Okay." His look is neither reassuring nor discouraging.

Of course, back inside, the music's switched from swing to this recent sappy slow song. The floor is crowded, surprisingly, with a lot of couples, fewer people ringing the room than before. I stand just inside the door, looking, wanting immediately to bring Joel in here, to try again. But he stays outside, and it's obviously too weird for me to go back out. So I stand there, hoping no one's looking at me, knowing what I've just come inside from. In the crowd I see Olivia with her big arms propped on the shoulders of some boy with too-long short hair and one of those T-shirts that has a necktie and jacket printed on it. Flannery is over near the stage, still dancing with Joel's friend, which makes me suddenly, wildly happy.

Not happy enough to find anything funny about Violet and Brynn, though, who are dancing together, arms straight, hands gripping each other's shoulders like awkward middle schoolers. They're singing the lyrics loudly and dramatically, pretending to gaze deep into each other's eyes with cheesy feeling before they bust up laughing. They look completely stupid. I wish Violet would just stop showing off.

I'm also wishing I had a watch, so I'd know how much longer I have to be here. I just want to go back to my bunk and be lulled to sleep by the chatter of shared stories. Even teasings and jealous encouragement would make me feel better. I'm about to ask someone what time it is when the music jacks up again and everyone starts bopping up and down, giving up on the swing theme and just dancing in whatever way. There aren't any colored lights swimming across the floor or the crowd, but it feels like there should be. And then there's Vivi bobbing in front of me, bouncing up on her toes, head wobbling like a jack-in-the-box, this huge grin on her face, grabbing both my hands and pulling me out with her.

I don't really feel like dancing, but I guess it's better than just standing there, watching everyone. I do scan over Sissie's shoulder to try to find Joel, but after a few looks I know I'm looking desperate, so I just leap around and waggle my head like my sister. Brynn comes over from wherever she went, links elbows with the two of us, and jumps up and down too. Even though she's weird, I let her make me bounce along. A couple more girls from Violet's cabin join us, and I see Manon and wave her over. At some point Rutger comes over too, and we spend half a song trying to jump up in the air and click our heels together. By the time the song ends, I realize I'm actually having fun.

"Okay, folks," the dance instructor Margaret says into the microphone as the lights come up. A bunch of groans and "Aw, man's" come up from the crowd. Margaret smiles and presses our noise level down with her hand. Her face is gleaming with sweat too, though you wouldn't have to be dancing for that to be the case in here.

"Now, at the beginning of the night we gave you all tickets. Right?"

A few shouts of "Yeah!" and some other, less enthusiastic sounds of agreement.

"So I want you to take out your ticket now and find the person who has the same number you do. All right?" She has to raise her voice, because we've already started moving, asking everyone around what their number is. "Find the person with your number, and when you've found each other, join hands and hold them up in the air." We can hardly hear her, everyone moving and laughing around the room together like bumper cars. I hear Brynn say to my sister, "Can't we just trade tickets with whoever matches you, and we can be partners?" But Violet pushes her into the crowd and heads off to find her own matching ticket.

I bump myself into Montgomery. Since she's standing right there, I ask what her number is.

"Ew," she says, scrunching up her nose. "You should be asking the *boys*, duh. Girls don't have the same numbers as other girls. Look." She jerks her glossy brunette head in the direction of a few pairs already standing together, hands raised. "Don't you get it? Why don't you go over and ask your boyfriend Rutger what number he has? Or—I forget—is it Joel you're with? Or, hmmm." She presses a finger to her lips. "Too bad *Coach* isn't here, huh? Must be very confusing for you." Her eyes are hugely, fakely angelically wide. She bats them a few times. "Unless you're more like your sister, that is." She tosses a vile, pointed look at

Brynn, who's found her partner and is doing everything she can to have as little contact with him as possible. "Everyone knows they're gay together."

I'm so shocked it takes me a minute to even be embarrassed. Montgomery flips her hair and turns off, while I just stand there. It's like when Vivi and I get in a fight. All my systems shut down, including my Sense of Humor Valve and my I Know You Are But What Am I Button. I'm just too stunned. Yes, I'm humiliated, too—why would she think anything was going on with me and Rutger? He's a senior. And he has a girlfriend back home. And he's eight feet tall. And there's just no way. And then, Coach? What the hell was that? And so what if Vivi and Brynn were gay? (Though I'd wish my sister would pick a better girlfriend, if she were.)

My temporary paralysis is broken only by a finger jabbing down into my shoulder, poking several times. "Excuse me?"

I turn. Behind me is a kid I've seen in the dining hall. I think he's in Muir. One of those normal-looking, blend-in-with-the-crowd kind of guys: neither cute nor ugly nor weird nor interesting, just normal.

"Are you number forty-one?" he asks, holding up his ticket.

My own ticket is wet and mashed in my hand from where, I guess, my fist was just trying to squeeze it into a pulp. I straighten out the disintegrating mess and squint at my number.

"Yep, I guess I am," I say back, offering what was my ticket as proof.

"I'm Andy," he says, putting his hand out for me to shake.

My own hand is still lead, my arm useless rubber, but somehow I manage to shake his. I'm sure Montgomery is watching this, thinking, I guess, what a slut I am. Me, the slut who just got grossed out kissing behind the building.

Margaret divides us into three groups of lines, partners facing each other. The Whitman girls all find each other, of course, squealing, linking elbows with each other and their partners, refusing to be split up. Andy leads me around the far side of the room, to the line that seems to have the most trouble forming. When we pass the second group, my eye catches the edge of Joel's face, but I don't look up. Instead I try to listen to Margaret explain how couples are going to march down the center, twisting. There are more complicated directions about how then they'll move over a group, but I just look at Andy and shrug.

"It's okay, I got it. Follow my lead."

He smiles, and then this crazy song about Pierre and his mademoiselle comes on, and the first pairs move down the line. People are giggling and hooting, and only three couples down it's obvious this is going to be an out-twisting-each-other competition. Andy is unfazed, even though in two more couples it is our turn. I want to try to see what Joel is doing, find where Flan is, look if Violet is having fun with this, but with everyone wriggling and jostling it's really hard to see anyone. I wish Calla were here. Her dazzle and excitement are always contagious, making it easier to have a genuine good time. But all I've got right now is Andy. So I focus on this place somewhere between his shifting shoulders and his sternum, and just try to copy what he's doing.

"Okay, ready? Follow me," he says, taking my hands and twisting us both together down between the columns of couples. My knees move like his knees. I'm not looking anywhere but directly at him, at his easy face, his eyebrows going up and down like yeah-yeah-yeah. I'm praying he's not going to stop in the middle and break-dance or flip me over his head or anything like what other couples have tried to do.

Instead when we get there, he goes, "Okay, on three, pause—and patty-cake." I look at him like he is crazy, but he is just giving me goofy jazz hands. "One, two, three," he insists, and right on the beat, exactly together, we go stop-slap-clap-slap, hitting knees and hands together, and then moving right back down the line in complete flawlessness. I'm so surprised, I give him jazz hands and a grin right back.

It goes on like that for a couple more songs, enough for Andy and me to work our little patty-cake routine into the other two groups, and enough for me to forget to care where Joel is or even if he's having a better time with his twist partner. At the end of the last song, Margaret hollers, "Okay, good night, twisters! You were great! Lights-out in twenty!" We all groan and waffle. Andy gives me a bow and then a high five. When he says, "See you around," before heading over to his cabinmates, I think I might actually be glad to. Not in that way. Just because he was nice.

Which is when Joel passes right by me—close enough for our arms to touch—and says nothing. He doesn't even look at me. His jaw is clenched a little, so I know he knows I'm there. The numb feeling takes over. I don't even look at his back as he pushes past. I want to say something, but there I am, not moving.

I look around. I need Violet. She would say just the right thing about Joel right now. But she is probably way ahead, or hanging far back, with Brynn. Or James. When I finally make it outside and find myself beside Flannery, I'm so relieved. I ask her how her twist went.

"Ugh. Sam Tarkinson."

"Ouch."

"Tell me about it. He's so weird," she says, laughing a little to herself.

"Too bad you got separated from that other guy." I elbow her. She can't stop herself smiling. "Do you think he's cute?"

"Definitely."

"Your twist partner anyone good?" She wants to take the focus off herself.

"Some guy named Andy? I think he's a junior, maybe."

"Cute?" she wants to know.

"Not in a way you'd notice. Just sort of nice."

"So, everything awesome with Joel? I saw you go outside. What happened?" She is puppy-excited.

We're near the cabin. The other girls are already clogging up the door.

I shrug. "I don't know."

"You're still together, right?"

And I look at her, realizing everyone must've already thought we were together. And now we're clearly not together, before we got to *be* together.

"I'm not sure," I tell her, holding open the screen door. I remember seeing Joel the first time this week, how great that was. The way his hand snuck over to mine at karaoke. Smiling together at breakfast. And then the wet, probing grossness of his tongue; his clenched, don't-talk-to-me jaw. "I really don't know what happened at all."

Saturday & Sunday

CALLA

Not having to get up at six on Saturday morning is so luxurious. Even though I conked out with my book immediately after dinner last night and probably slept almost eleven hours, it's delicious not to have to jump out of bed at dawn. Since I don't have to report anywhere until this afternoon, I also get to do the most amazing, terrific thing and just lie there after my eyes open, no requirements except my own drifty memories of past Saturday mornings, when all the cabins went into town: wandering in shops and rock-hopping with Duncan in the creek that runs beside the main road. I wonder if Vivi and Daze are doing that right now, and how the swing dance went for them last night: if Bot's hooked up with anyone, or how things are going with Dizzy and the white-haired fox. I feel a little bit of a pang, having missed it all. But I could barely register much of anybody at dinner last night, let alone muster energy to dance. I was so tired after having pulled myself through Hangover Day that not even Duncan was really on my radar at that point. I did make myself give him an A-OK sign when I dragged myself and my tray by his table at dinner and he looked up, all attentive and concerned, but even getting embarrassed seemed like too much work.

I decide I should probably get moving now, though, see what's going on and re-enter reality a little bit. Maybe do some laundry. I head out into the lounge, listen for Kesiah or Lucy, but the doors of both their rooms are wide open and everything is still. I bet with campers gone into town by now, they're all down by the lake, taking advantage of the early quiet.

I let myself enjoy the treat of another long, hot, luxurious shower. I even sing as loud as I want, thrilled that nobody can hear me. Midway through "Southland in the Springtime," though, I find myself wishing a little that Dizzy or Bot would come and sit on the toilet and sing with me like they do sometimes at home. This completely bums me out without warning, because really there's only going to be a couple of weeks between the end of camp and my heading off to Smith. I wonder if it'll even occur to them, or to me, to do something as goofy as singing in the bathroom together before I leave.

I'm glad I'll get to be with them during games this afternoon, at least. I hope, when their teams are at whichever station I get assigned to, that we can hang out a little, cheer each other on. But for now I need to figure out what I'm doing in the meantime. After pulling on some shorts and a tank top, I head outside, where the sun is bright and beautiful and it's immediately warming and delicious on my skin: totally the most perfect morning for just lying around sunbathing, reading stupid magazines, and chilling out.

Which is what the instructors are pretty much doing when I get down there.

"Heeeyyyyy," Chad says, seeing me come down the beach. Ed looks up and waves too, and Kesiah and Lucy give me big good-morning smiles. Helene, Steffie, Nadine, and Margaret are stretched out on towels with them, along with Nathan, and Dizzy's coach, Sterling. And yes, he does look as good as everyone wishes without his shirt on. I have to make sure not to look at him very long.

"Morning, everybody. Thought I'd see what was going on."

Kesiah pats an empty corner of her towel, and I sit down with her.

"Oh, we're just doing our little elephant seal act right now."

Ed is lolling on his stomach, stretching his pale, fleshy, and very hairy legs out behind him. "But there's been talk of volleyball. We had a lovely dip. You should've been down much sooner."

I stretch my arms up over my head. "Totally slept in. Which I completely needed."

"Yeah, were you okay the other night?" Chad asks, squinting against the sun at me. "You were a little . . . toasty."

A raging blush must take over my whole face. I'm sure everyone's heard now about my amateur drunken behavior, the High School Kiddo Who Threw Up in a Trash Can.

"Aw, cutie," Lucy says, rubbing the top of my head. "It's okay. We've all been through it. Rite of passage, baby. Rite of passage."

"I was kinda hating it yesterday, yeah," I admit to them.

"She's a toughie, though, right?" Lucy gives me a gentle punch in the arm. "Jump right back on that horse tonight with us, huh?"

"Ugh. I don't know if I want to repeat that or not."

"Well, you certainly can't throw up in my trash can," Ed guffs.

"But still, you should come. No Hook 'n' Mouth for us— we're going into town," Chad crows.

"Oh, bless you, T.G.I. Friday's and your giant margaritas," Ed says, pressing his hands together up under his chin like he's in church.

"Gotta earn that thing then, man," Sterling says, hopping up from his towel and clapping his hands together once. "Who's ready for some volleyball?"

I'm still not feeling up for a lot of physical activity, so I tell the girls I'm thinking of doing some laundry while the campers are away. Nadine, Steffie, and Lucy all say that sounds like a great idea.

Before going down to the basement where all the machines are, I veer to my room to grab my laundry bag. I toss my makeup pouch on top for good measure, too. I didn't bring with me to camp near the amount of nail stuff I have at home, but I didn't want to spend the whole summer with naked or chipped toenails, either, so I do have three different polishes. I figure we can have a little girlie laundry party, gossiping and doing our nails.

I'm not the only one with this idea. Steffie offers up a big bag of those nasty Doritos—the kind that are supposed to be guacamole and sour cream or something—and some Tootsie Pops, plus a squeeze tube of peel-off mask that she says will totally rehydrate our skin. So, while our clothes spin and swish in their cycles, while the dryers hum and buzz around us, we hang out, sitting in the molded plastic chairs, me listening to them swap bad drinking experiences—which morphs into bad boyfriend stories—eating junk food, and playing spa, just like a spend-the-night party back home. I think, if college is half as fun and cool as this is, I totally can't wait.

I'm even feeling good about going into town with everybody later. Somehow, I guess—maybe it was Command Jenga—something with me and the other instructors has turned a corner, and now I don't feel like some kind of stupid sidekick, but instead a little more like one of them. Almost like a friend.

We carry our fluffy warm laundry back to our various rooms, and I change from a tank top to a camp T-shirt for games, feeling relaxed and happy. Since the counselors all play with their cabins, the staff serves as umpires and referees for the afternoon. I'm not really sure how to ref a kickball game, but since I've played plenty, I guess it won't be hard. I'll just have to remember to pay attention to the game instead of Duncan, whom all of a sudden I cannot wait to see either. We used to get really competitive with games, even when we got paired up on the same team. He'll certainly have something to say about me being the one with the whistle now, and I'm already grinning, thinking of how I'll torture him about it.

Only, when I get down to the field, Deena spots me and heads over right away, with her I Need Something From You face.

"I thought Gatorade would be a good idea," she says.

"The water coolers aren't enough?" I'm squinting past her narrow shoulder, checking the fields. Daisy's cabin is at the one closest to ours. I can see her along the first base line, waiting for her turn at bat. She hates any game that involves swinging something, so I hope the pitcher is a nice one who'll either throw to her easy or strike her out fast.

"Alexander put them out, but I've been out here and it's so ungodly hot. I just thought that might be a nice treat."

I'm trying to picture myself hauling a hundred fifty bottles of Gatorade out of the store. How do you even get that many in a shopping cart?

"Alexander'd go on his own, but I thought it would be better if you helped."

I finally spot Duncan, running up the field in flag football with his team. He's got his bandanna on, holding back all his messy curls. His real game is ultimate Frisbee, but I can see from here how much he's loving it, trying to lead his boys to victory. *But I wanted to stay and watch this*, I want to whine.

"You have your Jeep keys with you?" she's asking me, one hand shielding her eyes now, even though she has sunglasses on.

I check my pockets. "Up in my room." I feel like it's a gross oversight on my part, not having brought them.

"Well, he can take the van. If you go now, you should be back in time."

"Any particular flavors?" I'm already stepping back, wanting her to see how ready I am to help.

"Not important, but thanks." She turns back to the field, heads in the direction of Duncan's flag football game.

Completely not fair, I think before I can stop myself. But this is what I'm here for, what she needs me to do. What did I imagine? That being her assistant would mean lolling around in the grass, cheering while the boy I love frolicked around and showed off his jumping catch?

I find Alexander, and we drive to the Walmart together. A hundred fifty Gatorade bottles are a lot. It takes us a while to get them, plus ice, out of the store and into the giant coolers Alexander was smart to bring. By the time we get back to camp, games are almost finished. We pull the van right down onto the field so we can just hand them out as campers come over. They're all so hot and thirsty, I'm just grabbing and giving, grabbing and giving. I don't even realize Violet's in front of me until she says, "Thanks, Sissie," and wipes her bottle dramatically across her brow.

Everyone takes off with their drinks, back to cabins to clean up before the cookout. All I've seen of Duncan is his grateful, flushed face before he herded campers off. I'm left helping Alexander dump out the Gatorade coolers, plus retrieve the other water coolers on the field and gather all the discarded cups. When we're done, I need a shower too, and then I'm going to enjoy a well-earned night out. But not before I stuff myself on barbecued chicken and Binky's awesome baked potato salad and banana pudding.

Before I can even smell the charcoal on my way down to the lake after cleaning myself up, Duncan runs up and slams me with a hug. "I'm so sorry I couldn't get away this afternoon," he pants, overwhelming in his urgency. "I thought I'd see you at breakfast yesterday, and when you weren't there, I worried you were still feeling bad. But we had to help with setup for the swing dance, and then in the afternoon we did archery, and you know I couldn't leave Nathan and Arrow alone with them for that. I thought I'd see you at lunch. And then you looked so tired at dinner, and weren't at the dance, and games are always so gaaaaah, you know." He finishes with, "Are you all right?"

He's so concerned and goofy, and it's so nice thinking he's been spending so much time looking for me that I have to laugh a little. Maybe it's from hanging out with the girls and listening to some of their drinking stories today, or maybe it's how over-the-top his concern is, but I'm not even embarrassed about my vomitous episode anymore.

"Yes, I'm okay. And really, thank you so much. For helping me, I mean. It was completely sweet of you."

"Well I couldn't have you choking on your own puke, you know? I mean, what would I have told Daisy and Violet?"

"Yeah, well, still. Really, I—" Now I'm embarrassed a little.

Now I can't look at him. I think, *If you would sit with me while I puked, and then clean it all up, and still be all worried about me the next day, not totally disgusted but instead genuinely sweet and wonderful, and come running up all concerned that we hadn't seen each other in twenty-four hours, then I think I might have to love you even more than I did before.*

"I got your back, Cal," he says, wrapping an arm around my shoulders and squeezing me close. "Always."

I let myself lean into him a little, and we just stand there like that together, watching kids from his cabin sword-fight with drumsticks and pile too much potato salad on their plates.

"You're on my team tonight, right?"

I have no idea what he's talking about. He sees my confusion, and his face deflates.

"Flashlight Capture the Flag? Four-team smackdown? I just thought after last session we would automatically—"

"Uh. Of course, Capture the Flag. I mean, of course and right. I just—of course I will." Even though I was really, really looking forward to hanging out with my instructor friends after this. But how can I say no to Duncan? When tonight might be the night, working together to ambush unsuspecting campers, that he decides to show me how all his "I've got your back" stuff really means "I love you and let's be together"?

"There's your sisters," he says at the same time I see them

coming, their cabins entwined in a mass group with a third collection of girls, all of them singing the "Bee-eye-eee-eye-eee"
song as loud as they can. "So. See you later?"

I nod, forcing myself to look cheerful. I decide I'll wait to
tell Kesiah I'm not going out with the instructors tonight—
maybe even blame it on wanting to stay with my sisters. Seeing
them see me, watching them wave and move together to head
over and wrap us up in a three-girl hug, I think that wouldn't be
so much of a lie.

DAISY

Seeing Violet and then Calla at the cookout, I almost want to run to them. But it's good enough to pool together, hug, and start talking all at once, getting ourselves in line for food. We find a place on the beach where we can sit, just us, and it's like taking off a tight, hot, sweaty pair of sneakers. It's not that today was so bad, really. Games were all right. When our team faced Joel's cabin in kickball, he ignored me, so I ignored him right back. It sucked, but I thought of kicking Rutger's butt in that spin class, and steeled myself against it. Signing up for the Olympics during break was weird, though. I guess Montgomery and Olivia are my enemies now, because after I said I'd run the relay, there was an awkward moment when they purposely didn't sign up for it. Our counselors kept having to say, "So, for the relay, who else is going to run? Because if no one signs up, we'll have to forfeit that one, which is stupid since this is what Daisy won last year." Eventually Manon said she'd go, which was nice of her, and then Savannah just looked at Jenny, and then they both agreed to do it too. It was fine. Well, it got fine. Overall, it wasn't a bad day, even with the parts of it that were. It's just that somehow, everything feels a lot better when I can be with my sisters.

"So how was the dance last night?" Calla wants to know right away. "I'm sorry I didn't show up, but I was just completely exhausted."

"It was so fun," Violet says back, telling her some of the details: dancing with Brynn, twisting with that friend of hers, Satch.

Calla looks at me. "And, missy, what about . . . ?" Her eyes are looking for Joel out there, excited.

Violet and I swap glances.

"It was fine." I shrug.

Then Violet and Calla swap glances. Which means they'll talk about me later. Which means I might as well tell them.

"I don't think we're . . . into each other the same way as before." I don't look over to where Joel and his friends are sitting. I want to ask my sisters instead if kissing is always so disgusting.

I want to tell them how fun it was, dancing with Andy and not thinking about the rest of it. I want to know if it is always so stupid, the back-and-forth of liking someone, the games you have to play. But I also don't want them lecturing me, don't want them leaning in and telling me I deserve so much more, gushing about how it'll happen for me eventually, and what I need to do to get over him. I don't want them zeroing in on Andy just because I danced with him, or trying to get me to like someone else. I don't want their fuss. No, thanks.

But I can feel them looking at each other again. Fine. They can think what they want. I don't care. I don't want to get into it.

"What about you and James?" I ask Violet, to take the pressure off me.

"Wait, what?" Cow immediately says, grabbing Violet on the knee.

Violet tosses an I Am Going to MURDER You face over her shoulder at me. Oh yeah. I forgot. Big oops.

Violet doesn't look at either of us when she answers, "It's just really, really good to see him back at camp, you know? There's nothing else."

Calla is not convinced. "But you want there to be." She narrows her eyes.

"I'm not stupid." Vivi takes a big bite of her chicken, chews.

"She's too busy hanging out with Brynn, anyway." I try to

change the topic. But then Violet glares at me again, Brynn apparently being another forbidden bit of conversation too. But it's not like I'm dumb enough to tell Cow about the whole sneaking-out thing. She'd freak.

"She was in the office yesterday, again," Calla says, shooting her eyes at Violet.

"She was just horsing around."

"She totally flipped a canoe! Somebody could've completely drowned!"

"We have life jackets. Nobody got hurt."

"I don't even know why her parents sent her here." Calla won't let go, and it's uncomfortable to watch. "It's obvious she totally hates it and is just doing what she can to get attention and prove to everybody how stupid camp is."

I want to trade looks with Violet then, but she's concentrating on her plate, scraping up remnants of baked potato salad, just waiting for Calla to run herself out. I know what she will say later about Cow and how judgmental she is. I know what Cow would keep saying about Brynn if Violet weren't pretty much ignoring her right now. I know they'd both be a little bit right.

Mostly, I want them to cut it out. "So, you haven't said anything really about, you know." I look down the beach, find Duncan and his wavy blond curls.

Calla blushes. "Oh god, it was so stupid. You won't believe

it, you really won't. But you *told* me to go out," she says, drop-ping her knee down to knock Violet's. She tells us about play-ing some game Thursday night with the instructors, and then going up to the fire pit, about how fast she got drunk without even knowing it, how she—uh, gross—ended up throwing up in a trash can. My eyes go over to Violet more than once dur-ing all this.

"But he was totally sweet about it, y'all," she finishes. "Like, just now he was all like, 'Are you okay? And will you be on my team tonight?' And, 'I was looking for you at the swing dance,' and all that. I mean, he's always been sweet, but this was *really* sweet. Like, uncharacteristically so."

"Here we go," Violet says.

"No really, Shaz. He still hasn't hooked up with anyone else, and I think—" She looks straight at him, without having to even search the group. "I think maybe finally he really is feeling the same . . ." She might as well have doves and cupids flying around her head. "The same way as me."

Again I want to look at Violet, and I can tell she has an eye-ful she could give me, too, but we stay stock-still, both of our heads turned only on Calla, as though she is the fox and we are the hunting dogs.

"Can I be on your team tonight?" I can't help blurting. It would be so much better for me if Duncan just grabbed me and singled me out with Calla, so I wouldn't get stuck in some bunch with Montgomery and Olivia by accident. Or, god, Joel.

"Of course, duh," Calla says. "We're all three teaming with him, right?"

Violet's uneasy. "I think I want to, you know, hang out with—" She says "my friends," but both Calla and I know she means Brynn.

Calla swallows and tosses her head a little. "Be on whatever team you want. Be on *James's* team."

Violet doesn't say anything back. I hate when they get like this with each other—mean and not talking instead of working it out. I never know what to do, because all I really want to say is "Quit being so stupid," which means they'd just tell me to butt out. But it doesn't matter, because it's time to clean up and get ready to divide into teams. We bunch up in groups of as many as six, and then the four captains—two guy counselors and two girls—select different gangs of kids, pointing and picking. Violet punches us both in the arm and says, "*Semper fi*, girls, but may the best team win," before she disappears to find Brynn. Calla lets me bring Flannery and Rutger over, plus Lena and April, and right away Duncan picks us for his team. While we wait for everyone else to get sorted out, Cow keeps looking over at Violet and Brynn, but when she catches me watching her, she smiles and pretends everything's fine.

I don't really get into Flashlight Capture the Flag the way a lot of people do. For some of the boys, this seems to be almost the entire reason they sign up for Callanwolde in the first place. A lot of the girls can get pretty territorial about it too. Once the game starts, everyone wants to be the boss of what we do, so a lot of times it just disintegrates into chaos, in spite of the elaborate rules.

We tie on our blue bandannas, head to our territory, and then crouch together, dividing up into offense and defense and discussing our strategy. At one point Calla brings up that it'd be a good idea to set up some kind of decoy flag guard, to give the other teams something else to aim for. Duncan looks at her like she's the goose who just laid a golden egg or something, and I understand then how she might think this summer it could actually happen between them.

The game starts. We scream. We run around. We turn on our flashlights and hiss at each other to turn them off. We crouch between bushes and behind trees. We leap out at people. We get pegged. We tackle. We have no idea how the rest of our team is doing, or what's happening down at the lake. At one point two girls on our offense rush by, chased down by two other kids on the green team, and there's a triumphant cheer when Rutger and Lena leap out to tag our opponents.

Eventually we hear the "game over" signal—four quick

whistle blows in succession—and we all stop and head back to the beach in front of the main lodge. When we get down to the beach, a Whitman girl is holding the yellow flag up over her head, hoisted up on the shoulders of two of her team. Half of them are soaking wet. They're jumping up and down and shouting their "Yawp." The boys from yellow all look pissed, and cowed.

After that we head up the hill to the fire pit, for singing and marshmallows, and I feel a heaviness press back down on me that I didn't realize was gone before. In the woods with Calla, Duncan, and my other friends, it almost seemed like we were somewhere else. Somewhere we're just kids having a ton of fun. Now, passing Olivia and Montgomery chattering together, passing Joel kidding around with his friends, I remember exactly where I am.

VIOLET

During pretty much the entire cookout, while I'm sitting there with Daze and Cow, listening to Calla go on and on about how stupid it is to think camp isn't 100 percent supercalifragilisticexpialidocious every minute of the day, I feel like I'm going to burst into flames. James is down by the water, sitting with a bunch of his campers and their friends from other cabins, but he's facing up the beach, staring pretty much straight at me. *When am I going to get you alone?* is all I can think. I'm trying not to look over there, trying not to be self-conscious, but with that burning gaze of his coming up the beach at me, it's hard not to.

During Capture the Flag, all I want to do is find him, talk to him, throw him down, and kiss him, but Brynn has other ideas. She gets into the game about as bad as half the boys do, wanting to smear our faces with mud and everything. I convince her no, by reminding her our territory's the boys' cabins, and that probably every inch of dirt is soaked with decades of boy pee. Emma Jane assigns us to border patrol, but Brynn gets bored, so we abandon our post and sneak deep into yellow territory around the farm.

We spend basically the whole time crouch-running and then plastering ourselves against the ground and freezing, hiding in the wide open, which is easy in the dark. We look, wait, listen, and then crouch-run some more. It's pretty scary, because any minute we know we might stumble on a guard, or have someone pop out, blinding us with their flashlight, but it's actually kind of cool how close we get before we're discovered by this freshman girl who screams when she finds us, and then tags us so hard I can feel the bruise that's going to form.

We spend the rest of the time hanging out in yellow's jail, talking, not really caring whether or not we get rescued. Brynn's in a talky mood. She tells me about the guy she broke up with before she came to camp, about how glad she is to be here, not having to delete all his *I don't understand* texts. She only stops when the Whitman girls swoop in and snatch the flag like a herd of blond Amazons, which is pretty cool. They pull a total sneak, three of them going in for the flag and then all coming out of the barn looking like they're carrying it under their shirts. The boys guarding of course all split up after them, which leaves the flag—covertly dropped by one of the first girls just outside the barn door—pretty much unguarded so that the fourth and fifth girls can come running in, pick it up, and bolt straight around the farm and across the road, safe into their own territory.

As we take our time walking toward the fire pit for marshmallow roasting after the whistle, Brynn complains that she was hoping to find somebody to distract herself with here at camp, but so far she hasn't seen anybody decent.

"Not anybody?" I can't help asking.

"Pimple-faced monkey boys who smell like the ass end of the Great Outdoors?" Her face squinches. "No, thanks."

"There are some seniors who don't look so bad, come on."

"And counselors." She bumps me with her bony shoulder. "What's your deal with him? It makes me feel weird, knowing something's up but not knowing."

I look at her a second, struck that she might be actually hurt.

"Well," I start. "Two summers ago James was a junior and I was a sophomore, and we got paired up the first night in the get-to-know-you games. The only thing I registered then was that he was going to be in my concentration, and that he was funny, and nice."

"Go on."

I explain how no-nonsense it was that first night: how you'd think you couldn't really connect with someone on any kind of deep level while you've got a yardstick tied between your waists, trying to coordinate your hip swings enough to get the marshmallow hanging from it on a string to wrap around the stick, but by the end of the evening I just felt like I knew him. The rest of session, hanging out in Vis Arts, we were just no-brainer pals. We made a good team at Pictionary. We admired each other's work. But we had other friends and other things going on at the same time, too. It didn't occur to me to like him. It didn't occur to me that he might like me back.

I think she's going to laugh when I tell her all of this, but when she doesn't, I go on: "When camp was over, we were like, 'That was great. Have a good life.' He wasn't back at camp the next summer, and I had enough boy drama then as it was."

We've stopped walking and are just sitting on a couple of the big rocks on the side of the hill.

"But when I saw him Sunday, there was just this undeniable draw." I tell her about the balloons-from-the-ceiling feeling, about blindfold hike, about dying to be with him and at the same time worrying, once we talk, that he's going to just turn back into this . . . buddy.

"Dude," Brynn says, jumping up and pulling on my hand.

"We have *got* to get you two together. Right now. I can't believe you've been here all this week and haven't completely jumped him. That is just too romantically disgusting for words. Have you seen him look at you? I mean, really. Dreamy-eyes at each other all week and that's it so far?" She's dragging me up the hill the rest of the way to the fire pit. "You are sneaking out with him tonight if I have to haul you out of your cabin myself, do you hear me?"

Which is how we end up, much later, at the now-extinguished fire pit, squatting in the dark with James and a bunch of other counselors. A few other seniors have snuck up here too, and I can't help but wonder a little jealously if our intimate group is going to just get bigger and bigger as the session goes on, making it less secretive and less interesting. But I guess I'm counseloring next summer, I should know what it's really like.

Next to me Adele and Sage talk about the games today, about how annoying it was getting kids to sign up for Olympics. Arrow and Carpenter compare Capture the Flag strategies. Everyone complains about another whole week of off-sites and activities, how they wish it would rain. I'm listening, or at least pretending to listen, though I'm not really focusing. At the marshmallow roasting earlier, Brynn went right up to James, grabbed him aside, and told him I'd be there tonight after hours, that after a while I would get up and leave, but would really go down and wait for him at the boathouse. Then she came back and told me the same thing. So there it was, done for us.

Now I'm just not sure how long I'm supposed to wait. I don't want to cut out too early and be obvious, but I don't want to waste the whole night up here when I could be with James. Plus, I'm not sure about ditching Brynn, even though that's what she wants me to do. I keep waiting for the right pause in the conversation, the place where I can stretch and say, "Gosh, I'm more tired than I thought," but it takes a while. Finally Anjelica and Whitney do get up to leave, so I stand up with them too, purposely not looking at James, but at Brynn instead. I give the jauntiest, "I don't care I'm just trotting off to bed like normal" wave I can, and then I head down, not looking back. I don't look back either as I walk toward the cabins, waving a last good night to the two counselors when they peel off to theirs. Nor do I look when I stop just shy of my own cabin and take a sharp right, beelining down to the lake where it's darkest, where I can follow the edge back up to the boathouse.

While I wait, I crouch down between two racks of canoes so that no one can see me, but so I can also keep a decent view of the path. Being out after hours with Brynn, I've learned that when it's quiet like this, you really can't sneak up on someone and pop out of nowhere. Someone can pretty much hear you coming a good ways off. Still, it takes forever before I hear his footsteps crunching on the path. Long enough to get slightly chilly, sitting still for an extended time. Long enough to wonder—just a little—if this is ridiculous, if he decided this was too risky and stupid, if he thinks the reality of being together won't be as good as the fantasy we've been playing at all week.

When I stand up he starts a bit, and then bursts into a smile that pushes all my doubt away. We don't say anything, but grab hands and head immediately together to the lower field, dodging lights and ducking windows and walking as quick as we can.

As soon as we get out into the deepest, darkest center of the field, where we're sure no one can possibly see us, it's as though someone turns off some kind of switch—this switch that has held us robot-rigid and stiff with each other practically all week. Now, in the dark, we are liquid rubber: sliding and bending and moving together seamlessly—mouth to mouth to neck with hands sliding up arms and stomachs meeting, knees bending together to adjust to pressing hips. It's completely all-encompassing immediate. I need him. All of him. It's like I honestly can't get enough of him close enough to me, and am just grabbing and pressing him as hard as I can. The best part is, he's grabbing me back.

Meanwhile we are both talking at the same time, saying how amazing it is to be back here together, how crazy it is to have missed someone you never knew you missed.

"You have no idea," he finally says, holding my face in his

hands and stepping back to get a look at me. "Is this really what I think?"

I smile and kiss him, talking at the same time. "I know, I know. I couldn't believe it when I saw you Sunday. I couldn't believe you were here. And then all week I wasn't sure if I was making it up or not, if I—"

He shakes his head. We are kissing, kissing, kissing and our hands won't stay still on each other. "No. No. You were absolutely right. I just don't know why we didn't do this *before*."

"Stupid, right?"

We both smile. He brings me down to the ground. The grass is deep and cool and a little itchy against my legs. His hand slides up under my T-shirt, over my bra, and everywhere he's touching is warm and right and reaching out to him. My already bare feet wrap around his shins. Our chests are pressed together. He's telling me about how crazy it's been, seeing me and not talking, not touching, not finding out. I tell him I tried to pretend it was a game, a game I was constantly losing.

Before long our shirts come off. Immediately it's so much better, pressing our stomachs close. We're telling each other as much as we can, but meanwhile I'm hooking my chin over his bony shoulder, pressing my hands flat against his back, squeezing him against me, just holding him because it's so incredibly nice. His hands slide up my back, my neck, my face. Then soon again we are kissing and kissing and every time my mouth is away from his, all it wants is to have it back. I want to kiss him all over—forehead, neck, Adam's apple, shoulders, fingers, chest. There isn't enough of me to cover him or enough covered by him. The kissing is enormous. It's everything.

Our eager, hungry fingers are tracing lightning patterns down each other's stomachs and backs. I'm not even really thinking about what's happening and what it means, why it is so perfect—I'm just doing it because it's the only thing I want to be doing. Soon our shorts are just getting in the way, and his warm hands are undoing mine and I work to undo his. When he slides mine down it's chilly in a way I didn't expect. He is kissing me again, though, and his chest lies against mine and his legs tangle in mine too, and our bodies are pressed close and so warm that I can't really tell where his begins and mine stops. It's the best feeling—the best feeling ever to just be sliding skin to skin with him and the grass and the sky and the whole world around us.

When his fingers curl over the edge of my underwear, it's a surprise that makes a hot place even hotter. Everything down there is slippery and burning, and his mouth on mine is something I need. I'm pushing against him—my whole everything. I take small little bites along his collarbone, the side of his neck. I cannot get enough of him.

"Do you want to?" he asks me, suddenly very still.

I surprise myself and just nod yes, because without even thinking, that's the absolute best answer—the friend sweetness suddenly caramelized into something so much more intense—and then I pull him back down to me, press my hips up against where his hand is.

"Okay, gimme a second." I think I can hear him smile. He keeps one arm around me but rolls back a little to reach for his shorts. I don't know what he's doing until I hear the clink of his belt buckle moving against itself and I realize, *condom*. It's kind of gross that he thought to bring one—that he thought we'd go this far in just one night—but at the same time it's kind of terrific and great that he knew. Or at least hoped.

There's some more fumbling and moving on his part, some sticky sounds, a small blanket of embarrassment covering us for a minute while he does what he needs to do. I don't look at him but past him and up at the stars—the black enveloping sky with its bits and flakes of the universe sprinkled and glittering across it. *Remember this. Remember this. Remember this*, I tell myself, though none of me wants to be examining anything. Instead I just want to slip into the melted dark beauty of my body and his.

He leans back over me then, hand back where I want it. He's ready now and so am I, and I don't want us to lose the moment or change our minds or talk or think too much or anything. I don't know if he knows this is my first time going this far, and

245

I don't know if I'm supposed to tell him, if it matters or if he'd want to know. But I don't want to ruin this, don't want to say anything as he brings his hips down and closer and then pushes and presses and connects us in the best way possible.

It hurts. It definitely hurts. But then he just stays there, still, a moment, and the hurt starts to fade. Moving together is painful in a different way, and I kind of feel like I have to pee, but soon the feeling-right takes over the duller ache. He covers my shoulder blades with his hands, and our chests are melting into each other. I link my ankles around his. I feel exactly how and where we're connected. He is kissing me again, kissing and kissing, all over my face, eyes, lips. I cannot hold him close enough to me. Everything in me is pressing—against him, against the ground, against the sky. I have never felt so much gravity.

He moves and I move and we move. We are moving together. I keep my eyes, my mouth, everything on his face—his blissful face and everything open. His hands, his knees, his everywhere is with me. I am thinking, *Remember this. Remember this.* And *James, James, James.* His breathing, the tautness of his throat, the sound coming out of him: "Oh."

Soon we are more still, and he is soft-kissing my face and I take his hand and press my lips to his palm and I realize it is over and it will never be over at the same time. It is—we are—always now.

"You okay?" he asks, quiet into my neck. I nod. He can't

see that I'm smiling. I say out loud that I am.

When he pulls away there is an embarrassing sound and we both laugh a little, nervous all of a sudden with the quiet night swimming around us. We hand each other what clothes we find. We dress, not looking at each other.

"I guess we need to go back," he says, standing, offering me a hand up.

"Thank you," is all I can say. I am looking up at him. He looks different to me now—more real.

"Are you kidding?" He wraps me in a big hug.

We take hands and walk slowly back to camp, not talking. I am trying to see if I feel weird, to see if there's any part of me that is unsure or wants something more, needs to know anything from him. But the only weird thing is that I don't feel anything but perfect.

We stop at the edge of the lights around camp. "I'll see you tomorrow," he says, kissing the end of my nose. "You really okay?"

And I am. I am. I am—something—but okay is definitely a part of it. I wish there was a way to tell him, because it seems like he wants me to say something reassuring, but anything else I could say would only be an attempt at explaining things, and therefore insufficient. And I'm not sure I really want to say anything. Because saying something would somehow break the quiet, calm good I feel inside, and I want to hold on to that for a while, until tomorrow, when everything will be noisy and different, and I will want to tell someone. So I just smile up at him again, squeeze his hands in mine.

"Good night," I tell him. "Have good dreams."

He makes an *mmmm* noise, and neither of us wants to leave but we have to. I squeeze again and then let go, turn and head toward my cabin. I don't look back. I don't want to see if he's looking. But my whole body is listening to the sound of his feet, carrying him, his slow steps out into the night.

CALLA

Sunday morning and I don't even sleep that late, am up, refreshed, and totally awake by seven—plenty of time to get dressed and ready for breakfast with the campers, maybe my sisters, but especially Duncan. Who is part of the reason I'm so well rested this morning, actually. As I pull myself out of bed and head toward shower preparations, I let myself just smile about all of that. I am so, so totally glad I skipped instructors' margarita night and did Flashlight Capture the Flag instead. Duncan was awesome. Daisy was awesome. We were awesome, even if we didn't win. The part where we sneak-surrounded half of the red team's offense was completely worth it all, especially seeing Duncan tag so many of them at once. We were panting and laughing, all of us, and I completely felt this total sense of right on—just free and crazy and wild and happy. Like camp—like time with Duncan and Vivi and Daze—is supposed to be.

After the game was over and the winner'd been declared, I sidled over to Duncan to see if there was anything going on after hours. I'd made a total, humiliating mess of it my first time, but that didn't mean I couldn't try again, and after how he'd been all day, it seemed like he'd want me to more than he wouldn't.

"Ugh," was all he said when I asked him, planting those hands over those knees and leaning over, shaking his head. "I'm beat, I gotta tell ya. The only thing I'm up for right now is bed."

And I let it go at that. It was cool. We were sweaty and dirty and happy and tired, and actually, once I'd high-fived everyone for the fiftieth time and then made my way back down, on my own, toward the instructors' lodge, I really felt it—happy. It was completely okay that I'd played tonight with the campers and counselors. It was okay that that was over now, and that I was headed straight to bed, alone.

And so it would be okay, I decided in the shower, if this morning at breakfast I just plunked myself down next to Duncan and ate with his cabin. We'd been together every summer before this for four years. Who cared if now I was a part of staff while he was with the campers? What did it matter, really, especially at a place where we're supposed to be making connections with people who aren't in our normal circles?

I'm so blissed with the idea that the half second of pause Duncan takes as I stand there over him with my breakfast tray, expecting him to jovially shove over and make room for me on the bench instead of just kind of blinking at me—well, it totally throws me. All of a sudden, with him there, looking up at me, kind of questioning what I'm even doing over by an all-boys' cabin on a Sunday morning when the only thing anyone's interested in is waffles and how many they can shovel into their faces, all I want to do is crawl back over to the instructors' table, or better yet, back into my bed.

"I mean, is it okay?" I find myself saying, standing there, him looking at me, no one moving over, his campers watching me too. I *am* not *a desperate girl trying to bag your counselor, boys,* I want to say to them. *This is Duncan. He is my* friend. *We've known each other since before any of you got your braces.* But they're already elbowing and snickering and watching and pretending not to watch, and I know it and Duncan knows it, and I can see on his face he wants to say, *Maybe this isn't such a good idea, Cal,* but what can he do, because there I am standing over him, like the biggest dork in the world.

So space is made for me. Boys shove hips against hips, and a space barely wide enough for my leg opens up next to Duncan.

He's already almost done with his waffles, I notice. I hope he's going to go back for a second round.

"So, uh—," I try to start. "Last night, huh?" My own waffles are soggy with syrup and suddenly totally unappetizing. I pray someone—anyone—takes my bait.

"Those bitches, man," this thick-haired blond boy grumbles. "They totally cheated."

"Knock it, Aves," the kid next to him says. "They won it for us fair and square."

The blond boy slams his fist down on the table. If we had pepper and salt, the shakers would totally rattle. "Dude, they had the flag. But then they dropped it. In our own territory, man. It should've been forfeit or something. It should've been taken back to the original hiding spot. Or, or—" He shakes his head, dumbfounded by frustration. "Or we should've hidden it again or something."

"We didn't see it, genius," another boy says from the neighboring table.

"Still, man," the blond boy says, shaking his head again. "Those girls suck."

From beneath his frustrated eyebrows he sneaks a glance over at me, looks half-apologetic. I'm emboldened again. I am my friend's best friend.

"Those girls do suck, man," I tell them. "Still, though." I

consider the bite of waffle on the end of my fork, dark and drippy. "Paybacks, as they say"—I pause a minute, look around—"are always hell."

A few boys smirk at this. Even Duncan gives me an elbow in the ribs. I'm a stranger here, a girl in their realm—and a staffer, to beat that—but I'm not, at least, a total idiot.

Duncan clinks his near-empty orange juice glass with mine. "What're you doing this afternoon?" he says, quieter, pressing his hands against the edge of the table and arching his back. I want, I want, to run my hand against those hard muscles, trace the outline of his vertebrae.

I shrug instead. "You know. Sunday stuff." I'm honestly not sure, having the entire day to myself. I'd ask him to go canoeing, actually, if he didn't have to stay around to half monitor campers on their free day.

Things are about to break up, we're about to move away into our separate mornings, when Duncan's knee, under the table, bumps against mine. "Fun last night," he says, leaning close so the boys can't really hear. "We make a good team, yah?"

And my whole head, my back, my chest, are absolutely going scarlet again with pleasure. I wonder if anyone's looking over, seeing us talking. I wonder if they can tell.

I nod, try to swallow. "We make an all right team."

He looks at me a second, and I swear—

"Okay, gang," he says, clapping his strong hands together. "Cleanup time, and then it's seriously cleanup time. There's a stinkage in the cabin no mother could love. We've got some elbow-grease work to do before there's any kind of"—he jerks his eyebrow up and down, shifty—"shenanigans."

There are groans and complaints, but they all obviously like him, because wadded napkins are tossed onto trays, glasses are gathered up, and one by one, his little brood of boys stand up and clear their places.

"Later, Cal," Duncan says, offering me a high-five hand.

"Later, Dunk." I meet his palm with my own open one. The sound of it is a healthy *smack*.

I wait for him to lean in, tell me something private again, maybe mention a meeting point later tonight, but instead he just turns and goes, bosses one of his campers into picking up a fork from the table even if it isn't his. Sitting there, looking after them, I'm suddenly aware of the vast empty space left by ten boys up and vacating the table, and I hurry to finish my now cold waffles, take no pains in clearing my own place and heading out.

Just as I'm leaving, I do see Violet, craning her neck a bit to catch my eye from where she sits, surrounded by girls who all clearly love being in her proximity. Seeing each other, we swap something that isn't quite a smile, isn't quite serious, either. She wants to tell me something, or she wants to know something I might tell her—I'm not sure which. It's a look we know, though. A look with intention. She can come find me later if she really needs to—I've had my fill of trying to insert myself into camper conversations. For now I just nod to her an "All's well" sign and hope she gets the meaning of it, walk myself out, and head back to my room for a little cleanup myself.

Not that I have that much to clean up, really. I can't stand a messy space—never could, after Violet and I stopped sharing a room when I was, like, nine, and all three of us got our own rooms upstairs. Violet doesn't care much about her environment, but I do. I can't stand laundry on the floor and not knowing where everything is. At camp, with limited wardrobe and limited stuff, there really isn't that much to make a mess of. Unless you count my trash can, and that Duncan cleaned out the other night.

Kesiah and Lucy have their doors and windows open, and the Dave Matthews Band drifts into our common space on Kesiah's iPod, but they're both also prepping plans for their concentrations this week, and it's clear they're not up for idle chat. I don't really feel like reading, or going for a walk, so after a few paces between my already clean and straight closet, and my perfectly made bed, I decide to sit down at the desk and write a few letters. I knock out postcards to Madeline, and our friend Nalia, plus a light, funny one to Laurel, who's going to be my roommate at Smith next year. After that I'm warmed up and can settle into a real letter, to my parents.

Dear Folks, I start, on some handmade paper with dried flowers pressed into it. It's nice, eco-friendly paper and all, but after even only those two words, I see it makes the pen bleed like crazy.

Second session is going well here at Camp Callanwolde, I'm sure you'll be glad to know. I pause, considering that, looking at my stupid, too-fat handwriting. *Going well*, I read. And I think, *Is it?* I mean, it's well so far with me. Well as it can be, anyway, with the weird not-camper/not-counselor situation. They would be glad to know I've made better friends with the instructors, that I feel like I'm fitting in, though I think probably the whole drinking-game thing they'd be equally glad not hearing about.

Would they be glad to know about Violet? How she's got some kind of crazy senioritis streak and has made friends with the wildest girl here? I can focus on how Daisy seems to really like her concentration, at least. That she's hitting some kind of stride, even if it's one that's surprising to us all.

Mom would be glad to know I've stayed connected to Duncan, too. She's met him, of course, several times, and she knows everything I think about him. But whenever we talk about it, she just says vague things like, "Your happiness is what matters the most to us," and, "Whether he loves you or not, there isn't much you can do to control either." Maddening, wise and Zen things like that. Things that don't help me figure out what to do, whether to follow Violet's advice and just tell him how I feel, or stick to my own reluctantly cautious guns.

My friends here, what they're like and what they're into, is the safest bet. I start on that when a knock at my open door startles me so much I almost drop my pen. Turning to find Daisy standing there makes me put it down flat on my desk.

"What's going on? You okay?" I'm half out of my chair already to hug her.

"I just wanted to—," she says, but doesn't finish. She shrugs, small, not looking all the way at me.

"Free time start already?" I try, my brain swimming over the schedule, trying to remember what everyone's doing now, if it's okay for her to be coming to hang out with me, or if she needed to get permission.

She nods, comes into the room a little farther, looks uncertain, sits down on the rug in front of me. I mess with my iPod, fool around until I find a playlist of things Violet made for me over spring break for us to listen to. When it starts, Daisy makes a sound that I'm not sure means she recognizes Violet's signature DJ-ing, or is just some kind of throat clearing. I look at her, her bowed head, her hunched back, her not talking. I decide to take the direct route.

"So what really happened with Joel?" I go over and sit behind her on my bed, start raking her long yellow hair between my fingers, choose a small section to braid.

She lets her head fall back, shrugs. I can think of five hundred different things she could say. And then: "Why are boys so . . ." She flounders.

"Stupid?" I finish for her, and we both laugh. I see her ease a bit around her shoulders, even though she gathers her knees up, presses them to her chest. I hate that that's the main word she's got so far to describe the boys in her life.

"I don't know." She shakes her head a little, and it's weird how tired of everything she sounds. "At school it's different, because you see each other all the time. There's a schedule. There's a routine. You know when he's going to be at his locker. You know what time he has lunch."

Part of me wants to say that I know *exactly* where Duncan is, every day, down to the minute. I know when he'll have a space where he can consider taking a nap, or if he's wrangling campers into a van. But I figure that's not what she needs to hear from me this second. I pick another section of her hair, start braiding again.

"Here it's like . . . everything is so . . . impermanent, you know? Like we only have these three weeks and already one of them is over. It's not even the whole summer. It's no time at all.

And then we'll all vanish and go back to our lives. This isn't really anything, what we're doing. It's just . . . a flash."

I keep quiet, not saying to her what I feel, which is, *Well, for some of us, it is completely the whole summer. It's the whole summer, and it's our* lives. But again I don't think that'd be totally helpful, so I wait instead, try to listen for what she actually needs. This is something I've learned from Violet, really—the listening thing. Because sometimes she and Daisy are a lot closer than me and Zee are, or even, from time to time, me and Violet. I've figured out that listening instead of talking can really help, especially because with Daisy you have to be careful. She's like a fish: You can't move too soon or she'll disappear. You have to hold still, have to let it all be about her, let her control how much and how far. We've learned this, Vivi and I, over a long period of time. We've made mistakes. We've said things we shouldn't've.

Dizzy shrugs again, becoming even smaller. "It's like this tiny period of time, right?" she says, not needing me to say yes or no. "But for that time, it's also your whole world. An eternity. Not small or little but completely big."

I think she's not just talking about Joel anymore.

"There's a microscope quality, yes," I say slowly. When she looks over her shoulder at me, I go on, "Objects in mirror are closer than they appear."

The song switches: the National now. We look at each other, both missing Vi.

"Sissie, is everything okay?" I feel the need to push. There's a reason she's in here. I just have to figure out how to get it out of her.

She picks at her cuticles, looks around at my empty cinder-block walls. "I don't think they like me," she finally says.

I think about this. "Who doesn't like you? Your counselors?" She shakes her head, doesn't go on.

"The boys, then? Is that what you're worried about? Because Dizzy, listen, you are so completely beautiful, and smart, and, like, completely talented. I mean, look at you—who'd've thought you'd be this amazing athlete. . . ."

But that isn't it either. She shrinks further. I hate myself for not being able to be what she really needs. I wish I could just take her in my car, drive down the windy road and get milk shakes or something, go shopping at the T.J. Maxx.

"It's nothing," she says, trying to shake it off.

"But Zee, really—" I want my voice to convey all my worry. Don't want, at the same time, to worry her for my sake. Because she hates making people concerned.

"People just take stuff so seriously sometimes, you know?" she asks, not even really to me. "And it's like, whatever, but when they're all so serious it's impossible to really *be* whatever. I mean, Vivi, she's all like—"

I can't—I really can't—help the disgusted noise that comes out of my throat. Daisy looks at me, nods in this knowing way.

"Thank you for that," she says.

"I mean, the whole Brynn thing? Like, what is up with that?"

"Yeah, right? I mean, who *is* she?"

"And why is Bot all totally Siamese-twin best friends with her, you know?"

"You know?"

I consider. "But it's not just about her, eh? Brynn. I mean, really?"

The music changes now to some U2. I can't help it—for a second I think somebody must be wondering where Daisy is by now.

"I miss Mom," she says, sighing. It makes me miss Mom too.

"You going to make it?" I am worried, somehow, with me and Vivi trying to be all hands-off and everything this summer, with leaving her to her own devices, maybe we were wrong.

"It's just three weeks," she says, shrugging. "And I mean, at least I don't have to worry about Joel anymore." She is funny and bitter. She is strong in a way she doesn't even recognize. In a way that's sometimes even hard for me to remember. I look at her legs—tight and lean. Legs that look good in shorts. Legs that boys surely notice. Legs I'm not sure where exactly she got, and when.

"On to the next boy, right?" I make it light.

She looks at me. "*You* on to the next boy?"

I'm again that uncontrollable blushing everywhere. But this is Daisy. "You know there could never be anyone else." I am honest. There isn't anything else to say.

"Well, he's a dumbass if he doesn't totally grab you this summer."

I picture that, him grabbing me.

"Could be the summer of dumbasses." I'm meaning Joel. I hope she knows.

"Yeah, it could."

The song switches again. It's too sad being here without Vivi all of a sudden. Sad we're not all three together upstairs in my room listening to this—that we won't be until the middle of August, when I'll only have a little time left.

"I should go back, I guess," she says. "Thanks for letting me just get away from it for a minute."

Her hair has six small braids now, all twisted together. I watch them start to loosen themselves from each other. I want to know, really, what she's hiding from.

"It's all right," she tells me. "I mean, Joel, whatever. You know?"

I nod as though I do know. But she seems old to me, older than me and Vivi put together.

She stands up, stretches. Even her hips are thinner, her stomach hard and flat. "You look awesome," I blurt out.

"You're silly." She shakes her long bangs around her face, pulls her T-shirt down.

"No, you're hot. He's completely stupid."

I hug her. I want to surround her totally, want to find all the places where she feels empty and find the exact thing to make her whole. I want to make her giggle, make her silly, make her smile. But mainly I just want to make her be okay.

"It's going to be all right," I say into her yellow-honey-white-gold hair. She and Vivi both, they think I don't get how sad they are sometimes, but when I'm faced with it, the only thing I can think is, *I* have *to undo this sad in them.* Because who can stand to see her sister sad? And if I can't be the one to fix things for them, to show them the ropes, to guide them through, to make them okay—then who will?

"Camp sing-along never gave nobody the blues," she riffs in this crazy slang. I crack up, not wanting to.

"I'll come tonight if you want."

"You could," she says, wanting me to and not wanting to need me to.

"We'll see, then," I say.

"Okay, we'll see."

"Keep Vivi away from that awful girl," I tell her, switching.

"Schyeah," is all there is to say about that.

"Okay, I love you."

She goes into the hall then, walks out, leaves me, heads toward her cabin and her counselors and her whole life happening outside of mine right now. And she's totally right, I think: It is the whole world in three weeks—it is so much. And yet it is so much nothing; it is not even halfway real. Not as real as me and her and Vivi's music in the same room. No way as real as that.

DAISY

I don't know, really, why I went to talk to Calla yesterday. But being there in her room, away from everyone else for a little while, did make me feel better. Better enough to get me through to this morning, when I can't find my underwear.

I know I had them yesterday. After I came back from talking to Calla, I made it into the laundry room as the few people before me were moving their stuff over to the dryers. Manon came in at the same time, and we spent the rest of the time talking in the grass, just chatting and joking around. Montgomery and Olivia and Esha walked past at one point, on their way to wherever, but like I said, talking to Calla had helped. When the dryers finished, Manon and I dumped all our stuff on one table and just stood there together, quiet, taking out our own things and folding them. Afterward we still had time to go down to the lake and swim a little bit with Flannery. It was nice.

I can even remember rearranging my clean stuff: socks on the left, shorts and T-shirts for running together on the right, cuter stuff for evening activities in the middle. My clean, fluffy panties and bras I put along the front of the drawer for easy reach. Dirty would go in a plastic bag shoved in my suitcase under the bunk. It was organized, and still warm. I can see myself doing it, sliding my hand out of the drawer, leaving the cotton pile there for the next day.

Now my hand is moving back and forth, feeling nothing but sport bras. I check under my tidy stacks of clothes, along the back—nothing. I am trying to do this in a way that no one notices, but of course I feel like everyone is watching. Especially the two girls who I'm sure know exactly where my underpants are. Especially them.

"Okay, girls." Jill claps, sounding a lot like Coach. "Let's get hopping."

Flannery sees me fumbling by the dresser, asks if I'm okay.

"I'll shower after running," I tell her fast, wanting her to go ahead to the bathrooms, stop bringing attention to me. I get my face wash and toner, press a T-shirt, sports bra, and shorts to my chest. I'm not sure I can bring myself to wear the same underwear two days in a row. I'll have to check them out. I make like I'm just going to use the bathroom in the cabin to wash my face.

"Winthrop, what's up?" Nyasiah calls.

"Showering after running, remember?" I say, trying to look like everything's normal. Trying to move my mouth through all this numb.

I know—I know—Olivia is watching me. I can see the smirk barely hidden on her face.

Nyasiah isn't pleased. She doesn't want me staying behind, but at the same time, she sees my logic.

As soon as everyone's gone, I'm stuffing my hands under mattresses, figuring somebody just swiped my panties and stuck them under there. Lots of girls get pranks played on them in camp. This doesn't mean I'm being singled out, doesn't mean I'm hated. But mattress after mattress and I find nothing. I stand in the center of the cabin, looking around, trying to think. The ceilings are all plywood, so it's not like they could be hidden behind a ceiling tile. Everything else is solid. There aren't any trapdoors. *Think, think, think.* I pretend I hear Montgomery cackling in the shower. I imagine her, for no reason, telling Joel about this.

I check my drawer again, just to make sure. There is nothing there. I reach under the bunk and pull out my dirties from yesterday, but yeah—just too sweaty. Already I hear a few girls walking back from the bathrooms, squawking with their morning chatter. I want Violet here, want her to be angry, instead of my stupid inability to move, my numb face and hands. They are coming back. I have to get dressed. I go to the tiny, mildew-smelling bathroom. I pull on my jock bra and my T-shirt. I pray no one can tell I'm commando under my shorts. I splash water on my face if for no other reason than to bring some color to my cheeks. I do not want to be frozen and pale. I do not want to look frightened.

When I come out, they're all there, working on their bunks. I go straight to my own, start pulling the sheets tight. But my running shorts aren't exactly long, and I'm too aware of being up high, on the ladder.

Being underwearless isn't nearly—not nearly—as uncomfortable, though, as knowing that there are at least two people in the room who know I'm underwearless. And there could be more. They could have told. They could've had helpers.

I make my spine steel, my face an impenetrable mask as we file out of the cabin. I am pretending I can't feel how weird it is to have nothing between me and my running shorts. I am pretending the air isn't a different kind of cool. I am walking beside Flannery and Jordan, who is gushing about her dream last night, about how she knows it means she has to try to make something happen with some junior in her concentration, instead of the boy she set her sights on the first day. I am not looking at Olivia and Montgomery six steps ahead of me, am not paying attention to the way Olivia keeps sneaking glances back at me, how Jenny, Abby, and Esha are all in line with them.

Breakfast and I am nothing. At least my lower half goes under the table. I have cornflakes. Or I have Rice Krispies. Or I have toast. I have something I don't even know what it is. I'm not paying attention. I am not looking around for Calla or Violet, am not sending out any signals of distress. If my cabin-mates are doing something mean to me, I am numb to it. I am completely not anywhere they can touch me with their petty stupidity. I am definitely not naked underneath these shorts, about to go running.

When keynote ends, I take off before Olivia or Montgomery can even look my way. I hardly hear Flannery telling me she'll save me a spot at lunch—I am just moving where I have to go. Where I have no choice but moving. There is no getting out of this. I just won't look at them. And I will be numb.

When Coach comes in with his CD player and his yoga mat though, the hot feeling comes again. I cannot do Downward Dog today. I just can't. Or Half Moon pose, or even half the stretches. These aren't leggings or anything—they're shorts. If I stand up straight and still, fine. Two giggling, mean-ass girls may know what's up, but probably no one else does. But if I have to bend over? If I have to raise my leg above my head? I didn't worry about it before, but that was when I had, you know, underwear.

Coach gets the music started, and I step to the back of everyone on their mats. I don't have to fake a headache—I can barely see.

"Um, Coach?" I mumble, wanting no one else to hear, knowing everyone does in the tiny room with only the noise of the fan and reggae.

"You okay?" he wants to know, too concerned, too serious, too worried about me. I shrug away from his friendly hand on my shoulder. I can hear them laughing even though they aren't.

"I just don't—" I see everyone else, already in Warrior Pose, their chins high, their chests breathing deep.

Coach's eyes go where mine do. He wants me to be doing what they're doing.

"I mean, I feel like I need to take it easy today. . . ." I won't look at him. I can't. He's too kind. He's too concerned.

His other hand goes on my other shoulder. "You need the clinic?"

"I just—" Beyond us everyone is switching into Triangle Pose.

I pretend I don't see Montgomery, smirking underneath her arm.

"I can still run, I think. I just need to start slow." This is not a real answer or explanation for him, but at least it keeps me from total mortification.

Coach isn't pleased, but he lets me sit at the rear of the room, faking like I'm doing a few light stretches, back against the wall. He probably thinks it's my period. Christ. I should've worn my bikini bottom, even if it was still damp.

During running, I am just grateful for being with Rutger again, getting three laps around the whole camp instead of two, getting to focus on nothing else, not even what Montgomery and Olivia think about me and Rutger running off together into the woods. They can say what they want. But for forty-five minutes I can be away from them and not care and just do what I came here to do: run. And I run better than both of them put together. Even with sweat crossing my body in ways I've never felt before, I can run. I can do that at least.

When we get back though, and have to do sprints with everyone else, finishing up with stretches in the grass, I almost break. I almost do. Because Montgomery makes sure to sit directly across from me, and even though I don't mean to look at her, at this one point I do, and she's totally waiting for me to make eye contact. When it happens, her face scrunches up as though she smells something bad, and I want to die then right there. I want to die.

When Coach finally lets us go—it is so hot, we are so sweaty, it is so unfair—I follow Lena and Rutger and the others, sticking close

to them, staying in the center, and I don't look at Coach. He wants
to say I had a good recovery, I can tell—but I can't stand it. I can't
stand being his favorite and everyone knowing it. I want, immediately, to not have done as well as I did today. I want only to get back
to the cabin, look around again. They're not that smart, my panty
pilferers; they're just mean. And unless they threw my underpants
in the trash and Alexander already emptied everything—which he
doesn't do until after lunch anyway, I know—then they have to be
somewhere, right? They can't've done something awful like spread
them all over the boys' side. They can't have done that, right?
Because they'd've had to sneak out. And people would've been talking about it at breakfast. And they just couldn't have done that. Not
to me. Not really. They couldn't have.

But when I get to the cabin, Nyasiah's coming out the door
and is definitely in a Don't Mess with Me mood. Before I even
say anything she sighs and goes, "You've been really dragging the
last couple of days, Winthrop." And I'm trying to just blankly
stare down her disapproval. I'm trying to channel the stillness
I can sometimes get in the middle of one of Vivi's meltdowns.
Remembering Montgomery's mean face though, and the glint
in her eye, for a second I unfreeze. And I find myself telling my
counselor all of it. Right there. Quiet but still talking. Not wanting to name names, but explaining why I need to go back into
the cabin for a minute.

Her dark eyes slide over me, and I don't know how she knows who I'm talking about, but immediately she hisses their names, rolls her eyes. And I feel my face go flat again. I force myself not to cry.

"Go on in, then," Nyasiah says. "And let me know what you do or do not find."

Which is, of course, nothing. I'm there, alone in the cabin, digging through my drawer, through everyone else's drawers, looking under pillows and even ducking to look in the crawl space under the cabin itself, really panicking now. I can't find anything. I have no idea what they did with them. I imagine a ritual fire, some kind of shredding ceremony, but at the same time none of that makes sense, because the only time I wasn't with everyone was during the half hour or so I was with Calla, and that was before I even did laundry. I put it away—I know I did. Maybe there was a spot of time between dinner and sing-along—or did they get up at all during dinner? Pretend to be heading to the bathroom? I wasn't paying attention. I didn't know I had to. But still, it's not like they could've done anything too crazy, unless, like Violet's been doing, they'd plotted something while I was asleep. And then—well. Then there's nothing I can do.

After I shower I put my still-damp bikini bottom on under clean shorts, don't even pay attention to what tank I have on.

Headed to lunch I'm defeated, numb, angry, wishing Calla's fingers were in my hair, wishing I could just go put my head in Violet's lap and listen to her talk crap about everyone in my cabin (except for Manon, Flannery, and I guess Jordan). When I make my way over to our table, both Nyasiah and Jill look at me, but I just shake my head and sit down.

"What's going on?" Flannery whispers, low, next to me.

"I just . . . " I don't even know what I just. "It's nothing."

But it's not nothing. For one thing, now the whole main office knows I've got no underpants, and someone will have to go get me some—probably even Calla—which is just awful on its own, not to mention the merciless smirks, sideways comments, and discomfort that'll go with them getting delivered to me. I want to put my head down on the table. Right in the middle of my three-bean salad. But that's nothing compared to what happens after lunch.

Because then it's not nothing, because Jill and Nyasiah won't let it be nothing.

"Ladies, we have a problem," Nyasiah says when we're back at the cabin.

"Respect of others is a pretty crucial element to our time together here at camp," Jill continues, staring over her red glasses at everyone. "It's a pact we make. It's something we uphold and cherish."

"But it seems," Nyasiah goes on, "it seems like not all of us in Emerson are up to speed on what that means exactly. Like not intentionally excluding people, for one." Her eyes go around to all of us. Jenny looks quickly down at her feet. "And for two, respecting each other's property."

Flan looks at me. No one else even budges.

"Some stuff has gone missing," Jill picks up again. "And we need to get it back. Some of you, we have reason to believe"—Jill looks at Montgomery, who doesn't even blink, just keeps staring her down, alert and attentive—"may know where your cabin-mate's belongings are."

I can tell Flannery's dying to ask me what of mine could be missing. Manon's face is concerned and baffled, and Jordan can't figure out who Jill and Nyasiah are even talking about. But no one else moves. I picture my underwear strewn hither and thither across the camp. I picture a pair floating in the lake.

"Until one of you lets us know where it is," Jill says, "I'm afraid all of us are going to have to sit out this afternoon's activity."

Now there's some action, some noises of protest, some glances around the room. Montgomery's mouth is set in a line. She wasn't expecting this. I'm glad she's at least a little pissed.

"What're we going to do instead?" Savannah pouts.

"And say . . . someone . . . gives the stuff back, can we go then?" Abby wants to know, her voice making a clear point. Everyone is thinking of riding horses. The gorgeous sunshine. The cool breeze. The chance to mingle some more with a boys' cabin. I feel, maybe unreasonably, like they should at least let me go.

"If there's time to, sure," Jill says, leaning back on her own bed. "I mean, I want to go riding. I know most of you do. So if you know what's missing and where it is, you can just pipe up right now and we can all head out."

"Come on, guys," Manon groans. "This is stupid."

"Whose stuff is missing?" Jordan wants to know. I remember how she helped some random girl the other day who got stung by a yellow jacket—how she volunteered to walk her back to the main lodge and then her cabin to lie down for a little. How she's helpful like that, in ways you wouldn't expect.

All the other girls, though, including Olivia, are looking at Montgomery, waiting for her to volunteer what she knows. But she sits there on her bunk, arms crossed. She won't even make eye contact with the rest of them, just keeps her face focused—calm and hateful—on Nyasiah's.

My insides feel like cold liquid, and my throat feels dry and hot. She's not going to say anything, and she's not going to let anybody else say anything either. This is going to be a long afternoon.

Esha sighs and reaches under her bed for her book, and a few other girls move to do the same thing until Jill's bark stops us: "Oh no, no." She waves her finger back and forth, like a teacher or a librarian. "I didn't say we were going to read this afternoon. Or write. Or draw. Or anything else. I said we were going to *sit out* this afternoon's activity. In fact, let's circle up down here on the floor."

Now everyone is really groaning, even Olivia. Montgomery doesn't look at anyone. As she crosses her legs underneath her, her face is stone. I know now she thinks, on top of being a slut I guess, that I'm a tattletale, too. And now we're all being punished. She and the girls on her side who didn't like me for whatever reason before are going to really hate me now.

I raise my hand.

"Yes?" Jill looks surprised.

"It's my stuff that's missing," I say, like most of them don't know. "And I really appreciate it, what you're doing, but I don't think it's fair for the whole cabin to miss out on our activity because of this. I mean, it's replaceable. I'll be fine. So I don't think—I mean, it's really okay."

Nyasiah looks over all of us. "That's sweet of you, Daisy, and I hope whoever stole from you will take note, but we are a unit here, and when one member does wrong to another, then she may as well have done it to all of us."

"And if there's someone who didn't steal from you, but knows about it," Jill continues, meeting eyes with Nyasiah, "not telling is just as bad as doing it. So thanks, Daisy, but this whole thing reeks of a bigger problem that we need to make sure doesn't grow. We're here for another two weeks together, ladies. We can't be having this kind of thing in our community."

I feel a few girls looking at me, maybe sheepish, maybe mean. I don't look back at them to find out. I couldn't see them if I did anyway, because I've just gone totally numb again. I can barely even feel Flannery's hand as she squeezes my wrist in sympathy.

We wait, all of us, staring at the floor or our feet or the ceiling, picking at fingernails or toenails or scabs. Esha huffs out a big sigh every ten seconds or so, braiding and rebraiding the same strand of her long brown hair. Jenny keeps crossing and uncrossing her ankles stretched out in front of her, maybe trying to signal to Montgomery somehow, get her to fess up. But it's like you can *see* Montgomery's will to stay silent surrounding her like a force field. If we have to sit here for three hours, she's going to make us.

"Come on, you guys," Manon says again. "This is bull crap."

"Hey." Jill's voice is sharp.

"I'm sorry, but it just is. Stealing somebody's stuff? What are you, in fifth grade?"

Olivia giggles, I think out of nervousness.

"Yeah, I guess so." Manon's face is disgusted. "I guess for you kindergarten little girls it is funny. But the rest of us don't think so. Can we have pieces of paper?" she asks Nyasiah then, getting an idea. "If we know anything about all this, we can write it down on a piece of paper, anonymously, and nobody will be ratting on anyone else."

Jill looks over at Nyasiah, and you can see they both wish they'd thought of that first, instead of waiting for a camper to figure it out. Jill rips some sheets out of her journal and hands half pages to each of us while we dig in our own bags for pens. I don't care anymore who's looking at who, or what signals Montgomery's sending through her evil brown eyeballs—all I want is for this to be over. I don't care about my underwear anymore, even, or what they think of me. I just want this awful business to be over and finished. Really what I want is to go home. Because I may get my underwear back, but after this, I'm still going to feel naked.

"All right, you ladies can turn around and face the wall if that'll make you feel better, so nobody can see what you're writing. But you have to write something. Even if it's 'I don't know.' When you're done, fold it in half and hold it over your head."

Everyone turns around or at least shifts a little to cover their paper. I don't have to write anything, of course, but I figure writing "Size 4" will at least let them know what to get for me, if someone hasn't gone already. Montgomery doesn't even look at the piece of paper. Instead she is glaring at the bunk across from her as though she might be able to burn a hole in it.

Jill goes around and collects the papers from everyone. When she gets to Montgomery she waits, her face full of impatience, until Montgomery huffs and scratches something down. When Jill finishes reading through each piece, she snorts, then hands them to Nyasiah, who looks at them and sighs.

"Guess we're in for a long afternoon then, ladies," is all she says, dropping down onto her bed and reaching for her own magazine.

"Not fair," Esha wails.

"I'm sorry." Nyasiah blinks, innocent. "But I don't think I'm the one who's protecting a thief in this cabin, am I? Maybe after a half hour or so we'll see if you ladies feel like changing your tune a little."

And Esha's right. It's not fair they're doing this. I know they're trying to help, and they have "camp togetherness" to worry about and all that, but sitting there, staring, I start to think about Violet, and what she would do. Violet wouldn't even care if she had to go commando all week. She'd have barely batted an eye or said anything in the first place. She doesn't care what anybody thinks about her, "especially not bitches." And Calla's too friendly to have anything like this happen to her, either. If she even gets a tiny hint that someone's halfway thinking about maybe being a little bit mad at her, she'll bake them cookies or take them out and win them over as friends. Neither of them would understand or sympathize with me right now, and actually, they'd probably laugh. Sure, they'd say, "Oh Daisy, that's terrible—those girls are awful," to my face, and then as soon as they were alone together, they'd roll their eyes over how immature I am.

But they don't have any idea of how hard things are sometimes, even though they think they do. I feel like a fool for going to Calla yesterday, even. I know probably first thing she can, she'll be talking to Vivi about how I can't handle things on my own.

But the truth is, I can't handle it right now. I do really need them both. I can't handle it enough to make it fixed. I can't charm or scare Montgomery into telling what she did with my underpants, or Olivia and the others into betraying their leader. Instead I'm left here on my own, trying not to feel the edges of my skin, not to mention the hateful eyes of everyone else roaming over it.

VIOLET

It's not until camp charades tonight that I really get a chance to talk with Brynn, can thank her for pushing me and James together this weekend. Yesterday she'd come over to hang around our volleyball game during free time, but for some reason she wouldn't play. I could tell she wanted to talk to me, but I had too much "dear god all I want is to kiss him again" energy I needed to burn off, and plus I wanted us to be private when I told her. I thought I might be able to at the campfire sing-along, but Daisy was being all weird and clingy, and Calla showed up, and James would not stop looking over at me, and even though part of me wanted to yell it from the rooftops, I didn't really want him knowing I was telling anyone about us yet. Brynn probably would've given it away, anyhow. It was hard enough not saying anything to my sisters. Now, after sneaking out last night again with him, and all day of barely suppressed smiles at each other during meals, seeing Brynn it's like I want to burst, in the way you feel when you just have to tell somebody something, and you see your friend—any friend—and you think, *Oh, thank god.* Even if I don't tell her all the way, I still owe her the most gigantic thanks.

She sees me too across the room and winks, pats an empty spot beside her. I split from the rest of my cabin and put myself down cross-legged next to her, my knee touching her bony knee in a nice way, in a way that feels like camp.

"Fire pit was kind of lame last night," she says.

All I can do is shrug, trying not to blush, thinking about last night and what I did instead. When she'd asked me about sneaking out at the campfire, I'd lied and said I felt like the other girls in my cabin were catching on, that I thought it was better to lie low. Which was true. But it didn't mean I hadn't snuck out anyway. Just not with her.

"So what'd you write about today, Write-y?" she wants to know, while the head counselors work on sorting out the teams. James gets up to say something to a couple of his rowdy campers, and I can see him smirking, not looking over at me. A million swirls go over my skin.

I wrote about everything except what I really wanted to write about, I want to tell Brynn. I wrote about being at our grandparents' house in Asheville, about an afternoon at the Biltmore, and then going up to some beautiful cabin on a hill surrounded by all this grass and amazing wildflowers, feeling like I was in *Little House on the Prairie*, when what I really wanted to write about was the way he emerges from the dark—this slow-motion comet across the blank of a summer evening—the way he looks me in the eyes before he kisses me, the way he moved against me again last night, when everyone was safe asleep in bed, late, when I felt like I didn't care anymore if I got in trouble or I got caught, I just wanted this and this. I wanted to write about that.

"Ah—just a picnic near my grandparents' once." I shrug. "Not even Calla remembers where we were, only that it was this magical field full of all these flowers."

"Ah, nostalgic childhood youth." Her voice is bored. I usually like how cool she is, but this is a little annoying. I want her to be excited. I want her to ask me what's up.

A counselor, meanwhile, is pointing in our general direction, looking for people for Team Four. We raise our hands, both get chosen, high-five each other.

"You and your sisters are like some kind of coven, aren't

you?" she says out of nowhere. "I saw you last night," she goes on. "Tight."

It's a little odd she's still not asking me about James, and a little like she's making fun of me and my sisters by saying that, but honestly, it was tight. At the fire pit, doing sing-along, it was really, really good. Daisy came straight up to me as soon as she got there, sat next to me on a log and took my hand like when she was little, like when she was afraid she'd get lost from us. A minute later Calla came up behind us, and it was this incredible surprise. We made room for her on our log, and when the guitars and singing started, Calla took my other hand and the three of us joined in.

Even though everything was so crazy charged with me and James at that point, singing with my sisters is so soothing, it's almost hypnotic. Calla's the high part most of the time, with me and Daisy going back and forth between the lower harmonies or joining with Calla. We love it so much that sometimes, especially if one of us has had a bad day, Cow will drive us around town after school, going nowhere, driving and singing, song after song. When we sing together, everything else just falls away. Good and bad.

And it was like that last night, around the fire. As soon as we started singing, it was just this incredible *yes*. Everything else faded into the background, and it was all yes. The same yes I felt on the floating dock with Brynn last week. The kind I have with James's mouth on mine, or when I'm so into the writing that the rest of the room disappears. The interior yes that transcends the rest of everybody's no's and maybe's and I-don't-know's and do-I-have-to's. It was just yes and singing and us and yes.

But I guess, to people outside of us, to people like Brynn who have no sisters or even siblings who they can (or have to) share everything with, maybe it's kind of strange. Too intimate and close. Or something. Maybe it makes them feel weird. Outside.

Not for James, though. He'd been perfect the whole night. We didn't even really have to say, "Let's meet again tonight," after everything was over—the singing and all that. I was just happy and holding hands with my sisters, and then I looked over and he was looking at me and our eyes knew exactly what the other was trying to say, and then it was bedtime with our cabins, and faking sleep for this forever amount of time, and then sliding out of bed into the dark and meeting by the boathouse and then—ah. Just like that. Not hardly a word. Just—that. Yes.

So it's irritating that Brynn's still not feeling the yes of camp too. That she always has to have that wry smile, has to hold herself at arm's length from everyone, even me. And I want her to get it. I want her to understand. I want her to feel as good about everyone here as I do. I want her to know—really know—that

the connections you make here are just somehow more significant than those you make anywhere else. That this place, being
here, is wonderful. That being here will change our lives. If we
let it.

"We are tight, but isn't it tight with everyone here?"

She looks at me like I just suggested she swap cabins and
become a Whitman girl.

I try again. "You don't feel sometimes like—I don't
know." I shake my head. "Like this time here is something—
monumental?"

Okay, maybe "monumental" is a little hyperbolic. She
knows what I mean though, even if she won't admit she does.

She squints at me. The counselors leading the game erupt
into America's Next Top Charades Player introductions on the
stage. Brynn doesn't say anything, just nods her head in the
slightest way.

I feel a little bit goofy, a little bit overwhelmed by everything
that's happened in the last couple of days. I also feel a little self-
conscious, and like I definitely can't tell Brynn about James right
now. And it makes me miss Calla horribly. Because all I'd have to
say to her would be pretty much one word—"monumental"—
and she'd remember the talk we had out on the floating dock
my first year, would remember how weird it was coming back
to our regular friends at home after three weeks of camp. She'd

know everything I was meaning in just the right way, and she'd say something back that was perfect. Perfect because she knows me. Because she gets it.

I almost want to get up then, go find her, tell her everything about me and James. Because no matter what she thinks about counselors and campers, I know ultimately she would understand, like nobody else.

But then there's Daisy up onstage, weirdly in the one pair of jeans she brought. She's in a team of about six hyper underclassmen, but also this tall, hulking guy I think she knows from running. They're glommed together, watching their teammates uncertainly. I break into this big grin, seeing her. Brynn can get it or not, I guess. I'm still glad she's here, is a part of it. I'm glad ZeeZee is up there too, having her own monumental moments.

I put my fingers between my teeth, whistling. This is my last summer as a camper, and I don't care if it's hokey. I want to have as much of this experience as I can possibly have. I want to grab it all, even sour, sarcastic Brynn, and get the most out of it I can get.

CALLA

This morning there isn't time for a real breakfast. I run in, grab a banana, and don't even look around, because I'm still behind from yesterday. Being sent in the Jeep to Walmart to fetch some stuff on Deena's list (including a pack of underwear for some poor camper who lost hers) hadn't helped, but the whole day was chaotic anyway, and this morning I have to finish a bunch of things before I even start on my regular work. When our official lunchtime comes, Sally heads down to the dining hall because her husband has a dentist appointment and can't meet her for their regular lunch date. I go down with her but only to get a big sweet tea to take back to my desk. Over her paisleyed shoulder Sally says, "Honey, you ain't stayin'?"

"I want to go over those new entries again, make sure there are really no mistakes this time," I explain. *Because I thought Deena was going to tear me a hot fresh new one yesterday when I printed those labels and she saw I hadn't put periods after all the "Dr's" and "Ave's."*

"Lunch at your desk—honey, that's for later in life," Sally tsks.

I shrug and thank her, promise her I'll grab some scraps before Binky shuts the kitchen down. She shakes her head but smiles, heading off.

Equipped with enough caffeine, halfway back up the stairs to the main floor I hear two staffers talking together, their voices quiet and serious. I don't want to interrupt them, barging up the stairs, so I duck my head down, prepare to cross over to the upper staircase in a few quick steps, let them know I'm neither listening nor intruding. But then I hear one of them—the girl— say "Daisy," and my body just totally locks up. I freeze, halfway up the stairs. From where they're standing and where I am on the staircase right now, they can't see me. With the getting-lunches noise coming up from the dining hall, I hope they haven't heard me either. I crouch myself down a little so I can sneak up a couple more stairs, get closer.

"—not saying anything to me even, but that's part of why I'm concerned."

"Like I said, she mostly seems okay in concentration," the guy—must be Coach McKensie—says. "Good runner. Very serious. Keeps to herself, yeah, but—"

The girl says something back. Words I don't catch.

"Mmm," is all Coach McKensie responds. I can picture him rubbing that handsome beard stubble of his, thinking.

"Well, I'm going back up to the office, see if they have more ideas to help me and Jill defuse things a little better. Letting girls be girls doesn't seem to be working much in Daisy's favor. And since she, like you said, keeps to herself mostly—"

"Sure, yeah," Coach says. "And I'll keep a closer eye in running."

"Thanks." I think now it must be Nyasiah who's talking. There's something else I don't hear. Then, "For another whole week, you know?"

"Well, sure, and you're right—singling her out can just, uh, make it worse, I guess."

"I'll keep you posted, anyway. You going down?"

I freeze to a whole different degree, not sure if I should bolt up, or maybe trot down a few steps and make it look like I was just now coming up. Turns out I don't have time to do either, because suddenly they're at the top of the stairs. I do that thing where I pretend I'm tucking my hair behind my ears, keeping my chin low, not making eye contact, hoping they don't notice who I am before I get past them. Fortunately, they don't pay me any attention and I slip by, head up to the office, and let myself in. I sink down into my chair and stare at the spinning screen saver a full minute, just staring and thinking, trying to imagine what's going on with Daisy, trying to think what it is I can do, trying to remember Sunday, the things she said—what it might've been that she needed, and me there, not knowing. Not knowing the whole of it.

When Nyasiah comes up later, I'm deep in what I'm supposed to be doing, and Sally's back from lunch, so she's the one who sits there and tsks and clucks, listening to Nyasiah asking about defusing bullying. I don't know if Daisy's counselor doesn't realize I'm sitting right there and can hear every word, if she doesn't remember that I'm Daisy's sister, or what, but as she's heading back out of the office with a book and some printouts in her hand, I can't help saying to her, "Excuse me," before she acknowledges my presence. At first she looks down at me, not knowing what I'm about to ask, like I just don't compute in her brain.

"My sister Daisy's in your cabin," I explain.

That's when her face shifts, recognizing me.

"I know Daze can be really quiet and stuff sometimes, and I

just wanted to make sure she's getting along with the girls okay? I mean, if they're having some difficulty I just wanted to make sure . . ."

I see her wondering how I know that Daisy is the reason she's here.

"Do you and Daisy talk a lot?" she asks, squatting down so we're more at eye level. "Are you pretty close?"

"Of course." Randomly I remember this rainy weekday last summer when Vivi was gone somewhere with a friend or whatever, and I just scooped Daze up in the car and took her to the movies. There was no one else in the theater but us, and so every few minutes we'd scream out "Change seats!" and jump up and run over to another aisle. I can't remember what the movie was, but I remember that it was sad at the end. We held hands, crying, and when it was over we looked at each other and smiled.

"Have you talked to her recently?" Her eyes are hoping I'll tell her something that will help.

"Well, I really only get to see her at, like, meals and stuff, when everyone's around. . . . " Her asking has made me wonder, for just a second, if Daisy is the one picking on someone else. But then I see that she's being concerned, not critical.

"Is she okay? Can I—?"

She waves me off, though nicely. "We've got some things to resolve, I think, but now that I remember you're up here, I'll let you know if there's anything you can help with." She stands back up, cracks her knees. "Don't worry," she tells me, seeing my face. "Daisy's a great kid."

"Oh, no—she's the best one." I try to smile at her, try not to ask more questions.

But an hour later I just keep thinking about Daisy, thinking about her being all withdrawn and tense, not saying anything, not tattling or complaining. It makes a big lump go in my throat that I can't get rid of, remembering the times, back before we renovated the upstairs and we all got our own rooms, when Vivi and I would stay awake whispering and laughing with each other long after lights-out, and how Dizzy's tiny figure would appear there in the doorway, her thin body outlined under her night-gown from where the bathroom light we always had to keep on for her shone through it. I remember her hands clutching that smashed-flat bear of hers, knowing how scared she was of get-ting out of bed, how she hated having any part of her body not under the covers once Mom and Dad left the room, how scary that must've been for her, getting down out of bed, crossing her dark room, coming into the hallway and standing there to hiss at us in her baby whisper, "You *guys*. I need you to be quiet. I can't get to sleep." How Vivi and I would lie there a second, staring at her and saying, "Okay," barely waiting for her to disappear from our door before we erupted into mean-sounding cackles. How we still make fun of her for that, how she will just sit there and take it, at the dinner table, as Bot and I crack each other up to the point where we can't speak, relating that story to any visitor at dinner with us.

I can't stand it. Me and Vivi laughing at her is one thing. Anybody else should have to answer to both of us.

"Sally, my eyes are totally crossing over here," I finally say. "I think I'm going to go take that stuff into town to storage and maybe pick up a sandwich. You want anything?"

"No, hon, I'm fine." She smiles up at me. "Good for you, getting some fresh air. You need help carrying those boxes?"

"No, I got it, but thanks."

I tap lightly on Deena's office door. She's on the phone, but she looks up and waves me in. She's clearing things out of the office—old files Bob and Tina kept for years and years, their notes on different programs and the renovations. The file boxes are lined up by the low bookcase. It takes me five trips to get everything down the stairs and into the Jeep, since I can't carry more than one box at a time. Once they're packed, I know I should get going in order to make it back before four thirty, which will basically be the end of the day.

But I have something else to do first. When I get down to the lake, there Vivi is on her big ugly Elvis towel, legs splayed out in front of her and leaning back on her hands. She's talking to two other girls but stops and squints at me when I get over to her.

"Can I talk to you for a minute?" is all I say.

She glances over to her counselors for approval, but when Natalie looks my way, she just gives me a wave. Nobody really cares what you do during free swim, so long as you don't drown yourself or someone else. Violet shrugs. "Have a seat."

"I mean, can I *talk* to you," I say, looking pointedly at the other two girls, who are trying to pretend I'm not totally standing over them.

"Sure, I guess." She stands up, pulls her shorts on over her swimsuit, follows me along the edge of the lake, moving away from the screaming and splashing.

"Have you talked to Sissie?" I ask her.

"I saw her at breakfast this morning. Why?"

With her sunglasses on I can't see her eyes. Can't tell if she's annoyed or maybe a little concerned.

"Did you know the girls in her cabin were picking on her?"

She snorts. "They are not."

"Yes, they are. Her counselor was in the office after lunch."

"What did she say?"

"Well, she didn't really tell me anything, just that they had some issues."

Violet snorts again.

"I wish you would stop doing that."

"Stop doing what, Cow? Daisy's fine. She's just sulking."

"Sulking about what, exactly?"

I catch myself staring dumbly at kids jumping around in the water. When I look back at Shaz, she's pursing her lips the way she does when Dad's being unreasonable about something she wants.

"I don't know. . . . What isn't she ever sulking about? You know how she is. She always has to be unhappy about something."

"Why does her counselor think something's really wrong then, smarty?"

"Because she's never seen such a colossal *pouter* before, maybe? God, Calla. You're always wanting to do this—always trying to run in and protect her from any bad feeling, from any kind of disappointment. No wonder she doesn't know how to handle it if she's not Queen of Popularity in her cabin. It's not enough, I'm sure, for you to come marching down here about."

"You're not being fair to her."

"*I'm* not being fair to her?" Her arms swing out from her sides, cutting through the air between us. I realize I've just said the thing that's going to make the volcano boil over. Part of me is a little afraid, and part of me is sorry, but another part of me is just over it with Violet and her freakish football-player temper. I barely said three words about Daisy and she was already het up, already irritated with me. So before she can launch into how unfair it is, how she's had to put up with Zee so much more than me in the last year since I had the car and had to stay after school for chorus so much, how unfair it's been to her that I've been here all summer and I don't know what it's like with them cooped up at home together all the time, I know I need to cut her off.

"Just be quiet for a second, okay?" I drop my voice, say it nicely, try to make her hear me out. "Can you just listen to me for one minute?"

She starts to say something, but I don't let her.

"Do you think you could hang out with her a little more?"

She snorts again, and I want to shake her.

"Just sit with her at the bonfire more or something. Get her on your team at games. Like I did for you at first? Just make her feel, I don't know, like you're happy to be here with her and stuff."

"First of all, how would you know I'm not doing that already, and secondly, are you really saying you want me to baby her again? Even though she told us both that she wants to try things on her own? You want me to baby her like you had to baby *me*?"

I have no idea why she's lashing out at me.

"I didn't baby you. I was totally thrilled, ecstatic, to have you here with me, and everybody in both our cabins knew it. You knew it. I made sure you knew it. Even Binky knew it. Don't turn that into babying you, just because you're too cool now to hang with our sister."

"You didn't want to hang with me if you could hang with Duncan," she says, low.

My face is suddenly hot. "That was your second summer. Your first summer, I—"

"So what if I have someone I want to hang out with now, huh?"

"Who? Brynn?" I don't mean to say it in such a snotty way.

"Yeah," Violet says, looking away from me. "Well, Daisy doesn't like her either, so." She scrapes her top and bottom teeth back and forth against each other, biting back other stuff I can see she wants to say.

"You don't have to hang out with her every night, I mean—"

"It's not just Brynn, Cow," she says, her voice really quiet now, her face placid and, I realize, sad.

And it hits me that she's talking about James. That she's been lying about what's up with them and that something is, totally, up. I can't help it; it's the first thing that comes into my head and it's all I can say: "Have you—you know? With him?"

She doesn't answer me, even though that's a pretty ridiculous leap for me to even make, so then I know that means she did. For a second I'm furious at her for pretending there was nothing going on, and then I'm wickedly jealous that it happened to her before me, but then everything switches these crazy gears inside me and I just want to say something great to her. I want to ask her how she is and did she use protection and is she happy and did he treat her okay and was it weird or scary and is she going to tell Mom, and I see the small breeze moving her wild curls around just slightly, just at the edges, and I wonder does he like it when she's all a-tumble like this, when she has her guard down and is calm and quiet, does he understand how easily her feelings get hurt, without you even thinking you're doing the smallest thing to her, does he know how ticklish she is, how she hates her feet? And wondering that, looking at her, I'm filled with this crazy-sad feeling, knowing that I understand all these things about her and she understands all the same kinds of things about me, but I didn't know she'd had sex for the first time. I didn't even know that.

"I know what you're going to say," she says, not even giving me a chance.

"No, you don't. Shaz, I—"

"You're going to say that's a long way to go with a summer boy."

"Well, I mean, you know that's what I think—" I want to punch myself in the face for saying that, even though it's true.

"See?"

"Gah, Sissie. That wasn't what I was thinking. Jesus. You're so smart, but you can be so totally stupid sometimes."

She rolls her eyes and holds up her hand at me, and I can't take it.

"What is wrong with you? I mean, Violet, I am trying to *talk* to you."

"Doesn't feel very good, does it?" she fires back.

"What doesn't feel very good?"

"Doesn't feel good when you're trying to tell someone something, and they aren't really listening to you, does it?"

"What the hell are you talking about?" I'm trying to sound as pissed as she is, am trying to scare her back. But nobody's as scary as Violet when she's mad.

"I'm talking about me trying to tell you I think I'm in love with James and you telling me I can't be because he's a counselor, that's what."

My brain is rewinding as fast as it can, trying to replay all the conversations we've had in the last week. "You haven't tried to tell me that. And I wouldn't—"

"Well, I am now. What do you think about that, huh? Think you're doing a good job of listening, sister dear? Think you can hear me now?"

"You don't understand," I try, which doesn't really have anything to do with anything, but also definitely does.

"*You* don't understand."

"Okay, well, we just don't understand right now, I guess. All I know is I do understand that our little sister is having a rough time, and if you could take ten seconds to stop trying to prove how much *cooler* you are than me all the time, you might understand that, too."

My voice is totally shaking and I feel like my chest is closing up, though I'm not sure why. And even though she just told me this big-deal thing, and though I want to talk to her more about it, with her being so impenetrably pissed at me right now, I can't give her any sympathy.

"I have to go," I tell her.

"Of course you do." That dead, flat voice, soaked and seething with disdain.

"No, I like, *have to* have to. It's, you know, my job. Not everybody can just lie around by the lake and sneak out at night to hook up with counselors or whatever else it is you're doing."

"That was low." She glares at me for what feels like a million seconds before she turns around and starts walking back.

And I know it was, and I already wanted to take it back before I was even saying it. Because I don't want it to be like that, and I don't want to be saying any of this, really. When I've pictured talking about our first times, I wanted it to be great and sisterly and wonderful. I wanted to be the sister who would already know what it was like, and who could then say all kinds of helpful, knowing, funny things about it, could be there and listen to her. I wanted to swap details and giggle and be in awe of each other a little, for doing it. But I also didn't, you know, think it'd be at camp. Not even for me and Duncan, if and when we got to. I mean, first of all, where did they even do it? It's not like you can go back to the cabins. And obviously she had to sneak out, and so how did she manage that? All these things are rushing now into my head, and I'm stomping after her and wanting to ask them, but then I get pissed again because she is the one who derailed this and we were supposed to be talking about Daisy, not this big-deal thing in, like, the five minutes I had before having to hightail it.

She's walking so much faster than me, I have to practically run to get beside her.

"Vivi, I want to talk about this more—"

"No, you don't. You just want me to calm down so we can get back to your agenda. So just—go do whatever it is you have to do, okay? Just go on. The rest of us will be just fine without you. We already are."

Which shocks me so much I just stop. Somewhere deep, deep, deep, I know that she doesn't mean it; I can hear my heart telling my brain that she doesn't really mean that and she's just talking out of anger, that, like Mom says, Bot needs me so bad

she has to say stuff like that sometimes. But most of me is ringing like she slapped me across the face. I watch her striding off,
back to her friends. I can see her drop down onto that hideous
towel, and I wonder what she's going to say to the rest of them
about me, wonder if she's already told them all about James.
Them instead of me.

VIOLET

As soon as Calla disappears, marching off to wherever it is she "has" to go, all I want to do is go find James, sink my face in his chest, smell his clean-laundry, boy-cabin smell, and make myself forget anything else. Of course I'm worried about Daisy; of course I don't want her to be having a bad time, but Calla's been so caught up in her own stuff this summer, and all I've been wanting to do really is sit down and talk to her about what happened with James, even if she got weird about it at first. Because there's nobody else, really, I want to tell—not even Brynn—which is how I felt all day, honestly, so it was kind of like a magical mirage, seeing Calla come down by the lake just now.

But then she focused so hard on Daisy, and after that thing she said about going too far . . . Couldn't she, for once this session, have just been *there* for me?

"What was all that?" Trinity wants to know when I get back to my towel. I don't want to be sitting here. I don't want to be surrounded by curious girls. I want to be alone. I want to be with James. I want to be able to go after Calla.

"Family stuff." I shrug, lying on my stomach and resting my head on my arms so she won't ask me more about it.

After dinner, though, when we're all milling around in front of the main lodge, waiting for the counselors to get the vans pulled around so we can all go farther up the mountain to tell ghost stories at this old abandoned church that has this creepy, ancient cemetery with graves you can barely see anymore, I spot Daisy standing off near the edge with Flannery, and I decide I need to talk to her.

When she sees me coming, though, she has this weird look on her face. It's almost like she takes a step back, away from me.

"You creeped out?" I ask. Cemetery ghost stories is actually really fun, but part of the reason it's fun is that it is so spooky. Even the guys get freaked out after long enough up there, and if there's an owl or something? Oh my god.

Daisy and the dark don't get along very well to begin with. And while I was looking forward to sitting with Brynn tonight, now I realize that Calla, much as I hate to admit it, might've been right. Daisy might need me with her instead.

"What's up?" ZeeZee says, crossing her arm over her stomach to grab her other elbow, scrunching her face at me like she doesn't know why I'm here.

"I just thought—," I start. Flannery isn't looking at me either, but instead down at her shoes.

"Are you—okay?"

"Why wouldn't I be okay?" Her face is almost mad.

"Well, because . . ." I glance at her friend, not wanting to embarrass my sister.

Last year me, Daisy, and Calla sat clutched together in the cemetery with Duncan, all three of us grabbing on his arm, squeezing our eyes shut, laughing out of fear and almost wetting our pants.

Now all she does is shrug.

"You want me to—"

She starts shaking her head before I even finish. "You can be with your friends. It's really okay."

She's so weird and stiff and obviously annoyed that I even came over to her, so I just reach for her hand to squeeze it and then step away. "Well, if you need me, I'll be—" I twirl my finger up and over in the general direction of Brynn, who's waiting for me by the last van.

Daisy nods, her lips in a line. She drops her head and follows Flannery into the van—one behind the one the rest of their cabin is getting in.

"More secret sister code talk?" Brynn wants to know when I get to her. We push our way to the very back, where three freshman guys are already sitting. Brynn just looks at them, points to the seat in front of it, and they're up, unbuckled, getting out of our way.

"I don't know what's wrong with either of them." I sigh, feeling a weird combination of mad and sad and frustrated and lonely all at the same time. "Calla comes to me today and she's all like, 'Something's wrong with Daisy. You have to hang out with her more.' And we get in this fight about it, but then I see Daze and she does look weird, but when I go up to her she treats me like I'm a leper."

"You and Calla are fighting?" Brynn says it like she's concerned, but when I glance at her she looks more . . . thrilled.

"She's so caught up in her own crap," I mutter. "She's totally in love with this boy here, and since it's their last summer before college, she's extra obsessed with him. Although she's always obsessed with him. It's gross."

"Who?" she wants to know. And I know I shouldn't tell her, but whatever, it's not like she even knows him really, and besides, I'm still mad about this afternoon and the way everything went.

I meant to be telling Brynn about James now, but with the loud, wiggling boys in the seats in front of us, that doesn't seem like a good idea either. So on the rest of the ride we hunch way down in the seat, and I whisper to her about Calla's thing with Duncan, how she always gets so into him every summer and how he always breaks her heart.

"It's sad, sort of, I guess," I finish.

"It's pathetic," Brynn says, looking at me. She's shaking her head a little, her face a combination of perplexed and disgusted.

"What?"

"You Winthrop girls just don't know how to make anything happen, do you?" she says under her breath, as the vans park in the clearing in front of the church. Everyone starts making ghoul noises around us, the volume rising so much Brynn wouldn't hear anything I had to say, even if I could think of what.

DAISY

First thing in the morning, after washing up, my underwear is on my bed. It's in a muddy plastic grocery bag, and on top of it is a damp note that says: *Thanks for the snack! Your lover, Brynn.* The letters are in this exaggerated scrawl—like someone was trying to make it look like a serial killer wrote it. Nobody says anything, so it's even easier to hear the silence of suppressed giggles throughout the cabin.

I don't even look at Jill or Nyasiah—I just snatch the bag, grab it to my chest, and head back up to the showers so I can check everything in private. I have some new ones now, sure, but I'd like to not have all the crotches ripped out of my old favorite pairs either. After yesterday, after the horribleness of sitting there in the cabin, doing nothing, everyone hating me more and more as the minutes went by, I just—turned off. More than in a fight with my sisters, more than being embarrassed in class. I have to be here for another week and a half, and the only way I can pull through it is if I totally shut myself off. I'll still be doing whatever it is we have to do, but I'll stay out of everyone else's way. I'll go through the motions, but I'm not going to be here anymore. I'm gone.

So it's not even relief I feel, seeing my panties there, all still clean, stuffed into the bag. I don't wonder where they hid them. I don't wonder who put them back. I just take the bag back to Emerson, put my underwear away, go back to the dining hall and sit at the end of the bench, eat my breakfast. Go to keynote. Do yoga. Run. Blindfold hike in the afternoon with I don't even know who.

After dinner though, when Flannery and I are just standing there together, waiting for the vans to take us up to the cemetery, I see Vivi see me, and I feel something under all that numbness shift. Violet's walking over, so coolly unkempt in her cutoffs and her plaid boy's shirt, that concern on her face. And I want to just fall into her, but then the iceberg in me freezes again. Because if I show Violet I'm feeling anything, she'll put her arms around me and ask if I'm okay, and I will not be able to keep from crying.

Flannery might lean in, maybe Manon would come over. Montgomery would finally see me crying, and after that, I wouldn't be able to stay here. Absolutely not.

I hear—from what feels like underwater—Violet ask if I'm okay. She's only checking on me because she thinks I can't hack it at graveyard storytelling. And I *was* scared last year. But now I feel nothing. And she doesn't really want to sit with me. She's just doing her sisterly duty. She doesn't need to worry about me, though. She needs to just go away. Because now I'm not here and so I know nothing can freak me out. Not a bunch of stupid high school boys and their stories they stole from a bunch of horror movies. Not anything.

And they don't. The stories. Freak me out. Surrounded by woods, it's pitch-black except for the flashlights a few counselors are holding, and there are skittery noises in the brush, and everyone's squealing and yelping and going "Bwooooohhahahaa," but whatever. It's stupid. It doesn't faze me at all.

Doesn't, I guess, until this one guy tells a story about a strange light in the woods that lures people deeper and deeper. Really the light is the lantern of this old, psychotic railroad worker who coaxes people into the woods and then cuts off their heads to use as shooting-practice targets. The guy telling the story uses his flashlight as an extra prop, turning it on at different points and shining it on unexpected people. They scream when he does it, of course, but that's not what makes my hair stand on end. It's when his beam falls right on Montgomery. And Montgomery is sitting next to Esha. Who has her hand entwined with the boy's next to her. Who happens to be Joel.

A bunch of stuff happens then, all at once. Montgomery shrieks stupidly with the light shining on her lap, and everyone around her giggles. The guy telling the story talks louder, getting to the part where the girl who knew enough not to follow the light is now bringing the posse of her boyfriend's entire football team up into the woods to investigate. The flashlight beam falls on someone else right as the psycho attacks with the rest of his psycho union who hide out with him in the woods too, and then there is this loud, crazy pop. And another. And another. Not really gunshots, but firecrackers maybe—enough to scare everyone to death. The storytelling guy drops his flashlight, and the kids around me have their hands up around their ears, crouching down. Or jumping up. In the screaming and the chaos and people going, "What the hell was that?" I can hear Brynn's hysterical laughing. In all this I see the white flash of Joel's hair and I just do it—I open my mouth like everyone else and scream and scream and scream.

CALLA

In the morning there's a note from Deena asking me to help Alexander wash the vans again, because they're totally dirty. And really? It's fine with me. Yesterday afternoon was just a mountain of horrible—not only fighting with Violet, but also there was some kind of roadwork going on in town, so it took me forever to get back from the storage place. By the time I parked the Jeep, everyone was already heading into dinner, and I just didn't feel like trying to insert myself into a conversation with instructors that'd been going on for fifteen minutes. What I really wanted to do was tell Duncan everything that had happened with Violet, and my worry about Daisy, but I knew he'd be occupied with dinner and ghost stories. I ended up just reading in my room, eating the few Wheat Thins I had left.

Doing something active—and getting to do it with Alexander, who is always talking, even if it isn't about anything—seems like a good thing for me this morning. Maybe it will take my mind off the situation with Daisy and Violet and everything else. Maybe I can purely zone out, listening to Alexander and his monologues about the weather and fishing.

"Morning, morning, morning," he says to me when I get over to the mini-lot where we keep the vans. "Good morning out, don't you think? Not like last session with that rain! Whooee. Clear as a bell now, though; stay that way through the weekend, I believe. Good for the kids then, their games. Swimming. The farm, though, I don't know if those rain barrels have got enough in them, you hear what I'm saying? Collected plenty last session, but they must be down near to empty now. Tomatoes need a lot of water. A *lot* of water . . . "

In all this I see he's already washed the first van and is on to the second. We have four of them that hold fifteen people—which is why they have to go in shifts for the ghost telling and big trips like that, why off-sites have to rotate between cabins. I grab a sponge from one of Alexander's big white buckets, enjoy squeezing out a squishy handful of sloppy wet suds before I lean into the opposite side of the van from Alexander, start sloshing the door and windows.

"Whoo-ee! Somebody filming this?" Duncan's voice surprises me. He comes trotting up behind me from the right.

"What are you doing?" I try to sound carefree, though I'm so relieved to see him. He is wearing loose shorts and one of those tight ribbed tank tops, making his legs look even trimmer, and his chest and arms even more cut. He is tan and smiling. He is totally beautiful, and he is so, so obviously happy to see me.

"Getting things together for this afternoon while the monsters are in concentration," he says. "But more importantly, what are you doing?"

He eyes my dripping hand and wrist, my already soap-splashed shorts.

"What does it look like I'm doing? I'm filing all the camp's tax documents for the last five years."

"In alphabetical order, I hope."

"Well, alphabetical by the first letter of the date filed, yes."

"Excellent work then, Winthrop. I'm sure that everyone's impressed."

We smile at each other. The way I feel, standing there with him—that grin on his face—everything with my sisters flies from my mind. It would be so easy right now to just say, *Guess what, I'm in love with you,* to throw my wet arms around him and kiss him. I need to be really sure before I take the plunge, but maybe that would make things better with Violet, too.

"So . . . now that we're into the second week of second session, are you—" I fumble a minute, not sure how to find out what I want to know. He still hasn't mentioned another girl, but that doesn't mean he isn't working on one now. "I mean, are you still having a good time?"

"Yeah, yeah," he says, nodding hello to Alexander, who grabs the hose and blasts the van with a violent spray. Even from the other side, Duncan and I get hit with the cascade from over the top of the van. Duncan reaches out and guides me a few feet away, his fingers light but warm on my forearm, pulling me out of reach.

"It's definitely different," he goes on, keeping one eye on Alexander and his enthusiastic hosing. "I didn't realize how immature we were back then, to be honest. Seeing these kids, it's like, whoa—really? Is that *really* what you want to do, dude? But, you know. It's cool, too."

"You're still getting time on your own though, right? Or with everyone else?" I can't make eye contact with him, asking that. "I mean, you know. It seems like you are. Enjoying yourself. When you aren't, like, babysitting drunk staffers."

I don't want to make him picture that awful night again, but I also figure it's in my interest to act like it was no big deal.

I don't want him to picture having fun with too many other girl counselors, for that matter. But I also don't want to make the move Violet and Daisy think I should make, if I'm going to end up looking like an idiot because he's entrenched in somebody else. I want to know if he's crushing—I need to know—and at the same time I totally don't want to know. And I don't want to look like I'm trying to know. But he's never kept me from knowing before either.

"I mean—" I'm rushing. I'm trying to cover my own stupid, obvious tracks. "I guess, it seems like the other girls—and guys—are cool. But it doesn't seem like there's anybody . . . special?"

When I bring myself to look at him again, he's still got that bemused little grin in his eyes and across his lips.

"Nobody more special than you, Cal," he says in this annoyingly friendly way. But then he keeps going, not taking his eyes off mine: "I'm hanging out with people I want to be hanging out with, don't worry. You know. It's different this summer. I mean, it's different and it's not. You feel a lot more responsibility. So you want to . . . I don't know." He looks away then, pushes his curls back with one hand. "You want to be with people who get that. Not just anyone. But people who get you. Who you can trust."

When he turns back, our eyes lock and there's this conversation between us, without either one of us saying anything: this gaze that extends between us that means, *Yes, I get you in all these ways I'm not sure I even want to be seen, but also in all these ways I am dying to expose.*

"Duncan—," I start, when at the same time he goes, "Which makes it cool, you know, the guys and everything." He is clearing his throat, shrugging. He is looking away. Standing there with Alexander able to hear every word we say probably isn't the best time for us to declare our undying love, anyway. But the next time we are alone—

"I should let you get back to it," he says.

"Yeah."

"I'll see you, though." He reaches to brush my forearm again before he heads off.

And the rest of the morning I can't wait—I cannot wait—until I get to see him alone again, because this time, I know I'm going to be able to show him everything I really feel.

DAISY

After last night, after Brynn and those stupid pop caps she had at the cemetery, scaring everybody to death, I feel like something else has to happen this morning. I was waking up maybe every hour or so, thinking I'd heard someone sneaking around to sabotage me again. But showering, getting dressed, going to breakfast—nothing remarkable happens. Montgomery doesn't sneer at me, and Olivia keeps her eyes to herself, which is abnormal but at least not wholly sinister. Everyone's acting so blasé, it's almost strange. It keeps my shoulders and neck tense all through keynote.

At concentration I align myself with Lena and April—putting

some space between me and Rutger, in case Montgomery and Olivia have more snarkiness up their sleeves. But they don't even look at me. They just get their mats and go up to the front, start doing some preliminary stretches as though they actually care. Lena and April are talking about last night. Lena explains to April that no, it wasn't anything dangerous, just those stupid things kids throw against the sidewalk to make noise. They don't even flash or anything. But then that gets her into telling about this guy last summer, Scott, who actually brought real fireworks with him and canoed out to the floating dock on our last night, lit them when we were coming back from the dance. I'd forgotten about it, forgot being at first scared by the sound and then running excitedly down to the lake with Calla and Violet, the three of us holding hands, standing there by the water, watching these colored explosions in the sky. Until his counselors canoed out there, of course, and made him stop. It's funny how different that summer feels now. Far away.

During yoga I'm thinking about what the last day of this year's session might be like. Violet will be wrapped up in James, I'm sure. Hopefully Calla and Duncan will be together. Flannery and I will hang, I suppose. Maybe even end up slow dancing in a funny way, like Violet and Brynn at the swing dance. But then I remember that guy Flan likes, from that night. Probably she will dance with him.

"Well, gang." Coach claps, bringing us out of our yoga

stupor. "We're going to round ourselves up"—*clap*—"head out to the vans, and get ready for another off-site."

"Oh god no," Finch says, collapsing back down on the floor. "No more spin class. I can't take that woman another time." I don't show it, but I can't believe I thought I might be able to like such a whiner.

Coach smiles. "I think with these ladies you'll do just fine. And actually, uh, I forgot. I need you guys to hustle back to your cabins and grab your swimsuits."

We all look at each other. Coach takes out his stopwatch.

"I'm going to give you eight minutes and thirty seconds to hit your cabins, grab your suits and a towel, and meet me back up at the vans. Starting—" He doesn't even pause, doesn't give us a minute to ask questions or put our mats away. "Starting . . . now."

We are immediate action, all of us rolling up our mats as fast as we can and getting them in the closet. I immediately jog off to Emerson, not wanting to be alone in the cabin with Montgomery and Olivia. I make it there before they do and slip inside, get my bathing suit and my swim towel, and trot up the trail to the vans. I pass them, ambling along together, not in any kind of a hurry. I don't look at them, and they don't look at me. My shoulder blades will not, however, unclench themselves. It occurs to me that now they'll be in the cabin without any super- vision. My underwear could disappear again, or worse, though after last night it seems like mostly what they want to do is just ignore me.

I can't worry about it, because I'm certainly not going to go back there with them now. I get up to the vans and am surprised by Calla there, sloshing a big soapy sponge over one of them with Alexander, who is doing the same thing on the other side. She sees me and breaks into that enormous grin of hers—the one that got her voted Best Smile in yearbook superlatives. Falling under that smile feels like a beam of sunshine just radiated all over me, making the numbness crawl away. She drops her sponge into the bucket and wipes her hands on her shorts, comes straight over. I am wrapped up in the biggest, strongest hug. I let myself be enfolded. I feel like I could melt.

"You're better than them, you know that, right?" she says into the top of my hair. It trickles, her voice, down into my whole head. I nod, my face in her shoulder, not sure how she knows and not caring.

"Your real friends know that too. You stick with them. Those other girls are just—"

"Bitches," I say before she does.

Calla pulls back a little, to look me in the face. She's smoothing my ponytail. She can't ever keep her hands off my hair. I shake my head a little to get her to stop. Montgomery and Olivia and Coach will be coming soon, and though it's better here for a minute, with Cow, it's not like she can stay with me the rest of session. I can't thaw out too much. But I try to send her messages out my eyeballs. *I want to go home. With you. And Violet. Right now. Please.* But I'm also nodding, giving a small smile and a shrug. "What doesn't kill us makes us stronger, right?"

"That bad, huh?" But she has a tender smile now. She is relieved. Who could stand it, to disappoint Calla?

She sees Coach coming up, steps back from me a little. We are just talking now. "You want me to come to decaths tonight?"

I shrug. It's not like she could really do anything, besides sit there and cheer. It's not like she can join in, since we have to be on teams with our cabins. But it would be good to have her there, jumping and clapping on the sidelines.

"Only if you want to."

Everyone is here now. Coach is embroiled in a run-on conversation with Alexander, but I have to go soon.

"That them?" Cow says, narrowing her eyes at Olivia and Montgomery, who are standing a little behind us. Calla barely moves her lips. Only I can hear what she's saying.

"Yes." But it's not like she can do anything.

"Got it."

"It's okay. Mostly now they just ignore me."

Coach claps, rounding us up. I have really got to go. I wish I could stay here and wash vans with my sister. I don't want to go back to handling things on my own.

"You are so way prettier than both of them put together. Like, total no contest."

I snort. It doesn't help anything, but it's funny how Calla is.

"I'll see you later," she promises.

I tell her thanks and try to seem reassured, but once I've turned away I don't look back, because if I did I'd have to smile at her, and now I don't think I can move my face.

Coach drives us to the Y after that, where apparently we are taking a morning water aerobics class. We change, put our stuff in some lockers, and head to the pool, the shallow end of which is full of ten or so older ladies. They have flowered one-pieces and flabby arms. They are bouncing and drifting around together, and smile at us when Coach leads the way into the pool, pointing for us to spread out across the back.

And the class ends up being pretty good. Sure, it's funny to watch these ladies bouncing around to techno, but they obviously know all the moves, and before long several of us are struggling to keep up with them. By the end we are all panting and smiling, surprised, at each other. When Coach lets us have a few minutes of free swim before we head back to camp, it's even kind of fun.

At lunch Montgomery and Olivia are still basically pretending

I don't exist, which is fine with me. *Bitches, bitches, bitches*, I let myself chant. I can almost believe that's all they are. I concentrate on getting my food, finding Flannery and Jordan. I'm starting, I think, to feel a little better.

That is, until post-lunch cleanup and downtime are over, and Jill and Nyasiah are telling us what we're doing for our afternoon activity. Half the cabin erupts in cheers.

For me, though, it's like the room suddenly expands and I shrink down small, smaller than before. I absolutely cannot do zip lines. Last year my cabin went on the same day as Violet's by some miracle, and she did this great job of talking circles around the zip line guy and the counselors, faking that I had some medical condition and acting all perplexed that our parents hadn't included that information on my forms. Violet's good like that in a problem. I can count on her to navigate me through anything, even if it's something she's never done before either. We didn't tell Calla about it, because she'd just've been disappointed. But Calla doesn't understand, the way Violet does, that I simply cannot. No way.

I'm in a minority, though, because even Flannery looks excited. I feel like I'm in slow motion, but the rest of the room has speeded up. Everyone's so pumped that Jill makes us scream one of our Spirit Splurges on the way to the vans, to blow off some energy. Meanwhile I'm trying to sidle up next to Nyasiah.

It's too loud for me to ask her privately if there's some way I can sit this one out, though. My mind is swimming with things I could do instead—find Calla and help in the office, maybe. I'd peel potatoes in the kitchen with Binky if she'd let me.

My desperation increases when we get to the vans and Alcott's there, waiting for us. They've heard us coming and are screaming back one of their own chants. I can't separate her voice from everyone else's—not really—but seeing that girl Brynn, her mouth wide and happy and yelling along with everyone else, it's as though I can.

"Oh god," Jordan says behind me to Flan.

"I know, right?"

"Just ignore her," Manon puts in. "That girl just wants attention."

And I do not want to be anywhere near her when she tries to get it. I don't want to be caught even close to her wake.

"Nyasiah."

My counselor finally looks at me.

"I really don't feel great. I wonder if I should head to the clinic and—" I'm making my face as pitiful as I can.

"Oh, come on, blondie." She hooks her arm over my shoulders and gives me a half hug. "We're all scared when we do zips for the first time. But it's just like the high dive. Do it once, and you'll be running back for more. Trust me, it's completely safe. And we'll all be waiting for you down at the bottom."

Which is, of course, part of the problem. I am not excited about facing Montgomery and her friends at the end of the most terrifying experience of my life. I'm not enthusiastic about them being behind me in line, either.

"Hey, you're Violet's sister, aren't you?" A voice comes toward me. I know who it is. I don't want to look. It doesn't matter; she's there next to me before I know it.

"The younger one, yes."

Brynn eyes me like she is a tailor and I have come to her for a suit.

"Sit with me," she finally says, pulling me into the line for the nearest van. I don't have time to pull away or tell her no or look for my friends. Her strong hand just takes mine. And then we are among other girls in front of and around us, and then we're in our seat. Two girls from her cabin squish next to us.

"You guys sing a lot, huh?" Brynn says next to me, after the van gets going and we're down the road from camp.

I don't know what to focus on: her voice and her face right in mine, or Esha and Olivia in front of us, straining to hear every word Brynn says to me so they can report back to Montgomery. Brynn's witchy leg is pressed against mine in the tight seat. And her two cabin friends are there, leaning in and wanting to hear. I try to make myself disappear. But their eyes are on me. Their ears want to know. It is impossible to vanish.

"We sing, yeah. Sometimes."

I'm not looking at her, but I can feel Brynn giving me that appraising look.

"You play guitar, too? Any of you?"

I just shake my head.

"I just wondered if it was Von Trapp family singers or something at your house."

She is not trying to be mean. She is smiling. She wants to be nice.

"No. No yodeling, I'm afraid."

"No yodeling." She laughs. "That's good—yodeling. Funny."

I can see Esha going back to Montgomery, telling her Brynn and I sweet-talked about *The Sound of Music* of all things.

"Your sister's, like, way in love with that guy, isn't she?"

I look at her. She raises her eyebrows a little.

"They're close." It's all I'll give. I don't know, really, what kind of friends she and Violet actually are. I don't know what Violet's told her.

"Yeah, it sounds like it." She nods. "You like him?"

It's weird how she's being. Like, nice and genuine and almost sort of sadly sweet.

"If he's good to my sister, I guess. Otherwise he's not worth much. In my opinion."

By the look on her face, if she'd been chewing gum right

now, I can tell what I just said would have made her stop.

"She'd deserve better, right? Move on to more fish in the sea." She is thinking about something, but I don't know what. "You ever do this before?" She juts her chin toward the window. We're pulling into the park now.

"No," I admit.

"Me neither." She grins. "I absolutely cannot wait."

The weirdness of talking to Brynn—sitting so close to her, being under her gaze, knowing Esha was eating it all up—was enough to almost take my mind off the zips. Now we are here, parking, getting out of the van. The trees and platforms are high above us. There are two guides waiting. This is completely real.

"If we're near the front, they might let us go twice." Brynn's hand is around my wrist again, pulling. I imagine digging in my heels, making myself either limp or stiff. But I'm so numb now I'm apparently just following her. It surprises me to wonder if this is how Violet feels.

We move near the front, and I hardly see anyone around us, barely hear the instructions. *I am not doing this. I am not doing this. I am not doing this.* I can almost hear the words coming out of my mouth, but my lips won't move. Flannery shows up beside me, grinning. All I say is will she go ahead of me, so I can see how it's done. I can't believe I'm even moving, but buffered now in a Brynn and Flannery sandwich, I don't really have much choice.

I watch as the girls ahead of us get strapped into helmets, gloves, harnesses. We go through instructions, checks, rechecks. There's only buzzing in my ears. *I am not doing this. I am not.* They start the climb up the huge tower of stairs—did someone say sixty-five feet? A hundred? Brynn is close behind me. It's like a warmth comes out of her that pushes me ahead. I'm climbing up. I want to shut my eyes. Somewhere behind me Montgomery and Olivia are laughing with Esha. Somewhere back at camp, Joel's wondering what Esha's doing, instead of me.

We climb and climb. Everyone is excited, gasping. I can barely see. And then the guide clips the first girl's rope to the cable and *whoosh*, she is gone, and it's like you can feel the drop of her, leaving.

"I can't do this," I feel myself say. But I'm not loud enough. I crane my neck, look behind me for Nyasiah. I don't care if my parents already paid for this. I don't care how much fun it will be at the end. This is way, way, way too high, and all I can think now is I'm going to fall. I'm going to fall because Brynn will be monkeying around, playing a prank, and I'm going to tumble off the edge before they clip my rope. And everyone will laugh. Or my rope will get clipped, and then somehow it will break. It will break and I'll fall and see only laughing faces, peering over the edge.

Two more girls go. Flannery is next.

"I can't do this," I say again.

"Of course you can." Brynn's face is over my shoulder. "Look at you. You can do anything you want."

"But I'm not doing this."

It's like she sighs. Or grumbles. She inches closer to me on the stair, as though she'll push me with her whole body if she has to.

Flannery's rope is clipped to the cable. She hangs on with her gloves. She looks down past her swinging feet and grins, gives me a thumbs-up. She is gone.

"Okay, you're next," the guide says, waving me up to the platform.

I can't move. I can't move. I can't move and I can't breathe. My hands are on the railing, but they are ice and they are frozen shut. The only thing moving is my rabbit heart, racing.

"You will do this," Brynn says, almost mean. "Because I'm not letting you back down behind me, and they won't let you stay up here." Somehow at the same time she also doesn't sound mean. I remember bouncing up and down with her at the swing dance. "Listen to me. This is perfectly safe. They wouldn't bring us here if it wasn't, dummy. Now get moving, because there's me and fifteen other girls who aren't too pussy to take their turn."

It's the word that does it. That *P* word I hate. Violet called me it once when she first learned it in sixth grade, and I was so mad and surprised I actually hit her. And then we were both so shocked, we just looked at each other for a minute before we started laughing. Hearing it from Brynn, my body does the same thing it did that first time—it just acts without me thinking. I'm up on the step, taking the guide's hand. He's checking my harnesses again, making sure I know what to do. *I am not doing this. I am not doing this.* But then my rope is clipped and the guide's asking am I ready. And I see Brynn behind his shoulder, and she is really smiling. And I am nodding somehow, and then— *whoosh*—I am gone.

VIOLET

I hung out with your sister today," Brynn says when I see her that night at decathlons. At first I think she's talking about Calla, up in Deena's office, where I know she had to go this morning after the whole thing last night at the cemetery.

"You should've seen how scared she was at zips. It was funny. I practically had to push her."

I'm shocked. Daze went down the zip lines this year, after all the machinations we had to do last time?

"Was she—?" I am looking around the field now, past all the different tables set up for our various events. I want to find Daisy, see how she felt about it, tell her I'm amazed and glad. Simultaneously I'm thinking, *See, Calla? Daisy's fine on her own.*

"I wouldn't say she'd sign up to do it again anytime soon, but she did go through with it." Brynn's looking for Daisy now too.

I turn my eyes on her, on her scrawny neck arching, her black-and-turquoise hair pushed back from her face with a plaid headband. She seems so earnest, and kind, even. She seems like she's really being normal.

"Hey, listen, I need to talk to you," I say.

She grins sideways at me. "My dress for the last dance is going to be pink." Her eyelids flutter crazily. "So you can get me either roses or an orchid, I don't care. Just no carnations."

"Damn." I snap my fingers. "You're going to have to go with another girl, then," I kid back. "Seriously, though. I just—just whatever. At ice cream? After this? Come sit with me, okay?"

"Okay," she agrees, though now she's looking at me strange. Our counselors are whistling for us all to form up, so she gives me a high five in departure and trots off to join her cabin.

Decathlons are pretty ridiculous, but since they're on the low field, with lights and everything, it's kind of fun, making it feel like a real football game or something. There are ten events, all manned by different instructors, which means that our counselors actually get to do the competitions with us. Some of the events are all-cabin ones—balloon shaving, for example, and blanket carry—but for others each cabin picks just a couple of competitors, while the rest of us cheer. Besides prizes for the three top-scoring cabins, there's also a prize for most cabin spirit, so yelling is a big part of it.

Tonight, for me, is all about cabin bonding. The relay stations are too spread out to really pay good attention to events besides your own, so it's not like I can be watching out for Daisy, or making eyes at James. I know I'll see him later tonight, anyway, and that knowledge releases me to focus on my friends. While I'm clapping for Trinity and Mysha in the three-legged jump rope, I do scan the crowd, see if Calla's around anywhere. Not because I want to even talk to her, or because I need her cheering for my cabin, but because all the instructors are out here tonight, and I don't like to think about her alone with her book, even if she is a jerk.

If she's here I don't see her, but partly because the water balloon toss gets really intense when we manage to be one of the few cabins to get as far as twelve feet apart. We're all chanting and screaming our heads off, coaxing Bo and Aislin to go even farther. Ava in particular looks like she's about to bust a vein somewhere.

In the end we come in third, which isn't bad, considering that we're the only girls' cabin that places. We're all high-fiving and hugging and bragging how we will stomp everyone during the Olympics next week. We shake hands with the two other winning cabins—Sierra and Muir. When Duncan shakes my hand, he says, "Your sister get to see all that?" And I tell him I don't think she's out here. And then I note that he was asking. With real interest. It's not enough to convince me, but I'd be happy to actually be wrong about him this year.

After the march of winners around the field, when we get our silly ribbons pinned on our T-shirts and head back to the dining hall for the ice cream smorgasbord, I finally see ZeeZee, attached at the hip to Flannery. Most of me wants to rush up and squeeze her and lift her in the air and tell her how happy I am that she conquered the zips today, but I don't. I got enough of the cold shoulder from her the other night, and it's clear if Flannery's around, Daisy doesn't want me to be.

I have to work on keeping my face indifferent while James and I are basically across from each other at the topping station, anyway. When we both reach for the butterscotch ladle at the same time, I swear a spark jumps between our fingers. "Sorry," he says, in this way that makes my belly button hot. I know he knows my cabin won. I know he was watching me as I cavorted around with my cabinmates, acting all crazy and victorious around the field, and knowing that already made me practically incandescent. If my eyes meet his now, I think there'd be some kind of thermonuclear reaction. We decided to take a break from sneaking out the last couple of nights, mostly because we needed some sleep, but tonight we'll meet up again, and all I want is to be alone with him. When we're in situations where we obviously can't, it's almost better for me to pretend he isn't there.

"You got some badasses on your team," Brynn says, appearing next to me with an already melting bowl of what looks like Neapolitan, covered with chocolate syrup and rainbow sprinkles.

"I know, right?" I grin at her.

"Alcott's full of a bunch of babies."

"You seem to have a decent time with them, though. I mean, some of the time."

She shrugs. "More fun than damn kitchen duty this morning, that's for sure."

She leads me over to a corner instead of a table. We sit down together on the floor, away from everyone. I'm aware of people seeing us. Everyone's pretty fed up with her, I think. But whatever, I don't care.

"So what's this big serious talk you want to have?" She licks both sides of her spoon, starts mashing her ice cream into an even more soupy, runny moosh.

I can't help it. Now my eyes go back over to James, sitting three tables down, scooping ice cream into his mouth.

"Oh Jesus, really? That?"

"What do you mean, 'oh Jesus'? I thought you wanted me to get with him."

"Whatever." She hunches into her ice cream, which is a bizarre shade of green-streaked brown.

"Wait. What?" She was the one who pushed us together. And now she's being all weird about it? Before I've even said anything?

Her eyes come up at me. "Are you serious?" She is mad to the core. And I feel shocked and a little freaked, like a wildlife documentarian who realizes he's way too close to the Komodo dragon. Watching her go from sweet to pissed is like—well, like watching myself.

"'Wait. What?'" she mimics in this nasty voice. "Let me spell it out for you, then. Until I worked my campfire magic, you were stuck in retardo do-nothing land. But as thanks for that, you have completely shut me out of everything. Have kept me at arm's length for days, even though you've had plenty of chances. You haven't told me one thing about him since Capture the Flag night, and in camp time that's, like, four months or something. And now you want me to be all excited for you? My excitement wore off forty-eight hours ago, honey." Her eyes never leave mine. They are burning and serious.

"We would've snuck out together if you hadn't gotten in trouble last night," I protest, though it's not wholly true. "And besides, I didn't think you'd noticed, really."

"Okay. Yeah. Right. Because we're not friends or anything."

And that hits me—her calling us friends. She's right. I have been holding things back from her a little. But if I don't treat her like a good friend, she's certainly not going to become one. So I confess about Saturday night. And Sunday, too, which is a little rough since I'd told her I wasn't going to go out at all, but she deserves the truth. I tell her how incredible he is and how huge being with him makes me feel. I tell her things I haven't even told my sisters yet.

When I'm done, she looks away, over her shoulder. Maybe at James. "Well, ain't that peachy," she mutters, raking her spoon over the edges of her scraped-clean bowl.

Which is not exactly what I thought she'd say.

"But—why is James and me suddenly bad?"

She gives her head a terse shake. Scrape. Scrape. Scrape.

"No, really. I thought you'd be—I don't know. Proud or something. I mean, I finally did something."

She snorts. Her eyes come up at me. "Yeah, well, whoop-de-do for you."

I feel stunned and shocked and a little like I can't move, like I've been cornered. And then I start to get mad.

"What the hell?" I can't help slitting my eyes at her. "What is wrong with you? I thought you'd be happy for me. You know, like a friend."

"Oh yeah?" Her spine straightens again. Her face is full of righteous tension. "Well, I don't know exactly what's wrong with *me*," she spits between her teeth, "but I do know that any friend of mine who claims to be having all these 'monumental' feelings, and then, come to find out, is mainly talking about the monumental *deep dicking* she's getting every night at the boathouse instead of doing something 'monumental' with me, isn't really a friend at all."

I'm shocked. And she's glad about it.

"I mean," she goes on, "sure you're a total camp groupie and everything, swooning and swirling around all this togetherness. I know you've got the whole sister bonding and family legacy and sense of entitlement thing, but what I didn't know was that all your babble about significant bonds was really about him. I thought maybe you meant your friends. I thought, for a second, you might mean me."

She stands up, so I do too. I think she's going to keep going, or at least let me say something, but she just turns and storms off before I even get a word in. I'm left there, staring, holding my stupid ice cream bowl, empty. And it's infuriating. Because she's completely wrong, and didn't even give me a chance to explain. But also part of what's infuriating is that she's right. And now here I am, monumentally on my own, having pissed off pretty much everyone, and it monumentally sucks.

Second Thursday

VIOLET

At least as soon as it gets enough past midnight, I can slide out of my bunk and rush to James. At first, when we get out to the field, we're obviously all about the kissing, but I can't stop thinking about Brynn, and Daisy, and Calla, and so when we lie on the grass together and he holds me against his chest, I let myself spill it out. And it's so great, because he holds me and listens, and asks a few questions, and offers up a couple of good points, and in the end I feel so much better. It isn't the big hot night we thought we were going to have, but when he kisses me a last time before we go back to our cabins, in a way I feel like it's even more fantastic between us.

Keynote in the morning is, funnily enough, also all about forgiveness. My writing instructor, Kelly, is up there, talking about finally forgiving a friend who dated the boy who was Kelly's first love. After a few weeks of anger, Kelly realized she'd lost the boy either way, and she'd rather not lose her friend, too. I think of how I felt last night when Brynn walked off, leaving me alone. I think of what James said, about giving people the benefit of the doubt. I think of Brynn standing up in that canoe, and talking to me in the dark on the floating dock. I did mean her when I said that stuff about how amazing camp is. I need to tell her that, at least. I need for her to know.

It's after we finish lunch when I get my chance. Walking back to Berry, I see her ahead of me, chatting happily with some girl from her cabin, and I move to catch up. On the way I pass by Daisy and Flannery, but I don't even wave. I can only deal with one reconciliation at a time.

"Hey," I say at Brynn's elbow, not wanting to look too eager, not wanting to act like yesterday wasn't a big deal, either.

She squints at me, has this sideways grin. "Hey, Write-y."

We walk a little bit. She doesn't introduce me to the girl she's walking with. Everyone else is talking about the talent show. Somebody complains about not having the right costume.

"Catch up with you?" Brynn says to her cabinmate as we're nearing Alcott. She touches the girl on the arm, like they're close. I feel this twist of jealousy that is completely stupid. The girl winks and nods. I wonder if this is going to be Brynn's new sneak-out partner.

"'Sup?" Brynn says, facing me, rocking back and forth.

I don't know where to look. I hadn't thought about or practiced this part.

"I just—want to apologize, I guess."

"Okay." She watches girls from other cabins, moving past.

"And—" My counselors go by us, eyeing me. I am going to have to make this quick. "I'm sorry I didn't tell you things sooner. And you are definitely a part of what makes being here so amazing."

I sneak a glance. She is amused. And not saying anything.

"So, I just wanted to say that if you had any, you know, interesting ideas, I'm totally in. No boys, no nothing. Whatever."

She still doesn't say anything. Her eyes are slits. Her mouth is crooked.

"You. Want to do stuff. With me? Just us?" She draws it out.

"Sure." I shrug. "Of course. It's our almost-last weekend. I mean, tonight I think we should still keep things chill, but I—" I'm about to apologize, about to say more, but she stops me.

"Okay then. Boathouse. Tomorrow night. Same time. And just wait until you see my talent show act."

She winks then, like the other girl did at her, and turns on her heel. I feel like I have whiplash. I mean, I'm glad we're fine. I'm glad there wasn't any weird silent treatment, or more of a fight, but also it's kind of fast, her turnaround. Still, I'm seeing her standing up and walking away from me last night, acting like I was nothing. She didn't apologize about anything yesterday herself, didn't say anything more on the matter. She just left, with me standing there watching her, now having to trail along behind the last few girls heading into their cabins. Eventually I'm joining my cabin, trying to be open to everything and fill myself with forgiveness. But I can't get rid of this nagging feeling that some caution might be a good idea too.

DAISY

Something about the zip lines yesterday—I don't know exactly what. "Empowers" is the wrong word. It's more like I'm just not afraid anymore. Or, more than that, not bothered. And not because I wasn't terrified the entire ride down the zips. I was. I was afraid I'd fall, afraid my rope would snap, afraid my gloves would disintegrate and burn my hands down to raw bone and blisters, afraid someone—anyone, it didn't have to be Montgomery—would jump out at me at the bottom, make me wet my pants or have a heart attack. I was afraid I'd never see Violet and Calla again, or Mom and Dad. But then none of that happened. It was like this incredible release. I got to the end, and I landed on the ground. They unclipped me. I gave up my helmet. I was done and I was safe. Flannery was hugging me. I was smiling at Abby for no reason. Brynn came down about five minutes later. There was this sense of individual triumph, but also some kind of larger *yes*. I was there. I had done it. And so had everyone else. And there we were, together.

I felt—I just felt calm.

And for the rest of the day, it stayed that way. We piled into the vans, all of us talking about how awesome that had been. No one was on anyone else's side. We were all together, as a cabin, even me and Esha. I forgot, for a second, that she's now technically with Joel. Flannery's face could not stop smiling. Jordan and Jenny were buzzing a mile a minute. Even Olivia was in on it. And we went back to camp, and we ate our dinners, and we went to decathlons. We even won a few things. It wasn't perfect. It wasn't like zips had totally undone the discomfort of Monday, the torture of that silent afternoon. It didn't make Montgomery and Olivia my best friends. But it feels like—it really feels like—we might be able to overcome it. I'm starting—a little—to feel about camp the way Calla does. The way she always wants me to.

In concentration this morning, Montgomery and Olivia just ignore me like yesterday, and it's totally fine with me. Again, it's normal, not vicious. We do Upward Dog. We struggle and shake through Half-Moon Pose. We concentrate. We feel exhausted and invigorated at the same time.

And then we run. Rutger and I peel off without really needing much instruction. We're going farther than we've done before—six laps around camp—but we just swap eyes, nod at each other, find our pace. It's like an order of things has been established, like we've all settled in. Okay, so Esha and Joel are together, and okay, I hate it. Okay, Olivia and Montgomery probably hate me, but I'm making good friends with Rutger now, and Lena and April. I'm feeling a little more normal. Less numb.

In the afternoon we have ball sports with Carson cabin. There's some debate at first about what we'll play. Basketball is out, because everyone's intimidated by this senior girl who plays varsity back home. Kickball is briefly considered, but there's too much complaining, and finally somebody suggests soccer.

So we divide up into teams. Flan and I are on the same side, with Manon and Jenny and Abby and a mix of girls from Carson. This isn't exactly how I wanted to spend my afternoon, doing more running—but it's warm and not too humid. There is a good camp feeling. I can kick a ball around a field for an hour or two, even if I don't wholly understand the penalties, or the rules for that matter.

The first game goes on forever—back and forth, up and down the field, with no one really scoring. Their goalie (the basketball champ) is too good. Our defense is—surprisingly—too aggressive, and everyone keeps hogging the ball when they're not supposed to. By game two it's hot, and we're tired. We want to have free swim instead of soccer. Flannery and I are on offense— up near the center line, running ahead, deep into their defense. Neither of us is very good with the ball, but we're fast, and when I kick an awkward pass to her, she manages to get control of it to head down the field, a bunch of girls after her. When she's almost at the goal though, she flails and falls to the ground. I think at first it's the ball getting in the way of her feet, but then from the corner of my eye I see Montgomery high-fiving some Carson girl. I realize they've tripped Flan on purpose.

I'm shaken—surprised—but it doesn't really get to me until it happens again, and again. Flannery's elbow is bleeding from another hit she took after the first fall, and though she shakes off the third slam, I know she's going to have a bruise up her rib cage. Everyone sees it. The counselors don't get there quickly enough with their whistles, though. Flannery is too amenable. She jumps up too fast. Doesn't want to make a fuss.

But the way Montgomery stays on her defensively—not even looking at anyone else on the field—I know what's going on. I know what Montgomery's doing, and I know it's because Flannery's my friend. So things aren't normal, after all.

When we're down by the goal, four of us batting the ball

back and forth, trying to get a good angle, none of us able to sneak in, but none of them able to keep us far enough away, I actually see it myself. Though, yes, things are close, and there's some crazy footwork going on between Flannery and two other girls, it's plain from even five feet away that Montgomery's elbow goes intentionally up and into Flannery's jaw just as Flannery's moving in with an overdramatic move of butting the ball with her head, trying to keep it away from the goalie's reach. You can hear the impact. Flan goes down on the ground, flat on her back. Montgomery stands over her, asking is she okay, with this look of satisfaction on her face. The counselors' whistles blow. Other girls move in. Flannery can barely get her breath.

And that's it for me. I don't see the other girls. I don't see the counselors. I don't focus on the ball, rolling off somewhere past the goal. All I see is Montgomery. Her smug face. All I see is her feeling like it's okay, what she's doing. To me, to Flannery, to everyone around her, even her "friends," who she just bosses around. I don't even see the girls I shove past. I just see Flan on the ground, and I see Montgomery's dark ponytail, her sweet ruddy cheeks. And I am one step, two steps, and I am putting into my hands every ounce of frustration I've ever had about anybody making a girl feel inferior just for being herself. My arms are stiff as cadavers. I am out of my body, watching myself push Montgomery as hard as I can. I watch her collapse a little into herself before she falls to the ground, and then I see myself standing over her, daring her to stand up. Daring her to make me push her down again.

I am dizzy with adrenaline. Montgomery is on the ground, looking at me in complete shock. I am waiting for Jill and Nyasiah to come up behind me, grab me by the scruff of the neck, haul me off to Deena's office, get rid of me for good.

But the only thing that happens is that Nyasiah blows her whistle. There's a foul. Some kind of onside kick or something. Montgomery pulls herself up without the help of any of her teammates. Flannery's okay, but they make her sit on the bench to ice her jaw, anyway. I feel like everyone is smiling, though no one is looking at me. Not even Flannery. It's like she—anyone—can't acknowledge what I just did. As if calling attention to it will suddenly undo the greatness of it. I wipe my hands on my shorts. I hunker down, get ready to play again. Sweat is beading on my forehead. It is blinking into my eyes.

For the rest of the game Montgomery doesn't come anywhere near me. We slaughter them, winning 8–3. It's like a steam train arriving at the station after a long and difficult haul. We don't jump around too much. There isn't a lot of screaming. There is just this sense, on my team, of universal satisfaction. It's like maybe now there will be some peace.

CALLA

Maybe it was lame of me not to go to decaths last night—maybe it was woozy and dreamy and stupid—but I didn't want to be around Violet, Daze would be okay, and I really didn't want to watch Duncan jump and leap and slap hands with everyone else, either. I wanted him for myself. After everything that's gone on this last week, I know it's going to happen. And last night I didn't want to do anything but wait for it. I was fine with holing myself up, keeping myself separate, putting myself just a little out of his reach, because I knew—I knew—he was going to grab for me any minute. Definitely by this weekend. So I want to draw out the anticipation as absolutely long as I can, because once it's over, I know I will look back on these hours with wistful feelings: *Ah, those days of camp when I knew you were going to knock on my door.* My last days of hoping for him. I want to savor them. I want this to be a story we'll tell each other, and everybody else who asks how we met.

And anyway, after preparing the camper/parent exit surveys we'll give out next week, plus all my regular work craziness, I have to say that most of what I am is just plain ready to be in my own space at the end of the day. I don't know how the counselors do it, surrounded by people all the time. I can barely take the two in my office.

Dinner tonight is lasagna and garlic bread, which is carbohydrate heaven. The staffers all want to get up near the front to make sure they get big slices, so I'm swept up in their rush, but on the way back to the table I do see Duncan waiting in line with his kids. I make a goofy gesture, like I'm stuffing my face with lasagna already, but he looks like he can barely eat. I'm worried until he gives me a small, simple smile, and after that *I* can barely eat. I completely know what it is. He's nervous. He's nervous about telling me how he feels. The rest of dinner, I could be eating sawdust, or ambrosia, and I wouldn't be able to tell.

After dinner, to distract myself, I play some Uno with Kesiah and Lucy in the lounge until about eleven, the whole time thinking about next semester. He won't be able to get away to say anything until Saturday or Sunday, but after that, Duncan and I will have another six weeks of blissful summer together, so separating for college might be a little hard at first. But Ithaca isn't that far from Northampton, and at least we'll both be experiencing our first Frozen Winter together. Duncan's all gung-ho about how gorgeous Ithaca is anyway, and I bet on a break I'll be able to drive up and let him show me himself. Hike around. Study together in his favorite coffeehouse. After I miss two Skips and a Reverse in the game, though, Lucy and Kesiah catch on that on top of being distracted, I can barely keep my eyes open. We record the scores and peel off to bed. Washing my face, I prep myself mentally for when Duncan says what it is he has to say. Sunday, at the absolute latest. It's okay. I can wait.

Just after I get back in my room and into my pj's, a knock at my door scares the crap out of me. All I think is *Daisy*. Something else awful has happened with those girls in her cabin. I don't care what the rules are—she's staying the night with me.

When I open the door though, it's like I can't figure out who's there for a second. I mean, it's Duncan, obviously, but the disconnect of it not being Daisy and instead this big hunk of elbows and curls—this boy I've been *waiting* for—makes me sort of just pause stupidly.

"Can I come in?"

"Uh, of course." I hold the door for him and watch as he

goes to sit on my one little chair, fists on his knees, jaw working, foot tapping. But he's only there for a second before he launches up, starts pacing.

"Do you—want some water or something?" I slowly shut the door and put my back to it, watching. He's so nervous. It's totally sweet. I completely love that he just couldn't wait.

"No, thanks. I want you to come over here and sit. Just—sit with me for a second."

It's pointless to point out that he's standing. Standing and pacing. I go over to my bed and sit up on it with my legs crossed, in case he decides to sit back down again, which he does. I am completely open and listening. Four years of waiting have been totally, absolutely worth it, looking at him here now. Here in my room, telling me. Finally.

He reaches over, grabs my hand. Squeezes it hard. "You know I love you, right?"

I just look at him. This was not—at all—the way I dreamed and hoped and imagined that this conversation would start, but oh my god, here it is. I have to pay attention.

"You are . . . so . . . just, great. And I love that we get to see each other every summer, and that this is our place and we're always here, together. Right? You know that. And that will always, always be true."

I'm scared to move or say anything, in case none of this is

somehow real. I can't even say *I love you, too,* or ask why now or anything. I can only look at him. Because even though part of this is exactly what I wanted, there is also something very wrong with his face, and it doesn't connect at all with what's coming out of his mouth.

"But I don't . . ." His hand lets go of mine, goes up into his curls, squeezes and scrunches as though he's trying to press something into his skull.

Then he faces me squarely, says it: "But I don't *love you* love you. And it's not that I haven't thought about it. Or even tried. And wanted to sometimes. But there's something . . . I don't know. Different than with other girls. And I don't know why. I don't really think I want to be with anybody like that this summer, anyway. At all. I just want to not—be attached. And probably we should have talked about this a long time ago. I guess I should've told you somehow, but I really didn't think, especially not anymore, that you still felt"—he looks again at me, hesitates—"that way."

I.

Am.

Horrified.

All I can think is how totally, stunningly humiliating this is. And, like, *what*??

After about ten seconds though, looking at him and realizing he's not going to start laughing, is not going to tell me this is a joke and what he really means is that he loves me and can't imagine being without me—when none of that happens, then the embarrassed rage kicks in and the only thing I want is to get him out of my room.

But I still can't move. I can't even look away from him, I'm so numb. The pain on his face registers with every nerve in my body. That face full of agony trying to tell me he loves me but *not that way*. Not the way that matters, not the way that I have tried and tried and tried so many times to not love him. He doesn't love me *that way*, the way that makes me ache whenever I even look at him, let alone touch him or hold him. The way that makes me want to have him mine, all mine. Not that way, the way that makes me stay by him, whether he loves me back or not. He doesn't love me *that way*, and the anger and embarrassment in me is so strong (Oh god, the way I've totally thrown myself at him, gotten giddy-stupid whenever he was around, told myself every touch was sending some secret message, thought our eye contact meant something else, sat here waiting for him to come tell me he loves me, planning our damn future), I feel sick.

"I wish you would say something," he finally says.

And then I can't look at him. And I am certainly not going to *comfort* him. I am hoping that if I stay still and silent long enough, he will just go away.

"Cal, you are such a good friend, and I—"

"Shut. Up." I can't help it just coming out. Loud. Fierce. Not me.

"Okay, okay." He shakes his head. "Listen, maybe it is weird. And I know you're probably embarrassed. But you don't have to be. That's what I wanted to come here and say. When I got your note this morning, I thought I could just let it blow over and not do anything. I thought we could just roll along like we've been. But then I told myself, *It's our last summer,* and I wanted us to be square, and honest. And I couldn't think about you hoping for this thing that I'm not sure I can give to anyone right now—"

I'm staring at him, hard, but I don't see him. I don't even really see the room. "My *note?*"

He sees my face, holds out his hand like I'm a dog that's about to bite him. "Cal, you don't have to—"

"What. The hell. Did it. Say?" My throat is trying to close on itself.

"You know. I mean, it was just there this morning and I—"

"Give it to me." My own voice is so harsh and mean I think it scares us both, but I don't care.

"It said—" But he stops; his hand is holding it out, the humid piece of notebook paper. I glance at it, don't even need to read it, notice only that the handwriting isn't mine or my sister's. But I still know this is Violet's doing.

"And you . . . believe this?" I say to him, voice trembling, giving me away.

"Calla." His face is so gentle I want to slap it. "I mean, come on—"

"I mean, it could be anyone writing this. It could be anyone—" And I know my voice is climbing toward shrill librarian hysterical. Worse than that, I know it was a very specific someone who did this, and it still doesn't change him being here, in my room, telling me he doesn't love me. Not that way.

"Cal, look, I—" He shakes his head. "I should just go. I want you to know I love camp with you. I thought we'd be able to . . ." He's looking forlornly at my lamp. "I just thought . . . something. And so, no. And I get it, I do. But you have to know you are the most—" And his eyes go up to mine, searching, wanting to find some warm connection with me again, stabbing at things that I hope—for my sake—aren't there in my face.

"Anyway, you're my best friend here, really. And it's been so weird not hanging out like before. And I don't want there to be . . ." His hands go up into his hair, and at that point I want to take them in my own, hold them and hold him and tell him it will be all right. But my cheeks are burning and my legs won't move and all I have in my head is, *Not that way I don't love you that way Violet told him just tell him how you feel I don't love you that way.* And all I want is to be alone. All I want is to throw up and die.

He gets up, slow, like there's something painful in his joints. He stoops over me a little, opens his hands as though he wants to give—or get—a hug, but when I just sit there glaring down at the floor, he shuffles back, turns to the door. Where, of course, he pauses, dragging this out, taking his time, not loving me *that way* enough to know how much this is killing me—him being here in my room not in love with me.

"I won't . . . bug you. I mean, you just let me know how you want to play it, okay?"

"*Play* it?" Beams of hatred are coming out of my eyes. I can't stop them. They will laser him in half if I don't look away.

"Just—whatever. I understand this might be weird. But just know I meant what I said, and I hope we can—" He sees my face about to crumple, about to undo itself, and now I really can't look at him anymore. I pull my knees up, bury my face in them.

"Okay. Okay. I'm sorry, Calla, I really am."

I'm only about the crying now. It's all I can see or feel or know or can think of wanting to do, and it's coming whether I want it to or not, so I just give in. I don't even hear the door close, just hear my own sobbing and sobbing into my knees, my shoulders and back heaving and my face hurting from squeezing it all out. I cry and cry and I think I'm done and then I remember that stupid limp piece of paper in his hand, the way he held it out, and it comes all over me again. I am wailing and wet and messy and I don't even care. At some point I lean over, curled up gripping my pillow, knees up to my chest, still crying. It's easy enough to figure out what happened, easy enough to picture Violet deciding to be smart, to get back at me for the other day. It doesn't really matter. What matters right now is—and the crying comes up in me again—Duncan doesn't love me. He doesn't love me that way.

CALLA

In the morning I still completely want to die, and I feel like maybe part of me already has. It's worse than my hangover day—a hundred million horrible times worse. I fell asleep crying, and now, awake, half of me wants to just stay here, never moving. I never, ever want to get out of this bed. I don't want to go out and face anyone. Certainly not the sunlight.

But the other half of me—the half that's getting up, heading down to the shower, operating as though everything's totally normal, as though my heart isn't completely broken, as though I could ever somehow manage to get over what happened last night—is pissed enough to drag the rest of me down the hall.

Pissed at Duncan, of course, for being stupid enough not to love me back, and pissed at him for thinking that we could be friends after he humiliated me, but more than that—a hundred fiery hot furnaces burning with hatred more—I'm pissed at Violet.

My sister has totally betrayed me.

Yanking a comb through my wet hair, smearing on some lip gloss, I start to cry again, thinking about it: picturing Bot making fun of me with her stupid friend Brynn. *She's so pathetic, the way she pines after him every summer.* They both probably had a really good laugh over the fact that Violet's been bagging the boy of her dreams, while meanwhile her poor spinster sister just stares longingly out her window, hoping Duncan will show up and confess his true love. Who knows how long Vivi's been laughing at me? Probably from the first day. All that advice about how I should tell him how I felt—probably she was just trying to move things along, trying to up the pathetic factor so that she and Brynn would have even more to laugh about.

And the thing is—I throw my comb at my reflection, am startled at the noise it makes—she's right. I am pathetic. So, so, so extremely, painfully pathetic. But your sisters aren't supposed to prey on you when you're weak, no matter what they really think. They're supposed to support you, and understand. They're not supposed to gloat about their triumphs and make your failures look even larger. They're supposed to help you out, be by your side, double-cross anyone who tries to cross you, not hand them the ammo with which to gun you down.

But I'm not—I'm so totally not—going to sit here anymore, crying about it. Violet wants me to say how I feel? She better be ready.

It doesn't take me long to find her at breakfast, thank god, because then I don't have to spend too much time not looking at any of the boys' tables, not making eye contact with Duncan and not having to see his stupid awful apologetic face all wondering am I okay and everything. She and her cabin are only two tables away from the main entrance, so I manage to slip right up behind her without anyone noticing, and before I lose my nerve.

"I need to talk to you." My hand is at her elbow. I know my voice is totally cold.

"What is it?" she's asking me as we go up the stairs to the main floor, out onto the wide front porch that wraps around the whole building. "Cow, you're freaking me out. Come on. What's going on?"

"Don't, don't—do *not* say anything to me. Do you understand?" I have to say it fast. And strong. With barely a breath. "I don't want to hear a single thing you have to say. I just wanted to tell you—the only reason I came down here—was to say that I am never—not *ever*—telling you anything again, Violet Hawthorne Winthrop. Not. Ever."

"What are you talking about? What did I do?"

I try to snort like she does. The anger has come up in me so hard and fast I feel like I'm kind of outside my body, even though most of me is completely shaking.

"Fine. You need me to say it? Well, Duncan came to my room last night, for your information. He had a note. A note that said I don't even know what all—that I'm in love with him or whatever. I couldn't look at it, I was so sick. He came over because he thought it was better for our friendship if he was honest with me about that fact that he"—and here's where I lose it, where I choke, where I can't look at her and I can barely say it—"he doesn't feel the same way."

"Oh, Calla." Her voice is soft, and astonished. My whole face is hot and pained from trying to hold the crying in, and seeing her empathetic face, seeing how she knows how very incredibly awful this is, I sort of just want to fall into her. I'm still mad, but here I am with pretty much the only person who could make any of this better, even though she's the one who made it such a mess. Really, all I want is for her to just hug me and make jokes about how stupid Duncan is, what an idiot, how many more boys I will be able to break the hearts of now that I'm free of him. I want her to be at home with me, on the couch, watching romantic comedies and stroking my hair while I cry into her lap. I want none of this—none of it—to have ever happened. I want us to be okay, though even as I'm standing there, wanting it, I'm not sure we ever will, because I don't know if I can ever forgive her for this.

"I won't be bothering you with Duncan again," I manage, choking on my own voice, feeling awkward, not knowing how to finish. "I won't be bothering you with anything. Ever."

"Calla, I didn't—"

"I just—" But I start to sob. I have to get away from her.

I jump down the stairs and run the whole way back to my dorm, because I don't want her trying to follow me, don't want her coming after me, attempting to apologize and explain. I just want to finish crying, get ahold of myself, splash some cold water on my face and go into the office, focus on my work. If I'm going to have nothing and nobody—not even my own sister—I might as well have some productivity to show for it. If I'm never talking to Vivi again—the miserable feeling swirls up inside me—right now I'm not sure I want to do anything that would make me even tempted to tell her about it.

DAISY

his morning all anyone can talk about is the talent show tonight. Or else, like Montgomery, they're not talking about it, because they want their routine to be a surprise. Yesterday and what happened at the soccer game's been usurped by tonight, which I guess is fine with me. And to be honest, it seems this morning like more girls are talking to each other than they were before. Though that might just be the excitement about the show. I haven't really thought much about it since we had to turn in our camp forms and I purposely did not send in the one signing me up and describing my routine, but everyone else has apparently come fully prepared. Esha takes out her tap shoes and shows everyone. Abby brags that she's doing the monologue from *Our Town* that she did in her school's spring play. Olivia gets out her baton, and Montgomery just sits there and purses her lips, crossing her arms, insisting she's not going to reveal what she's doing.

I'm just glad performing isn't some kind of requirement. Maybe I would think about singing something if Calla and Violet were doing it with me like we did last year, but Violet said if she did anything she'd read some poems, and I know she didn't end up turning in her forms, anyway.

I'm not in the majority, though. A lot of people get involved. Even Rutger, in running this morning, asks me am I doing anything for it tonight. I just give him my crazy look, and he laughs.

"Winthrop, I'm sure you got all kinds of hidden things you can do."

"Yeah, like *not perform in a camp talent show*. That's a big hit of mine."

"More time for me, then."

"What, and your ballet routine?"

He screws up his face around his smile. "Good one, 'Throp."

We run awhile, not saying anything. He so wants me to ask him what his talent is. But I am not going to give in. I focus, speed up, take the edge of the lake faster than we have before. Coach isn't really serious about timing us, but we do keep track, and I like to improve every day if I can. Mainly what he's been giving us is more distance. I want to increase my distance *and* my speed.

"Okay, okay," Rutger breathes beside me after a while. "You just have to promise not to laugh."

"You're doing it in front of the whole camp, man. If you're worried about people laughing—"

"Magic tricks," he blurts out. "I do some really good magic tricks."

And I almost do laugh, but not because it's funny. More out of surprise. I know Rutger's pretty disciplined, but I can't picture him sitting in his room, making a coin disappear over and over. I can't imagine him wanting to spend his time that way.

"A guy came to our school," he goes on, "and he was wicked good. I mean, you wouldn't believe it, the stuff he did. And so after, I went up to him and asked him how he learned those things. Turns out there's this old guy teaches classes in the upstairs offices of the gym not far from my school. Harold. Used to do shows on yachts and at country clubs. I think he toured a little. Walks around some restaurant now on weekends during their brunch, entertaining people while they're waiting in line to pile their plates with food. He's a cool guy, Harold. I'm learning a few things. Thought, you know, it'd be good to practice in front of a real audience."

It's so sweet, and so unlike the Rutger I know, that I can't help smiling.

"What?"

"I just think it's really cool," I tell him.

"You do?"

"Sure I do. I've never met anybody who studied magic tricks before. It's—distinctly unique. And surprising. But, you know, in a good way."

"Distinctly unique," he mimics, obviously liking the sound of that. "You're something, Winthrop. You know that?"

By the end of the run, we've slowed to a comfortable jog, and I'm listening to Rutger tell me about some of his easier tricks, how hard it was to learn how to hold two cards in the palm of his hand without anyone seeing, what it was like going to a pet store and trying to buy a white pigeon. As an exchange I'm telling him about being in the musical this year with Calla, all the chorus-girl dramatics and disasters in costume and makeup. Stuff I didn't even think was funny or ridiculous until Rutger was chuckling at it. We make terrible time, but I'm happier than I'd be if we'd done well.

When we get back to Coach, Montgomery and Olivia are huddled together, away from everyone else, but I honestly don't care anymore. There are boys who surprise you with magic tricks here. There are soccer games that show you what you're made of. It's possible to do things you don't think you can do. Two immature babies and their playground politics? Whatever. That feels like years ago.

We cool down, stretch, listen to Coach read to us from *Born to Run* as inspiration for the weekend before our final week. When we break for lunch, Rutger gives me a high five. I tell him I'm looking forward to tonight. And I am.

Later at the lake, lying on the beach to dry off after a good splash-around in the water with Flannery, letting the sun bake my skin and relax my muscles, I think about the last time we had free swim, when I was out here with Violet. It was only— what?—ten days ago? But it seems like it's been a year. Looking at everything that's happened, it strikes me that I wouldn't be as calm and happy as I am now if I hadn't gone through all the awfulness, too. It's stupid and annoying, because it sounds like something straight off the camp brochure, but lying here, watching the girls on the floating dock try to do backflips off the edge, I realize that it sounds like the brochure because some of the brochure is actually true. The stuff you go through here, the people you meet and what you experience, living with them this way, it really does kind of make you . . . better. Stronger. More . . . something. In a way that's different from school or family or home. It's been terrible and it's sucked, but I've proved things to myself I never would've known otherwise. I'm a good runner. I can keep up with Rutger, even become friends, and he's one of the best runners I've ever met. I don't like Joel and I don't like having to pretend I like him, or anybody. Mean girls freak me out, but I can stand up to them too. I can go down the zip lines. I'm a real contender in the egg-in-a-spoon race. I like doing things without my sisters hovering around me, but I miss them when they're not there. I may never be the total, pro-camp cheerleader Calla and Mom are, but I can sure appreciate where their enthusiasm comes from.

It's a great, calm, be-here-now kind of feeling that I actually can't wait to tell Calla about. She'll be so proud. I let the feeling carry me all the way through dinner, through everyone's hyper scrambling and screeching in the cabin, getting ready for the talent show. It's on my face, I hope, when I see Violet in the auditorium and she heads over, immediately, straight to me.

We hug right away. It has such a homey feeling to it, until I realize she's clinging to me, and practically crying.

"I'm so, so sorry," she says with her face pressed against my ear. "I am completely sorry for hanging out with Brynn so much instead of you. I hope you don't hate my guts. I don't want you to not be with me in our last week. I know you have your friends and everything, and I promise not to suffocate you, but I hate us not being together, and it's so much better when we—"

"Wait, wait." I sit her down in one of the nearest seats.

"What happened? You haven't been hanging out with Brynn too much. I was just thinking this afternoon how—"

"But I *am* so sorry. I mean, I thought I knew better than you and Cow or something, or maybe I just—"

She's so upset. She's squeezing my hand. I don't have any idea what's up.

"Why don't you start over and tell me what happened."

She takes a deep breath. She's so obviously grateful I'm even talking to her. It's a thing about Vivi we forget sometimes—how sensitive she really is, how much she feels things. She's so tough all the time and so confident. It feels good, actually, to be able to be there for her. To know she needs me to, and that I can.

"So, I was pissed at Cow, I guess. She was being this, you know, total judgmental jerk about James and I . . . " She stares off, lets out her breath in this slow, careful stream. "Well, no, really I was being a jerk. I was mad because she wasn't doing cartwheels, I guess. I don't know. But I was mad at her, and Brynn was there and I just—vented. I forgot it wasn't you I was with. But I never thought she would—"

The counselors jump up onstage to do some crazy intro dance, interrupting us for a minute. We hunch down in our seats, not caring, and she tells me the rest. How Calla found her at breakfast this morning, so furious she was crying. How someone apparently wrote some note to Duncan, pretending to be Calla, telling all about her crush on him. How he went to talk to her last night. What he said.

"Oh my god." My hand goes up to my mouth. I know how hideously embarrassing it is to see the face of a boy who doesn't like you anymore. But I can imagine it was eight million times worse if it was Duncan. My stomach twists. Poor Calla. And stupid, stupid Violet for saying anything to Brynn about the two of them.

But Vivi's big brown eyes are huge with regret. "I know. And now Calla's not talking to me. And the thing is, she has every right not to. I've been so horrible and selfish. And I don't know how to tell her. She said she doesn't want to hear anything I say. Ever."

I can't help it. I don't blame Calla. But at the same time, she doesn't know how easy it is to think Brynn's your friend.

"We should go," I say. "Right now. Cow's probably in her room. Screw this stupid show. It's retarded anyway." I pull on Violet's hand, start to stand up. We can say we need to go to the bathroom or something. I don't have to be afraid of doing what I know is the right thing.

"I can't." Vivi pulls me back down. "She's so mad. She isn't going to want to see me. I don't know what to say to her."

"You'd rather sit here and watch this than try?" I jut my chin out over the seats in front of us, at some girl onstage singing in a way her mother must tell her will win her a place on *American Idol.*

"You don't understand. You didn't see her face."

"Look, I know you're scared," I whisper to her. "And yeah, you messed up, but the only way to get through it is to face it and just go tell her all that. You can't have this kind of thing sitting between the two of you. You can't be scared. It's not worth it. You have to just tell her the whole truth."

My brain totally switches then. I should stay focused on poor Calla, but I can't help it. "You did with him, didn't you?" I have to ask.

Her eyes are still sad, but she smiles in this small, special way and nods. I squeeze her hand. "Is that what Cow was mad about?"

She nods again. Everyone around us claps when the *American Idol* girl finishes, but it's mostly out of politeness. "Or at least, kind of."

I look at her, my sister, who is now totally different. "Are you happy?"

"Not about Cow, but yeah, with him?" Another smile flits over her face—a real one. "It's pretty terrific."

I want to ask her everything then. What he said, how it felt, where they went, what it feels like looking at him now. I want to know what it is that makes you want to do any of that with anyone—how you get there with them. How you let yourself totally go.

But when the emcee hollers out the name of the next performer, we both straighten up. We can't help it. It's Brynn. We swap glances, crane our necks to see better. She's already up onstage, taking the mic.

"Hey, everybody." She waves, rocking her hips. She has a canvas bag slung over one shoulder. She's wearing a plain tank top and some shorts. "So, y'all know now about my Janis Joplin fixation."

A few claps go up, and a hoot.

"And I know you know I'm not scared to be a little . . . different." She wry-smiles at everyone. More people clap and cheer, some girls around us roll their eyes. "So I was going to get up here and do another Janis song for you, but I thought you guys might want to see what I've got in my sack here instead."

She's grinning into the enormous amount of applause. Then she reaches into her bag and pulls out—it takes a second to see—a hammer, and a giant nail practically the length of my forearm.

"Back in Janis's day . . ." Brynn drawls, quieting everyone down. She keeps one eye on Deena and the counselors at the edge of the stage, who are ready to jump out and haul her off, but also curious themselves. "Back then there was this song going around about 'If I had a hammer, if I had a nail.' Well, Camp Callanwolde, here's what I'd do if *I* had a hammer and a nail."

She holds the nail up to her left nostril and, to everyone's shock, eases the shining tip of it in, back into the open space of her sinuses. Into her skull. The counselors are looking at Deena, not sure what to do. They could go and grab her, but now she has the better part of an inch of sharp metal in her nose. What if she fell, and it went the rest of the way in, to her brain? The hall is noisy with everyone's cries of surprise and disgust around us, and they only get louder when Brynn brings the end of the hammer up to the nail and starts—I am not kidding—pounding it in, straight back. Slowly, carefully, but still. She is banging a four-inch nail into her head.

Nobody knows what to do, or say, so they stand up, start cheering. Violet and I have to stand up too just to see. Guys from somewhere start chanting, "Pound it, pound it, pound it!" And Brynn obliges, tapping the nail in until only about an inch of it sticks out, perfectly perpendicular, from her nostril. When she's finished, she stretches her arms out, twirls around slow, lets us see that it is, in fact, not a trick. That she really does have that thing up there. She smiles at all of us. She absolutely does not give a shit. And I can see, completely, what both Vivi and I have found so compelling about her. But also why trusting her over our own sister is definitely not worth it.

She's not up there long. She tilts her head back a little, grabs the end of the nail, and pulls it, slowly, out of her face. Everyone groans and squeals. No one can believe it. When she takes a bow, brandishing the gleaming wet nail and hammer over her head, everyone is stomping and screaming and laughing. Deena gets her offstage pretty quickly, but the clapping takes a while to die down after her.

Vivi and I give each other *What the—??* faces. I put my arm around her waist and squeeze. I really wish Calla were with us. I wish we never had to go through anything that made us stronger without each other. I wish we never hesitated because of our fear of those very things.

Since everyone's standing up, it'd be easy for us to slip out right now, go find Calla and fix everything, make it right, but the emcee is calling Rutger up next, and I can't leave. I have to watch him. I have to be able to tell him how well he did. As he lopes up the stage stairs, I wish I could do that finger-whistle thing that Dad does. Rutger is sheepish. He doesn't want to have to go after Brynn.

"Well," he says into the mic, once the applause has died down and it's just him in the spotlight. "I was going to make a nail disappear too, but . . ."

Immediately everyone is dying laughing. I am grinning so hard. Up there is one of the real friends I've made here. Vivi and Calla have their problems, but I know we'll work them out. Since Cow's not here, that probably means she wants some time to herself, anyway. And letting her cool down isn't a bad idea. Violet is horribly sorry for her part in it, and I'll make Calla realize that somehow this weekend. We only have one week left here. Now that I'm really on board, now that I get it, I am going to do everything I can to make it a good one. This will be a last summer we'll neither forget nor regret. For now, though, I'm going to do the thing both my sisters have been wanting me to do probably for years, what I've been trying to do all session. I'm just going to stand here and do exactly what I want, unafraid.

VIOLET

It takes forever for the talent show to end. And then for everyone to shut up about it and settle down. I have to wait until well after midnight before I can leave the cabin, but when I get to the boathouse, Brynn is there, waiting. She has a flashlight. And in the light of the security lamps I can see she still has on all that makeup from the talent show. I want to choke her.

I really wasn't even going to come out here. But I had already promised I'd meet her tonight, and this way I have her alone so I can tell her exactly what I think of her. "What did you say to Duncan?" I demand the second I'm close enough. I don't care really if anyone hears. I don't care if we get caught. I'm not going anywhere with her—I just want her to tell me what happened, what exactly she did. Before all this, I liked her and I had fun with her and thought we were real friends, but I am not going to let her or anyone else mess with my sister. I don't care who she thinks she is or what she tries to do to me.

She chuckles. "Cat's out of the bag, huh? C'mon." She starts down to the water.

"No," I hiss. "I'm not going anywhere. What did you do? And god, Brynn, why?"

"Suit yourself." She shrugs without hesitating, leaving me. Not caring.

I stomp after her. "Where are you going, anyway? There's nothing out here but woods and swamp."

"Yes, but after that," she trills.

She means the Hook 'n' Mouth.

"You're an idiot. That's, like, a mile and a half away. Through the dark. There isn't even a trail."

She clicks the flashlight on and off a few times, as though signaling to someone in Morse code for her answer.

"We could be wandering in the woods until morning."

I was angry all day, but now I'm getting even angrier.

"Don't be stupid. We just follow the lake neck to the skinniest part, and then cut left and go straight. We'll probably see the lights from a hundred yards away out here."

I'm following her. The lights of camp are getting farther behind us. There isn't much of a moon. I'm wearing flip-flops. If I don't get her to turn around, I'm either going with her or I'll be stuck trying to feel my way back to camp in the dark. And it won't be as fun as blindfold hike. I know—I know now—this girl isn't worth it, but sometimes, like now, it doesn't feel like I have much choice.

"Why are you like this?" I hiss, though at this point no one can hear us.

"Why are *you* like this?"

"Why do you have to work so hard to drive everyone away from you?"

"Oh, that's charming. You been talking to my mother?"

"I mean it. I'm really pissed at you. You had no right to do that to Calla. You don't know anything about it—her. You don't care about her feelings. You treated her like crap. And she's my sister. She's not even talking to me."

"She probably feels a lot better now though, knowing the truth, don't you think?" She aims the flashlight into the trees ahead of us. I can see that there is, actually, a thin little trail between the bushes and skinny trees. It doesn't make me feel any better.

"No! Now she has to be here all summer with this between them, and it's going to totally suck."

"What would suck more, do you think? Wasting your whole summer pining after a boy who doesn't love you, or spending that summer getting over that boy and moving on to something else? Something better?"

I have to think about that for a second.

"Besides," she goes on, "you're just mad you didn't think of doing it first."

"You are such a bitch," I spit.

Again, the chuckle. "I'm not really a bitch. And you know it. Why else would you be following me?"

"Because, in spite of what a complete jerk you are, I don't want you to get into trouble."

"I *am* in trouble," she says wildly. "We're all in trouble." Her voice is harsh, breaks a little.

"Yes, I am in trouble. Thanks to you I'm in deep trouble. I don't know if Calla's ever going to forgive me."

Brynn stops then, whips around. Her face is eerie and shadowed beyond the glow of the flashlight. "She'll forgive you," she says, fierce. "She probably already has forgiven you. Do you even know what you have, with the two of them? You have something nobody else can get even close to duplicating or penetrating. Ever."

She's trembling. I can't see it, but I can hear it. And I don't know if it's anger or sadness or what, but it practically knocks the wind out of me.

After what feels like a minute of just staring me down, she turns around, aims her beam on the trail again. I don't say anything. She's not turning back, so I can't either; I just follow her, staying as close to the light as I can, so I don't trip over any roots or sticks or rocks. We walk like that, listening to the sound of our horribly loud footsteps, both of us keeping our eyes on the circle of light ahead of Brynn's feet and not looking anywhere else. I'm only aware of the huge span of black to my right—the lake—and the dark mouth of woods to my left.

I know she's right. It is better for Calla to know. I said so myself. I don't want my sister wasting her summer—her life— going after a boy who doesn't know how great she is. I don't want her not getting to have the kind of feeling I have when I'm with James. But Calla should've gotten to tell him on her own terms. If she was going to be pushed into it, she should've been pushed by someone who actually cares about her.

I don't have long to think about any of it, though. It turns out, getting to the Hook 'n' Mouth really isn't that hard. The way they talk about it at camp, you'd think there'd be razor wire and booby traps every step of the way. But there are no bogey-men jumping out from behind trees, no snakes dangling from limbs, and no pits to fall into. Just a very long, skinny, twisting trail, a bunch of frogs in the dark, and then a sagging old dock and a beer joint at the end of it.

We can hear the music and smell the beer and cigarettes before we even go in. For a wild minute, when Brynn's tendon-y hand grabs the handle of the screen door, I panic that we'll walk into a roomful of instructors all turning around to look at us. Counselors may be cool with a few campers sneaking out to join them at the fire pit, but walking all the way through the woods to get to a seedy bar is a lot different. We would get marched back to camp. We would get sent home.

But only one guy even looks up when we come in, and that's because he's facing the door and is about to take a pool shot. Brynn doesn't even glance at him—just walks straight past the table like she knows where she's going, into the back room, where there are some video games, an air hockey table, and a few plywood booths.

"Get us some quarters," she says breathlessly, leaning against the air hockey table and handing me a ten-dollar bill.

"What are we doing?" I say between my teeth.

She flicks her hair back and smiles. "We're playing air hockey, duh." Her eyes go over the other people in the room. There's a booth full of saggy women with bleached hair, too much blue eyeliner, and T-shirts cut up into tank tops, smoking long white cigarettes and cackling over a pitcher of beer. Behind them a wrinkly guy with a big, gray bushy beard and a camouflage baseball cap sits alone, sipping from his own mug. On the opposite wall there are two younger guys—maybe in their twenties, maybe seventeen; it's hard to tell because their backs are to us, both of them concentrating on some video game involving shooting a bunch of aliens with fake plastic pistols.

"Why didn't you just stop at the bar when we came in?" I'm trying to sound calm.

"Because, duh, I didn't want to pause long enough for them to ask to see our IDs. Unless, of course, you have yours with you."

I glare at her. We both know I don't have a fake ID.

Lucky for me though, there is a change machine between the bathrooms and the pay phone, which I didn't even know people had anymore. I stuff the whole ten into the slot, jam my pockets heavy with the quarters that come spilling out.

Brynn lines the quarters in stacks of four along the edge of the air hockey table. She's acting like she's measuring, making sure they're evenly spaced, but I can see her eyes going over to the guys at the video game. One of them cusses, stomps on a metal pedal on the floor.

"I intend on fully kicking your ass," I tell her when she pops the first dollar in, and the table starts to hum.

"You better have more quarters, then."

She winks at me. She freaking winks at me. So now I'm going to show her. Though it takes a second to get the hang of how fast the puck can move across the table, though twice in a row I manage to hit it into my own goal and give Brynn early points, after a few back-and-forths, I get a lot better. It feels good, slamming my plastic doohickey against the hard, flat puck. I pretend it's her face. I'm keeping my eyes fixed only on it, my hand, Brynn's hand, the table. The sound of it—plastic against plastic—makes a hard, satisfying *thwack* each time. I start aiming for the sides of the table, angling my shots. I start to beat her. I start to wipe that smile off her face.

We're into the fourth game before the video game guys come over.

"Play the winner?" the blond one says. The longish hair sticking out from under his ball cap is dirty. The other one has close-cut, wavy hair, and a wisp of a mustache.

"You got money?" Brynn says, cool, smiling only a little.

Wavy Hair reaches into his jeans pocket, pulls out a five, and drops it on the table. Brynn laughs, throaty, though I don't know at what. She shrugs, leans back over, getting ready to defend my next shot.

The guys tell us their names, but I immediately forget them. They look at each other. "You ladies want anything?" They shift a little toward the front room.

"Bud if they have it," Brynn says, light. "What about you, Tanya?"

I'm shooting laser beams out of my eyeballs at her.

She doesn't even flinch.

"I'm fine, thanks, Tiffany." I punctuate it with a mean giggle.

The guys go away, then come back with a beer for Brynn, shots for everyone. If they aren't twenty-one, the bartender obviously doesn't care.

"Ooh, goody," Brynn says, stopping in the middle of our game to rub her hands together, take the shot glass from what's-his-head. She kicks the golden liquid back just like they do in the movies. Then she follows it up with a big slug of her beer.

"Your turn now," the blond guy says to me, holding out the small glass.

"I can't. I'm allergic." I smile, like it's an affliction I'm ashamed of.

"She's a pill-head anyway." Brynn giggles again. The boys are looking at me with a new respect. I want to punch her. In the face.

"Whose go is it?" I'm no-nonsense. She might have brought these jokers over, but I don't have to talk to them. All I want to do is finish and get her out of here. Leave.

"Well, if it's gonna be that kind of party . . . ," Wavy Hair drawls. Both boys chuckle. I decide it's my turn again, even if it isn't. The guys bring stools over, watch me and Brynn play. At her end of the table, Brynn can't keep her hips still. When she makes a shot, she jumps up and squeals, like she's in Whitman or something, and when she misses, she pounds her fists on the table, pouts. Two shots later and she's beating me. When she scores the final point she holds her hands over her head in victory, the hem of her T-shirt riding up and showing her stomach.

"My go," Greasy Blond says when the game is over. "You getting ready to *lose*." He points a finger at Brynn.

I sit down on the stool, which is still warm from Greasy Blond. Behind us one of the tank-top ladies brings in another pitcher, and I feel somehow relieved a little.

"Y'all not from town," Wavy Hair says next to me. It isn't a question.

"Where're you from?" I don't have to answer him.

He juts his chin, indicating somewhere just outside the bar, I guess.

"It ain't far. We could go hang out awhile, drive you back." He smiles without showing his teeth, eyes dropping to my boobs, my lap, then moving over to watch Brynn with her butt in the air.

I follow his gaze. She is giggling, slugging her beer. She is actually kind of into these guys. I do everything I can to keep my face perfectly neutral, though I feel like all the blood has suddenly drained out of me.

"Our friend's meeting us here," I lie. I don't think I can even blink.

"She can come too." He smiles again, eyes staying on Brynn.

"I should—" The light over the hockey table is suddenly too

yellow, and bright. I swallow, my throat dry. Maybe they're harmless. Maybe we'll just play and go, maybe they're just bored and interested in new faces. But that closed-lip smile and Greasy Blond's eyes on Brynn make me feel something very different. I know Brynn would go with them, if they asked, and I know it wouldn't be good.

"I should call her, then." I feel myself getting up, reaching for the quarters. I don't know if Wavy Hair is watching me, but I feel like he is. Greasy Blond cusses and laughs. Brynn slams her beer can down. The back of my head is tingling.

At first I'm afraid the pay phone isn't going to work. And I doubt very much these boys have their iPhones with them. But two quarters, three, and then I punch in the number Mom and Dad made me and Daisy memorize before we got to camp. We groaned then, complained they must think we were babies.

The phone in Calla's suite lounge rings and rings and nobody answers. After maybe thirty rings I hang up, fish my quarters out of the coin return slot, feed them back in. Over here by the bathrooms, I don't think Wavy Hair can see me, but him watching twitchy Brynn isn't any better. The phone rings and rings. I hear more beer cans opening behind me. I squeeze my eyes shut, will Calla to answer the phone, instead of Kesiah or Lucy.

"Hello?" a bleary voice answers.

"Calla—" Her name is like a release in me. There's so much to say besides what I have to say to her next. Not just about Brynn, and Duncan, but everything—how hard I've tried to not be like her, when she's one of the only people in the world I really admire. How I've hated the other boys I've gone out with, because really what I've wanted is James—someone who's my friend first, like her and Duncan. How horribly, horribly bad I'm going to miss her when she goes away to college, and that I'm sorry I threw her Polly Pocket out the car window that time when she was seven. I want to tell her all of it, and I hate myself for not being able to say those things first, hate Brynn for making me be here, instead of sneaking out to make up with Calla.

"What happened?" She's immediately awake, serious.

I'm starting to cry a little, mad and scared and ashamed and so, so sorry. "Sissie, it's so stupid, but I'm at the Hook 'n' Mouth. I followed Brynn here. And there are these boys and she's drinking and I'm really sorry but I need you to come get me."

"Who are they?" She is flat-voiced. Stern.

"I don't know. Some guys. But I think they want us to go to their place. And I don't think I could keep Brynn from going with them. I'm so sorry. This is all my fault and I know it and I'm sorry." I'm clutching the receiver with both hands, pressing it as close to my mouth as I can, as though, by pressing in, she'll somehow be able to hear and feel exactly how much.

"I'm coming."

I stand there with the phone to my ear after she's hung up,

pretending I'm talking, just until I'm sure my tears are really gone. Then I go back to Brynn, who's sitting now on the bar stool, watching the guys and sipping her beer, looking like someone I don't know. The two guys are neither smiling nor cussing, but are tense-browed, serious. I take Brynn's beer from her hand and down a swig—better me drinking it than her, I figure. She leans into me, smiles. She has no idea how much I hate her right now.

When Wavy Hair loses, Brynn bounces up. "My turn! My turn!" She's like a girl in a sixties movie. She should be wearing a halter top and waving a flag. Except I'm glad she isn't. We only have two more stacks of quarters on the edge of the table. I don't know if that includes Wavy's fiver or not.

When he sits back down next to me, he doesn't say anything. I'm still holding on to Brynn's beer. He only looks over, once, when I raise it to my mouth and swallow. We both know I'm not allergic. I don't know if my lie matters or not. The game goes on and on. It stays a tie forever. Brynn's forehead and upper lip are shiny with sweat.

"Dude, score already," Wavy says to Greasy, an edge of impatience in his voice. Greasy frowns, hitches up his jeans. Brynn is shifting back and forth, rocking on her feet. She throws the puck down on the table. She is not going to let this guy win. And, by the looks of him, that might not make him very happy, losing to this sassy drunk girl. He might get mad. He might—

"Hey, y'all," Calla says breezily behind me, her voice a bucket of daisies. Brynn looks up, shocked. Greasy Blond gets the shot.

"We've got to go," Calla says, jerking her thumb. "Todd's really pissed, and Kevin's trying to calm him down, but they made me come get you."

Wavy and Greasy glance at each other. Brynn still looks startled, like a little girl.

"Didn't you tell them where we were?" I move over to Brynn, take her elbow.

"Yes, but still. You know how they get." For a crazy second it's almost fun, like being in some little play with Calla.

"Well, thanks, guys," I say to Greasy and Wavy. "You can have the last game."

Brynn's looking at me, at the guys, at Calla. It's like she's catatonic suddenly or something. She looks like she might cry. I don't know what's up with her and I don't care. I pull on her elbow. "We're leaving," I say. "Now."

She blinks at me with that blank, frightened look, and then suddenly she clicks out of it, tosses her head, gives a little wave to the boys. "Well," she huffs, moving out now on her own feet, playing along, "I don't want to spend another Friday in the emergency room, that's for sure."

"Sorry again, guys." Calla shrugs, giving an apologetic smile to Greasy and Wavy, like they're nice boys at a dance in suits.

They're just standing there, looking, and for a second I feel like they're going to lunge after us, but they just watch, hands hanging down by their sides, as Calla hustles me and Brynn out the door.

The Jeep is there, right out front, parked half in one space, half in another. Calla punches the key chain's unlock button probably sixteen times. Brynn gets in back and lies down on the seat, drapes her arm across her eyes. I buckle fast, wanting us to get out of there, but when I look over, Calla's just sitting there, staring out the windshield. Her breathing is weird, and she's shaking.

"Calla—?"

"Just . . . ," she pants, eyes wide. "Just . . . give me a second." She grips the steering wheel and squeezes, swallows. She takes in several breaths, each one a little more steady than the last. I realize how scared that made her, marching in like that. I feel awful. Worse than before.

Finally she looks at me. "Do not. Ever. Do that again. Do you understand me? Not ever."

And I don't know if she means sneak off to go to a creepy dive bar to almost get roofied by two townies. Or tell my sister's secret to a pseudo-friend who will then blab it to the one person she shouldn't. Or give up something stable for something completely unstable. Or lie to your sisters. Or all of it together. It doesn't matter what she means. I just say, "I promise." And I mean it all.

She nods then, checks the rearview mirror. She turns the key in the ignition, and the engine roars up around us, dark and comforting. We drive back, not talking. There isn't any more to say.

Second Saturday

VIOLET

"Winthrop, you're needed in the office," my counselor Emma Jane says in the morning, giving me a single shake. I can't believe it's time to be awake. I can't believe I ever got to sleep. Last night when Calla brought us back, as soon as we were out of the car, she slammed her own door, said, "Go to bed," and left. I was so tired and ashamed I just listened to her. I can't remember if I even said, "Thank you." I didn't say anything to Brynn.

I felt so awful I almost wanted to get caught sneaking back into the cabin. I wanted someone to have come after us, to have found out, maybe even called the cops. I lay there for I don't even know how long, staring into the dark, wanting someone else to know how truly terrible I've been.

Now with Emma Jane's meaty hand on my shoulder, it's like a relief. Somebody's cashed in all my chips for me, and I'm out of the game. I'm about to finally be punished. I can't wait to face my sentence, so I can start working on redeeming myself. I don't know who clued everyone in so early in the morning, but I don't care, not even if Calla went to Deena herself. Whoever it is, I half want to hug them with thanks. I slide out of my bunk and into whatever clothes are handy. Nat stays with the rest of the girls while Emma Jane takes me, wordlessly, up to Deena's office. She's sleepy and bleary too. She didn't want to wake up to the news that one of her cabin kids is in trouble with the director. I wonder if Brynn's already up there, silent and hostile as last night.

But it's just Deena at her desk, waiting.

"Good," she says when I come in, her face and neck tight with the strain of her managerial smile. "Can you shut the door, please?"

There are two other chairs crammed into the office across from Deena's desk. She extends her thin hand toward them, and Emma Jane and I both sit.

"Well," she says, swiping at her hair as though it needs to be brushed back from her forehead. "I need a little clarification here, Violet."

It surprises me that she knows my name.

"I got a call first thing this morning, reporting that some campers chose to go off-site in the middle of the night." Her eyes turn almost merrily from Emma Jane to me. "Do you know anything about that?"

There's no point in lying. To be honest, she can't bring the ax down fast enough on my neck. "We snuck out. I thought just to mess around by the lake—"

"You are aware that being outside your cabin after lights-out is against camp policy?" She's doing that thing grown-ups do where they act surprised and astonished about something that is really kiddie-pool obvious.

"Yes, ma'am." My neck tightens. I understand she has to punish me. But she doesn't have to be such a bitch about it. But I make myself swallow down the physically automatic *screw you* I always feel when anybody acts like this, like I'm not as *whatever* as they are. I know I messed up, and I can take it. "I do."

"But you chose to ignore that," she says, nodding, her voice fakely pleasant. "All right, well, okay. Continue." Her eyebrows go up, waiting.

"I was mad. I didn't want to even do it. But I had told Brynn I would meet her. And then she was marching through the woods and headed—"

I stop. I'm not sure how much she knows. I'm not sure how much I have to or want to tell her.

"And I'm sorry, Emma Jane?" Deena interrupts. "You and your co-counselor were completely unaware of this?"

Emma Jane doesn't like Deena's clippy little tone either. "I'm afraid so."

"Huh." Deena's lips purse together, and just the smallest, slightest frown dips along the edges of her eyebrows while she takes a deep breath and looks down at her desk. When she exhales, her face comes back up with that smile. "Thank you, Emma Jane. Violet and I can take it from here. You and Natalie, I will speak to later."

Emma Jane's mouth drops open just a bit, and her hands go forward as though they want to offer an explanation or apology.

"Thank you." Deena doesn't even wait. That strained smile. "I'll send Violet back directly."

Emma Jane shakes her head and yanks open the door. "Oh," she says with surprise, opening it wider. "Should she come in?"

Deena and I look up. It's Calla there, waiting outside. Seeing her, all at once—all over my body—I miss with horrible ferocity the weekends when Mom and Dad would be out and she would make popcorn from scratch on the stove for the three of us, and we would climb together on the couch with pillows and blankets—stuffed animals, sometimes, in Daisy's case—and we'd watch movies until our eyes crossed with sleepiness, sometimes staying there in a pile until Mom and Dad arrived home and carried us, one by one, up to our own rooms, our bodies curling against them to try and connect again to the warm pile the three of us made. I start crying.

Deena greets her. "Calla, you got here a little faster than I expected, but you may as well come in."

So it wasn't Calla who called in this morning. Realizing that, I immediately know what Deena is going to say to her, and I can't stand it. I don't want to be here to watch Calla get fired because of me. I can't. I can't watch Deena's ringed hand pointing Calla into the chair Emma Jane just left. I don't want to be the reason Calla has lost everything she cared about this summer, even though I am.

Deena clears her throat. "I wanted to ask you about Alexander's call to me at seven o'clock this morning, saying that last night he woke up to the sound of the camp Jeep—the Jeep you have been entrusted with keys to—pulling back into the driveway, after one in the morning. Why he identified you, your sister, and a third camper getting out of that Jeep."

"Yes," Calla says quietly, simply, though she has to clear her throat around it. "I know about it. My sister called me. She was scared and in trouble. I went to go get her."

Deena waits a second, as though there might be more.

"And you didn't think about alerting anyone else last night? The instructors in your suite, for example? Violet's counselors? Alexander, even? Any of the other adults who are here to help when there are problems like this one? Anyone with authority?"

Calla looks pained. *She knows already*, I want to shout. *Leave her alone.*

"All I knew was that my sister was on the phone, and she was freaked out. I knew where she was; I knew how to help, and I went to go get her."

Deena just stares.

"I—I don't know what else to say, really." Calla shrugs. It's like she's broken, and I know I'm the one standing over all the pieces, a hammer in my hand. I have to squeeze my eyes shut to keep from crying harder.

"I know you have to dismiss me, and I understand. And I'm sorry. But I couldn't do anything else but what I did. It was my sister."

"Well," Deena sighs, the meanness suddenly out of her voice. I bring myself to look up at her. She shakes her head a little. "This is truly, truly disappointing." Her eyes swim at Calla. Calla has to look away.

"You probably haven't eaten yet, huh?" she asks us, quieter. "Your cabinmates should still be at breakfast. I'll call your parents. Of course you understand I have no other choice, for either of you. I assume, if they left now, someone could be here for you sometime after noon?"

Calla nods. I can't believe this is happening.

"I'll need you to gather your things and return here to wait with me. I don't think it's necessary to disrupt everyone else's Saturday activities."

She really does look sad. Sorry.

"Are we the only ones being sent home?" I can't help asking.

"My only regret is not sending Miss Polonowski home sooner." Deena sighs. "Brynn is packing her things now. Her parents don't live incredibly far."

So Brynn's already been summoned and dismissed. I feel a little satisfied that she got in trouble first, that she was the one Deena hauled in before us. But then I wonder what Brynn might've said. It doesn't matter, really, because Alexander identified us all anyway, and Calla is the only other person besides him who has keys to the Jeep, but I wonder if she told the truth about how it all happened, or if she blamed it on me. If she made sure to mention Calla's name. Or if Brynn just sat silent, saying nothing, while Deena went at her with accusations. I wonder if she was even a shred of sorry, or if she'll be glad to get back to her pool, to pizza with her stepdad. I wonder why, for a girl who was supposed to be my friend, I don't know anything for sure either way. I wonder, too, if none of this had happened, whether we would've traded e-mails and phone numbers at the end of camp. I wonder if we would've used them.

"Do we get to say good-bye to Daisy?" Calla asks.

Daisy. God. Of course Calla would think of her first.

Deena doesn't really know how to handle this. She looks away, out the window. And for a tiny second I feel almost a little sorry for her, running a camp she doesn't know or care much about. Sorry for her not knowing what a beautiful place this can be.

"I suppose it would be best for her to hear it from you," she says. She twists one of her gold rings around its finger with her thumb. Her nails are just long enough: thick, glossy, and creamy. You can picture her going to get them done. Maybe even with her own sister.

"Thank you." Calla sounds like Deena has just handed her a glass of water at the end of a desert race.

"I can't tell you how disappointing this all is," Deena says again.

"I know." Calla can't return her gaze.

"I'm sorry too," I offer, though I'm looking at my sister, not Deena.

"You can both go on," Deena prods us, brushing back her hair again, straightening her spine. "Get some breakfast."

"Do you want anything from down there?" Calla, my ever-caring sister, makes sure to ask her. I don't see how she can manage to be nice at a time like this, why she thinks it matters. But then again, of course it does.

Deena smiles sadly, shakes her head. "I ate already."

We stand up and bobble awkwardly, trying to let the other one out the door first. Calla is still stiff, and won't look me in the eye. She's turned and headed back to her room before I realize she really isn't going to say anything to me.

"Aren't you going to get breakfast first?"

She halts. Pauses a few seconds, finally turns around. Walks right past, toward the dining hall. I know I deserve it, but I wish she didn't have to be so pissy, not even give me a chance to apologize. I do not want to have to ride the four hours back home in the car with her. But then again, I don't ever want to be too far out of her sight, either.

"I'll talk to Daisy." She is a robot. "You better make it quick with James."

James.

The tears come up in me again, but I wish they wouldn't. I'm walking just enough paces behind Calla so she doesn't have to see. It's selfish and horrid of me to think about how awful it's going to be, having to say good-bye to James now, when we thought we would still have a whole blissful week together. It's hideous that I'm feeling sorry for myself the whole walk to the dining hall, my heart sloughing away from itself in paper-thin sheaves of ash, the all of me going empty, when everything Calla ever wanted has disappeared in front of her already.

But James. And writing. And my cabin friends. I realize I have to leave them, and I'm not ready. I want to do anything else but this. Especially not with Calla walking stiff and solemn in front of me, having said good-bye already to the one she loved before she was ready. I look at myself and hate my own weakness, hate all the things that aren't as good and solid and brave as she is.

She holds open the door for me, but that's it. I want to say something but know better. She walks to Daisy's table without a word. I don't watch. I deserve to be the one on the outs, and Calla will explain it all better anyway. Daisy will know why I can't face her right now. And I'll write her as soon as we're home. In the meantime, Deena said we should eat, but I can't imagine having an appetite for anything. I'm not sure I want last night's chicken pot pie to be my Last Supper of Camp Callanwolde though, either. Leaving. God, I'm leaving. This is my last summer as a camper and now it's my last morning, and I wasted everything leading up to this, did everything so wrong, messed it up in so many ways that I can't undo. There's no way to keep myself from crying, I'm so miserable. I can barely hold this plate.

All I can hope is that I look a little like I might just be trying to decide between cream cheese and peanut butter. And then he's there beside me: a scent before I see him, a feeling before he speaks.

"Violet, what happened? You look—terrible."

"Can we . . . ," I murmur. "Go . . . outside?" It's impossible to get it all out. It's impossible to face him.

He looks over his shoulder and makes some kind of gesture to one of the guys at his table. I put the plate down somewhere— anywhere. I don't give a crap about bagels. I follow him outside to the back patio. He moves around to the farthest rear corner, where no one can see. The misery pours out of me. I can barely stand the sound of it.

"I h-h-have to . . . leave," I manage to heave.

He's trying to look me in the eye, even though I can't meet his. "What happened? What do you mean, leave?"

I tell him about sneaking out with Brynn, about Alexander, Calla, and my mom on the way.

He doesn't say anything, just reaches forward, takes me in, holds me tight against his chest. I don't deserve this. I don't deserve it and I don't think I can ever let it go. I grip the back of his T-shirt in my hands. I claw him as close to me as I can. Around my shoulders and neck, the muscles in his arms tighten. His heartbeat is in my ear. We cannot press each other hard enough.

But eventually we loosen. We can't be out here forever.

"I'll write," he says, face serious with sadness.

"No, you won't." I am teary, messy, honest.

"You don't know that."

"Yeah, but you don't either." My face twists up around more tears.

"Well, we'll have to find out who's right then, right?" He's wanting me to smile, but I can't. I so can't.

"You just need to know, no matter what happens next, that you—this—" I'm fumbling. I can't breathe. "Was . . . the most incredible." I'm gasping. "Thing. And I will never . . . forget. In here." I push my hand to my heart. Maybe it will help slow the sadness coming out of me.

"Shhh now." He pulls me to him again. He is rocking me a little, slow. I can't see anything but the white of his shirt around me. I want to memorize this moment, this smell. This absolutely everything.

But then I feel him letting go, feel the gaps where his arms separate from mine.

"I have to get my things," I say, to say something.

His eyes are sad. But he's smiling a little. Sweet.

"I *will* write," he says.

"No, you won't," I laugh-cry finally. It makes him smile wider, at least with his mouth.

"And I won't forget either," he says. "Not ever."

He puts his hand, for a second, up over his heart. We gaze at each other a minute, and underneath the sadness, the heaviness, the awful black hole of leaving him like this, I can feel the tremor of lightning—the kind you can see from far away, in a summer sky, without any thunder.

"You go now," I tell him, wiping my nose with the back of my hand. "I hope the rest of the week is great." I manage a wobbly smile.

"All right," he says, still looking at me.

I can't stand it though. I reach out, squeeze his hand. He pulls me closer and kisses my forehead, practically leaves a burn. Then he unfolds from around me and turns. I wait until he's gone back inside before I make myself walk away, head back to my cabin, pack up my things. I don't want to go back inside to see anyone else, really. Not besides Daisy, and even there I don't want to have to explain. Like I've been telling Cow, Dizzy'll be fine. Way better off without me around to mess things up for her like I seem to do. Mom will be here in a few hours, and then Calla and I will be in the car, driving away from here, for—I realize and understand, considering what's happened—the very last time. Daisy will finally be able to have this place to herself.

I let myself take my time folding my T-shirts, pulling my bathing suit down from the shower rack where it was drying, checking to make sure I have all my toiletries. I project myself into it already—the going. There's so much I've felt and been—so much I don't want to walk out of just yet, so much I'm going to miss. There's so much I regret doing and not doing, so much I feel.

I imagine that each thing I'm packing corresponds to something I'm leaving behind. One T-shirt equals being stretched out in the sun at the lake, talking to my friends. These shorts are the awesome energy of Writing, and how much it sucks I won't be there for the final presentation and reading. The bandanna I use to hold my hair down and back when I just can't deal with it—that's the first day I got here, with Calla three summers ago: the hopeful, excited, scared, curious, and "at last, I'm here" feeling that overwhelmed me then, still fluttered when we drove up the first day this session. The gingham bra? That's my nights with James: his body, his everything. These flip-flops are that canoe trip with Brynn. My pajamas, they are singing by the fire with my sisters. Each thing, I fold up and put away, press down into the dark and silent parts of my heart.

I think about Calla, in her room now, packing her things. Of the packing she'll be doing in several weeks—leaving us for college, leaving our home. And I realize she's been leaving us all summer, and we've been leaving her, too. Daisy and her independence, her distance—she's getting ready for Calla to go, to be left alone with just me. And I'll be leaving her too, eventually. This mess of a summer, it's all been the awful preparation for the leaving. All session—probably all year, if I think about the fights we've been unable to stop having—we've been doing the hard and terrible work of packing each other into boxes, beginning to move away from the safe, sweet house of our growing up together.

I take out a sheet of the stationery I brought, write a quick note to everyone, and leave it on Nat's bed, saying sorry and good-bye, and to kick ass in the Olympics. I leave my e-mail and phone number too, though probably I'll never see those girls again. We may keep in touch a little, but our friendships were here, at camp. I don't know what we have, really, outside of it. The sadness of that washes over me—that these people mean so much but not as much as the one person I've hurt the most so far. I can't stop crying. I make myself zip up my suitcase, everything secure inside.

The door to my cabin opens. Daisy's standing there.

I'm stunned, seeing her bags over her shoulder. "What are you doing?"

"You don't think I'm staying here without the two of you, do you?"

"But you can't leave. Your cabin, your friends. What about running?"

She shrugs. "I think I've gotten as much out of this place as I need to."

The relief surging through me is so forceful I almost laugh. Seeing Daisy standing there, looking at me as though I'd be crazy to think she'd stick around without us, it hits me plain and simple that there are two people I will never fully pack away. Calla and I were fighting, and she still came for me when I needed her last night. Daisy just heard what happened, and here she is, ready to go wherever we go, to leave everything else behind.

It doesn't change what's happened, and I know there's a lot I still have to make up for, still things Calla and I will have to get through, but as I shut the door of my cabin and walk hand in hand up to Deena's office with Daisy, it does make me feel a little better—the way being with my sisters always does.

CALLA

I've never been a failure at anything. Okay, maybe that C in chem last semester was completely devastating, but then I took Mr. Evans up on his offer for extra credit, and I made Dad sit down with me and those stupid flash cards, and by the final six weeks I had a B+, and my GPA was somewhat repaired.

But honestly, that's the closest I ever got. And even then it wasn't exactly failure, more like embarrassing. Which is how most things like that are for me. And it's not because I'm so awesome or anything. It's not like I haven't had, you know, setbacks. But I've just never seen them as real obstacles. Challenges, maybe. Frustrations, yeah, but I'm not one of those girls who spends a lot of time crying and whining and getting afraid. I just feel like, I don't know, there isn't anything that isn't somehow solvable. There isn't a mess you can't clean up somehow, can't turn back into sparkling and new.

But sitting here in my room, listening to Kesiah and Lucy going down to breakfast and not coming in to see what just happened in Deena's office, to see if I'm all right, because really, why would they after Deena's phone call to the suite at seven thirty this morning, after her serious voice and what I'm sure she told them, after the terrible sinking feeling in me when Kesiah knocked on my door, and how fast I got dressed, and how I couldn't look her in the face? How could there be anything they could really say, now that they know and there's nothing to say about it? Though I felt I was starting to become one of them, now I'm marked with this dark gray ashy *X* on my forehead—condemned. I won't be invited to come back as an instructor. I won't get invited back, ever. And I can't undo it; I can't change the decisions I made last night. There isn't anything for me to do but pack my bags and get out of here, let them assemble and talk about me, talk about what a stupid kid I was, how inept with responsibility. Now there isn't anything but my dishonorable discharge, the ring of Deena's awful word—disappointed.

That's not why I'm a failure, though. I mean, of course it is. Partly. I broke all the rules and messed up and paid no regard to the system I signed on to uphold, made everyone believe I revered. I knew better. I *knew* better. And then I just trashed it all the second I hung up the phone with Vivi, the moment I grabbed my keys and headed out the door. Not telling anyone where I was going. Thinking I could solve it all myself. That I could, I don't know, clean everything up without anyone having to see the mess at all.

But sitting here with all of that on me—looking down into the open mouth of my pink flowered suitcase, trying to make myself get up and take the folded T-shirts out of my drawers, shove my dirty laundry into my drawstring bag, tuck my shampoo and my toothpaste into the side pockets, swipe all my hair bands into their zippered case—I know that's not even the half of it, and it's like I can't move. I feel like, in one way or another, this whole session I've been nothing but a giant screwup scoring big, fat Fs in pretty much everything. I've failed at making any new real friends, failed at connecting with anyone else here at camp, including and especially my sisters. I've failed Deena and Sally (big help I am, leaving in the middle of the summer with no time to find or train another assistant), failed at helping Daisy solve the problems in her cabin. I failed myself, failed in making this a Summer to Beat All Summers. And was I there for Violet in one of the biggest moments of her life? Nope. Just another whopping F. The business with Duncan has had fail-fail-fail written all over it, probably since we met. I have done nothing but completely, absolutely, hideously fail in all ways. Abysmally. Rottenly.

And now I have to leave—disgraced—without a chance of redeeming any of it. Sitting here, staring but seeing nothing, it's all so heavy on me, so impossible, and I know there is no way to make a right out of any of these wrongs—not even one of them, let alone all—so I'm not sure I can ever get up from this spot, face myself or anyone else again.

I lie back on my bed and stare at the ceiling, wishing I could somehow stop myself, stop time, cut off my own heartbeat and brain, freeze everything still until Mom gets here and whisks me away, out of sight.

Which is when somebody knocks at my door. I stare a minute, holding my breath. Maybe Duncan put two and two together when he saw me talking to Daisy and no one else, and now he's run over here to say good-bye, he's sorry, he didn't—

But I know it's not him, and I know that's ridiculous. Even if the story is all over camp already, he's likely halfway to forgetting me, anyway. He'll be here, and I won't anymore. I won't be that hard to replace, no matter what he says.

Tears prick up. I don't want them, but it just still hurts too much. I can't open the door. If I sit here, quiet, whoever it is will just go away.

But the knock comes again, urgent, sharp, and I decide, if nothing else, I can say buzz off; I don't want to talk. Nobody expects someone who's a colossal failure to be sweet and chipper all the time. Even if it's Daisy, and I let her in, she'll just sit here, watching me pack, and I'll be reminded how I've let her down too.

A third knock comes, and this time it pisses me off. Who knocks three times? You knock; no one answers; you take the hint; you go away. So now I will have to get up and tell them off. But it's all right. I'm a failure now. I can be nasty if I want to.

When I open it I can't believe who it is. She is so skinny, like a licorice girl. Even toned and sinewy, you wouldn't think she'd have the strength to do half of what she does. You wouldn't think she could make such a mess.

"My stepdad's here," she says, as though that explains anything.

I just look at her. I have nothing to say.

"He drives fast when he's mad. Mad and worried." She looks off for a minute, sad. "But I made him wait. I told him I had to—" She looks into my room, my open suitcase on the floor. Her eyes go back to my face. She has the biggest nerve of anyone I've ever met or even heard of.

"Look, I just wanted to tell you sorry. To your face. I thought about writing you a note and putting it under the door, but I figured that might not—"

I don't look at her. I can't.

"He's an idiot," she starts again. "And he's going to regret it, I swear. But your sister's right; I shouldn't have . . ."

She has to think. I just stand there and wait. I have no feeling left in me to even hate her. There is so much neither one of us should have even attempted.

"You just should've had a chance to tell him the way you wanted. I know that. I do. But I guess I thought, in whatever crazy way . . ."

I sneak a glance when she pauses. Her eyes are far off. We aren't seeing each other at all.

"I dunno. I thought I was giving you something. At least, that's what I was trying to do."

I have nothing to say to this. I don't know what she's doing here.

She jerks her face toward the end of the hallway, like someone's called her name.

"I gotta go now. I just thought I'd try. You know, so you might one day, a long time from now, when you're done with all this—you might eventually think something nice about me."

My eyes flick then, just for a second, back at her. She is so tiny and fierce. She is so awful and unavoidable.

"You ruined it," is all I can say. "Everything."

"I know," she says back. And like some kind of octopus,

some kind of sea creature half salt and half skin, she disappears out of my door frame. Her feet make slipping sounds down the hallway, and she is gone, forever, from my entire life.

I can't say, standing here, the door still open in my hand, that it changes anything. I still feel the same paralysis, the same inability to craft any kind of silver lining in all the gray clouds swirling around me. There is no glimmer or glitter. She has not waved some kind of magic wand. Everything is still the steely gray of reality—of the awful mess of things, of all I've failed in doing right. But now that she's gone, I do turn around and face my suitcase. For whatever it's worth, she has put my body into motion. Without thinking much—about Vivi or Daisy or Duncan, about Sally, who I'll never see again, or Deena's let-down face—I begin assembling my few belongings, packing myself together. With these small motions, I do begin, slowly, to leave. The next time I come back will be years from now, as an alumni, if they let me. It's so upsetting. It hurts my throat, my eyes, my heart. Brynn and her stupid apology hasn't made any of it better, and won't. She hasn't fixed anything, and I don't know how I am going to fix any of it myself.

But against my will or because of it, I am at least moving. I am making whatever motions I can toward facing what I have to face. I finish packing, make my room as tidy as it was when I got here: empty, swept clean of every trace of me. I leave a note to

Kesiah and Lucy on the lounge table, thanking them and leaving my e-mail, even though I don't think they'll write.

Outside, I take a look at the lake one last time before I go up to Deena's office. Campers start coming out of the dining hall, laughing and calling to each other, completely oblivious and happy. It's almost funny, thinking how their day is stretched out in front of them with nothing but swimming and games and gossip, all capped off with a bonfire later tonight. Though everything has changed for me, nothing's changed for them, and they totally have no idea. I wonder if I'll end up being able to feel as carefree about this summer, by the end of it, as they do now. If, later on, I'll be able to forget the dread that weighs down every memory now.

Walking up to the office, heavy and glum, that thought does make me wonder: If everything I've done has been a failure so far, maybe totally failing myself will be something I'll fail at, too.

DAISY

All I can think about from the second I wake up is Calla and Violet and their fight. They're both wrong. And they're both right. And I think, probably, I'm the only person in this whole camp—them included—who understands that.

Which makes it frustrating, and a little weird, when neither of them is at breakfast. In line I go up to Rutger and bump fists, tell him what a good job he did at the talent show. Flannery and I heap our plates with pancakes, sit with everybody at the table, and listen to rehashes of last night. It's a good morning, and it'll be a good day, but I keep sneaking glances over to the instructors' table, to Violet's cabin.

Finally I see them both come in the back door of the dining hall. Violet looks like she just got touched on the forehead by Voldemort, and Calla's face is serious and tight. Something's wrong. Something's happened to Mom and Dad. I feel the dread numbness sweeping over me before I can even blink. I'm standing up to go over, but Calla gets to me first.

"Tell me everything's okay at home," is the first thing I say to her.

"Everything's okay at home. Can I talk to Daisy a second, please?" she asks Jill. Jill sees how wrong Calla's face is and just nods.

I'm able to get up and follow Calla out into the hallway, but the frozen feeling is still all over me. If everything is okay at home, it's something else. Maybe something worse.

I watch her face as she tells me. It's the only thing I can focus on. Violet and Brynn and the Hook 'n' Mouth. The Jeep. Deena and this morning. That they're both going home.

"You'll still have a great week," she says, hugging me. But I kind of can't move. I don't understand the whole of all she's said, really. The Hook 'n' Mouth? They have to leave?

"I love you, and I'm really sorry," she's telling me.

Mom's coming. They're going away. Both of them, together, with everything so mixed up and wrong. Somehow I'm hugging Calla, telling her yes, I'll be fine, am sitting back in my seat.

Calla's going out the door, up the stairs, to her cabin. I don't see Violet anywhere. I don't know what's happening.

I picture the rest of the week without them. I picture the two of them at home, not talking. Picture me, here, at the bonfire with Flannery and Rutger, Manon and Jordan, but no sisters. Picture going harder and faster in running, with neither of them here to know about it.

"I've got to go," I'm suddenly saying to Flannery next to me. Her mouth is full. "What?"

"Something's happened. It's okay, but I've got to leave. My mom's on the way."

She throws her arms around me. "Who am I going to hang out with?"

"You'll be fine. Stick with Manon. And now you've got your boyfriend."

"Yeah." She smiles a little, blushes. But then she goes all super serious: "Leave me your e-mail, okay? Maybe I can come and visit you."

I tell her I will. I still am kind of not sure what I'm doing. I go squat next to Jill. "I have to go to Deena's office," I tell her. "My sisters are there."

I can't believe how easy it all is, how fast it's happening. I think of going over to Coach McKensie, saying good-bye, but that would take too long, and I can e-mail him anyway when I've had more time to think about how to really thank him. For now I have to hurry. I don't know how fast Mom is going to get here. I don't want them to leave without me.

I fast-walk to my cabin, my mind still pretty blank, though it's different from feeling numb. Instead I feel really alert. Really focused. I throw my stuff in my bag, cram my pillow and blanket into their sack. I should be looking around, memorizing things, taking my time to say good-bye, lingering and remembering, but like the zip lines I'm not thinking anymore—I'm just falling down the line of where I need to go.

Vivi's still in her cabin when I get there. She looks a mess. She keeps looking around at everything and crying, like she just can't control it. I don't blame her. She has a lot to cry about right now.

When we get up to Deena's office, Deena's just as surprised to see me as I am to be there.

"Daisy, what's happened here doesn't have any impact on you."

"It has every impact on me," I'm telling her, my voice stronger than I've ever heard it. "And anyhow, I don't think I could get any more out of my time at Camp Callanwolde than I have already. Especially if my sisters can't be here too."

"There's no alternative than to send them home. I hope you understand that."

"I understand. But there isn't any alternative for me, either. Much as we love it here, they need me more than I need this place."

We look at each other. My breathing is slow and calm, and I thought my heart would be racing, confronting her like this, but it isn't. I can't believe what I'm saying to her, even though I know I believe it with every thawing-out part of my body. It doesn't matter one bit, that disapproving look on her face. I know how to make my own decisions, to do what's right for me even if it's scary—even if sometimes I need a little push. I'm not intimidated anymore by girls who think they can boss you around. I am free to do absolutely my own thing, and this is absolutely it.

"There's some paperwork I need you to fill out, then." Deena sighs, frowning.

When I'm finished writing out the explanation that I'm leaving of my own accord, and that I understand the consequences, I go back and sit beside Violet.

"I can't believe you're doing this."

"I can't either, kind of."

We smile at each other. I take her hand. "It's going to be okay," I tell her. "I promise. All of it. We're going to be okay."

She's biting her lip, but she nods. "I'm really sorry."

"I know. And we're good. Now you've just got to tell her that."

Which is when Calla comes in with her bags. She looks at us a minute, confused and astonished. She walks over, drops her things beside mine. Her lip pokes out in a little-girl pout: a sad but sweet face. She looks completely helpless. She looks like she needs us. Vivi and I stand up, grabbing her in a three-person hug. We stand like that for a long time, arms and breath—everything—entwined. We're leaving here, and we're sad about it for our own reasons. There are things to fix and to mend, and we'll probably have more broken between us in the future, but right now we're leaving the way we would choose to do most things, the only and best way we can—together.

Acknowledgments

No way could this book even think about existing without my two sisters. To Erika and Brae, thank you for your trust and your support, but more than that, thank you for, absolutely, making me who I am, and for being the only other two people who fully know who that is.

Sisterly thanks also go to my fabulous editor and collaborator, Anica Rissi, as always, and to Amy McClellan, without whom this book would have no plot.

The entire Simon Pulse team gets another three cheers of thanks: for the belief in my writing, and all the work to make it the best possible.

A Spirit Splurge of thanks also goes to Laurel Snyder, for that talk we had about normal girls and how they sometimes do bad things too.

Scott always gets thanked last. But he is certainly not least. Thank you, among other things, for knowing that even tough triangles need support, and for being the person who makes me a stronger leg.